WHEN YOU BREAK GIRL CODE

SOMETIMES LOVE HAPPENS

BOOK 4

J L LORA

Larimar

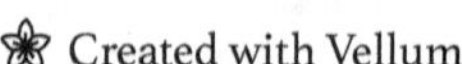 Created with Vellum

When You
BREAK
girl code
J.L. LORA

1

———————

Baltimore, 2021

Alis

No one can disappoint you more than those closest to you. I stare at my father wondering why—and how—I continue to expect better of him. Not even on my brother's happiest day can he manage to not be a complete asshole.

Maddie's soft fingers wrap around my chin and pull my face until I'm snared into her hazel eyes. Her blonde hair catches the soon-to-be-setting sun's rays and reflects them over her head. Here, standing under the atrium with her face illuminated by the skylight and her hands touching me, the world is picture-perfect. *She's* perfect in every way. *And she's mine. Finally.* Soon, I'll have the two things I've always wanted: Madison Summerville in my arms and Ellison Corp under my leadership.

She leans in and whispers in my ear, "Best man, don't listen to the negativity. You're going to do great."

She's positive and sensitive, making it easier for me to deal with my colder-than-granite parents. I trap her hands with mine and smile back at her. "I'm already a winner. Be back."

My Aunt Leila winks at me as I head to the wedding party table. I lift my knife to tap my wineglass.

With two hundred sets of eyes on me, I begin. "Everyone is looking for someone who can speak fluently to his soul. We want a connection with a lioness, a copilot, and a second self. Weston and Dahlia have found that in each other." I look at my brother and new sister-in-law and smile. They're happy and in love. "For those of you who don't know me, I'm Alis Ellison, the doctor's brother. Weston's not just my twin, he's also my big brother. On the day we were born, I snoozed, and he raced out of the womb ahead of me."

Everyone in the reception hall laughs.

"He had fifteen minutes to soak up extra knowledge, and he used them wisely. No hard feelings, but I've slept with one eye open ever since."

Laughter again.

"Since that fateful day, Wes has conquered a long series of firsts. Weston found someone beautiful, inside and out, who completes him while shining in her own light. My brother is lucky to have found someone who matches his spirit and complements him perfectly. You all see the way they look at each other, right?" I point at them for emphasis. "Go ahead, Wes, kiss your wife."

The room breaks into kiss-kiss-kiss chants but my gaze lasers to meet Maddie's again. She's in conversation with my Aunt Leila, whose jaw tightens as she leans in closer to grab my girlfriend's hand. Maddie closes her eyes and nods at whatever Leila is whispering to her.

My stomach dips, Leila's rarely that forceful with anyone. *What did she see?* The room breaks into applause, forcing my gaze back to the union we are here to celebrate. "Their love is strong, beautiful, and everything a love story should be. Join me by raising your glasses to Dahlia and Weston."

The newlyweds stand. The bride hugs me first. "That was beautiful, Alis. I love you."

"Love you, too, sister."

Weston hugs me after. "Love you, Al. You and Maddie are next."

My gaze searches for hers again. She's watching us, but the smile holds none of the warmth of minutes ago. It's surgical, like she cleaned it and pasted it on.

A prickling breaks out at the base of my neck, and I shake my head. "Love you, too, Wes. But it's too early to think about that."

After the maid of honor's speech, the venue explodes into music, more laughter, and dancing. I set out to look for Maddie, but she's not at the table we shared with my parents and Leila. I spot her walking to the courtyard. I set out to follow but get intercepted by Aunt Leila. "You did a wonderful job."

"Thank you, my love. What happened between you and Maddie?"

She looks toward the door Madison just exited. "We had a little girl chat."

"About?"

"Girl stuff. Keep your eyes open." Her tone is serious and so is the pained look in her eyes.

"Okay, what the hell happened? Where is she going?"

Leila sighs. "She had a phone call."

Lately, she always has a phone call.

"Maybe it's important." I say it without inflection because Leila will pick up on any hint. As she loves to say, I can lie to my mom but not her.

"You changed your speech. There must be a reason."

I don't look into her eyes. Leila was the person I practiced my speech with. I was supposed to say that I hoped to follow in Weston's footsteps, but those words had dried in my throat. "It's Dahlia and Weston's day, not mine."

"There's no shame if the relationship is not what you thought—"

"It is," I insist, with more conviction this time. "The right time will come."

She places her hands on my shoulder. "It will, and when it does, you'll have no doubts."

2

Six months later

Alis

"I'm stealing away your soon-to-be Chief Marketing Officer," I say, gambling—watching the man across from me, examining his features —analyzing for a tell.

Madison has been worried about the selection process for that position. If I can get a confirmation, or a hint, that she got the job, I can set her mind at ease.

Or eliminate what I've been suspecting is an excuse.

Spencer Grayson's face is impassive, that famous poker face living up to its name. He gives me nothing. Instead, he points at the paperwork in front of him and smiles. "This project idea is amazing. It will make a world of difference in people's lives and elevate what both our companies have already been doing."

In two sentences, he summarizes the intent behind this project, states its central importance, and pulls my thoughts away from Madison.

"Thank you. At Ellison Corp, we are trying to get into the business of helping people as we help ourselves." I don't add that the trying has been...well, trying. Not everyone gets it like he does, especially those who love the status quo.

"I can't tell you how much I love it. I will take one more look and then move it over for review. Thank you for including Grayson Global in this initiative. I'm looking forward to this alliance. I'll be in touch."

I nod. "Thank you for being open to it. I'll get out of your way now."

He stands. "I assume you know the way to marketing. I would walk you there myself, but I have a noon meeting that just arrived."

"Working through lunch? Not even the devil does that anymore, Grayson," I say, alluding to *Big Apple Magazine's* newest article about him, where the reporter stated the devil works hard, just not as hard as Spencer Grayson.

His eyes narrow, but he laughs. "The second I get a chance, I'm going to beat the shit of that writer. Winter has gotten such a kick out of that ridiculous article."

His wife's name reminds me of something I wanted to ask him. I point at the portrait behind him. A man sits on the floor in a business suit as a baby crawls her way to him. His face is blank, but his posture and arms are open. If you stare long enough, you can almost see the baby moving and the man smiling.

"Please tell her I said hi and still want one of her originals for my house."

I leave his office and make my way to the elevators. The hallway is a visual voyage, with walls lined with images of the businesses Grayson Global is promoting. Right by the elevator doors is a bold splash of red with *Lash n' Gloss* scribbled through the middle. Inside the elevator, my eyes go directly to the opposite wall, where the words *Autumn Lush* are the last thing you see on each floor before the doors close. I know it's one of his pride partnerships. I'll have to ask Madison some more about it.

The receptionist in the marketing suite welcomes me and tilts her head to the door. I cross the threshold into Maddie's office, and there she is, standing in front of her desk. She's wearing a deep green blouse with all that gorgeous blonde hair tumbling down her shoulders. I don't rush to her like the boyfriend who hasn't seen her in three weeks because she's been way too busy. I stop short and wait until she notices me.

"You're early." Her smile is bright as she steps out from her spot behind her desk.

"Yeah. Grayson and I finished ahead of schedule."

She glances over at the reception area. "Cool. I'm ready."

Her gaze now shifts to the other side of the office. "Let me introduce you to my colleague. Alis, this is Mila."

I have to do a 180-turn, but when my eyes connect with her friend, my heart punches against my chest.

The woman on the other end of the room is all curves in a red fitted dress and glossy parted lips. But it's the smile that gets me. It's wide and bright, like the morning sun settling over your skin. She glides toward me, my eyes catching every move until she extends her hand. "Nice to meet you."

I shake her warm, smaller hand, and electricity flows through my skin. And for a second, there's a catch in those pretty russet-brown eyes.

"I finally got the two of you to meet," Madison says.

Mila quickly withdraws her hand, forcing my attention back to her.

Shit, I was still holding on. "I'm sorry. Nice to meet you too."

Maddie moves to stand closer to me, brushing a hand over my arm. "Mila's also a marketing director here. Her concepts and vision are poignant and human-centric. She always wows the boss."

"Thanks, Maddie," Mila says, looking from her to me. "I'm sure I don't have to tell you the powerhouse Madison is. She can sell a furnace in Miami in the middle of August."

I laugh at the analogy. "That, I know."

"Well, I'm going back to my desk. Mr. Grayson assigned me something to review—"

Maddie's phone goes off. She looks down and smiles. "Oh, excuse me, I need to take this." She rushes out of the office.

Now?

When my gaze returns to Mila, I peek at the document in her hand. It's the proposal I sent Grayson.

"You're working on the Gift of Life project?"

"You know about it?" She's already putting her hand down at her side. Grayson Global is famously tight lipped about the projects they embark on until they're ready to go public with it.

I lean in a little. "My company started the project. We are asking Grayson to partner with us to expand it."

"Oh. I just got his email. I like to print and highlight so I can understand where my emphasis should be and where to focus my recommendations."

I smile at her. "Do you normally get these projects?"

"My specialty is brand and social awareness campaigns." Her gaze shifts quickly to the door and then back. "Do you mind not sharing you saw me with these? This is a close hold."

Just as I thought. *But why didn't Grayson assign it to Maddie?* "Don't worry. Your secret is safe with me."

"Thank you. I'm excited just from the email. I love when we give back, especially to places where the need is so palpable. People rarely think of education as a dire need, but it has such an impact on economic growth and quality of life."

"You get it," I say. "It's a simple concept that so many cannot grasp. I know you'll do it justice and can't wait to see the new ideas. I hope you can involve Madison in this."

"Me too. Not to toot our own amazing collaboration horn, but Maddie and I are A++ when we work on something together. We make magic." Her laugh is soft, but there's a fire in her eyes that doesn't lie. She loves her job.

"We should go," Maddie says, stopping by her desk and grabbing her bag.

Mila clears her throat. "It was nice to meet you. Maddie, don't rush back. The meeting with the team is not until three."

Mila's smile is sweet and very enticing, sending a flash of warmth down my chest.

I look at my watch. "Weston and Dahlia will meet us at noon."

Maddie's smile wavers briefly. "Let's not keep them waiting."

We wave at Mila and turn to leave. A man in a striped shirt and glasses blocks the door. He nods at me and smiles at Maddie. "Hi. Checking in on my perfect alliteration."

"Hi, Greg. We're just leaving for lunch."

His gaze snaps toward Mila and back to us. "I figured you would go out. I came to see if I can rescue our miraculous Mila. Knowing her, she will stay chained to that desk until quitting time. She's all work, all the time."

"Oh. Good idea." Maddie hooks a hand on my arm and tugs. "We should get going."

"Yeah," I say, nodding at the man.

Greg walks to Mila's desk but looks at us over his shoulder. "Have a great lunch."

We move toward the elevator, but Maddie keeps turning back to look at her office door.

"Everything okay?"

She turns to me and smiles. "Yeah. I hope he doesn't start giving Mila a hard time."

"Is that her boyfriend?"

"No." She snorts. "He's a nervous Ned. I don't want her annoyed ahead of today's meeting and our presentation in two days. She'll get on me."

"About what?"

She flicks her hair from her forehead with her fingertips. "We have different styles of doing things and it's better when we work on our own. How was the drive up from the island?"

Yet Mila insisted they made magic together. "The drive wasn't too bad."

"Good." But her fingers are moving fast over her phone screen.

"Hey, what's the perfect alliteration?"

She rolls her eyes. "The two M's. Mila and Maddie. He's called us that since we started working here."

———

Mila

Greg's heading to my desk and I put away my printout before he gets closer. He's in his usual Clark Kent get-up—crisply pressed striped shirt and a jacket over it—ready to save me from my workload with some gossip or an invitation.

"Hi."

"Some of us are going to get tacos for lunch. You're coming?"

He's so sweet and adorable. I wish he gave me more than just homeboy vibes.

"Can't. Got some stuff to work on."

He rolls his eyes but smiles. "Remember what Grayson always says: the work will be here later."

Except Mr. Grayson works through lunch, middle of the night, and on weekends. I do as he does so I can be successful.

"Next time," I say.

His smile doesn't waver. "You always say that. I'm not even going to insist. Text me if you want me to bring you something back."

He pivots on his heels and leaves. One of these days, I need to join the group for lunch. I don't want to keep being the one that rejects the invitation. That day, though, is not today. I've got too much going on. But first, I need to have a conversation with God because, as they say in the streets, *'The math ain't mathin'.*

I chuckle at my own thoughts, but it's true. Mami didn't raise an *envidiosa*. No, I'm not the envious type. I'm the first person to be happy for my friends when good things happen to them. Yet instead of doing that, I'm sitting here wondering how fair life is. I need to understand balance. *Mami* always says what God doesn't give you, he compensates.

Except God gave Madison Summerville...EVERYTHING.

She's skinny without working out. If I only look at a piece of cake, it settles in my thighs for years. She was born rich with gorgeous sun-kissed hair. She has the same job I had to compete with thousands to get. And she's fantastic at it too. She walks into a room with her long legs and impossibly high heels, and people buy what she's selling without her having to utter a word. Meanwhile, I need to prove I'm smart before some people even acknowledge my presence.

If all that wasn't enough, she has the type of boyfriend I would set aside all my *vergüenza* for. Yes, I would set aside all shame and inhibitions to climb all over someone like Alis.

God, I think he was checking me out. His eyes did that quick scan over me that all the fine *Papis* know how to do from a young age.

Alis Ellison is an expensive cologne ad personified. He's pretty enough to evoke the feelings in a Ralph Lauren commercial where you can see yourself melting right into him while music plays in the background. But his body and how he moves is all Armani, manly, athletic, hot.

And he's got a girlfriend, your friend. Didn't you see he couldn't wait to get out of here with her?

So, stop Mila. Go back to work because this brief will not finish itself.

I have so many questions about him, though. *Girl, he is none of your business.*

I sigh and jump right into the brief. The *Autumn Lush* X *Lash n' Gloss* magazine proofs and the ads are everything I could ever want. There are five versions using diverse women in various settings. It vividly reflects the concept that came to my mind as I tried to burn lunch on the treadmill. The women were working out, targeting different areas of their bodies, some on ellipticals, others on treadmills or StairMasters. It's the perfect metaphor for how we all may have issues we focus on, but we are in this together.

I hope that Mr. Grayson loves it as much as I do. *Who am I kidding?* I want him to make me the head of marketing. It's been weeks and he hasn't decided yet. I must keep up my work quality, and his trust. These ads could go a long way to reinforce my portfolio and credibility with him.

I ping the graphic designer and request a few quick edits to the ads. I ask him to make *Autumn Lush* as big as *Lash n' Gloss*. Our boss has a soft spot for this collaboration campaign. It may be one of his favorites, and it should be. It's a smashing success that makes so much money for GG. I even subscribed to *Autumn Lush* Boutique since the service opened. I love the mixing of high-end and affordable. Though I make good money, I'm not a baller yet. Someday I will earn enough to dress like Madison without worrying about paying my rent and bills.

My desk phone pings.

"Mila." Sandy's Baltimore twang is verbal candy to my ears.

"Yes, ma'am."

"He asks if you can come to his office. He says you can finish your lunch first, but I assured him you're not eating."

She means our boss. The man who took a chance on me and the one I'm now trying to convince to promote me.

"You know me so well, Sandy. I'm on my way."

I smooth my skirt, check myself on my phone camera to make sure my hair hasn't gone rogue, and close my laptop screen. I hope everything is okay, and this is not one of those instances where Greg or Mary messed up on something.

No, we would've gotten an email first.

I ride the elevator up to the CEO suite. Sandy doesn't chitchat as usual. She points to his door as soon as I walk into the suite. It's her code for there's no time to waste. Is this about the Gift of Life project? I square my shoulders and walk up to the door. Mr. Grayson is sitting behind his enormous desk. He has that no-nonsense face and is paging through a folder. He's the embodiment of the boss who can fire me and flush my career down the toilet.

I knock on his door, and he looks up. "Come in, Mila, and please close the door behind you."

The drop in my stomach is instant. Everything from this moment clicks into place. It's lunchtime, and he summons me, has me close the door, and is not looking thrilled. *Oh shit.*

I do as he says but don't move from the door.

"Sit down, please." He waits until I sit. "Would you like something to drink?"

I shake my head. "Thank you."

"I know you're probably wondering why I called you here at lunchtime."

"Yes."

His small smile reminds me of the day he hired me. He was the last one on the panel, the hardest interviewer, and the one who told me at the end that he looked forward to "seeing you do all those things you spoke about at Grayson Global."

"Mila, I didn't mean to make you nervous."

I'm ready to deny it, but I can't. "You called me at lunch and told me to close the door. This sounds way too much like a firing."

He chuckles. "I would need an HR rep present, and since you're a phenomenal employee, probably a lawyer. It's quite the opposite. I asked you to close the door because I'm going to make you an offer, and it must be a close hold for now."

My chest squeezes tight because I may know why, but I don't dare speculate. "What kind of offer?"

"It was a long process with excellent candidates, but I am happy to say: Milagros Rosario, I am officially offering you the Chief Marketing Officer position here at Grayson Global."

I stare at him, unable to speak, but my heart takes off, galloping along the walls of my chest. I press a hand trying to ease the pounding.

"You're surprised?"

I bob my head up and down because I can't form words and my eyes well. I have to take quick, shallow breaths because there's no crying in corporate. The last thing I need is for my boss to think I'm unstable when he just offered me the job of my dreams.

I'm going to be the CMO.

"Since you came into this company, you have never ceased to wow me and everyone on the board. Your marketing campaigns are everything we could wish for and more. They're always thought-provoking, diverse, and relatable. Our partners are more than pleased. I can't tell you how many calls I've gotten about them, including from the owners of our signature collaboration brands. You captured their audience and what they want their brands to show the world perfectly."

I swallow to clear the knot in my throat. "My entire team is amazing. I can't take credit for that alone."

He nods. "I like that you give credit where it's due, but allow me to give you advice as a mentor."

A mentor? He's going to mentor me? I'm not going to make it through his meeting.

He smiles as if he can read my thoughts. "First rule of corporate is to be grounded but stop being so modest. The men in your team would take credit for everything if they could, but I know what you do. I've seen you here late at night. You are still in your office when I work late. I also know when you're logged on from home. I see the email threads. You follow a concept from inception to the final product and beyond, keeping tabs on all the campaigns you touch."

I'm floored. This is everything I've wanted since I learned about this company. *I can't wait to tell...*

It hits me. My coworkers, all of whom applied for this job, will be disappointed. "Madison."

"I have not had the chance to speak to her yet. That's why I want you to keep this to yourself. I want to tell each applicant myself and on my time. There are a lot of things that go into this part, such as feedback. I know you and Madison are friends, but for your protection, I would like to ask you to let me tell her."

That part doesn't feel great. I don't want to lie to her, but I understand what goes into this. If I tell her and she gets upset, it could lead to a scene and cause strife in the team. Turmoil, when I'm about to take over, is the last thing I want. "I'll keep it to myself."

"Thank you. Congratulations, Mila. I want you to celebrate because this is more than well-deserved. When we announce you as the new CMO, we will have a meet and greet in your honor—"

His phone goes off and he grabs it from the desk, but not before I see the image of Winter Grayson and the words *my love* appear on the screen. His smile widens. "Excuse me for a second."

He answers and it's a video call.

"Hi, Princess."

"Dada. Here."

And then there's a slight knock on the door, and it swings open.

Avelyn Grayson runs in as fast as her little legs take her, but she stops short when she sees me. Mr. Grayson rushes to scoop her up.

A woman with wild curls, jeans, and a sexy boho sheath top follows behind her. *His wife.*

When her gaze meets mine, she winces. "I'm so sorry. They didn't tell me he was in a meeting. We came to bring him lunch."

"When Winter and my Avy come, the staff would stop anything to let them in." He kisses the baby's cheek, but she's staring at me wide eyed.

"It's okay," I say and wave at Avelyn.

Winter steps in and closes the door. "Congratulations," she whispers to me.

"Thank you," I say.

"I saw your brief the other day. It was incredible. So beautiful and touching. You hit so many things that are important to women, single, married, and mothers, no matter the class or race. I knew it would be you."

"Oh," I say, placing a hand to my cheek. "That means a lot to me. You're so talented."

"Thank you." She looks at her husband, and the way they stare at each other is loaded with unspoken emotion.

It's time to go.

"I'll let you guys have lunch. Thank you so much, Mr. Grayson."

"Mister?" His wife laughs.

He shakes his head. "I keep telling her it's just Grayson. Especially now. You're a senior exec."

I nod and try to downplay how giddy I'm feeling. "Grayson it is. Bye, Avelyn, bye, M—"

"Winter."

I nod. "Winter. Good to see you."

I mouth "goodbye" to Sandy on my way out because I'm walking on a cloud. Also, I need to keep this quiet, and I would be too tempted to tell her. I'm back at my desk within minutes.

I grab my phone and dial the one person I can tell. I need to share it, or I'll think I dreamed it.

"Mami, guess what?"

"You got the job."

It sends chills down my arms. "Yes, how did you guess?"

I swear my mom has a crystal ball.

"You're the best one for that job. I know the talented genius I birthed and raised. My miracle baby."

There's nothing like the support of my mother. "I got it. I did it."

"Si. Y lo hiciste sola. No se lo debes a nadie mas que a Dios."

"I didn't do this by myself. Yes, I owe it to God... and you. If it weren't for you, for everything you sacrificed for me, I wouldn't have been able to do any of this." Then I remember Maddie. "I'm worried about Maddie, though. I hate knowing and not telling her. It doesn't feel right."

"Amor, there are things we keep to ourselves until the right moment. She will understand. She would do the same if the job were hers instead of yours. Concentrate on your presentation. Tonight, we'll celebrate virtually."

"Okay, I'll take advantage of the silence while she's out with her boyfriend."

"Which one?" my mom deadpans.

"Mami..."

"What? She told me about her two guys when I was there last time."

Yeah, she did.

"Nurse Rosario to reception." The intercom voice at her job signals the end of our call.

"I have to run. *Te amo, mi niña.*"

"Love you too. I'll call you tonight."

I turn back to my portion of the brief and put on the final touches. All we need is Maddie's part. We're cutting it super close now and she's not that fast of a typist. I flip through our shared document and find her portion blank. My stomach pitches. *Don't panic.* She stopped putting her notes and documents in the shared folder months ago. She likes to keep her ideas close to the vest until fully fleshed.

I'm the same way, but I never leave her waiting until the last minute.

3

Alis

I press Madison closer to my side as we walk through the door of The Birthmark. Sierra, the hostess, smiles. "Hi, Alis. They're waiting for you at your usual table."

"Thanks. Good to see you again and congratulations," I say, looking at her belly. She recently posted her pregnancy news on Instagram. We move past her. "You remember her, right? She was at Weston's wedding."

"Oh... yeah," Madison says. "You danced with her."

My brother waves at me from his table. Dahlia is sitting next to him, and both are chatting with Saona, Sierra's sister and the owner.

Madison's stiff as a granite column against my side and just as warm. It's been a year since she dated my brother. We've been together for a while and she was at their wedding six months ago. Things should not to be awkward between her and Dahlia.

Yet she's wound tighter with every step we take toward the table.

"Hi, you two," my brother says with his usual smile. He and Dahlia stand to greet us. My sister-in-law comes around the table and hugs me. She squeezes me like we've known each other all our lives. Then she goes to hug Maddie as well.

"You always look straight out of Vogue," Dahlia says to her. "That color does everything for you."

"Thank you," Maddie says. "You look great too."

Her smile is polite and casual. Dahlia, in contrast, is beaming from ear to ear. Marriage agrees with her, just like it does with Weston. They're fucking and it shows.

My brother draws Dahlia closer to him. "We are lucky this overworked detective pried herself from her workload to have lunch with us."

She rolls her eyes. "Says the doctor who has worked 72 hours straight."

They stare at each other as the seconds tick by. They lean toward each other, but Dahlia peeks at us and Weston settles for a kiss on the side of her forehead.

Madison's blue eyes meet mine and her mouth strains into a grimace. I'm starting to believe the tightening my gut. This is not normal. If this was a business deal, I would've cut my losses months ago. *Why am I still holding onto this?*

"How are things going at Grayson Global, Maddie?"

"Good. My counterpart and I are working on a campaign brief. Team meeting at three to prep. We're going to present it the day after tomorrow."

Mila with the radiant smile and silky smooth hands.

"She's also going to be the Chief Marketing Officer," I say.

Madison brightens. I want her to look like this at me all the time. If she did, I wouldn't have so much time and space to second guess everything between us. I want her to be present.

"Thank you. We're still waiting to hear, but my submission was flawless. I'm confident."

And she should be. The hours she's been putting into her work have kept us from being able to spend time together the past few weeks. "You've been working way too hard lately, and you're the best at what you do."

She beams. It's almost blinding, and I get caught up in it. Never mind that she's never wanted to show me her work. We talk about it but she's always insisted we keep things separate because I know Grayson and developed a friendship with him. I love to see her smile, to know that she's this pleased with me. It blurs the moments when I think this is going nowhere.

"So, Dahlia, how's the Baltimore Police Department treating you?" I ask.

She groans. "Busy, crazy. I don't know if you saw the article in the Gazette, but we had over three hundred people quit. It's all hands on deck right now with violence that won't stop."

"What does that mean for you?" She was already working too much. I can't imagine now.

"Way more cases than usual. Even cases that would not usually come to us are landing on our desk. There's a hiring initiative but you know that because of recent history, the vetting and clearance for detectives is now enhanced." She shrugs and takes a sip of her water.

Weston squeezes her close. "After the big scandals, only the cream of the crop gets in."

I lean in a little. "I'm glad the city is investing in more hires. Fresh blood is going to help clear the contaminated ones. I think the department is marching in the right direction."

"Hope things level out for you soon," Madison adds, earning a smile from Dahlia.

The waitress comes and takes our drink orders. And I'm feeling better. I put my hand on Maddie's leg and she covers it with hers.

"Let's talk about great things. Alis, I love your sustainability and adopt-a-village projects. Weston had me read the report. I'm in complete awe."

I wave her away. "Says the overworked detective who's also training an entire department on racial sensitivity. She's even got Mom talking about advocacy in our town."

"God. Mom is trying to plan another fundraiser," Weston adds, scratching the back of his neck.

Dahlia and I exchange an amused look. We tease him about how much Weston dislikes our mother's use of Dahlia's work as a pet project with her friends.

"She should spotlight Gift of Life. Leila and I were talking about it and gushing last night. Don't you agree, Madison?" Dahlia asks.

Maddie stops fidgeting with her bracelet to take a sip of her drink. "I... I don't know what you're talking about."

Dahlia's eyebrows squish together, and then she shakes her head. "You don't know, because this one is way too modest." She points at me. "But you know what? I'll tell you all about it. Alis has a sustainability program he's started with the company. He's spending a lot to make sure their materials are recyclable and not going to spend a lifetime in a landfill."

"It wasn't my idea originally. Weston brought it up."

"Weston's always thinking about others, isn't he? It's been like that since we were kids," she tells Dahlia.

My brother rolls his eyes. "I complained about one company. He created a whole initiative, got buy-in from the board, and developed an implementation plan we can now brag about."

"Can you tell him to stop being modest?" Dahlia looks straight at Madison. "He refuses to take credit for the great things he does. Adopt-a-village is brilliant. So are his efforts to bring clean water and make sure the children have what they need to go to school, supplies, food, and uniforms. Folding it into the Gift of Life and bringing in partner companies is going to be such an accomplishment. We are proud of him."

"That's great. You should have told me." She looks down at her purse, pulling out her phone. "Oh, excuse me. I have to take this. It's work. I'm also going to order lunch for my coworker." She gets up from the table and walks outside the restaurant.

The minute she's out of earshot, Dahlia's gaze lands on me. "I didn't mean to make this awkward. I think she's upset."

She is. I just don't know why.

"I didn't tell her because I didn't want her to think I was a bragging asshole."

"You didn't want her to think you're bragging... she already knows what you are," Weston says.

I laugh, like I didn't just utter the most pathetic of lies.

I had told Madison about the project. I wanted her to know about it. I wanted her to act like Dahlia just did, but that day, like most of the time, Madison's not present. She clearly has no memory of our one-sided discussion.

"Be right back. I need to ask Sierra something." Dahlia gets up and goes to the hostess booth.

My brother leans closer. "Is everything okay?"

"Yeah." I shrug, as if I can fool him. I'm also jealous of the nonverbal language between him and his wife. They don't even have to look at each other, and she gave us time.

Weston just stares at me.

"I think this is all for nothing," I blurt out.

"What do you mean?"

Now that I said it out loud, I cannot stop savoring it. "It's not working. I don't think she wants it to work."

"Maddie?" he asks.

"Yeah, don't you see how weird she's acting?" It's a question but it doesn't matter. I already got my answer.

Weston looks up toward his wife. "Dahlia thinks she doesn't like her. It may just be that."

I scoff. "How can she not like Dahlia? She goes out of her way to make us feel welcome."

Weston smiles. "She likes you and we're close, so she wants to have a good relationship with Maddie. They just need to get to know each other better. Maybe we should make this more regular..."

His voice drops at the end of the sentence. He must realize it's what we've been trying to do for months, but Maddie is always the point of contention. I can't deal with this much longer. I'm tired of making excuses for her. We could both do our own thing.

"This is like a slow brush-off."

My brother shakes his head. "Sometimes it's hard work. Give her some time. Maybe she's stressed or there's some other reason."

Or there's someone else...

The thought sneaks in fast, but this time I can't push it away like I normally do. It lingers and festers. On the drive back, it hangs tight and before I realize it, we are a couple of blocks from her job.

Neither of us has said a word since we left The Birthmark, and a moving car is probably the worst place in the world to break up, but I don't want to keep dragging this out.

"Maddie, listen. You're a great person, and I care about you a lot, but this is not working for us. Your head is not in this, so let's not waste each other's time. I respect you too much for this to become—"

"I know I've been distracted. My brain is on the job and it's just stuck there. I didn't want it to be weird back there. It's just odd going out with them. I don't know what to say to her and we have nothing in common. I care about you, too. Let's talk things out."

The doubts linger, and so do Weston's words about giving her time. Maybe I'm too quick to pull the trigger. She's just too preoccupied and I just need to give her a chance.

"Okay. Let's talk over dinner tomorrow night."

Her smile wavers but I don't relent.

She opens her mouth and then closes it. She finally says, "It's a date."

I kiss her before she gets out of the car, and she clings to me. Her hands press me closer, but she pulls away too quickly, almost abruptly.

"Okay, got to run. Mila is going to kill me if she sees how behind I am on our project. I'm going to distract her with this." She lifts the to-go bag from The Birthmark.

I walk Madison to the door, get back in the car, and speed away, trying to escape the thoughts. All I see is Mila all over again, swaying toward me, like a vision.

Damn.

———

Mila

The ding of the elevator door segues into the clip clop of stilettos. Not just any high heels, Louboutins. I know the sound like the back of my hand. Madison is rushing to finish her end of the brief ahead of the team meeting.

I look down at my computer like I'm reading. I'm not ready to face her. I don't want to be fake knowing I got the job, and she didn't. The last thing I want to do is hurt her.

She blows through the door like a tornado and heads to her desk. I can see her through the corner of my eye. I have my AirPods on so it looks like I'm listening to something but she doubles back, and before I can take a breath, she's standing in front of me.

"Have you been here the whole time?"

I look up and shake my head. "I took a mini walk."

To the CEO suite...to be told I'm CMO...

"I should've insisted you come with us."

I concentrate on her face and frown. She's flustered. The red is climbing high on her cheeks and there's an odd look in her eyes. She's so upset that she forgot to put her purse and shopping bag down.

"On your double date? No, thanks." After almost two years of friendship, I know teasing is the best way to get out of her funky moods.

She sighs and drops her butt on the corner of my desk. It's her usual signal for a bitching session and I'm so relieved I jump and come around the desk to sit next to her. One thing about Maddie, if we make it about her, I won't have to talk about me. "Why do you not look happy?"

"We went out with his brother and wife."

I wait for her to elaborate, but when she doesn't, I elbow her lightly. "Was that not the plan?"

"Weston is Alis' brother."

My jaw goes slack. I know the entire saga about the amazing Dr. Weston like the *Princesita Azul* lullaby my mom used to sing to me.

He's the guy she was seeing, and it stopped because he was hung up on his ex. And she's been dating his brother? No wonder she never talked much about Alis. This tea is on a new level of messy. "Whaaaat? You're dating the doctor's brother?"

She nods. "His twin brother."

Not just messy, but straight off the nine o'clock telenovela.

"OhmyGah. There's two of him." The words slip out of my mouth.

She smiles, wide and knowing. "I knew you thought he was hot."

I'm not a punk. "You know he is."

"Both of them are. In high school, they had the whole school crazy."

She takes any opportunity to talk about the doctor in that same forlorn voice.

"That's got to be awkward to date him after his brother."

She rolls her eyes. "It's the worst with the wife being there."

"Is she a jealous bitch? Does she mean-mug you because you're so pretty and stylish?"

She smiles briefly. "The total opposite. She's always nice and friendly with a huge fucking smile on her face. And she should be. She won. She fucks him every night. You should see how she takes any opportunity to touch him when we're all together."

It's shady as hell to date two brothers, but still be this resentful of the doctor's wife is on another level. "Are you still in love with him?"

She freezes for a second and shakes her head. "No, I'm with Alis now. It's just weird to be around her because Weston didn't even give me a chance. We went out a few weeks and he told me he was hung up on her. He didn't care what his parents or anyone said. He married her. It's incredibly so awkward and I think Alis notices it too. I don't want him to think I'm hung up on his brother."

"Are you sure you're not?"

"No," she says loud and then sighs. "You have to know Weston to see what I mean. He's good, and warm, and helps people."

I don't know what to say. "And Alis is not any of that?"

"He is, in his own way, I guess."

"He's got nothing to envy his brother about in the looks department."

She smiles. "Or any other department. He fucks like a wild animal. I just wish I was in a better place to enjoy that."

I press the back of my hand against her forehead. "Are you sick? Since when do *you* have to be in a particular mental place to fuck?"

She laughs. "Don't slut shame me, bitch."

I narrow my eyes and lean closer. We both end up laughing.

She sobers up. "This shit is too complicated. Like WTF, I can't deal with that right now."

I frown. "Why are you dating him?"

She shrugs. "We'll probably get married someday. I just want to have fun with Elias. There's so much of him I still want to explore."

Her eyes sparkle when she says his name and I don't groan like I want to. The mentor-mentee cliché sexual *situationship* between her and Elias Saunders is number one on her playlist. She cannot stop talking about this dude. Honestly, I don't know what she sees in him. Maybe it's a power balance thing, but his personality is drier than a pair of winter boots in July.

"I get it." But I never will. He's not at her level physically, financially, or personality wise.

"I know you don't, but he's so good when we're together."

There's that word again. *Good*. The doctor is good. Elias is good when they're together.

"I don't get how you still plan to marry Alis. Is Elias going to become your side piece?"

She giggles, her eyes glowing, and I know her. She's picturing it. "Our families are pushing for it. And he's not the guy I thought he was before. He's fucked his way through our town, but he's been really solid with me, not one rumor since we've been together."

"But you're not that into him."

She scoffs. "Of course, I am. You saw all of him. He's delicious all over."

I'm grasping at straws. "What is it then? Does he have a three-inch dick?"

She gasps. "Are you crazy? He's hung like my dad's racehorse." Her eyes roll back like she's feeling it. "Who wouldn't be into that? I just can't get serious with him. My mind is not on it. I need to give it some time after the whole Weston fiasco."

And the Elias *situationship*.

Yeah, she's a *loca*. Then again, I've always had a crazy friend on deck. "That doesn't make sense."

"It won't to you," she says. "You grew up different from me. And that's not a knock. Being born to wealth comes with all these ties. You always have to think about your money and who you marry it to. I wish things were simpler, like it is for you. Your mom is not trying to marry you off to make the family fortune grow and you guys are happy, even with no money."

Okay, this chick has officially lost it. "I guess?"

She links her arm through mine. "I'm not trying to offend you. You know I never would."

"I know." She can be a little clueless and bitchy sometimes, but she's solid. "But listen, let's set your first world problems aside for a minute and talk about work."

Her perfectly lined upper lip curls. "First world problems?"

"Yes, Miss I got-a-rich-hot-boyfriend-with-a-huge-dick-and-a-lover-I-can't-stop-fucking-plus-more-money-than-God-so-now-I-don't-know-what-to-do."

Her laughter rocks her whole body, and she slaps a hand over her mouth.

"Seriously, let's finish this brief for the presentation—I don't have your part of it—and we can go back to your boyfriends."

She sobers up and nods. I go around my desk, but she tugs at my arm. "Before we concentrate on work, I need a big favor."

"What's that?"

"What are you doing tomorrow evening?" she asks.

Working on my creative brief for my first campaign as CMO.

"I'm supposed to meet with my trainer to work out," I lie.

"Cancel it. I want you to come to dinner with me and Alis."

With the hung boyfriend she's not into? *No, thanks.* "I don't do third wheels."

"You won't be. He's bringing a friend and I'm going to be late, and I need you to distract him for me."

Oh fuck. Now she wants me to cover for her? Hell no.

"Madison. No. Why don't you just raincheck with him?"

She shakes her head hard. "Because I've been cancelling a lot, and after today, I think he's having doubts. I don't want him to think I'm not interested."

I don't scream *'cause you're not* like I want to. "He would understand."

"He won't. You had to see the look on his face after lunch today. He's always flirty and talkative. He was mostly silent. When he finally said something he was all like, I don't think this is working and blah blah blah. I needed to make it better, so I told him my mind was on the CMO job."

An itch breaks out on the back of my neck and I anchor my hand to my side to avoid scratching. She's worried about the job, not knowing she already lost it. "Maddie—"

"Tell me you'll help me. You just have to have a couple of drinks until I get there and then we'll have a nice meal, and after, I'll make it up to him."

You don't need this drama. It's not like it will help when she finds out about the job. You don't want to do this.

"Please, Mila."

I keep thinking about all the hours we spent working on our portfolios and how we commiserated as the interviews neared. She has so much talent and presence. She's a lot more polished than me. I know she will bounce back, but she'll hate it at first, and I hate that she'll feel that way. We still have to work together. I don't want her to hate me.

"Okay."

She hugs me. "You're the best. Just make sure you don't let anything slip, okay?"

I stare at her. "I live strictly by girl code. Don't worry, I got your back."

She brims. "That much I know. Love you."

I feel like an idiot. "Can you get to work now?"

"Aye aye, captain," she says and offers me the bag. "I bet you didn't eat lunch. I got you a steak and lobster with veggies. No carbs, so you're not sleepy after."

I push aside my doubts and smile. She's always so sweet to me.

4

———————

Alis

I look down at my phone and I have messages from my office, my mother, Aunt Leila, and Weston. But none from Maddie. The time stamp of my last message, telling her I left Luciana Island for Baltimore, confirms it's been over an hour. Despite the insane rain, slippery roads, and traffic, I managed to reach the restaurant on time. She has not bothered to answer me.

I search through my texts and get caught up, answering my secretary, then my brother and aunt, and by the time I look up, Mila appears at the door, by the hostess booth. I have to do a double take.

The blue body-fitted dress looks way different from her work attire, in a more casual way, with the kind of straps you can see yourself sliding over her delicate shoulders. Her hair hangs loose, brushing over her skin as she makes her way toward the table.

Where did that come from?

I should've cancelled last night when Maddie told me she'd invited her friend to dine with us.

"Go out with your friend? Absolutely not. Why?" The last thing I needed was to sit across from someone else when Maddie and I are breaking up.

"Alis, she doesn't have many friends here and I know it's supposed to be just us, but when she told me she needed to go out, I couldn't say no. She can really use a friend."

Just when I was about to protest, she stopped me with a question. "You liked her, right?"

"I did. I liked her, but you and I need to talk alone. It's time. We can't keep putting it off. Maybe we don't even have to talk right now. Let's just agree to go our own—"

"No, you're right. We should talk. We can hang out at my place after we drop her off...I have so many things I want to do to you." She used the same honeyed tone that usually got her whatever she asked of me.

I knew then all my instincts have been right. Her disregard was just more proof that she's not as into me as she says, but I figured we would go home to her place and talk, maybe fuck one last time. I should've said the words then, but I didn't want to break it off over the phone. Either way, it's going to end tonight.

And, of course, she's late. This was never going to be easy.

But thank God for that. How could I hide the way my body goes taut at the sight of her friend? I manage to stand as Mila reaches me.

"Hello," I say, mostly to make sure I haven't swallowed my tongue.

"Hi." She reaches me, climbs on her tiptoes, and presses her cheek to mine.

It's a cultural hello, and thank you, Aunt Leila, for teaching me about other cultures, so I don't assume she's coming on to me. Her scent invades my nostrils. It's full-bodied and decadent with touches of spice and earth. It's sexy as hell.

I step back and pull the chair out for her. "How have you been?"

She smiles, not too wide. "Happy to be out of the crazy rain outside and ready for a great evening. How about you?"

So, you're not down, depressed, and in need of friends? Got it.

"Same," I say and fish for something to talk about with her. "Are you all set for your presentation tomorrow?"

She blinks a few times. "Madison told you. Yes, I think we are almost all set. I can't wait."

"You're not nervous? It's a big presentation about your fiscal plan."

"It is, but I'm confident about this one. We've done so much work to prepare, and I think our plans can propel our marketing for our clients to a new level."

The waitress comes to take our drink orders.

I stick to my favorite, Macallan. But she surprises me.

"I'll have a Vieux Carré."

I raise an eyebrow. "That's different. I can't remember the last time someone ordered that around me."

"My uncle was a bartender. A few years ago, he moved back to New York, and he would make this drink for me. He used to tell me I needed to learn how to drink so I wouldn't get drunk on the first cocktail someone gave me."

"That's really wise. Is he still in New York?"

Her small smile is a little sad. "He died last year, but not before he shared his repertoire of drinks with my mom and me."

"I'm sorry for your loss," I say.

"Thank you. He wouldn't want us to be sad, so we'll drink to him."

"Deal. Next drink you'll order for both of us. We can try another one of his favorites."

"Yeah." She looks around. "Madison and your friend should be here soon. They'll have one, too."

Madison. Christ.

"I'm sure she'll love that." *But how the hell would I know?* She only drinks wine around me. *Did she say friend? What friend?*

"Yeah." She stares into my eyes and then looks away, tucking an errant strand of hair behind her ear.

I lose my train of thought. *Is it just me? Does she feel the electricity between us, too?*

"So, you're from New York?" I ask.

She fidgets with her bracelet. "Dominican from Jersey actually. My uncle lived in New York."

"Ah. I see the *Latina* part, but you don't look like a Jersey girl."

"What does a Jersey girl look like? And please tell me you're not basing that comment on Jersey Shore or the show with the housewives?" She leans forward and I strain to keep my eyes from drifting to her chest.

I raise a hand. "Guilty of Jersey Shore. I went to Italy one summer and caught a stomach bug. It confined me to my room for two days. It was the only thing on TV I could understand. Macaroni Rascals is what they call them there. I don't know what was worse, the pain of the stomach bug or the one from watching them."

She laughs and it's so contagious my lips follow along. She looks less lethal when she smiles, even as the top of her chest shakes.

I press my palm on the table and move closer to her. "Tell me what real Jersey girls are like."

"Confident, tough. We can get down when it counts. We don't pump our own gas, but that's because we know how to let people treat us like we deserve."

I find myself smiling harder. "Is that right? I always thought it was because of the self-service ban."

She shakes a slow and delicate finger. "Clearly, you know nothing about Jersey girls. I'll need to educate you."

God, please do.

I'm saved by the waitress, who places our drinks in front of us.

"Are you two ready to order?" She lights the candle in the middle of the table. "Also, we're about to dim the lights on the chandeliers."

Her tone is cheery, and she winks at me. *She thinks we're a couple.* Mila doesn't look up right away, but when our eyes lock, she's a little rattled.

I shake my head. "We are waiting for our...friend. Can you give us a few more minutes?"

The waitress looks puzzled, but nods.

"I'll text Maddie. She must still be stuck in traffic," Mila says.

"She is?"

She looks down at her phone but nods. "Yeah, she called me when I was on the way here. She said she would call you."

"She didn't." Anger flares up my chest. I pull out my phone and send her a text.

ME

Where are you? Mila and I already got our drinks and what is this about a friend? Did you tell her I was bringing someone with me?

I look up and Mila's watching me intently. She offers me a small smile. "Evening traffic in the Beltway is crazy when there's an Orioles game."

Nice try. "Is it the same when the Orioles are not in town?"

Her eyes widen a little, but she chuckles. "We had a hectic day at work. I was upside down most of the afternoon and was almost late myself."

Except you weren't. You showed up gorgeous and fresh. You turned the head of everyone you passed on the way to the table. Every man was staring at your body. Yet you're here, covering for your friend like she didn't lie to both of us.

"You're a good friend," I say.

"I'm just being honest, Alis." Her lashes drift down, and she reaches for her drink.

It's the first time she says my name, and Jesus, everyone should say it like that. Her accent flared out and colored it.

I need to get the fuck out of here because nothing good will come of this. But I can't make myself move. I lift my scotch. "Cheers."

"*¡Salud!*" She clinks her glass with mine.

The shadow of the candle flickers on her chest, and there's a droplet of her drink lingering at the corner of her smile. It drives home the danger of this moment and as it turns out, it's the final drop.

"Excuse me." I open my messenger app and blow up Maddie's text messages like I never have before.

ME

I'm at the restaurant like we agreed. You're somewhere else, not answering me.

It's obvious that this is not working for either of us.

I don't know why you're trying to avoid this. It's not like you want it. At this point, honestly, neither do I.

I didn't want to do this by text but I refuse to keep this up…

I refuse.

I'll always care about you.

But I'm done. We're done.

————

Mila

MADISON

Flirt with him a little. He's mad, but I'll get him over it.

This fucking bitch lied to me. There's no friend to keep me from being a third wheel. Alis looked confused when I brought it up. It took everything in me not to dial Maddie's number and tell her to get her ass here. And now she texts this shit?

ME

Are you crazy? I can't flirt with your boyfriend.

Except I have. We've been doing so without meaning to.

MADISON

Come on. He's trying to break up with me.

ME

I don't want to.

Well, that's not true. Flirting with him is easy and I love it when he smiles. It sends delicious shudders over my body. But I shouldn't. This kind of stuff doesn't lead anywhere good. And I'm trapped. It's not like I can tell him she's with another guy and I came to buy her time. I can't get up and leave. It wouldn't be fair. He got played. *Like I did.* So I play along, knowing I can never hang out with him again because we don't have the right to smile at each other like this is real and we're going to fulfill the promises our eyes are making.

"Maddie told you about what I do. Tell me something interesting about what you do."

His frown is brief. "I work for my family's company and the work we do is not as interesting as it is necessary."

"I'm sure that's not true. What about Gift for Life? It's such a wonderful idea."

ME

I can't believe you did this. I'm going to strangle you.

"We have holdings in different companies, we develop large scale projects and maintain them. Depending on long term vision, we keep some and we sell the rest. Gift of Life is my favorite thing right now. My brother brought up the idea of sustainable and humane practice with our construction materials. I researched it, found some places that use it, and I'm bringing those practices to every business under our umbrella. I want to use our power to do things that will go on and impact underserved communities worldwide."

His answer hits me right in the chest. Normally, companies dump money into causes but don't get that deep into them.

"That's one thing I love about working for Grayson Global. It supports programs that make a meaningful difference."

He takes a sip of his scotch and I swear it plays in slow motion. His lips wrapping on the rim of the glass, his tongue swiping his lip, his gaze pinning mine. Heat spreads over my skin like he doused me with an accelerant.

He sets his glass down but doesn't look away. "That's why I came to speak to Grayson yesterday. We already got started with some of our water projects, but I want to go beyond, including education and creating accountability. Our companies can do more together."

I nod. "It's a great partnership. We're already doing it by bringing Grayson's virtual classroom ideas to underserved districts. I put together our internal campaign last year. So many employees are now contributing. This will take it to a new level. Tell me about your water efforts."

So, that's why he chose her to work on Gift of Life. She's worked on his big campaigns.

"We are adopting villages. We identify poverty-stricken communities and provide one service they are in dire need of. We got started in Honduras with a small village where clean water was scarce, so we come in and build them an aqueduct with a filtering system. It's hard to get the plumbing to the actual houses, but what we did is install many drawing points. Then created splitter systems with underground hosing so all households could get drinkable water."

"That's wonderful," I say. "People don't know how difficult it is to get potable water in some parts of the world. Here, all we have to do is turn on a faucet and drink. We take for granted what is vital to others."

His smile is deep, reaching the corners of his eyes. "Exactly."

"Your family must be so proud of your efforts and your employees happy to be working in a company with this kind of consciousness. You're not only about making yourself rich, but what you can do for others with what you have."

He looks away. "We're not selfless, Mila. Our company was built in tradition. We make great profit."

"Yeah, and that's okay. We all work for profit. It doesn't stop you from doing good. That counts for a lot."

He stares down and only then I realize I placed my hand over his. *Shit.* I remove it like he burnt me.

"I'm sorry. I get carried away sometimes, Alis. I don't want to give you the wrong impression."

Stop talking, Mila, and keep your hands to yourself.

I clamp my lips together.

"I don't think you can give me the wrong impression. I like your empathy."

And I like your mouth.

"Thank you."

I breathe a sigh of relief when the waitress returns. "Are we ready to order now?"

I'm ready to ask for more time, but don't get to say it.

He looks over at me. "Ladies first."

I order the pan seared salmon. He orders the rosemary pork chops. As soon as the waitress is out of earshot, I turn to him.

"We should have waited for Madison."

"She's not coming, Mila." His tone is casual and detached. I don't get it.

Like I don't get how Madison has this hot man in her life who does good things, who is smart and likes her, but she chose to go out with someone who is not at her level.

"She is coming. It's the —"

"Traffic? If so, why isn't she answering my texts too? Is her reception good only for your phone? She stood us up. And it's okay. It wasn't working anyway, and now it doesn't have to anymore."

I have to look away because now I feel bad. I covered for her, but damn, he knows he got played. And most of all, I think I got played because she told me she would let him know she was running late but didn't. I don't dare ask him if he was bringing a friend. I don't want to make it worse for her. Did she plan this all along?

Why would you send your boyfriend to dinner with another woman?

Because she trusts you and you're not supposed to be this attracted to him, or notice the heat in his gaze when he looks at you. Your job was to play your part so she can get hers.

ME

> For real, this is fucked up. Get here now.

It takes her five minutes to answer.

MADISON

> Still tied up...not literally, though.

She adds a tongue out emoji at the end.

And now I'm pissed. I can't believe she's doing this. I'll do anything for my friends, but I didn't sign up for this shit. She's hanging me out to dry in a situation that's getting more dangerous by the second.

I look down one more time, trying to figure out what to say to her.

"You can stop looking at your phone. Don't stress it. Breakups are never easy, but it's not like she and I didn't see this coming. Let's just have a nice meal. And don't worry, Maddie and I have known each other our whole lives. We'll still be friendly."

This is exactly what she didn't want but she's so caught up, hanging with captain dry toast. He doesn't even look broken up about it. I wish I could do something to help her but how can I? She's not even helping herself.

"She'll show up eventually and we'll give her tons of shit about it."

He chuckles. "We're done. But, you're a good friend, Mila. She definitely needs to keep you in her life."

"Oh?"

He shakes his head. "What's a Jersey girl doing in Maryland where she is not getting her gas pumped?"

Jesus, this is like watching a car skid towards a crash but I can't seem to peel my gaze away. *Thanks a lot, Maddie.* All I can do is keep playing along. "Well, Jersey is great, but Grayson Global is where I saw myself growing."

"How did you get the job?" he asks.

"I applied for GG's National Recruitment Initiative. You submit your portfolio and go through the evaluation and search process." I take another sip of my drink.

He does the same. "That's impressive. I'm sure there were a lot of applicants."

"Over 10,000. But I've been studying GG and Mr. Grayson's work since my college business classes. He's a model to follow. I created my portfolio with his company values and different audiences in mind."

"That's really smart."

"I'm a smart girl, Alis."

He places an elbow on the table and leans his chin on his hand. "Oh yeah? What am I thinking right now?"

He's closer and those lips...I would just need to lean in some more... *Nope.*

I push back and cross my arms. "I said smart Jersey girl, not the Long Island medium."

He throws his head back and laughs. It's not loud, but it transforms his face and makes him look boyish.

"I'll tell you what I'm thinking. I wish I could steal you from Grayson and bring you to work for us. You could transform our marketing. I don't think he would forgive me, though."

Pride flares all over my body, but I know I can't trust this. We are in way too intimate a setting. It can affect what people say.

"How do you know I would go with you?"

"I would make the offer way too enticing. I don't think you could resist."

It's involuntary, but I bite my lip and look away.

"It would have to be the offer of a lifetime. When I first saw the call for marketing professionals, I got a chill all over my body, and I knew this job would be mine. I knew it was where I belonged. I would have to get the same feeling about... what's your company's name?"

"Ellison Corp." His last name. He's the owner's son.

"Did you always want to work for Ellison Corp?" I ask.

He nods, adamantly. "Yes. I've wanted to run this company since I had enough sense to understand mergers and acquisitions. My brother Weston wanted to be a doctor and take care of people. He's had no desire to deal with our company. I, on the other hand, always had a vision of what I want."

You can hear the motivation in his voice. "It's nice that you both follow your passions. Do you love it so much because it's the family business?"

"Not necessarily. It's a challenge and in a way a fixer upper. I think we have a lot of older practices that can be renewed, and we can do so much more, not only for communities like we were talking earlier. We can also earn more. There are untapped revenue avenues. It's not always a one way. When you have a product, you can diversify the ways it brings income to you."

I can see it clearly.

"And once you identify it and set up a process, it's a matter of marketing it in the right way to the right target audience."

He shoots me a crooked smile. "Exactly. Are you sure you're not auditioning for the job?"

Heat flashes over my neck. *Easy girl. He just broke up with your friend.* "I mean, the values are there. When someone speaks with so much passion, it's hard not to think about the possibilities."

His eyes seem to grow darker. "It's good to be understood."

Somehow, this conversation took a sudden detour, and I can't seem to look away. Now my throat has gone dry. The intensity of his gaze is making me feel exposed.

When the waitress places my food in front of me, I barely notice it. My eyes and attention are only for him. My body in tune to his every move. And I'm aware of everything I ignored when I walked in. The way the buttoned-down white shirt clings to his arms. He doesn't skip arm day. I catch myself staring at the scar above his eyebrow, his big hands as he cuts through the meat. He's so sexy and I'm in so much trouble every second I spend in his presence. Thankfully, this is the last time.

I bow my head to give thanks for the food but also to get away from that gaze and the warmth that floods my belly.

When I look up, there he is again, looking at me with clear eyes. "What?"

He shakes his head. "I was just watching you."

"Why?"

"Because you're beautiful."

Oh.

Oh no.

He's just saying that. Don't read much into it.

"Thank you."

He clears his throat. "I'm not being sleazy. It's just a fact."

"Thanks," I repeat like an idiot.

But there's a heaviness between us. Something that wasn't there before.

Fucking Madison.

Thankfully, we both go back to our food. When the waitress comes back to check on us, I don't remind him about Uncle Felipe's drinks. It feels like it would be yet another too intimate moment. He orders another drink and I do the same. I'm sticking to the same because I need a clear head. But I also need something to freshen my throat because I feel like I can't get enough liquids.

"Do you go back to Jersey often?"

His question takes me by surprise.

"As much as I can to visit my mom. It's just her and me. I try to spend as much time with her as both our jobs permit. She's the head nurse in a hospital."

"That's great. I have a lot of respect for people in healthcare, like my brother."

I know all about Dr. Weston.

"Are you two close?" I ask.

"We have to be. We don't always agree on things, but it's hard to beat the twin thing."

"That has to be so cool."

He shrugs. "Mostly but, too often people either believe we are the same person or believe the whole good twin and evil twin. You know, angel or devil."

"If that were true, would you be the devil?"

He chuckles. "Of course. Would you take me as the angel?"

I stare at him. "No, you would be the one tempting people to do..." I trail off because I can't think of a word that wouldn't be bad here.

"Do you think I can tempt you to do anything, Mila?"

Yes, that's why I need to get away from you.

"I'm pretty strong minded."

"Everyone has a weak point." Yeah, he's the devil on my shoulder.

Mine is hot men with pretty lips and corporate arrogance... *like you.*

I take a sip of my drink before answering. "Yeah, but you have to calculate the risk to reward ratio."

"Are your moves that calculated?"

I can't afford it not to be.

"Well, no. But I almost always need to consider what I get out of something, what I'm putting into it, and what could happen if it blows up in my face. Don't you?"

"Always."

5

Alis

I calculated the risk. I don't know how good the reward is going to be. But I've made my investment and I don't want to turn back. I want to find out what it would be like to have her.

The ball is in Mila's court. I'm giving her the chance to call all the shots.

Well... kinda.

I insist on driving her home. There's no way I would let her get in an Uber, though that would have been the safest thing for us. Safe is not what I'm going for, though. I left safe way behind after our first drink. Further cemented when I sent Madison the message breaking it off. She doesn't care enough to answer me. I don't care anymore, either. I did what I had to do and closed the door. Tomorrow, I will call her and make sure we stay friendly, for our families. She's obviously okay because she kept texting her friend. But she's gone right out of my mind because I'm pulling over in front of Mila's building.

"It's really nice of you to drive me home, and thank you for dinner." She's not even looking at me while she says it.

"Mila." I wait until she turns to me. "Thank you for a great evening."

She smiles like she's relieved. Then leans over to kiss my cheek and lingers. The warmth of her lips clings to my skin. The air conditioner breeze cools it down almost immediately. When she pulls back, the heat in her eyes that matches the one surging inside me. I see all I need.

I don't calculate. I don't leave it up to her. I swoop in and crush my lips to hers.

Her reaction is immediate. She opens her mouth for me and I taste our whole evening in her tongue, traces of sweetness, spices, desire, and danger.

She pulls back and we stare at each other. The message is in her eyes. We crossed the line. She opens her mouth, but I beat whatever she's going to say.

"Invite me in."

Her eyes round, her lips drift apart, but she says nothing.

And I should take that as her answer.

"We really shouldn't..."

That's not a no. She knows it too.

"But we want to..."

She nods.

"And we're going to." Again, not a question because my answer is her glowing eyes.

She nods again, and I throw my door open, go around the car, and open hers. The rain is picking up, pelting our heads and bodies. We move quickly, heading inside her building, passing the reception area with only a brief acknowledgement to the person behind the front desk.

The second her elevator doors close, I'm on her. I press her against the wall, my body against her softer, warmer one. I feel her nipples against my chest and my hand finally gets to graze the curve of her hip. I don't stop there, I slide both hands past her hips to grab her ass.

Her hands bunch on my shirt and she pulls me closer, her mouth opening wider. Now I'm touching so much of her that my dick is getting hard. I'm so caught in the heat of her mouth. I'm pressing her closer as our tongues swipe against one another.

I flick my hips, needing contact with her. She leans back, pressing hers forward, rubbing herself against me. My hands drift down, trying to find the hem of her dress.

The ding echoes through my system, but I hold her tighter. She tugs on my shirt.

"We're on my floor," she pants.

I take her hand and head for the door. "Let's go."

She points to the right way. We don't talk, just walk fast, almost running until we reach her door. The second we're inside, she drops her purse on the floor. I close the door behind us. I turn around and spot her couch. I hug her from behind, burying my face in her neck. My hand glides over her chest and I push down her dress to free her tits. I feather my fingers over them.

"They feel so good."

"Your hands feel so good," she echoes.

"Are you okay with this one being a quickie?"

She nods. "As long as I come."

"That's my goal." I lift her skirt up, but her dress is tight, and it takes a bit for me to hike it over her ass. I bend her over the couch, and she braces on her elbows.

I take one look down at her ass in the air and the urgency seizes my body. I need to be inside her. I grab the condom from my wallet. Because I have a target, and her beautiful ass is not making it easy for me.

Her pussy is calling me and as soon as the condom is securely in place, I go to it. I probe with my fingers, parting her dewy folds.

"You want me."

She looks back at me, her gaze shifting from my dick to my eyes. "Yes. Give it to me."

I grab her ass cheeks and she pushes herself up a little, and in my next breath, I'm surrounded by heat, wet and tight. She moans and I brace myself to catch my breath. Then, I'm pumping inside her pussy, and I'm trying to give her the mix of slow and fast she needs. She has to come first, so I stroke and stroke while she begs me for faster until she screams. I keep pounding until I lose myself. I come so hard my entire body shudders. My seed pools hot at the tip of the condom, but I'm still squeezing her and pumping into her.

We don't move because she doesn't stop pulsating for a while. I'm pouring myself out.

When I finally take a step back, it hits me full force. I fucked her. I convinced her to let me in and I fucked her. There's no going back now.

She pushes back, her ass is pressing closer while she's trying to pull down her dress at the same time. I hold her hand and help her stand.

I glance down at her tits and she tries to cover up. I stop her hand.

"I have to...we shouldn't have... I need to..."

I put my fingers over her lips. "No regrets, no guilt, no talk about anyone else. We can face that tomorrow. Let's leave that for the morning."

Her eyes widen. Her glossy mouth opens but closes again.

I push on. "If we're going to feel guilty tomorrow, let's make it count tonight. I don't want to fuck you quick and leave you behind. You don't deserve that, and I need more of you. I've got to have more. Let's enjoy each other in the time we have. Can you do that?"

Her eyes are bouncing everywhere, but she finally nods.

"Good girl. Show me your bedroom."

She turns, but I stop her. "Wait."

"I didn't get to see all of you." I glide the straps down her arms and roll her dress down to the floor.

Then I discard my shirt, my pants, and my underwear under her unreadable gaze. When I'm fully naked, I arch a brow at her.

She smiles at me and offers me her hand to hold. We walk into her room hand in hand.

It's not dark. I can make out the tufted bed frame and I know where I'm going, but she flips the switch and the low amber light bathes the room and her skin.

"I'm going to take care of you the right way tonight, Mila."

"Tonight, I'm all yours."

I nod at her. "You shouldn't have said that. Now I have to fuck you like you belong to me."

I crush her to me and feast on her mouth with mine.

———

Mila

I forgot to close the curtains and now the light of day hits my face. I don't move because I don't want to wake him. I've never had a night like that, but the morning is here, casting the shadows, leaving my sins bare. I have to face what we did, what I've done. Maybe if I stay still and close my eyes, I can fall asleep again.

Maybe he'll leave and I can pretend if only for a few hours that I didn't fuck my friend's ex-boyfriend like an hour after they broke up.

Jesus, Mila.

All night. In multiple positions. Without a condom because we ran out.

Maybe I can pretend he didn't make me come in the shower and that I didn't whimper against the tiles. I wish I couldn't still hear my moans. I want to forget the feel of his cock pushing through my entrance and his groans of pleasure in the last strokes before he came.

He pushes out of bed. I hold my breath. But he heads out of the room into my living room and the rustling of clothing is the only sound. Relief pours all over me. He's going to leave. He's not going to say a word. I won't have to face him in the light of day.

Thank you to all that's good and merciful.

There's no need for conversations. We barely know each other, and after this, we may only see each other professionally if our work makes it necessary. I close my eyes and wait until I can't hear anything. Did he leave, and I just not hear the front door close? It's possible because my heart is pounding loud enough.

I get up from the bed, grab my robe from the bathroom, and make my way to the living room. Three steps in and I almost trip on my own feet. He's sitting on my couch, typing furiously into his phone.

"Is that Maddie?"

He looks up and I'm trapped there, feeling as naked as when I was in my bed writhing under him.

He shakes his head. "Still nothing from her."

"Okay," I say and go grab my purse from the floor by the front door.

"Don't look at your phone yet." His voice freezes me halfway there. He stands and walks up to me. "I have something to say to you."

My stomach dips and I shake my head. "No, you don't have to say anything."

"I want to. I had a great time with you, Mila. Not just…" He looks to my bedroom. "I wish it was under other circumstances."

The words thunder over me. I want to say I agree. I wish I could tell him how great last night was, the dinner, the conversation, the laughter, how good he made me feel. I can't be more disloyal than I already have been. "We knew what this was, and that didn't change."

He nods. "I should go."

"Okay."

He walks away but stops at the door, pauses, and reaches for the handle and goes out into the hallway, closing it behind him. I rush and slide home the deadbolt. Something I didn't do last night.

And in that exact moment, panic takes hold. I spent all night with friend's ex. I have to face her today. I'll see her in the office and present with her.

I rush back across the room and grab my purse. I fish out my phone and it's dead. I plug it on a charger over the breakfast bar in the kitchen and put on a pot of coffee. How the hell am I going to tell Madison about this? How do I even start? She shouldn't have left me alone all evening, but you should be able to trust your friend with your man or your ex, no matter the circumstances. I failed her so many times.

I can still feel his lips gliding over my skin.

Oh God.

The phone powers up and I have missed calls from Mami. I told her I would call her unless I didn't make it back in time.

My attention goes to the new messages from Madison. I dive straight for those.

MADISON

I'm sorry. You know how I get caught up. Sex makes me brainless.

I guess you figured I'm not going to make it.

Alis broke up with me. I'll make it up to him tomorrow.

For now… I have another session…

I'll tell you later..

You're the bestest. I'm buying you a Birkin bag.

I promise.

I read the messages over and over. I'm dying of guilt and this bitch left me hanging with her ex.

My stomach turns. Whatever she did is her issue. What I did is betrayal and I need to face the music. I fire her a text.

ME

Hey, we should talk. Can you call me when you get a chance?

I make a cup of coffee, but I end up pacing around the apartment. *Jesus.*

I grab the phone again and dial her. It goes straight to voicemail.

"Maddie, it's me. Please call me back. I need to talk to you. It's about Alis."

I hang up the phone and head for the shower, only to stop in my tracks. I can't go to work right now. I'm a wreck. I feel a full-on panic attack coming. I need to lie down and let myself settle my emotions.

I call the office and say I don't feel well, that I'm taking the morning but will be in the office in the afternoon for the presentation.

I plug the phone in my bedroom charger and climb back into the bed. Maybe a few more hours of sleep will help. God knows I got very little sleep last night. I snuggle up against my pillow, breathe, and count back from a hundred.

Unfortunately, my bed smells like him and my shower gel. Like the two of us, as we were all night. *Why did I say yes to Madison?* Now I'm the friend that fucked her ex, can't stop thinking about him, and is eaten alive by guilt over it.

The headache sets in, taking me by surprise, but it's the blessing I've been waiting for because it forces me to feel the pain and not think. I close my eyes and drift off.

I wake up three hours later, disoriented, and still groggy. I force myself out of bed and into the shower. I prepare for work and head out an hour later. I listen to the voicemails from my mom, and she tells me she will call me later. Thank God, because she would've known something was wrong.

When I get to the office, the receptionist takes one look at me and shakes her head.

"You should've stayed home."

"We have a presentation today. Let me go catch up with Maddie."

"Oh, she's not in, hon. She hasn't come in today."

I stop in my tracks. "What? Why?"

A mixture of suspicion and relief settles down on my chest. I don't have to face her just yet. I wonder if she knows. *Did Alis tell her already we spent the night together, and she is royally pissed?*

Also, there's the presentation this afternoon and her part of the work wasn't ready last night.

The receptionist flips her palms up. "I'm not sure. She didn't call."

"Thank you," I say and head in.

I sit at my desk and pull the presentation files. There's still so much work for her to do.

I open my phone again. No messages from her. I dial her and it's back to voicemail.

"Maddie, please call me back. We have to get ready for this afternoon."

I dig through my backup plan folder. I always have one. I've been burnt with project partners since college, so I am always ready to do their work when I need to.

I put my head down and, for the first time that day, expel Maddie and last night out of my head. I work on editing my files. She may be so pissed she's willing to let this presentation tank.

I can't, though, for her career and mine.

I lose myself in the work until all of it is done. Then I glance at my phone and still no signs of Maddie. I can't dwell. I review the presentation from top to bottom. Request the final edits from our graphics department. Too bad if she hates it.

When I'm satisfied with everything, I take a break to go get a drink in the floor kitchen. I find Greg leaning against the counter, sipping on coffee.

"Are you okay?" He frowns. "You don't look so good."

"I had a migraine earlier but shook it off."

His gaze narrows on my face. "Glad you're feeling better. Are my alliterated ones ready for this afternoon?"

I grab a coffee pod and put it in the machine. "We are."

He stares at me like he's not buying it. "You sure? When I checked this morning, there were chunks of the presentation missing."

"You should check now. All the pieces are complete. As always, we will hold up our end. Make sure you guys have your part ready."

"Worry not, tigress. We got this."

We share a laugh.

"Just making sure because, trust me, you don't want to be on the wrong side of *His* critique." He means our boss. He's been on the receiving end of Grayson's criticism when his team had a communication breakdown and failed to deliver. Greg's been obsessed with perfection ever since.

No one wants to be in that position. That's why I take his advice to heart.

"You know, Mila. You're so good at this. You're a great coworker and you got your priorities straight. You're definitely going to get the promotion. Can't wait to see you as the next Chief Marketing Officer."

I'm stunned by his words, but I don't dwell on them. I can't. Little does he know I was already chosen, but I can't say anything. I haven't even thought about that today.

"Thank you for always being so supportive," I say, flicking a cat hair from his jacket. I shoot him a smile, grab my coffee and head back to my office.

Five minutes before the presentation and still no Maddie. I put on my blazer and make my way to the conference room with in my brief in hand.

I'm prepared to present. I just wanted to be on the same page with her before we made another move. I guess that's not going to happen.

6

———————

Alis

The morning from hell keeps on giving. My father held me in a meeting for two hours. Thankfully, I could spit out the answers to all his questions from my report. Madison is not answering my calls or texts. Mila must have already told her. She was so wracked with guilt that I can picture her calling her the minute I left.

Mila Mila Mila.

The name has been in my thoughts all day. The last thing I should think about is her. I had her. It was better than I could ever have hoped but, from the way she looked at me today, I don't think there's a way I'll get another chance like to be that close to her again.

My brain can't accept there won't be a repeat of everything that happened last night.

Accept it, though. You already fucked up way too much.

I dial Madison again and get her voicemail.

"Look, I get it. You're pissed. I didn't want to break up over text, but you keep disappearing or changing the topic on me. Someone had to call it so we don't waste each other's time. But we owe it to ourselves to talk about it in person. Name the time and place."

I hang up just as a call comes through, but it's not Maddie, it's my Aunt Leila.

"Hi," I say.

"What's wrong?" She would figure it out from one word.

"Nothing."

"Everything," she insists. "I didn't get a hello, my love, from you, and that's not right."

If there's one person I can be honest with it's her. "I'm having a rough morning, beautiful."

"Hmmm. I know it's not work because you have that company in your pocket. If only your father did the right thing and retired, you would be King Alis. So, the issue's Madison. Again. What's the problem this time?"

"It wasn't working. I finally saw what you've been saying. I finally messaged her last night and told her I'm done."

She's silent, which is unlike her, but I don't press.

"It's about time you figured it out," she finally says.

"I knew you would say that."

"It's the truth. You've been trying to show her you're not a player anymore, but it shouldn't be that hard. That girl has other priorities."

"She was right all along about me, Leila."

"It's been a year, my boy. Your brother got engaged and married..." Her pause brings it home for me.

I sigh. "You don't think she's over Weston either?"

"I think she has an idealistic view of him, but they only went out a couple of times. I don't know what's going on with her, but it shouldn't matter at this point. It's too early for you to be trying to fix things between the two of you. You should be barely making it out of bed. Are you two even having sex?"

"Leila." I hate how right she is.

"What? Sex is natural, healthy, and good for the soul. Makes your skin glow and all that." She laughs.

"I'm not talking about that with you." Because she's too close to the truth. And because my soul had been singing at the top of its lungs last night. I needed that. "Anyway, I broke up with her and fucked up."

"How did you fuck up?"

I rub a hand over my face. "You don't want to know, but it's bad."

"Talk to her. Make sure you stay on good terms. Our families are close."

It's everything I've been telling myself. "I'm trying. She's not returning my calls. I will get to her, eventually."

"Good. So, who is this other woman you *fucked* up with?" Her voice is a little too intrigued.

"Bye, Leila."

She laughs. "I hope it was good. But seriously, I'm sorry it didn't work out. I thought the two of you would have a great chance once she realized she wasn't compatible with Weston. She just has crazy ideas about him being a saint, like most of the girls in our town. It's the doctor thing. Good luck with the new girl."

"Stop. By the way, your brother wants you here for the next board meeting."

She sighs. "I'll book a flight, but only because I want to see my boys."

That's what Weston and I are to her. She's the mom in our hearts because God knows my mother is something else.

"I love you."

We hang up. Leila's in Spain, and she could see from Europe it wasn't working out with Madison. I still feel lower than dirt that it went down like it did last night. But I don't regret it.

I just need her to call me back so we can put a bow on this and move on.

My thoughts drift to Mila. I can call her office and ask if Maddie called her. Maybe that's why Maddie is not responding to me. She'll see it as a douche move.

Instead I call Grayson Global and ask for Madison, but am told she is not in.

I give up for the moment. By the time I leave the office, I'm tired because I slept very little. I fucked my fill out of Mila, knowing it would be a one-night thing, wishing things were different, not wanting to leave anything behind.

A friend hits me up to go out for a drink, but I say no and head straight home. I spend some time in my home gym, trying to exhaust the little energy in my body. I check my phone between reps and nothing. I shower after, grab dinner, and go to bed.

My TV is on but I'm not paying much attention because my head is mostly in my memories. And it's all about last night.

I re-live every moment like a hypnotic trance — from the time Mila walked into the restaurant, with that radiant smile and glossy lips. She was so open, the conversation so natural, sometimes I think I imagined the pull between us. The Dominican from Jersey who shows people how to treat her right. Everything about her was overwhelming, her brain, her sass, that body.

By the time I bent her over her couch, I was already mind-fucked by her. I've never been an ass man before. Tits and legs are my thing, but Jesus, I'm a convert now.

And before I know it, my cock is in my hand and I'm stroking, picturing her mouth around it with the water from the shower dripping down her face.

Why did I look at her? It would've been better if I hadn't. If I had let it be a faceless blowjob, but how could I not? Everything about her is etched in my memory. I can see her arching her head for my mouth or grabbing my face and kissing me while her legs opened wider for me to go deeper.

This is not good.

I fucked the woman all night, and it hasn't been a full day and I'm jacking off to the memory.

But I stroke and picture her tits swinging over my face. All the times I caught one in my mouth while she rode my dick hard.

I come so hard it rattles my body and there's so much cum in my hands it shocks me. *How the fuck is this possible?*

If I'm already beating off to her, did I really get my fill? I really need to have my talk with Madison and figure out how to see Mila again. Or I could just wait. Yeah, I'll just wait and see. It's my last thought before I fall asleep.

———

Mila

Something's really wrong.

Madison never showed up for our presentation yesterday. She didn't return any of my texts. She was AWOL all day. I was seething, thinking she was letting me hang professionally because of what happened with...

Nope, not thinking about him.

This morning our supervisor calls and asks me if I've heard from her. Since I don't think she'd completely blow off work just because she's pissed at me, I find her sister's number and call her.

"Hi, Mila, thank you for your call. Maddie's probably taking some time off. She's been whining that she needs a vacation but didn't want to come with me to Cabo. She does this kind of shit when she's annoyed or tired."

"Okay... But she would have never missed yesterday's presentation."

"Oh." Pregnant pause. "Look, I got an appointment, but I'll call her after and tell her to call you."

Elias comes by an hour later. He looks at me but says nothing, but it's like he expects me to provide whatever it is he's seeking without having to ask.

He tilts his head toward Maddie's desk. "Do you know where she is?"

I shake my head but don't elaborate.

He doesn't move.

"When was the last time you talked to her?" I ask.

He doesn't answer me, just stands there like he wants to but doesn't dare. Does he think I don't know they've been hooking up for a while now? Everyone here knows.

He finally says, "I've been trying to get a hold of her."

I'm tired of the bullshit so I'm not playing coy. "Well, last I heard she had a *meeting* with you."

He shifts his gaze to the door and then back to me. His face goes red and there's now an odd look in his eyes that I can't decipher. The heavy feeling in my gut is instant. He takes a few steps forward, but he stops short of my desk and leans in. "You need to be careful about what you're insinuating. Careers are on the line."

I scoff. "I'm Maddie's friend. She tells me everything."

He smiles, mockingly, like he knows something I don't. "Sure. Tell her to call me when she comes back."

Like I'm his fucking secretary. "If I talk to her, I'll let her know. If you talk to her first, please tell her to call me."

He doesn't even acknowledge my words, leaving me more confused than anything.

I don't hear from her by nighttime when I leave work. My head is killing me, so I take a melatonin gummy and go to bed. I wake up in the middle of the night, sweaty, and panting. I had vivid dreams. My face was against my couch, but I wasn't feeling claustrophobic or panicking. I was moaning and begging Alis to go deeper.

I don't close my eyes after that because I don't want to dream about it. I head to work early and there's still no sign she's been there. Our common files are untouched. I don't want to keep texting her or annoy her family by calling again, so I log into my terminal and go over what we have coming. Now that we got the okay to move on, there are a million pieces to tie up. I begin to set up our campaign grid and files. It's time consuming, and by the time I look up it's ten in the morning.

And my heart drops. Now I *know* something's wrong.

I close my computer, jump to my feet, and head to human resources. They try to brush me off, but I insist on talking to someone about Maddie. Our assigned rep tells me we needed to wait until the family files a police report, that she is probably just taking time away.

I don't want to sit on my hands and do nothing. I call the Chevy Chase Village Police myself. She's been missing for too long and someone needs to do something about it.

"When was the last time you saw Ms. Summerville?" an officer asks.

"Two days ago, at work."

"What makes you think something's wrong, and she's not just taking some time off?"

Is time off everyone's go-to answer?

"This is not like her when it comes to work. I spoke to her sister, and she doesn't know where Maddie is. I don't think they realize the gravity."

"And what's the gravity, Ms..."

"Rosario. I'm Milagros Rosario."

"And what is your relationship with Ms. Summerville?" he asks.

"I'm her friend and coworker."

"Do you have any reason to believe Ms. Summerville could be hurt?" He's popping his gum in my ear and it's annoying me like his questions.

I shake my head like he can see me. "I just know this doesn't feel right. Can you just please do a welfare check?"

As I say the word welfare, it hits me why this feels so weird and why I'm all knots. I'm worried she may be hurt at her place. It's my uncle Felipe all over again. I was too busy here at work. Mami had long days at the hospital. Neither of us realized how much time had passed since we heard from him.

"Okay, Ms. Rosario. We will do that. Please give me her address and a contact number for you."

I give him the address to Maddie's place and my contact information.

"You live in Baltimore?" He sounds like it's the weirdest thing he heard.

"Yes."

"But the missing woman lives in Chevy Chase?"

WTF does this have to do with anything? I don't get angry and yell because I'm sure this man already thinks I'm neurotic or even crazy. They won't look for my friend if I prove him right.

I turn on the charm instead. "Yes, she does, but she works here in

Baltimore. She's a responsible employee who would never disappear from work without calling. I know I may be wrong, but I'm just so worried about my friend. Can you please check?"

"Sure, ma'am. We will try to reach Ms. Summerville at her residence and will contact you with our findings."

I hang up and go back to work, but my mind is not on it. Has Alis heard from her? Maybe I should contact him and see if he has.

I don't have his number but could find it by googling his company.

My fingers freeze halfway to the keyboard. Nope.

God, I need a distraction.

It comes in the most unexpected way when I get the proof photos and the models are all wrong for the campaign. I walk to the graphics department. Jerrod, my usual graphic designer, the one who gets all my concepts, is not there. I have to deal with his substitute. And God knows I hate working with this guy.

He questions every fucking thing, never understands a pun, and if you so much as look at him sternly, he calls his supervisor. Unfortunately, I haven't taken over as his boss yet, so I have to suck it up and tap into my patient side.

After an hour of explaining that we didn't want brushed up stock models and clarifying our concept to the designer, I return to my office. I have little faith in Tim, but thankfully, Jerrod will be back tomorrow.

I shoot him a text just to make sure and head upstairs.

When I get to the office, I find our HR representative waiting for me. Her face is unusually serious. She signals to the office I share with Maddie and closes the door behind us.

"Madison's family called. They reported her missing."

The air goes straight out of me. "Missing?"

"Yes, it seems you were right. Nobody's heard from her in two days and her phone goes straight to voicemail."

"Oh God. I was hoping she was just somewhere mad or with a friend, but she's actually missing."

She nods. "You did a good thing alerting us."

I shake my head. "It accomplished nothing. No one has heard from her."

"Well, hon. Now everyone's looking for her. You hang tight. They'll find her."

But there's a feeling deep in my chest that cuts off my breath. I hope I'm worrying about nothing. Except something tells me this will not end well.

7

Alis

I'm throwing the shirt over my head when my alarm system pings. Weston called thirty minutes ago and told me he was on his way. That's not enough time to get here from Baltimore, which means he must have been nearby when he called.

I leave my bedroom and meet him halfway to the living room.

I'm not shocked to see him inside. He and Aunt Leila have keys to my house. The part that stops me dead in my tracks is the lack of color on his face.

"Good, you're here still. I was afraid you had gone to the office."

I frown. "You told me to wait."

He nods and swallows thickly.

Dread creeps up my spine. "What's wrong?"

He breathes, and just like that, he schools his feature and his body.

"Let's go sit."

He's got the doctor's face, which means he's about to give me bad news. Someone's dead.

"Is it Mom or Dad?" Even as I hear myself ask the question, I know it's dumb. I would know before he does because I still live in the same area as our parents. Then my stomach turns and I'm rooted in place. *No.* "Something's happened to Leila."

He shakes his head and turns toward the family room.

"Just fucking talk, Weston."

"Dahlia came with me. She and Matt are on the way to the Summerville home."

I snort. "What the fuck for?"

"They have news about Maddie. Al, they found her."

His detective wife and her partner came all the way to Luciana Island with news about Maddie? It can't be good when two detectives show up. They come to people's houses to deliver the worst of news. *Death news.*

"She's dead." The words rush out of my mouth. I hear them but I don't get them.

"Yes. They found her in an alley in Baltimore."

"Maddie's dead?" I ask him.

He nods again.

I open my mouth to ask again but can't brace for the flash of cold that creeps over my body. I'm staring at my brother but can't feel my legs. He grows taller right in front of my eyes as I sink into the armchair.

"It's not true."

"It is," he says. "They think it's been two days."

I shake my head. "Two days ago, she was texting with her friend, and she stood me up."

"What friend?"

"Mila. We were supposed to have dinner, but she invited her friend and never showed up. Mila and I had dinner and...Maddie never returned any of my texts or calls. Lindsay called earlier and asked me if I'd seen her... Oh God, Lindsay. She can't be dead, Wes."

My brother grabs a glass of water and comes to stand in front of me. "I'm sorry. Drink this."

I squeeze my eyes shut, but when I open them, my brother's still standing in front of me. I shake my head, wanting to obliterate this moment.

She's not dead.

"Take me to see her."

"I can't. Her family is being notified and they will arrange everything."

This is stupid and ridiculous. "We're not having this conversation."

"Dahlia thought it was better you heard this from me. She wanted me to break the news and be with you."

"How did she die?"

"They don't know the exact cause of death—"

I push to my feet. "Don't give me that shit. You're a doctor and she's a cop."

"I didn't examine the body. A proper autopsy has to be performed." I stare at him until he relents. "They're thinking she was strangled."

The air whooshes out of me and, in that second, I wish I hadn't asked, that my brother had lied to me. *Maddie strangled.*

"By who? Why?"

Weston shakes his head. "I don't know, Al."

"It has to be a mistake."

"I know. I can't believe we just saw her three days ago."

"The last time I saw her was when I dropped her off at work. If I had known, I would've—" I can't even finish the sentence. I should've stayed in town and waited for her after work. "Maybe if I had insisted we talked that day. I could have asked her to come back to the island. She would've been back here and not in Baltimore."

"You can't do that."

I walk to the other end of the room. "I need to know what happened. How is someone alive for lunch one day and then disappears the next, only to turn up dead?"

My brother doesn't have to say anything. It's all in his face. This happens all the time.

The questions keep coming. "What did Dahlia tell you on the way here?"

"They don't even know when it happened. She's only on this case because of the staff shortages. Also, because they were the detectives called to the scene. She recognized Maddie right away..." Weston blows out some air. "They're going to tell the Summervilles and come here."

"To get you?"

He shakes his head. "No, I'm going to stay for a bit."

And it hits me. "They're coming to talk to me."

"They have to."

I nod. As much as I can't breathe or understand this, I know this is procedure. The significant other is always the number one suspect until a stronger candidate comes along. Until the killer...

"Who could've done this?" I ask. "Maddie had no enemies. Everyone loved her."

We exchange a glance and again, no words are necessary, but what we don't say stands between us. Obviously, not everyone loved her. Someone ended her life brutally. *But why?*

"You said they found her in Baltimore?"

He nods. "In an alleyway downtown."

"Jesus, Wes. What the fuck was she doing there? Is this why she didn't come to the restaurant?" Except, it can't be. "She was texting Mila. She told me Maddie was running late."

"We should call her. She may need to talk to Dahlia."

Call her?

My thoughts return to Mila. How hard she tried to cover for Maddie that day. And what happened afterward.

Maddie. Christ.

I think of our time together, how long I was after her. The harder to get she played, the more I wanted her. And I got her. Never would I have thought it would end this way.

My throat clogs and I take a hard breath. I sink into the chair and bury my head in my hands when emotion takes hold.

She's dead. The girl I've known most of my life. She's gone.

And I need to know why.

———

Mila

The office was a madhouse after the news broke that Maddie's missing. No one can believe it. I stayed late at work because the thought of coming home alone chilled me to my bones. Eventually, I pried myself away from my work laptop and headed out. I grabbed a sandwich, came home, showered, and propped myself on my couch. I called the Chevy Chase police twice, but no one has any news. They asked for my address and I gave it.

I catch myself thinking she's doing this to punish me because she knows what happened with Alis. That's what I'm praying for because I'm terrified of voicing my fears. There's nothing on TV so I grab my laptop and start browsing through companies. I like to see what marketing trends others use. It gets my muse going.

The knock on the door stills my hands on my keyboard. I'm not expecting anyone. I'm always careful, though. I grab my phone and open the security app for the building. I pay extra to see who's at my front door. A dark-skinned woman and a white man, both in suits, are looking up at my camera. I don't even move from the couch.

"Can I help you?"

"Milagros Rosario?" the woman asks.

"Who are you?"

The woman lifts her hand and flashes something metal toward the camera. "I'm Detective Dahlia Wicker of the Baltimore Police Department, and this is my partner, Detective Matthew Hunter. May we come in?"

I zoom in on the badge and it looks legit but anyone could get a fake badge online. "Let me see your ID as well, please."

Both flash their IDs and I zoom in. The names match and I take a snapshot of their badges and store it in the cloud. I push my laptop onto the coffee table and head to the door. I don't open the door all the way. "What is this about?"

Their faces are impassive, but the male says, "We want to ask you some questions about Madison Summerville."

They're here about Maddie. I open the door wider. "Please come in. I would do anything I can to help you find her."

Detective Wicker steps in first. She glances around the room. It's fast, but I've seen this type of quick scanning before. I would bet my life this detective absorbs everything in a matter of seconds.

"Thank you for letting us come in."

Since when can anyone refuse the police?

"Of course. Please sit down. Can I get you some water or anything?"

"Water would be nice," Detective Hunter says.

I go to the kitchen and come back with two bottles wrapped in a paper towel. They exchange a glance but take them.

"Thank you," Detective Wicker says. "When was the last time you saw Ms. Summerville?"

"Three days ago. She left work early that day. We texted throughout the day, but she stopped responding after that night. We were supposed to meet for dinner. She never showed. I sent her several text messages and left voicemails after. She never answered."

"Is that why you called the Chevy Chase Village Police?"

I nod. "I called them a few times. We had a big presentation the next day, and she didn't come in. That is not like Maddie. This presentation meant a lot to us and the team."

"Do you know where she went the night she didn't show up?" Detective Wicker is eyeing me intently, like she doesn't want to miss a thing.

I hold her gaze. "I'm not at liberty to say."

"Can't say or won't say?"

"It's Maddie's private business. I'm not betraying her confidence."

"Ms. Rosario, we need you to share this information with us… it's important." She pauses and leans closer to me. "I'm sorry to tell you this, but Madison Summerville was found dead in the early hours of the morning today."

I'm frozen. I don't think I heard her right. "What did you say?"

"I know it's hard to hear, but Ms. Summerville's body was found earlier today. Now we are trying to figure out what happened. Do you know anyone who would hurt her?"

One word makes me freeze. "Who?"

Meaning someone hurt her.

"Oh God."

Someone killed Maddie. My stomach sinks, taking my body down with it. I brace myself with a hand on the coffee table. Detective Hunter pushes a bottle of water into my hand.

"Drink."

I shake my head. The bile is rising. I have to take several breaths.

"Why?" I ask.

"We don't know. We are hoping you can help us."

"I want to—" But the sobs beat me to it.

My friend is dead. Someone killed her.

I need a few minutes to get a hold of myself. The detectives wait patiently until I calm down.

Detective Wicker squeezes my hand. "Milagros, I know this is tough, but we need your help. We need to figure out what you know."

"I don't know anything. I haven't seen her since that day I told you about. But she was a good person. She is smart and gorgeous."

"Did she have any enemies?"

"No. She made friends wherever she went. In the streets, restaurants, the dressing room at Lululemon."

The words don't even sound like they're coming from me. There's a tightness in my chest and I'm fighting to get them out.

Detective Hunter levels me with a look. "How come you were so worried about her? It's like you knew something was wrong."

I shake my head. "I had a bad feeling, like a premonition. When she didn't show up for work, didn't even call... I never thought it was this. Who would do this to her?"

Detective Wicker shakes her head. "We intend on finding out. And we're going to need your help to do that."

I can't think of anything but, "How did she die?"

"It's too soon to tell. We are waiting for the official word from the coroner's office. Where was she going the last time you saw her."

"She was seeing someone in the office, Elias Saunders. No one can know because he was her mentor." The word sounds so final that it sets off the pain in my chest. "He came by yesterday asking about her ..."

The detectives exchange an odd look.

"And?" Detective Hunter asks.

"I told him I didn't know anything."

He makes a few notes. "How did Elias seem?"

"His usual self. Cold maybe annoyed."

He takes his gaze from his notepad to examine my face. "Why annoyed?"

The whole thing starts to get to me. "I told him last I knew Maddie was with him. He didn't like that."

"Why is that?" Wicker asks.

"We have strict rules about dating at Grayson Global, especially when it involves power dynamics."

"Do you have Elias' contact information?" Wicker asks.

"No." The whimper fills the room and I don't know where it came from. I press my fist against my mouth.

Detective Wicker places a hand on my shoulder.

"Do you have someone you can call to come stay with you?" Detective Hunter asks.

Both are staring at me, waiting for my answer, and I just shake my head. "Maddie was one of my few friends here."

"We're sorry for your loss," Detective Wicker says and there's warmth in her eyes. "Is there anything we can do for you?"

I sniff, shaking my head. "Thank you."

She produces a business card from her pocket and hands it to me. "If you remember anything, I want you to call us."

I nod.

Both detectives stand and head for the door. Before she opens it, Detective Wicker turns around to look at me. "We'll be in touch."

After they leave, I engage the deadbolt and the chain. Then I retreat until the back of my knees hit the couch and I plop down on it.

Madison's dead.

The woman who had everything is no longer here.

And my heart shatters thinking of how she won me over with her sweetness and girl talk. How she took me out to lunch our first week at work and declared we needed to team up against all the other broke hoes. And I never asked her for forgiveness.

I don't know when I pick up the phone, but my mom's voice fills the other line, and I let myself cry.

"What's wrong, *amor*?"

"*Ay Mami,* she's dead. I was hoping she was mad or in her own world. But Maddie's gone. The detectives just left here."

My mother gasps. "What? How?"

My phone pings and a message notification drops from the top of my screen. It freezes everything. My tears, my sobs, my capacity to hear my mom.

At the top, in a green bubble, are six words.

UNKNOWN
You better not break girl code.

8

———————

Mila

The heaviness in my chest threatens to drag me down. I need to keep moving even if the place I'm going is the police station. The call from Detective Hunter came right as I was getting ready to go for a walk. They want to see me at the station.

"We have some questions about the timeline that you may be able to clarify for us," he said.

Unease settles in my spine. Instead of sneakers, I throw on some flats, take my purse, and get going. As I park outside the East Madison Station, my phone pings again. I don't even unlock my screen.

UNKNOWN

Keep your trap shut. You break girl code, I
break you.

My throat squeezes. Second text from some unknown five-digit number. Last night I didn't take it seriously. I get crazy spam messages all the time.

Eliminate 37 lbs. Follow this link.

Your package is ready. Follow this link.

I'm horny. Click here to see my video.

Robotexts are a way of life in the modern age, but there's something eerie about these new ones.

You're paranoid 'cause of Maddie. And how ironic is this? I'm at the East Madison St. precinct to talk about my friend Madison's death.

I step out of the car and look around me. There's a couple of uniformed officers by the door. They stop talking when I approach and then smile like drunks at a club.

I nod at them and walk into the precinct. At the reception desk, two women stand arguing with the officer behind the desk.

One woman is screaming at the officer. "I know he's here. He's a minor. Did you know that? I need to see him now."

My phone pings again.

SANDY

You okay? It's a weird day.

I nod like she can see me and text her back.

MILA

Hanging in there. I'm glad we don't have to be in the building.

The three dots appear, and I wait for her response.

"Hi Milagros, thank you for coming." Detective Wicker is right in front of me.

"Please call me Mila."

"Okay," she says and gestures for me to follow her.

We walk through a threshold and it's straight out of the *Law & Order: SVU* set. Desks everywhere, people on the phone, uniformed officers hanging around.

We stop in front of a door and go in. There's a table with a chair on one side and two chairs on the other. Detective Hunter sits on one side. *This is official.* "Am I being questioned?"

"It's just a chat, Mila. We want to clarify a few things."

I hesitate. *Do they consider me a suspect? Should I ask for a lawyer? Would that make me look guilty?*

Detective Wicker waits patiently. Her face is pleasant, like the doorman in my uncle's Upper Westside building. She lets me make up my mind, and because she doesn't push, I decide to cooperate. I have nothing to hide. I want them to find who did this to Maddie.

Detective Hunter stands until I sit. Then, he goes back to his chair and flips open a folder while Detective Wicker takes the chair next to him.

"Like I said on the phone, we want to go over the timeline. Tell us again about the last time you saw Madison."

I go over the story again, stressing our dinner plans and how she never showed up and stopped answering my texts.

"Where did you say she went?"

"She was going to hang out with the guy she's been seeing at work."

"Mila, there's something I don't understand. If she was hanging with that guy, why were you waiting for her?"

Her tone is soft, but the alarms go off in my head. I don't want to talk about what happened that night, but I need to at least tell them parts of it. Until it makes sense.

"She was going to dinner with her boyfriend and asked me to come along. We were waiting for her, but she never showed. I kept texting her because he was catching on, but..."

Detective Hunter leans in. "Catching on?"

I close my eyes and try not to wince.

"Look, I told her this was a bad idea from the beginning."

"What was a bad idea?" Detective Wicker presses.

"She invited me because she wanted me to keep her boyfriend company while she met with her office guy. Their meeting overlapped with her date."

They exchange a quick look, and I know that look. They smell the tea.

"Meeting?" Detective Hunter arches a brow.

I wince this time.

"So, what you're saying is Madison had two dates. One with her official boyfriend and another with a guy she was having an affair with from the office."

I nod. I hate that this is coming up.

"Why wouldn't she just reschedule the date?"

I sigh, frustration getting the best of me. "That's what I asked, but she didn't want to. Madison feared her boyfriend was getting suspicious and wanted to break up with her. Anyway, she kept insisting, and I gave in. The plan was for me to go to the restaurant on time and meet him and stall until she got there. She told him I would come along."

"How did he take it?"

"I don't know. She said she had told him she was stuck in traffic and that he was supposed to bring a guy friend. But she didn't let him know she was late, and he had no clue what I was talking about when I mentioned the other guy."

This sounds so stupid. *Jesus, why did I listen to her?*

Detective Hunter writes something on his pad. "Was the boyfriend angry?"

I shake my head again. "I'm not sure. He seemed... resigned?"

Yeah, he dumped her right then and there and didn't seem mad at all.

He leans closer. "Resigned? That's an unusual word. How about you, Mila? Were you upset with her?"

I scoff. "Yeah, wouldn't you be? She hung me out to dry. She didn't tell him she was running late and there was no friend coming along with him. She put me in an awkward position."

"How mad were you?" Detective Hunter asks.

Huh? Oh, I see.

"Not that mad." Cause I didn't get a chance. I was mostly guilty because of what I did with *him.*

Detective Wicker looks at her notes. "But you texted her saying you were going to strangle her."

"I did not—" Then I remember the texts from that night. "That was just me blowing off some steam because she jerked me around. Don't you ever say stuff like that to a friend?"

Wicker shrugs. "Yeah, but none of my friends have ever shown up dead and me looking like I made good on my promise."

Maddie was strangled. My throat starts to close like someone's squeezing it. I force a breath run a hand over my neck. *She thinks I did it.*

I see red. "You can't believe I had anything to do with this. Maddie was my friend." My voice rises and I don't care.

"Where were you that evening?"

"I told you. I was at the restaurant. You can call and they can vouch for me."

Wicker nods. "We will. What about after?"

"I went home."

"Alone?" Hunter asks.

"Why would I kill Maddie?" I ask instead.

"I don't know. She stood you up, didn't secure a guy for you, and you were mad at her. She was your rival at work, for what you've told many people is your dream job."

My stomach drops because they consider me a suspect. They've looked into me. They talked to people. It's like they're building a case. I need to talk to Grayson. He can set them straight. They probably won't believe me if I said I had already gotten the job and I don't want to lose that too.

"I spent the night at home. I have cameras and the building has cameras. The video can corroborate that."

"Were you alone?" Wicker asks.

I shake my head. "I had male company."

Hunter nods. "Get his number ready. We'll need to talk to him."

My throat thickens and I have to open my mouth to breathe. *Shit shit shit.*

"I don't have his number."

"You don't have his number?" His tone reeks of judgement and he can fuck all the way off.

"It was a one-night stand, Detective Hunter," I snap. "I don't usually have those, and I wouldn't want him involved. Wouldn't it be enough for you to look at the footage at my place?"

He shrugs. "Maybe. But you're keeping too much information for someone who is…"

He lets his voice drift off. And that's when I get pissed and shoot to my feet.

"A suspect? Is that what you're saying?"

"Mila, please sit down." Detective Wicker's voice is low and calm and none of the things I feel right now.

"No." I can't believe they think I could hurt Maddie. "If you're going to arrest me, do it. If not, I'm going home."

Neither moves, so I bolt for the door and throw it open. I walk toward the front door with so many things in my head. I need to call a lawyer. I need to call Grayson. I need to contact Alis. I need to stop dead in my tracks because he's standing across the room with a man who looks just like him. Both are staring at me.

My stomach churns. If I had followed my instincts and said no to Maddie, I wouldn't be in this mess.

No, if you had not been a *pendeja* feeling guilty because you got the job you worked so hard for, you wouldn't be in this position.

Yeah, this is my fault, but there's no way I'm going to talk to him. I keep going without a word and run right into Elias Saunders.

The police are looking at him too. He's must have been the last one to see her alive.

And is it because he probably killed her?

———

Alis

The two detectives show us in. They're friendly to Weston. Everyone knows him here as Dahlia's husband. They guide us to sit in the waiting area. I push to my feet because I can't sit anymore. We've been trapped in a car, driving from Luciana Island. I'm haunted by Mrs. Summerville's sobs, her husband's quiet devastation, and the new light in Lindsay's eyes. Her skin's so pale but she was gracious, receiving us and navigating her parents through the visit.

If only I had looked for Maddie. If I had gone to her place to talk. Since yesterday, the "what ifs" and "if onlys" have tortured me.

Where the hell had she gone? Who the hell could have taken her life? Could I have stopped it if I hadn't been with Mila? If we both had gone looking for her instead of —

A door swings open so hard we all turn to look its way and out storms a woman who heads in our direction. *Mila.* I freeze. She stops short when she sees me. Her eyes widen, but she quickly pivots and goes around the other side of the room.

"You know her?" Weston asks.

I nod but don't take my eyes off her. "That's my alibi."

At the door, a dark-haired man walks directly in her path. He stops her, his hand on her arm, but she flinches, recoiling from his touch.

"What did you say?" he asks, his eyes narrowed on her face.

"Get the hell away from me." She stalks right past him.

"Come on in, Mr. Saunders," my sister-in-law's voice rings out.

And I put it all together quickly. He's here to be questioned. Just like Mila was questioned. Just like I'm about to be.

Who is he?

The man walks towards Dahlia and I take off after Mila. Weston calls out my name. I don't stop until I get outside. She reaches her car and I run to catch up with her.

"Stop," I say.

But she opens the door with her key fob. I reach her before she can get in.

"Get away from me."

I shake my head. "Who was that in there?"

"Go ask him," she practically spits at me.

"Tell me. Why is he being questioned about Madison?"

"I don't know. I guess we are all here because we knew her." She's yet to look into my eyes, mostly gazing around me.

I put a stop to that, placing myself close and in her line of vision.

"How does he know her?" I repeat.

"We work together. I think the detectives are trying to put together a timeline..."

I shift forward a bit. "Yeah, with the last people who saw and interacted with Madison. Where does he fit?"

She backs into the car. "They had a meeting that evening."

I frown. "A meeting?"

"Yes, Elias is her mentor." Something in her tone tells me she doesn't want to say anything else, but I'm going to press her. Because the picture is emerging clearly.

"Is that where she was while we were at the restaurant?"

She presses her lips together.

"Look, we should talk—"

She puts a hand up. "I think you and I already did enough talking..."

And other things. She doesn't say it, but her words hang between us.

"I blame myself too."

Her face crumbles, but she manages to sneak a breath and puts herself together fast. "Let's just stay away from each other."

"I don't know if we can do that until they find her killer. I have so many questions."

"I can't do this with you, A—" She stops short of saying my name. "I'm sorry for your loss. I know you loved her."

"You did too."

She nods. "Yeah, and I failed her."

"This is not your fault. The killer is the only one at fault." But it's hypocritical. I feel the same guilt. It's been eating at me since I found out yesterday.

Her gaze is laced with pity. "Excuse me," she says, gets in her car, and drives away.

I'm left to watch the gray 4Runner disappear down the street.

I head back inside and find my brother waiting for me with Dahlia by his side.

She tilts her head into a room. "Let's go have a chat."

"What about the coworker?" I ask.

She walks into the room without a word.

"He *lawyered* up," my brother says, his gaze fixed on a door down the hall.

"That asshole did something to her." My voice is loud enough to bounce off the walls.

Dahlia tilts her head to the room closest to us and walks in. I follow her into the room. Matt is in there waiting. He gestures for me to take a chair. She closes the door.

We go through everything I told her yesterday about waiting for Maddie and her not showing up. I was careful to leave Mila's name out of everything.

"So... normally, I would start questioning you all over again, but we pieced a few things together and you need to clarify them for us. Tell me about you and Mila."

Her name is like ice water poured over my head. Lying to the police, even when the detective is family, is not wise. I already omitted too much the first time around.

"Madison invited her along with us to dinner. When Maddie failed to show, we ate alone."

"And after?" Matt asks.

I say nothing, trying to come up with a good way to get us out of this.

Matt sighs. "Alis, we are not trying to be salacious here. We want to find out who killed Madison and why two people who can clearly alibi each other are now looking suspicious because they won't come clean. We have already got the warrant for the camera footage in Mila's building and front door. But until we watch that footage, you're both suspects because you lied to us, and we can't understand why."

Shit. She's a suspect. I think of the agony in her face. It's the same anguish I saw today. What was that thing with Elias about? I need to find out, though my gut tells me Mila would never hurt Maddie.

"She was with me."

Neither moves nor acknowledges, but it's Matt who asks, "We figured that. From what time to what time?"

"From the moment she walked into the restaurant, around seven that evening, until around seven thirty in the morning, when I headed back to Luciana Island."

Dahlia nods. "Thank you."

"Why wouldn't she just say this?" Matt asks.

"Because she and Madison were friends and Mila broke girl code. Never touch your friend's ex. She knows this makes her look bad." Dahlia shrugs.

If she broke the code, it was only because I kicked her defenses down.

Matt grunts. "Did she really break girl code, though?"

His question has me snapping my head up and looking between them.

"Yes," Dahlia says and looks at me. "Why didn't you tell us about Mila?"

"I told you I was with a woman."

"The who you were with is as important as the where you were. You omitted a lot, Alis." Matt's tone is loaded. There's chastisement but also frustration.

I should've told them everything. I just didn't want to admit what had happened.

Dahlia flips through her notebook. "Thank you for coming and clarifying everything."

She's dismissing me? *Fuck that.* I have questions too and since I answered theirs, they can answer mine. "What did this Elias guy have to do with Madison?"

"They worked together," Matt tells me.

"I know they had some kind of meeting. Was he the last person to see her alive?"

"Did Mila tell you they met?"

"Yes, but she refused to say anything else. Tell me about him."

Dahlia doesn't move or blink, her gaze never leaving my face. "This is an ongoing investigation. We will let you know when we find—"

There's a knock on the door and a detective we saw earlier pokes his head in. "You're going to want to see this. It's going viral."

She and Matt step outside and I follow. Everyone is standing around a desk where there's a video on the monitor. My brother turns around and grimaces. I take three steps and all I see is the headline across the screen.

Source: Murdered Heiress Madison Summerville Double Crossed By Professional Rival And Boyfriend Who Spent The Night Together As She Fought For Her Life.

"Are you fucking kidding me? Who would put this trash out?" Dahlia explodes.

"That blog gets all the tea. I wonder who the source is?" someone asks.

Matt snaps. "This is bullshit, and they're trying to create a circus while we're trying to solve a murder." Matt snaps.

My thoughts turn to Mila. I need to warn her.

I move closer to my sister-in-law and take her by the arm, ignoring the looks from all others. "I need to talk to Mila. Give me her number."

She blinks a few times. "You don't have it?"

I'm almost ashamed when I say, "No."

She shakes her head. "I can't give it to you. This would violate her privacy and our confidentiality rules."

"She's going to be blindsided by this. I have to tell her."

Her face is impassive. "You need to let us do our job. This is a dumb gossip website. We will reach out to the FBI to have it removed."

"Fine." I walk away.

My brother follows me outside. I pull out my phone and call Grayson, explaining and then asking for his help.

He won't give me her number. He can't, but he tells me if I search well enough, I can find it. It takes me and Weston an hour, but we find it in her LinkedIn profile. I drop off my brother and call her.

"Mila, it's Alis. We need to talk."

"Please don't call me." She hangs up.

I try calling back a few times, but she doesn't answer the phone. I head to her apartment to tell her and to get some of the answers I need.

I'm a few blocks away from her place when the phone rings. On the car dash, the caller's initials fill the screen, J. Carey. She's our publicist at Ellison Corp. I tap to answer.

"Alis, where are you?"

"I'm in Baltimore."

"Did you see the blog story going viral? My sources tell me a couple of major news outlets are picking it up."

Fuck.

"Okay." I say.

"I'm trying to formulate a strategy. Is there anything I should know about you and Ms. Rosario?"

The hell if I know what to say or not these days. "We never set out to double cross anyone. It wasn't intentional."

"What does that mean?" she asks.

Even the truth sounds dumb right now. "I can't talk about this right now. Come up with something."

"Okay, standard response it is. We don't comment on gossip," she says.

"Jennifer, make sure not to throw any dirt on Mila."

"It's never my style. I'll be in touch."

I park in the same spot I did two nights ago, hop out of the car, and head into Mila's building. She may not want to talk but she's going to answer my questions.

9

———————

The pounding on the door echoes of the pounding in my head since I came home. The questions of the cops, the heartache over Maddie, the fear of losing everything I've worked so hard for, all of it had me taking three painkillers and laying down on my couch for thirty minutes.

It didn't work. I couldn't stop the thoughts. The police are now suspecting me of killing Maddie and it's all I can think about.

The pounding bounces off the wall. I get up and make my way to the door. I peer through the peephole. Alis is standing there, his eyes staring right at mine.

I clamp a hand over my mouth and take three steps back.

What is he doing here? How the hell did he get up to my floor?

"Open the door. I can hear you standing there."

I say nothing, hoping—praying—he will just go away.

He doesn't.

"Mila, I need to talk to you." His voice rises and all I can think of is everyone knowing he's out there.

I step up again, unlock the door, but don't remove the chain.

"Go away. We don't need to be seen together. Please don't make a scene."

"I hate scenes, but I'll make one, a big one, unless you let me in. We have things to talk about."

I'm losing this battle. He's obviously not a suspect. Meanwhile, I am.

I remove the chain and open the door all the way. He comes in and closes it behind him. We stand in front of it, but he doesn't move. I finally sigh and wave toward the sitting area. He takes a seat on the couch I just vacated, but I can't sit next to him on it, so I take an armchair.

"I was calling you to tell you that some website posted a salacious article revealing that you and I were together the night Maddie was killed. My publicist called me saying a media outlet reached out and they will feature the story."

He talks fast and maybe that's why it takes a little longer to catch up to his words.

Then I do. *Shit.* "No."

He waves a hand. "Unfortunately, yes. I wanted you to hear it from me and prepare before reporters reach out to you and the questions start coming in."

"The police already suspect me and now it's all out there. What exactly are people saying?"

"One, the police no longer think either of us is a suspect, or at least I don't think so. I told them we were together that night."

I swipe a hand over my face. This is not happening. "Why did you do that?"

"Because we need to be smart about this. I know this doesn't look good, but we are each other's alibis and there is a murder investigation. We have to save ourselves. I'm the ex-boyfriend and you're the professional rival who slept with me."

I can't sit anymore. I push to my feet and go stand by a window.

He follows me but doesn't come too close. "That's what they're saying. The boyfriend or ex is always a suspect. You and Maddie were obviously friends and colleagues, but you were in competition for—"

"We weren't. Not anymore."

"Both of you applied for the Chief Marketing Officer position."

I take my gaze off the old building across the way and turn back to him. "The competition was over. Grayson chose me. He asked me to keep it close hold until he told all the other applicants."

He seems taken aback. "Congratulations."

I nod, saying nothing else. The word doesn't hold the meaning it should right now.

"When did he tell you?" Alis asks.

"The day you went to lunch with Maddie."

There's a sad smile on his lips. "She was excited about getting that job."

I nod. "I was prepping for everything to go to hell. I needed to rack up points."

"Meaning?"

I close my eyes, and when I open them, he's a step closer. I back up. "Nothing would be the same between Maddie and me when Grayson announced I was selected."

"It's business, Mila." His voice is soft, like silk sliding over skin, smoothing over peaks and valleys.

I wish he didn't say my name like that. It's too much like that night. I suppress the urge to retreat and hold my ground.

"It's never just business when there's a friendship in the way. Maddie was a great person. She was also competitive and played to win. I hated not being able to tell her when she walked in after lunch with you."

"How was she that day?"

Hating your sister-in-law, worried that you could see the drift between you, still not caring, and wanting to go see Elias.

But I say none of those truths. "She was... herself. I was reminding her she needed to get ready for our brief that day and our presentation two days later."

"Is that when she asked you to come to dinner with us?"

I nod. "Yeah."

"And you came because you had no other friend in town and had nothing to do."

Huh?

"I went because she asked me to and I was feeling guilty and... she insisted. A lot. She even promised you were bringing a friend so I wouldn't be a third wheel."

He bobs his head. "She was going to see Elias Saunders, and she needed you to cover."

There's no point in lying anymore. "Yes."

"So, she was never coming, and you were just playing a game with me."

Heat bursts all over my face. "I admit I covered for her, but she told me she was coming and would be a bit late. I'm a girl's girl type of friend. I live by girl code... at least I did until that night."

"Why go through all this?"

I can't stand the way he's staring at me. There's something there. Pain? Maybe anger? "I asked her the same thing. I don't think she wanted to lose you. "

"She was sleeping with someone else."

I open my mouth and close it.

"Don't bother. I already know. I'm not stupid. She wasn't fucking me regularly. She must have been getting it somewhere else. Not to mention all the time we were spending apart."

I don't know what to say, so I say nothing.

"What about you, Mila? What was your part in all this? How far did she ask you to take it? Did you sleep with me as part of the cover up?"

My jaw clenches. "I'm not that good of a friend. It turns out I wasn't a good friend at all. She wanted me to pacify you so you wouldn't break up with her. Instead, I ended up sleeping with you."

"There wasn't much sleeping," he says and smiles a little when I pelt him with a look. "It's the truth. A truth neither of us can change. We need to learn to live with it and not let the guilt land us in jail."

I hang my head. He's right. "I didn't want to lie or omit anything to the police. This just looks so bad. Grayson will clarify the job thing. He assured me of that. But this whole thing with you—"

My phone pings, but I don't move.

"One night ruined everything. It feels like it's ruining my whole life."

He shakes his head and moves closer, this time putting a hand on my arm. "It will not ruin your life."

The electricity breaks over my skin, where he's touching me. And I fight to stay still, to not lean into his touch. My phone rings again and this time it's my excuse to break contact. I walk back to the sitting area. It's *Mami*.

I don't even get to say hello.

"I just saw it on the news. Madison's death. You and her boyfriend and now people say that you..."

"What? That I what?"

"It's awful. I need to come be with you. I don't want anyone to think this about you. How do I fix it?"

Her desperation is contagious, but I need to keep this together. "*Mami*, breathe. Calm down. I am okay. I need to talk to you about this. Just know the police don't think I'm a suspect."

"But the news and online..."

"*Mami,* just breathe. Go have some water. I will call you back, okay? Let me see what they're saying."

"Okay, *amor*."

I grab my TV remote and turn it on. It's only four in the afternoon, so there is no news on. I breathe a sigh of relief.

"My mom says she saw it in the news."

Alis is closer than I expected and he's looking over his phone. "My publicist just messaged me. It's all over social media."

I open the Twitter app on my phone. The messages are one after the other on my screen accompanied by hashtags.

Some fucking friend. #snake #JusticeforMadison

I'd beat my friend's ass. #Beat #backstabbing #snake

Wow, she was fucking Maddie's man while Maddie was getting killed. #JusticeforMadison #snake

He's not a snack. He's a Thanksgiving dinner with dessert, honey. #NotBlamingHer #snake

Girl, have you seen him? I would say fuck the friendship too. #snake

I'd slap my sweet granny for a night with him, #IWouldaFucked-HimToo #snake

It's the last two that break me. I plop on to the sofa. My friend's dead. I did her dirty. Now the whole world knows. I feel like the snake they say I am.

I bury my face in my hands. I don't know how much I was freezing until his arms go around me. I want to get up and walk away, but I can't. This is the first time I've felt warm since the morning he left. There's no way I have the right to take comfort in him, but I do what I did that night. I steal this moment until I regain my breath.

"You feel better?"

I nod against his neck. Then his lips press to the side of my temple. I close my eyes, let the sensation rock me. Then I pull back slowly, almost reluctantly. It would be so easy to kiss him.

And you'll be back in the hole again.

And you'll be losing worse.

He's coming out of this like a G but you're the snake. You'll keep being the snake.

I pull away. "You should go."

So many emotions cross over his face, and he shakes his head. "Mila, it's just comfort."

"I can't take your comfort. Not when Madison's dead, and I'm the snake. You're apparently so hot, everyone understands, but will still shit on me for it."

He winces. "I'm sorry, but I don't care about that."

"You don't have to care, Alis. I do. It's my life. My reputation. I need to figure out how to salvage all that. Thank you for being my alibi, for saying what I should have. But you have to go and you can't come back."

"I don't know that I can do that."

"I can't be seen with you. I need to talk to my mother and make sure she stops worrying. I also need to plan how I'm going to handle this."

He looks like he wants to argue but moves to the door. I go after him so I can engage the deadbolt and chain.

He opens the door and turns to me. "I really am sorry..."

I nod. "I know you are."

Then he says, "I don't think we can stay away from each other."

He steps out into the hallway, closing the door behind him.

And I stand there with my hand on the deadbolt. Except, unlike the other morning, I'm 100% sure I won't be able to keep him out.

———

Mila

I pace to the window and back to my sitting area again. After a week of being cooped up at home, I have walked the equivalent of the Sparthalon.

I have loved my rental since the moment I saw it. It's feminine and posh with its hint-of-pink walls, curved arches and built-in bookcases. It was everything I ever wanted. Now it feels like a cage. I don't want to go outside but I hate that I'm inside as well. I'm a finch flying back and forth in her gilded space.

"Mila?"

"I'm here, G. Just too much to think right now."

"Tell me how you're feeling. You have to let it out." Greg's voice is soft and warm.

I want to hold onto that because since I found out about Maddie, there's an Arctic chill I can't seem to shake off my bones. Except for a few minutes, but I'm not letting myself flash back to Alis's visit.

"I keep thinking it can't get any worse... turns out it can. And it has. And it will keep going." I don't grit my teeth or bite my nails like I want to. There's truly no point.

"Why do you think it will keep going?" he asks.

"Because she's gone and the grief should have been the worst part. Now I have to deal with the police and the internet and the..."

"Guilt?" he asks.

The pang breaks in my belly and I press my hand against it. Though I know he doesn't want to hurt me, his words still do. "Yes."

He sighs. "Mila, don't do that to yourself. You have too much going for you. Mourn the friend you lost but don't waste your time with guilt. It doesn't lead anywhere good. Plus, and you know I loved Maddie, but she was getting hers. She used you so she could cheat on her boyfriend."

He means well but I'm not in the mood for gossip. It's too soon, maybe will always be too soon.

"Do you want me to come over for a bit?" he asks.

I should say yes, because it would be great to have someone sit with me. Instead, I say, "Thanks, but I need to be alone. I'll take a pill and go to sleep."

"I'm only a phone call away, okay? Whiskers and Wolfie would be over the moon if you wanted to come by."

The thought of him and his cats actually makes me smile. "Thank you. I'm still waiting for that photo of Wolfie."

"I'll send it as soon as we fix that weird overbite he has going on."

I hang up and continue my wall-to-wall pilgrimage. One of the last things I said to Maddie was *I'm going to strangle you*. And someone made good on my innocent words. Someone killed her. Maybe Elias? That's why he was at the station. He was the last person she went to see. If she had only come to dinner instead of going to see him, would she still be alive? And if they hadn't arrested Elias yet, what did that mean? I run my fingers through my hair.

I need to get out of here.

My phone rings and Sandy's name appears on the screen. I pick up the Facetime call.

Her gaze lands on me and face shifts from surprise to sadness. "You don't look good, hon."

"I'm sure I feel like I look, broken. How are you?"

"Same," Sandy says. "It's bad all around. Even Grayson is off his game. He's making arrangements for Maddie's things at the office before he meets with her parents."

I'm thankful he's letting my team work remotely. I keep thinking the gathering of Maddie' things is one reason. He wouldn't want to traumatize the staff any more than we are. The other is probably me.

"Sandy, I know this looks bad, but I never meant... and I would never hurt her."

"Hon, stop this. You don't have to tell me that. I know it. We all know it."

"I don't even want to know what Grayson thinks about me."

"Not what you think. He made it clear that your personal life is no one else's business and no one in the company will risk going against him."

"Not to his face," I finish. Because the rumor mill at GG is big, like with any company.

"I know the nosy crowd has already started calling, but you just get them off the phone or don't pick up. Once the announcement is out, you'll be their boss and they won't bother you too much... and congratulations, hon." Her voice dissolves into melted honey at the end.

"Thank you." It feels so good to say it before the bitterness kicks in. Everyone will think it's default. "I'm sorry I couldn't tell you before."

"I've worked for Grayson for many years and totally understand. You deserve it. Have you seen him?" The change in topic is abrupt, but I know she means Alis.

"Not since he came by the other day to warn me about the story going viral. He calls. I don't answer."

"Maybe you should, Mila. The two of you are in a unique situation."

"This is all messed up because of what happened between us. Can you imagine if people get wind that we're even talking?"

"They're going to talk, anyway. You shouldn't care. That night is not the reason Maddie's dead."

I've told myself that a thousand times. It doesn't ease the guilt.

10

Luciana Island

Alis

My feet are heavy as we walk away from the fresh grave. The soft, wet grass muffles all our steps.

"They say time heals wounds but a month hasn't ease a dammed thing. This rain is just another sign of how wrong this is. My sister was brightness and sunshine. Livelihood celebration. In a way, I guess this weather is probably the best thing that could happen because Maddie's death soaks everything in our lives in perpetual sadness," Lindsay said in the saddest eulogy I've ever witnessed. She talked about her sister, her confidant, the one person who understood her. Her tears mixed with the rain and got carried away by the fall wind, but when she went back to stand by her parents, she was again stoic and in control.

"As if someone flipped a switch," Aunt Leila says.

"What?" I ask.

"Lindsay. She's being strong for her parents."

"Death makes you grow quickly," Dahlia adds, staring at the

Summervilles as the family gets in their car. They'll exit first. Everyone will file out after.

"I can't imagine what she must be going through." My brother meets my eyes briefly and I have to look away. That's when I catch the new direction of Dahlia's gaze. She pans out as if she's just looking around until I spot an SUV parked a block away, on the far end of the Summerville mausoleum. A gray 4Runner. *Mila.*

Why is she here? That's a stupid question. *You know why she's here. The same reason you're here.*

It's just a stupid decision. If these people were to notice her, they would subject her to so much aggression. But since no one seems to suspect, I'm just going to leave.

"We're going to the restaurant together, right?" my mom asks.

"We're driving that way," Weston says. "We'll meet you there."

The traffic director signals to us. We are next. My parents go first. Weston and Dahlia are next, but before they can get into the car, I make a split-second decision.

"Leila, go with Weston and Dahlia. There's something I need to do."

She frowns at me. "No. I'm not leaving you alone today."

"I'll be there soon. I just need some time."

Weston takes her elbow. "Come on. He'll meet us."

I'm so grateful that we can communicate without having to say a thing sometimes. What I don't love is the piercing look on his wife's face.

"A word." She hooks an arm to mine and walks to my car. Then she turns on me. "She's come to pay her respects. Let her do that in peace. The last thing the two of you need is to be seen together."

"I don't know what you're talking about. I'm leaving the cemetery after you."

"Alis—" She blows out a mouth of air as if she's measuring her words. "You're a big boy who's come out of this whole thing squeaky clean. No one is questioning your right to be here. Meanwhile, she's hiding to say goodbye to her friend."

"I know that." And though low, my tone is nothing near soft.

"Then you know what would happen if anyone realizes she's here..." She lets her words hang in the air.

I nod. But I can't let them get to me. I need to talk to Mila. This is the only time I have to do that since she doesn't answer my calls or texts.

I get in my car and drive behind them. As soon as we get to the first intersection on Memorial Drive, I break the procession and turn. I let all the cars pass and go back in the way I came. I park behind the mausoleum where my car is not in public view. I put up the hood of my rain jacket and make it to Mila's car. She's not there. I look around until I spot her beside the grave. She's standing there, under the rain. I grab the umbrella from my car and cross the street.

I move close but stay under the canopy. I want to give her time with Madison. I want her to get what she needs to say off her chest. When the rain picks up, she doesn't move. I open my umbrella and relocate next to her, shielding her from the downpour. She looks up at me and back at the casket.

"You shouldn't be here," I say.

She doesn't take her gaze off the grave. "I don't know where else to be. I may not have known her all my life, and I don't have her blood, but she was my friend. I needed to say goodbye."

"I know. I wouldn't take that from you, but if the press finds out... or the family and other friends..."

"I won't stay long. I waited until everyone was gone."

I nod this time. "I get it."

"Why are you here? If they see me with you..."

"I'm fucking tired of everyone saying that."

She humphs. "It's very easy for you to be tired of things. You're not catching the brunt of it. And trust me, I deserve some of what I'm getting, but not all of it."

"I'm as much to blame for what happened between us, but I didn't kill her and neither did you."

"No." Her voice is soft. "Someone did, though. I just want the police to find who did."

"Or maybe they have a suspect and are just not sharing." They have to be looking at Elias "that fucking asshole" Saunders.

She swipes a hand across her eyes and turns away.

I catch her arm before she can escape. "Wait."

"No, I stayed long enough. I don't want to be caught out here with you." There's no tone to her words, but they irk me just the same.

It's hearing them from Dahlia and now her.

"Trust me, I'm not trying to put you at risk." My tone is dryer than I intend and she bristles, trying to pull her arm free.

"Let me go. I'll head back to Baltimore immediately."

"Not until we talk."

"About what? Haven't we talked enough?"

"Not nearly," I say, and she gasps. I hold on tighter to her. "Not like that, Mila. I mean, we haven't had a minute to talk. You don't answer my calls, and I want to give you your space, but I really need to know things. Things that only you can tell me."

She sighs. "Fine, but just a few minutes."

"Thank you," I say, guiding her away from the grave. I head to the only place here where I've spent time. There's a small sitting area nearby that Aunt Leila insisted on installing.

"This is your family's." It's a statement, not a question, but I still nod as if to give her confirmation.

"Tell me more about Elias Saunders and Madison?"

She shakes her head. It's almost imperceptible, but it's there. "You already know. Maddie's dead. There's no need to rehash this."

"I need to know. Tell me."

She takes the bench and I hand her the umbrella.

"Elias works at Grayson Global. He's one of Grayson's lawyers. We met him at orientation. He came to talk to us about being part of the company. He and Maddie became fast friends."

"Why not you?"

She snorts. "I never liked him. He gave me social climber vibes. I also don't think he had any use for me, plus, I wasn't there for that. All I wanted was to get acclimated and learn about my job. Maddie was one of the few friends I made and mostly because she got on me."

"Why didn't you want to make friends?"

She looks away. "It's not that. I just had gotten a great opportunity in my life. I didn't want to waste a second of it. I spent my first six months in Baltimore researching, refining my ideas, submersing myself completely into every project."

"What about Maddie and Elias?"

"He came to talk to us during orientation like most higher uppers. He introduced the marketing ethics panel. We stayed behind to ask questions after the session and got introduced to him. I chatted up with Simone, another of the big-time lawyers. Elias got to answer Maddie's questions. He became her mentor soon after. He gave her advice and listened to her."

"When did they start sleeping together?"

Mila doesn't move or look at me. No reaction, but the tension is hanging between us. Still, she says nothing.

"She's gone, Mila. You don't need to keep her secrets anymore."

"I know," she replies. "It just doesn't feel good, but you're right. She's gone. She began sleeping with Elias right after... things didn't work out with your brother."

And if she sucker punched me in the stomach, it would've been less shocking. But I follow suit and don't move. I don't want her changing her mind.

"Go on."

She searches my face and then continues. "She was upset. She felt the doctor should've told her he was going through a breakup and not led her on. She was trying to get over the disappointment."

"Why did she agree to date me then? We started dating a year ago, shortly after her and Weston. Seems like the same time she began sleeping with Elias too." The anger seeps into my voice because I can't help it. She was fucking someone at the same time she was fucking me. "I guess I know now why she made so many excuses."

"Excuses?"

I shake my head. "Never mind. Keep going."

"There's nothing else, Alis." And there she goes, saying my name softly, staring at me with warmth.

"There's a lot more. She was with him that night. That's why the police are looking at him. I—"

She's taken aback. "They told you that?"

"It's only logical. He must have been the last person to see her alive. What I want to know is why you were covering for her?"

"My friend asked for a favor. I didn't want to do it, but she needed my help."

Her candidness pisses me off and I can see them both plotting and texting with each other to keep me there. "You're very generous with your favors, huh?"

She pushes to her feet and shoves her finger right in my face. "Fuck. You." She tries to move past me, but I stop her.

"We're not done."

"Yes, we are. I get insulted enough on social media. I'm not subscribing to get that shit from you. I didn't force you that night. In fact, you initiated it."

And I would fucking do it again.

The thought sneaks in so fast that I drop her arm. She storms away and I stand there like a fool before I go after her. Now for another reason—I need to apologize.

She is already near the road. I run to catch up with her and I'm a breath away, but everything happens fast. Out of nowhere, a pick-up truck appears as it intentionally speeds toward her. She has a foot off the curve and in the street, and I don't think, I grab her raincoat from behind and yank. She screams. We both end up falling on our backs. Mila lands on my leg.

The truck swerves at the last minute, missing us. I can only make out a single flower decal. Her scream is still in my ear, penetrating the pounding echo of my heartbeat.

"Oh, God."

I can barely hear her from the thrashing in my chest. "I think someone just tried to run you over," I wheeze out.

She lays her head on my shoulder. Her breath is ragged, washing over my neck in choppy hot waves.

Mila

The doorbell rings, and as if it's normal, Alis stands and answers it. I stay put on the sofa, with my throw blanket and my legs tucked under me like I'm not tired of sitting down. Detective Wicker, who I just learned is his sister-in-law, steps through the door, followed by her partner.

Detective Hunter once-overs me in that cop way where they see everything in one instant. Then his gaze softens. "Are you okay?"

"Yeah, sure."

He looks briefly at his partner. Detective Wicker shrugs.

"You should have gone to the hospital for a checkup," he says.

The laughter bubbles out of me. "In Luciana Island? Where everyone thinks I murdered one of their own? Where everyone has more money than God? Yeah, okay."

Why did I let Alis call them? Their presence is pointless.

"I get it. Not a good idea," he says, and I wince.

"I'm sorry. My manners are not usually this bad."

"You're not hurting my feelings. Wicker's my partner. If her coffee's not hot enough, there's hell to pay. You're pleasant compared to her." He hooks a thumb toward Detective Wicker, who nods.

And they've never been this friendly with me, which makes me distrust them even more. I sit up straight, and in the next second, Alis sits by my side.

Detective Wicker opens her mouth but then closes it. Because we all know what she's going to say. This is not a good idea when we don't want attention, but he saved my life. I don't know what I would have done if he hadn't driven me back and talked to me through this whole shitshow. I didn't even think to question him when he suggested we call them.

"Let's go over what happened. And for the record, the two of you should have called the police on Luciana Island instead of leaving the city."

"No," I say. "I was there only to pay my respects to Maddie. I don't want to turn the day of her funeral into a circus. Everything that's happened already has been enough, Detective. Her family deserves to bury her in peace."

"Call me Dahlia. I get that, but from what Alis said on the phone, the vehicle sped straight toward you and didn't stop after. That's a crime. Anyway, tell me how it happened."

I look over at Alis and he starts. "I went back to talk to her. I recognized her from afar. We went to my family's mausoleum."

"Why did you go there?"

Our gazes meet and I nod. "It didn't feel right talking by Maddie's grave."

My stomach sinks at the word grave. I watched her funeral, but it is still hard to accept she's dead and buried.

Alis clears his throat. "We talked, and she headed back to her car. I was running after her."

Dahlia stops him with a raise of her hand. "Wait, you're skipping a lot."

"You guys don't need to know what we talked about."

Detective Hunter nods. "That's true, but you were running after her. Were you arguing?"

Alis doesn't look at me. "She was telling me things I didn't want to hear, even though I asked. She headed to her car in a hurry. It took me a bit to follow, so I had to run to catch up with her. That's when I saw the car speeding down the road. I reached her before she stepped off the curb. The truck kept going. It never stopped. There was mud all over the place."

They turn to me, and I get to repeat the story from my side. Then we do it again.

"Who would want to kill you, Mila?" Dahlia asks.

I shake my head. "I don't know."

"Has anything out of the ordinary happened lately? Other than Madison's death, that is."

And I don't want to say it, but I need to.

Alis turns to look at me. "What texts?"

I stare into his eyes as I answer. "I guess threats."

"What the—"

"Let me see them." Dahlia extends her hand.

I grab my phone from the table next to my couch and open the texts.

"You better not break girl code again? Keep your mouth shut." She reads it aloud.

"What code? What are they talking about?" Alis asks.

Dahlia shoots me a pained look. "You slept with your friend's ex-boyfriend. That's breaking girl code. So that's one time. What else did you do to break the code? What do you know, Mila?"

"I don't know what that means."

"It's obvious this person thinks you know something. What the hell is it? What was Madison into?" Detective Hunter asks.

"Are you serious? Maddie was an affluent white girl from the richest suburb. What could she be into? She was sleeping with someone at work—"

Detective Hunter waves me on. "Keep going. I think we all know what was happening there."

Alis nods.

"I don't know anything else."

"Could it be someone at work because of your promotion?"

"Maybe?"

"We already spoke to Spencer Grayson. He's one of the reasons we dropped you off the suspect list. He confirmed he had informed you the day prior to Ms. Summerville's death that you got the job you were both competing for," Detective Hunter says.

"He did?"

"Yes. Mila, I want you to think long and hard about you and Madison. Sometimes we know something we don't know we know. We need to figure out what that is. In the meantime, you need to be careful. Is there someone you can stay with?"

I shake my head. I'm not bringing this shit to anyone else's door.

"We can post a uniformed officer outside the building. If you see anything strange, please call 911 right away. In the meantime, we are going to call in a favor and see if there are any cameras near the Luciana Island cemetery."

The detectives stand.

"That's it? A uniformed officer across the street. That will not protect her. Someone tried to kill her." Alis doesn't raise his voice, but the anger permeates the room.

"This is all we can do, especially when the two of you failed to file a report where it happened. There's no jurisdiction from here. But we will be watching. There are cameras in this building, and she has a camera outside—"

"Dahlia, that's not enough and you know it." It's the first time Alis addresses her by name.

She levels him with a look and then sighs. "I know you're worried. We are too. But all we can do is to investigate and post a uniformed officer."

"Thank you," I say to her like I'm not beginning to become really afraid.

Detective Hunter hands me a card. "Call us if anything pops up, even if seems small. Stay close to home."

Dahlia goes over to Alis, throws one arm around him, and whispers in his ear.

She then turns and shakes my hand. "Call us if you need to. No matter the time."

Alis walks them to the door and asks something I can't hear because I'm back to reading the text messages. I try to think about the stuff Madison and I used to talk about. In my texts with her, which I haven't deleted, we talked a lot about work, the people who get on our nerves, getting together for brunch on the weekend sometimes, clothes, her sex life. There's nothing I can think of.

"Are you okay?" Alis is back to sitting next to me.

I shrug. "I don't know how and what to feel. I can't bury my friend without some bullshit happening. Someone tried to run me over. I have to be on guard all the time. The texts are so ridiculous. How is this even my life?"

He leans closer, a hand pressing on the cushion next to my thigh, the other touching my cheek. "I won't let anything happen to you."

I shouldn't lean into his hand, but I do and allow myself two breaths. I'm scared and alone and his hand feels so good on my skin.

But it's not going to help in the long run. I slowly pull back. He does too.

"Matt and Dahlia know an ex-cop who works as a personal guard now. She's going to call him. I'm going to hire him to watch over you."

My pride yells for me to say no. I want to tell him I can take care of myself. But I can't. Someone killed Madison and that person now wants to kill me, maybe. I can't afford to be prideful. My eyes well, part frustration and the other so much gratitude.

"Thank you. You shouldn't be paying for stuff for me."

He places a hand over mine. "Stop."

His fingers squeeze mine and I'm trapped again in his gaze, his warmth, his touch. This is how we ended up in this mess.

"Alis—"

"I know." He pulls his hand away. "I'm going to stay until he comes. Then Dahlia will pick me up and I'll head back to Luciana Island."

I ignore the tug in my chest. "Hopefully, it won't be for long and I'll pay you back."

"You don't have to," he says.

"I will. I always pay my debts."

"Like a Lannister?"

I actually laugh. "Kinda. Less sinister though."

He says nothing, just stares for a bit.

"What?"

"It's funny. I can count the times I've seen you on one hand, but I miss the way you smile and laugh. I didn't realize it until now."

"Alis—"

"I'm not trying to take advantage. I'm telling you what I think and maybe I shouldn't but fuck it. We are already up to our neck. Might as well speak our minds."

I can't disagree.

He moves back. "When are they going to announce that you got the job?"

"In the next couple of days. Grayson is letting a few more days pass. He's been giving me a lot of new projects. I've been working on them, but it feels so…"

"Wrong?"

"Yeah. To put my head into it, even for five minutes, after all that's happened."

He nods. "I've been feeling the same way. But as hard as it is, make sure you allow yourself to enjoy your promotion and your new position. Maybe work can be where you get away from all of this."

"Like my sanctuary?"

"I wouldn't be that poetic, but yeah." He smiles at the end, flooding me with warmth all over my belly.

I lean back against my seat and the thought sneaks in.

I've missed the way he smiles too.

———

Alis

On the drive to her and Weston's place, Dahlia is unusually quiet. Normally, she and I have stuff to talk about. We've never had a tense moment until today. I don't think she wants to risk saying anything about the investigation, and I get it because she can't answer my questions. She's a good cop, by the book, but kind.

"Thank you for recommending your friend. He seems really competent."

She nods. "He is. Was a damned good cop, too. How is she?"

She means Mila.

"She pretends well. I think she's a lot more rattled than she likes to let on."

"She should be."

My head snaps to look at her. "Dahlia, tell me what you know."

"We don't know anything yet about Mila's attack and that's the full truth." She raises a hand before I can say anything. "But Maddie was murdered. It was brutal and someone is texting Mila about betrayal and telling her not to break the code again."

"You don't have to be a genius to put two and two together." My voice is calmer than I feel. I'm beyond pissed that someone is doing this to her.

"It was nice for you to hire a bodyguard."

I shrug. "It's the least I can do. She's getting shitted on while no one has dared to say an unkind word to me."

"You're a man. Enjoy the privilege."

"I don't want to fucking enjoy it." I take a breath. "I'm sorry. I should keep my temper in check."

She snorts. "Have you met me? I fly off the handle better than anyone. Anyway, I'm glad you don't enjoy the privilege at her expense."

"Who would?"

She stops at a light. "You would be surprised. Anyhow, to reiterate, it's probably not a good idea for the two of you to be seen together. It's only going to make it worse for her."

"I know."

She sighs. "But you will not stay away."

"I can't. She hates it, but—"

She scoffs. "She doesn't."

"What?"

She rolls her eyes at me. "She doesn't hate the attention from you. She feels guilty, and she knows people look at her funny because of what happened between you and Madison's death."

"Same thing," I say, ignoring the droplets of hope trickling inside my chest.

"It's so not."

We're silent the rest of the way. At her and Weston's house, my brother is waiting with Aunt Leila. My soul mom beelines for me the second I cross into the living room. She hugs me and clings to me tight. "How are you?"

"I'm okay," I say.

"Did you eat? We have dinner for you."

I rub a hand over the back of my neck. "We ate something waiting for Knox, the bodyguard."

"We?" Leila asks, looking between Dahlia and me.

"I ate nothing and I'm starving." Dahlia takes Weston's hand and they head to the dining area.

Aunt Leila stares at me but doesn't move.

"Mila. I had dinner with Mila."

"Is that wise? The two of you are already under scrutiny."

I swipe a hand over my face. "It was a soup while we waited. Nothing happened. Neither of us is thinking about that."

"I know, my boy. But if word gets out, she already has it hard. They're dragging her all over the internet, and she's the butt of jokes on TV. God, I can't even imagine what she's feeling."

I can let her in on that. "She's feeling guilty and scared. She tries to hide it, but I see it."

"You see her."

"I do." Then I frown. "What does that mean?"

Leila's smile is small and soft. "You tell me." She pulls me to the dining room. "Come have a warm drink and talk to us."

11

Mila

I settle against my pillows and bring the blankets around my chin. You would think I'm enjoying a good movie and not numbing on the cesspool that is the snake hashtag on YouTube.

"Oh my God. We were just waiting for them to start banging right then and there. The whole staff was watching," the somewhat familiar brunette says.

"What did you guys see? Be more detailed, please." The YouTube vlogger tries for professionalism, but the salaciousness creeps in his voice, and he gets louder with every word.

"From the moment she walked in, we knew she came for him. That blue dress was painted on her skin, and you know she's stacked, so there was a lot of hip swaying. Their eyes locked and me and my homegirl were like, *that lucky bitch*. All us waitresses were trying to make eyes at him before she came, but it's like we weren't even there. And then she walked in the room in her fuck-me dress and..."

"Stop, you can't keep cussing. YouTube is going to de-monetize my video." He laughs. "Girl, you know I got bills to pay."

She grimaces. "I'm sorry, Lamonde. You just had to see them. They were eating each other alive with their eyes only. I mean, who can blame her, right? If he looked at me like that, I would've dropped my panties."

"Girl, me too. I would punch a baby for five minutes with Alister Ellison in a bar bathroom. Keep spilling the tea. Were they drinking a lot?"

She shakes her head. "They had three drinks. They both can hold their liquor because they drank the heavy stuff, whiskey, and bourbon."

"Were they groping each other? You know, was she rubbing his leg to get him going?" Lamonde snickers.

"No, they were super classy, just eye-fuc—you know... but us girls were like, *they're going to smash in the car*."

Both laugh now.

I don't throw the remote at my smart TV screen like I want to. Instead, I continue down the path of self-destruction and find another video where they're talking about Alis and me. In this one, the gossip blogger is showing the elevator footage. It plays a few times. She slows it down, and it's almost frame by frame. I'm transfixed by that moment. I can feel his hands on me, his lips on my skin, and the fire spreads over my face.

Then the dissecting begins again.

They rewind the video, pausing and talking, breaking down every touch and the closeness of our bodies.

"I love how some of her coworkers are defending her, talking about how nice she is and the shame she feels. Where's the shame here? Look at how she's letting him feel all over her. Thank God the elevator stopped when it did. We would have caught the whole deed on camera."

They're not wrong. That was how it felt then. Who knows how far I would've let it go?

My phone rings and it's him. A month later and we're still doing this dance. He shouldn't keep calling me, but he does. I shouldn't pick it up, but I do.

"How are you?" His voice is casual and even.

"Pissed," I practically spit. "Did you see they have the elevator footage? I thought the police would not release it."

He sighs. "Yeah, I know. I called Dahlia and they can't explain how it got out. She promised it wasn't her department."

I roll my eyes. "You can't trust the police. Anyway, it's all over YouTube. There are tons of videos about us. The waiters from the restaurant are talking. This is bullshit. I'm a professional. I work hard. This is all people know me for."

"I'm sorry," he says.

His calmness reminds me to dial down my anger. This is not doing me any good. "I know and thank you. I just hate it. One slip and I'm defined by—"

"You're not defined by this. People will forget with time, Mila. How did the announcement go?"

I sink further into my couch. "It was good and bad. Special and a real shit show. A happy and a sad moment. All at once."

"How is that possible?"

I almost smile at the uncertainty in his voice.

"Grayson was great. He's always so sure of himself and he knows the right things to say. He talked about my accomplishments and the reason for his decision. He said despite the sadness and tragedy, we need to celebrate our victories and continue for ourselves and the team. Very inspirational, you know?"

"Sounds like it," he says, but there's something in his tone that gives me pause.

"You think it was just lip service?"

"No. I know Grayson. He meant every word."

"But?" I ask.

"You sound so reverent when you said inspirational. I mean, it's his job to stand by you and lead the company." He tries to go for casual again, but this time he fails. And something occurs to me.

"Are you jealous?"

"No," he says almost too quickly.

"He's married. Do you think I'm after every taken man in the world?" It's tongue in cheek, though I wonder what he thinks.

"Don't do that, Mila. I was there with you." My name on his lips, the coarse way he says it, makes my belly flop.

"I was kidding."

"There's a truth in every joke. Anyway, whatever people say about you, which is 100% false, they can say worse about me. I just don't want you fucking thinking about anyone else."

I smile, adding to the long list of shouldn't-dos in this call.

"I admire Grayson. He's my professional idol. However, I'm not one of the women who holds a torch for him."

I shouldn't be reassuring him, either. There's no point and it can only lead to the wrong place.

"I like hearing that."

You see? Change the subject.

"How's Maddie's family? Do you know?"

"They're trying to cope. My mother and aunt went to visit them. Her sister, Lindsay, has been very strong. She's holding the family together. It's surprising."

I frown. "Why surprising?"

"Lindsay never liked responsibilities. Maddie was driven, but Lindsay enjoys her family's riches."

"Maddie said something like that. She said her sister was about having fun and being carefree. She also said Lindsay was smart and she would bounce ideas off her all the time."

"She never showed her smarts around here."

I chuckle. "Is that what you boys were looking for from the Summerville girls? Smarts?"

"I'll be honest. I was not." I can hear the chagrin in his voice.

"Are you doing okay?" I ask.

"I'm fine. Work is keeping me busy. Too many unanswered questions. What was Maddie doing in that alley? Why Maddie just didn't tell me the truth. We come from a world where there don't need to be lies about this. She could've said let's go our own way and we can try later."

"Do you really feel that way? Would you have come back? Because that night you broke it off with her. Then again, scorned people make rash decisions."

He sucks in a breath. "Is that what you thought I was? Scorned?"

"Weren't you?"

"Not scorned. Annoyed? Yes. Disappointed? Definitely."

I don't believe him. "I saw the way you looked at her that day in the office. There was something there."

"Yes and no. I had a mean crush on her since I was a kid. I thought if I finally got her, it would be everything I'd been fantasizing."

"And it wasn't?"

"She wasn't there, Mila. She wasn't present and I'm not speaking badly about her. I just know it's like everything in life. When something's just not there, you can't force it. It never works out well. I'm an idiot who kept stalling and putting off what I needed to do. That's on me. I knew shit wasn't working between us. Instead of ending it, I made excuses. The thing is, Maddie wasn't shy, and she didn't conform to norms. Otherwise, she would've stayed in Luciana Island and married someone. I don't get her motive for dating me."

"She said someday you would probably get married."

"What the fuck? While she was fucking other men?" I can practically see his eyes glowing like blue fire pools.

"You just said it was typical where you both come from."

"Not for me, Mila. When you're with me, I'm going to be the only one fucking you."

"Like you were not fucking other women?" I throw it back at him. Men can be self-righteous like they're not doing what they accuse us of.

"Not since I've been with her." He pauses and then adds. "You're the only one."

He bombs us again and we fall into that awful silence mired in discomfort, sadness, and regret.

"Did you eat dinner yet?"

His abrupt change of subject takes me aback. "Yeah."

"Are you sure? What did you eat?" he asks.

"I picked up ramen from Ichiran on my way home. Did you think I was lying?"

"You didn't eat much the other day, just wanted to make sure."

The warmth in my chest is instant. He really is a nice guy. At least to me.

"Why did you say that you deserve three times the worst of the things that people are saying about me? I think you're a nice guy. You're helping me out when you don't have to. You could've washed your hands and kept on enjoying the fact that you're not getting crushed online."

He's silent for a bit, and then he sighs into the phone. "I'm not a nice guy and I deserve it all. You know why? Because you feel guilt and you feel bad about what happened between us. I feel awful Maddie died, but I would do it all over again. I would fuck you all night again and my only regret is I didn't stay to fuck you all day."

He drops that bomb and we're silent in the fallout. I can't seem to form words.

"You see? I'm really not nice. Good night, Mila."

I'm left staring at the phone, with the thoughts I couldn't allow myself to say to him. I don't regret the time I spent with him that night.

I go through my nighttime beauty ritual, asking myself one question. How can I mourn Maddie and still go hot all over thinking about my night with Alis? Something inside me says those are two separate thoughts but they're really not. They're intermingled and jumbled up together.

Back in my bed, I settle against my pillows and let the news play in the background. I'm barely paying attention because I'm wondering what he's doing. Is he thinking about what he just said like I am? No, that's stupid because I keep hearing the line from his lips over and over.

Then the headline on my TV screen freezes me, obliterating all thoughts of Alis.

One Person Dead Another Taken to the Hospital After Eating Noodles from Popular Baltimore Eatery.

My stomach clenches. They're in front of Ichiran, my favorite ramen spot. I ate food from there tonight. *Oh God.*

12

———————

Alis

Stupid.

That's what I am. I shouldn't have told Mila that last night. Even if it's the whole truth, because it is. I don't regret fucking her. I would do it all over again. And given the chance, I would do so right now.

I'm not a liar, but I'm still stupid. Getting into anything with her would be an invitation for punishment. Yet I would probably risk it all without a second thought. She plagues my every thought until I can't concentrate.

"Alis." My father's voice relegates Mila to the back of my mind. "Are you with us? Do you agree with Fred on his proposal? Do you need more time to read it?"

I should be annoyed that he's accusing me of not paying attention, but I wasn't paying full attention, just enough to hear what was said. I'm also tired of my father testing me. Especially that he thinks I would come to a meeting with him and Fred McConnell unprepared.

"I don't agree with Fred's proposal. While the land he's proposing we buy would be great to open the factory, he's overlooking that it would displace tens of thousands of poor families. Where would those people go? Are we going to finance their move somewhere?"

"Of course, not." Fred laughs, and so do others.

And to my mounting annoyance, my father joins them. "We are not welfare, son."

"No, we are definitely not welfare, but we should consider the consequences when we do things like what is being suggested. Since the families are not a concern, what about the environmental repercussions?"

"Well, I'm sure you can install windmills and find some of those other altruistic things you and your brother are always pushing," Fred says like the entitled rich idiot he is.

"Windmills won't fix it. Do you even know what they do? Never mind. This would destroy an entire community and tank the reputation our company is gaining for sustainability, kind practices, equality, diversity, and inclusion. Let me tell you what will happen if we go through with your proposal. Those families will fight back. The media will get a hold of this. The environmental activists and equal rights groups will descend upon Luciana Island. Be prepared to drive into work through the streets lined with them. Maybe they'll camp on the lawn outside the premises, or the lot outside the country club, since it's open and un-fenced, and where your cops can't remove them."

Fred swallows and some of the other board members adjust in their chairs.

"What do you suggest?" my father asks.

"I think we should backlist this proposal and look at the other three that won't compromise Ellison Corp's image. My recommendation is that we consider Franklin. We can install the factory there where it doesn't have the environmental consequences, and it is not a green sanctuary. We can also hire from the community, which can benefit from the 40,000 jobs we are creating. It would be a boost to the town, a better monetary investment, and we can keep our reputation."

"But the transportation would be much more costly. Not to mention the high crime. Who's going to guarantee the safety of the employees and product?" Fred's face is so red that I almost pity him.

I should probably throw him a bone. I won't. He doesn't deserve it. "Well, compromise is always part of any deal. We have security in all our businesses. I appreciate your concern for our employees, and I'll take you up on your offer to add extra security to our budget proposal."

He gets redder but my father jumps in. "I think we should vote."

Fifteen minutes later, I'm sitting in my office, looking through my phone. I have ten other messages but dig right into Mila's.

MILA

Hope the proposal goes well. What am I saying? You're going to rock that.

I don't get to message her back because of the fast-approaching steps. I drop my phone on my desk a second before Weston and Aunt Leila walk in with my dad.

Aunt Leila, as always, ignores my father and office decorum and comes around my desk to kiss my cheek and hug me. "You were brilliant. I love that you chose that community and all the thought you put into the proposal."

"Thank you, my love." I smile at her. I wish she wasn't leaving today.

My dad clears his throat, his way of chastising us without words. "I'm going to lunch with Fred to smooth the blow today. You're coming?"

It's not an ask, but I choose to treat it like it is.

"No, it's Leila's last day in town. Weston and I are going to take her to lunch and spend time with her."

My father's eyes glow in disapproval. "You were very hard on Fred today. With reason, of course. Your proposal is nothing short of ingenious. However, spending time with him can go a long way toward making friends on the board."

"I can see that, but after spending the night going over his ridiculous proposal, I feel like I've had all I can take of Fred. Not to mention, my favorite person in the world is leaving today, and if the last two months have taught me nothing else, it's that I need to spend more time with those I love."

Just not you.

"Fine, I'll deal with Fred alone. But this is the type of thing you can't avoid in the future as the CEO of Ellison Corp."

Like you're ever retiring.

"Thanks, Dad. Will do."

He says goodbye to Weston and Leila and walks out.

My brother wastes no time giving me shit. "Is this how you're planning to act as CEO?"

Leila chuckles. "No, he plans to scare them straight. God, did you see the fear in their faces at the thought of advocates and protesters lining the streets of Luciana Island?"

"I was probably heavy-handed, but it worked. Dad can take care of Fred's feelings."

"That old bat needs to retire. So does your father. You're practically running this company and in the right direction," Leila says.

"And keeping us from traditional and questionable practices," my brother adds.

"Let's not talk about this stuff. It was a victory. Thanks for your votes."

Leila rolls her eyes. "Like you needed them. The fear of activists got you an almost unanimous decision. Who would've thought activists is what would keep these prunes in check?"

We laugh and head out. Instead of going out to a restaurant, we have lunch at my house, on the patio.

"Thank you for indulging me. I didn't want to be out in public today. I hate the looks and the morbid curiosity of people here. Being on my best behavior is not my first instinct. I want to tell them to fuck off."

Leila puts her hand on my arm. "It's worse than morbid curiosity. I think these women are considering the appropriate length of time before they can start hitting on you. Every time one of them asks me how you're doing, I want to slap them."

"I have it so much better. Mila is going through hell."

She nods and her eyes go warm. "Poor girl."

Weston pours himself more water. "Dahlia says they're tracking who leaked the video from the elevator. Unfortunately, they can't do anything about the blogs and YouTube content. She and Matt think someone's feeding it to content creators. They can't figure out who is leaking out these videos."

My jaw hardens. These videos and blogs are making things so hard for her. I can't do anything and it makes me feel so fucking impotent. I want to offer them money to stop posting about her, but I worry it may backfire. "There has to be something we can do."

"With the internet, you just have to wait for a bigger story to come along."

I hate how right my brother is right now. "It doesn't feel right. We have so much money and influence. Yet my hands are tied."

We eat in silence.

"When are you coming back?" Weston asks Leila.

"I don't know."

"Fernando is keeping you from us," I grumble. She giggles.

We are happy she found someone. I just miss seeing her more often.

"You both can always come to me. Dahlia already promised me you and she will start working on vacation time to come to Madrid." She turns to look at me. "You haven't taken a vacation for a while. You should leave that place for a couple of weeks."

"They'd probably undo everything I've worked so hard for."

"They wouldn't dare." She smiles. "You can always invite Mila to come with you. In Madrid, no one will bother you."

I ignore thump in my chest. "You forget Mila and I are not a thing."

"Hmmmm," is all she says and winks at my brother.

Before I can ask them what that means, my phone pings. It's a call from our publicist. If she's calling and not texting, it can't be good news. I answer it.

"Alis, you told me to keep tabs on what is said about Ms. Rosario. I thought you should know her home address is circulating on Twitter. It's been retweeted thousands of times."

My stomach drops. "What? By who?"

"There are so many shares and comments that we have not gotten to the bottom of that."

"Find out and keep me informed." I clench my teeth so hard I feel it in my jaw. "Fuck."

"What's wrong?" Leila asks.

"Mila's been doxed."

"Oh, dear God."

Weston's already on his phone. "Hey, I thought you should know Mila Rosario was doxed."

I try to call Mila but she doesn't answer. I text her to call me as soon as possible.

"Tell Dahlia they need to look into that asshole Elias. He's got to be doing this. Why haven't they arrested him yet?"

Weston hangs up the phone. "They're looking into everything, including monitoring the activities of anyone they may or may not consider a suspect. Thus far, they've found nothing."

"Meaning they can't tie him to this online bullshit." I slam my hand on the table, enjoying the sting that breaks through my skin.

"It's going to be okay," Leila says.

"How? She's already getting threats. Now these crazy people know where she lives."

Leila shoots me her be-brave smile. "You just need to make sure she's protected."

I grip my phone harder. "She's going to fight it. She's already trying to pay me back for the bodyguard."

Leila puts her hand to my cheek. "She doesn't need to know all your moves. Tell her only what she needs to know."

And I nod because fuck yeah, I'll protect her.

———

Mila

"I want analytics to look at the data and dissect it. I want to know where the ads are getting the most engagement. Get me demos and geographical location. I want to AB test them and switch."

The words flow easily from my lips. I'm so calm that I amaze myself. To see me today, in my first meeting with my staff, smiling and talking about the projects we're tackling first, you wouldn't know the turmoil wrecking my insides. I tossed and turned half the night wondering if my ramen had been contaminated too. I was only able to sleep after the police announced it seemed like it was a targeted attack and not all the ramen was contaminated.

This morning I had to listen to my mom cry because she read what's been said about me. She raged about the bastards contacting her job to ask nasty questions about me. No one can imagine the waves of shame that are washing over my insides every time other family members tell me the media is reaching out to them. Someone even called Sandy today. It's bullshit.

To top it off, fifteen minutes before this meeting, I got the Google alert. I saw my address all over Twitter.

Now everyone knows where that snake lives.

We should wait outside her building.

Let's follow her and show up wherever she goes from now on.

The fear chewed at my insides, and I couldn't see anything but people following me when I got home or waiting for me outside my building.

I had to go into my new office, close the door, and sit on the floor breathing in the corner where people can't see inside. I should've taken the rest of the day off. I think Grayson would've understood, but I didn't want more of this drama to get in the way of work. I'm safer here, anyway.

I put myself together one breath at a time. I didn't tell my body-guard this was going on. He would find out soon enough, and if I talk about it, I'll lose my mind, so I kept my mouth shut. My phone hasn't stopped ringing since. I had to take out my AirPods because Siri keeps announcing the calls in my ear.

Mami, Alis, Sandy.

They all must know. I shoot a discreet text to my mom, telling her I'm okay. Minutes later, I spot Sandy waiting outside the conference room. I shoot her a small smile.

Now I just need to respond to Alis' text messages.

"When do you want all the reports by?" Karin asks. "We have to gather all the data and cross-reference with last month."

I make a mental note to call Alis after I get out of the meeting, put my phone away, and answer the head of analytics. "That's an excellent idea. Let's shoot for a week from now. We can tweak if necessary, ahead of the exec meeting the day after."

Karin smiles. Visibility is what everyone strives for, a chance to shine in front of Grayson and the board.

We discuss the action items and I adjourn the meeting. I don't rush out like I want to. Instead, I force myself to gather all my things from the conference table one by one. I stare at the items harder than I need to and then make my way out slowly.

Sandy rushes to me, but my attention is on the others. Everyone is staring at me like they're expecting something. They know. I push a smile on my face, hook an arm around Sandy's elbow, and walk slowly to my office. I pass my bodyguard, who's passing as a janitor. He taps his ear, code for he also knows.

I breathe after we close the door in my office, but I don't get to fully let it out. I can feel their gazes through the glass. I look up and no one pretends they're doing anything else. They're all staring.

I take one of the chairs in front of my desk and sit with my back to them. Sandy takes the other.

"Are you okay, hon?"

I shake my head. "I don't want these people to see me waver. I don't want to appear weak and become everyone's prey."

"I get you," she says softly. "You're so strong. I would be so scared."

I close my eyes for a second. "I'm petrified, but I have much more to lose if people at work feel I'm unstable."

"That's true. Grayson wants to see you. He knew I was coming to check on you and he asked me to take you back with me."

"Oh God. Let's get it over with."

I get up, but she places a hand over mine.

"Catch your breath, Mila. You've been on the go."

"I'm sure Grayson's so fucking tired of me and my drama." I massage my forehead with the back of my thumb.

"If anyone knows what it's like to be in the spotlight constantly, it's him. He probably wants to make sure you are okay."

I nod, not fully believing. Who would put up with this shit no matter how good the employee was?

My phone pings and I grab it. Another message from Alis.

ALIS

I'm coming to Baltimore tonight. I want to make sure you're okay.

The warmth spreads through my chest and I don't realize how cold I've been.

I start typing but dial him instead. The phone barely rings when he picks up.

"Are you okay?" he asks.

"Yes. I was in a meeting and couldn't answer."

"It's okay. I knew you were safe with Knox. He's still close by, right?"

I almost turn around to look. "Yeah."

"How are you holding up?" he asks.

"Not sinking yet."

"Not sinking is good." His voice is charged with something I can't pinpoint.

"How about you?," I ask. "Are you okay? Did everything go well today?"

"Yeah. I'm just pissed at this shit. Fucking people have nothing better to do. I don't like that your address is public."

"I know. I'm trying to stay calm," I say, hoping it calms him, too.

"You can't go back home, at least for now. I'm getting you another place."

"Are you crazy, Al—" I look over at Sandy, who is writing into the notepad on my desk.

Is that him?

I nod.

"Hear me out. You can't stay in that place and—"

I can't. It would get so much worse. "Don't worry about me. I can find a place. Listen, Grayson is calling me into his office. I have to go."

I hang up before he can say anything else and place my phone on my desk.

"What did he want?" Sandy asks.

I probably shouldn't run my mouth, but I blurt it out just the same. "He wants to find me a new place."

She smiles. "Damn, I thought it was just a one-night thing…"

"It was. It is." I struggle not to run my hand over my face. The last thing I need to do is look like a clown by dragging my makeup across my face.

"Seems like he doesn't think that way." She shakes her head. "You should let him."

My gaze snaps to her. "What? Do you know what would happen if word gets out that he's got me moved into some place? People would come with pitchforks after me."

"Hon, the pitchforks are already out. We got to get you protected. You can come stay with me for a while. Dave and the dogs may drive you crazy, but we got guns, lots of them. You'll be safe."

There goes that warm feeling again. It feels so good to be cared for. I can't take her offer.

"Thank you. That's really sweet, but I can't do that to you. The crazies are already calling you and bothering you. I'm not bringing this shit to your house. I'll think of something."

I just need to do it quickly because I only have a few more hours here.

"Let's go see the boss," I say, standing and grabbing my phone. I go around my desk and grab my purse.

We head out of my office, ignoring the trying-for-cover-but-failing stares. I tell my secretary I am headed to the executive suite. Sandy hooks a hand around my elbow and we head to the elevator.

The minute the doors close, Sandy turns to me. "I'm worried about you. Things are more tame here, but out there... you're alone."

"I'm going to be fine. I'm going to find a new place and I'll keep my new address a secret. Maybe I'll go into a hotel in the meantime."

Sandy nods. "That's a good idea. But, my basement is open and Dave's guns are *always* loaded."

I throw my arms around her. "Thank you. I would've gone crazy if I didn't have you."

Five minutes later, I'm knocking on Grayson's door. He stands when I come in, signaling for me to close the door.

Oh God.

He waits for me to sit and then takes his chair behind the desk.

"Are you okay?" he asks, staring at me.

"Yep."

"I called you in here because I found out what happened today. You've been doxed."

"I'm sorry for this. I hate that this is all bleeding into my work life—"

Grayson holds up a hand. "I'm not worried about this affecting the work. I'm concerned that someone may want to harm you."

"Oh. Thank you. I'll be okay."

"What is your plan?" he asks.

"My plan?" I repeat.

"Yes, Mila," he says. "Where are you going to stay?"

I consider lying, even saying I'm staying with Sandy, but he seems genuinely worried, and he's my boss. I don't want to lie to him.

"I'm considering going to a hotel."

"That's a good idea, but that's not really a long-term solution, not to mention it may not be as safe as you think. If you allow me, there's a place I can recommend."

I fight not to chuckle. Insulting my boss wouldn't be wise. "Grayson, I don't think I can afford any place you recommend."

"This place is owned by me. I can make it the same price you're paying now."

I frown. "Why would you do that? I know you care about all your employees, but I'm only bringing you problems."

"You would pay rent as you are doing with your current place. This is a more secure place with parking inside the compound and security. It's a gated community, and there are cameras throughout the perimeter. A club area and a reception office. No one can get in there without access. There's also a service room on each floor. Your bodyguard can stay there."

Something about this makes me uneasy. It's too easy. Too big of a favor. Why?

"I'm not expecting anything from you, Mila. I just want my CMO to do her job in a safe place. I also know that you're innocent."

"You have believed me from the beginning. You didn't even question it." Maybe I should have been leery about that.

"Let me be completely honest here, Mila. First, you had an alibi."

Heat flares over my face. Yeah, the entire world knows and won't ever let me forget.

He shakes his head. "I'm not saying that to embarrass you. It's only as a fact here. Second, I consider myself an excellent judge of character and you left here broken up about Madison knowing you got the job over her. Even my wife commented on it."

"I was. We were good friends. I didn't want that to affect our friendship, but please continue."

He nods. "Third, I'm aware of Madison's activities with another employee of this company. I'm not at liberty to reveal much, but there are things that will eventually come out that will shed some light as to why I've always believed you."

"Because Elias is a suspect?" I ask.

"I can't tell you that, Mila..."

"Okay." But it's not. I want to ask more. *Are the police still looking at him?*

"Let's talk about your move. Even though you have someone watching over you, I think you need to call the police and secure an escort to pick up your essentials today. You can hire a moving company to pack and take out the rest."

The headache is forming on the right side of my head and press my fingers lightly to ease it. "I have a lease."

"A good lawyer can help toss that thing in minutes. We can make a phone call."

"I don't have furniture. What I have now comes with the rental place." I don't know why I'm telling him that. He doesn't care.

"I rent the place to people who do business with me and need to travel to Baltimore for short-term periods. The basics are there. There's a sectional, a dining room set, and a bed in the unit. There's a built-in workstation with a desk and chair. There are linen and towels but I am sure you won't want to use any of that. You can get what you need as you go or order it."

It's a godsend. Too good to be true, but I think about all this. Everything that's happened lately. Maybe I need to stop dissecting everything. This can set my mother's mind at ease. I don't have to stay with anyone. I can also probably get a full night's sleep. "Okay. I accept."

13

Alis

"Thank you," I say, feeling rather foolish, but I would do it all over again. I would ask for this favor a thousand times if I needed to.

For her safety.

Grayson grunts. "I better not lose my best employee because of you."

I shake my head. "You won't. My lips are forever sealed, and she needs the help."

"Yeah, though she won't admit it, she does. I hope you understand that even if you're paying for the rental balance, I will not give you access, right? If Mila wants you to have access to her, she'll have to give it to you."

"I know." It bugs the hell out of me because I'm pretty sure she won't. "It's not about that. I just want her to be safe."

Grayson's silent for a moment and I get ready to thank him and say goodbye.

"You two have an uphill battle," he says.

"It's not like that."

"Isn't it?" He shoots the words right back at me. "I know she's probably not consciously thinking that because of this whole mess.

She's pretty broken, though I have to say she's her usual, on top of it all, at work. She has led her team through their project and even sent me new vetted concepts."

"You're lucky to have her." I shouldn't utter those words because it's just incriminating me more.

"I am, which brings me back to you. This may not be the best time for the two of you to try anything, but I would be a hypocrite to give you that advice. I fell for Winter in the weirdest situation anyone could be in, but every time I think about it, I know there was no other way. From the moment I first saw her, I felt it. Then I got to know her. I would have fallen for her no matter what."

And that brings back the words I said to Mila a few nights ago.

I would do it all over again.

"I don't know what I'm doing, Grayson. I just can't stay away from her. I wish the world would come after me. That they judged me. I could handle it. I have the money and ability to protect myself. She bears all the blame. I hate that."

"That's why you need to be careful. You need to make sure no more mud falls on her, but like I said, I would be a hypocrite if I told you not to go for her."

I close my eyes and savor the words. I tell myself to be careful at all hours of the day. Protecting her is slowly becoming an obsession. "I just want to see for myself she is okay."

"Good luck with that." He hangs up after and I stare at my phone.

I should head back home. She's already in a new place, under security, with Knox close by. I walk back to the living room and my brother is playing a video game with Dahlia's brother Teddy.

Weston looks up when I sit next to him on the couch. "So?"

"Already at the place. Knox is nearby."

"That's good," my brother says.

"Ya should probably stop talking in code. One, you're awful at it. Two, I already know what you're talking about."

"Teddy," Weston says.

"I'm no snitch. Plus, Dahlia would make good on her threat to beat the shit out of me if I say anything. Anyway, ya should reach out to Miz-Behavior. They always seem to get the drop."

I'm confused. "What?"

Teddy sighs like it's an enormous burden to explain and eyes my brother. "I guess I need to put on my proper voice for your brother. It's disappointing. I thought he had more game than that going by the video."

I open my mouth, but Dahlia beats me to the punch.

"Teddy." She only says his name, and he's immediately looking away, but she comes to stand between us in the room. "This is not a joking matter. They're making that woman's life miserable, bullying her for sport, and what happened between them is no one's business."

"I know. I agree. It's no shade. I was just saying that you should look into the Miz-Behavior blog. They always break news about everything first. It was in their thread where they doxed shorty."

"She's not a shorty. Anyway, how do you know about this blog?" Her tone is cutting enough he should be shrinking.

Teddy shrugs. "Ya know nothing. Miz-Behavior always got the celeb news first. On her blog, you find out first who gets arrested and who did something messy. They knew who set up MouseFly when they shot him downtown."

"Who's MouseFly?" I ask.

Weston runs a hand through his hair. "Teddy's favorite rapper. He was set up and got shot seven times a few months ago. He's lucky to be alive—"

Dahlia holds a hand, interrupting my brother. "Wait a second, Teddy's right. That blog broke the news. They're also the ones that released the elevator video and the first interviews with waiters. Lamonde is the blogger, right?"

Teddy nods.

She digs out her phone and walks out of the room. I open the Miz-Behavior website on my phone. The tag line at the top, on the banner next to a teacup under a palm tree, draws my gaze first. Come sit with us, we're spilling tea and throwing shade. All day, every day.

Assholes.

But this may be a good lead. If we stop these people from spreading the bullshit, things will get easier for Mila. Maybe I can send them a cease and desist.

"Thank you, Teddy," I say.

"Okay. I didn't mean any disrespect to your lady. She seems nice, like she's not a jump-off or nothing... You know, forget I said anything."

"You did something great by letting us know about Miz-Behavior," Weston says.

The kid shrugs and then looks at me. "You want next?"

He means the game and I shake my head. "I don't know how to play really well."

"You can't be worse than your brother."

Weston glares at him. "You're so disrespectful."

"It's no shade. Only the truth."

I laugh and my brother joins me. It's been a while since I laughed like that. When Dahlia returns, she looks between us three and smiles.

"Matt and I are going to follow up about our cybercrime division. I already contacted them about Miz-Behavior. We're going to see if we can find out where they're getting all their information."

"Good." I'm feeling hopeful for the first time, and I take my phone and go into the other room to call Mila.

She answers on the sixth ring.

"Hey, I was in the other room. I'm settling in."

"Oh. How is everything?" I ask.

"Honestly? Way better than my other place. This unit is gorgeous." The sentiment doesn't reach her voice.

"That's good to hear. You should be comfortable, though you hated giving up your place."

She sighs. "I'll make the best out of it. This place is beautiful and secure."

"But you hate it."

"No, really. I don't. It's just... I enjoy being free, Alis. I like walking around and going to get coffee and thinking. I do my best thinking walking down the streets and looking at people and buildings. Now I can't do any of that."

Grayson said her work is not suffering, but she must not realize that. Or is that not the type of thinking she means?

"I'm sure your muse is still around, right?"

"Yeah, I just don't want to go stale. I don't want to be that person who loses touch with what makes her authentic."

"I don't think that's going to happen and this will pass. It's only a matter of time. I was calling you to tell you we may have something. There's this blog that keeps getting information and the police are going to investigate how they know before anyone else."

She sucks in a breath. "I hope they find out how all this is getting started. I want my life back, Alis."

This is the second time she says my name on the call. Yes, I am counting and remembering. I don't get tired of that.

"Let me come see you."

She's silent for a few seconds. "I don't think that's smart."

It's not a no. I close my eyes and fight it because she is right. This can only invite trouble if we get caught.

"It's definitely not smart. I want to see you... are okay with my own eyes. Then I'll leave and head back to the island right after."

She's silent for so long, I think she's going to hang up.

"Yes."

———

Mila

I want to see you... are okay with my own eyes.

Those are the words that did me in. Part of me knows it's dumb and ridiculous, the other part ignores it. If we get found out, just talking, I'll get dragged and run over by people all over social media.

But I can't help it. I say yes.

And now I wait for him and I'm jittery. I should've changed out of my sweatsuit, but what else are you supposed to wear when you had to pack in a hurry while police officers wait? I only grabbed my clothes, toiletries, and essentials. When he called, I was ordering new pillows and sheets because mine won't fit the king-size bed here. Thank God we can order from GG retail, and it will get delivered tonight through my new executive privileges. I need to get more things to make this place comfortable enough, but I'll make a list tomorrow.

My phone pings in sequence with text messages from Greg.

GREG

Are you okay?

I called you a bunch of times. Why are you not answering?

I went by your place tonight. You don't live there anymore?

Send a smoke signal.

I stare at the messages. I've been meaning to reply to him, but I've been on the go. Every time I pick up the phone to send him a message something happens.

I start typing that I'm okay and safe but nearly get zapped out of my skin by the beeping of the intercom. I set my phone down on the couch and go answer. Instead of Alis, a man in jeans and a hoodie fills the smart screen in the reception area. I almost ask what he wants, but he looks up, and my heart thuds against the walls of my chest.

It's those eyes, that face, his lips.

"It's me," he whispers.

And I don't answer, just hit the button for him to come in. The one knock on the door is the code from Knox that he will stand watch and wait. In less than three minutes, someone knocks again. I look through the peephole and it's Alis.

I open the door for him, and he steps in. The minute he does, his gaze missiles to mine and his eyes go everywhere at once. It's nervous, like my mom's rescue cat when anything gets too close.

"It's a secure place. I like that there's a front desk where you have to sign in and call from there to get let in."

I'm only half listening. My attention is on his jeans, a zip-up hoodie, sneakers.

"Why are you frowning?"

"You're not wearing a suit."

He chuckles. It's soft and deep and it makes me smile.

"I'm not always in a suit. Plus, I thought this would be better. Less chance for me to be recognized."

It's a hard reminder of what's out there for us. "Yeah, that was smart of you. Where did you park?"

"My brother dropped me off on his way to work."

"Oh. How are you getting back?"

"I'm going to call a car service to his house. My car's there."

We stand there for a while, and it should be awkward, but somehow, it's not. I'm just getting my fill of him. I try not to be aware of how tall he is. I try not to stare at his lips. I try to zap away the images forming in my head. No, not images, memories. "Do you want to sit down?"

He hesitates and for a second I think he'll say no, but he sweeps his hand for me to lead the way and we sit on the sectional. I could sit on the opposite side, but at my old place, we sat next to each other and we should be able to do that here.

"I'm sorry. I'm pissed this is happening to you. These fucking assholes have no right. They need to get a fucking life."

"Yeah, I agree, but they're doing it all the same. I hate that they're going so far. I feel like this is just beyond ridiculous. They didn't know Maddie or care for her. Why are they going this hard?"

He flips his palms up. "They have nothing better to do."

"Yeah, and someone's feeding this. But who? And why?"

"I don't know, but I know the cops are investigating. Dahlia said as much."

It doesn't bring much comfort, but whining about it wouldn't either. "She was really nice today."

"She's pissed. She and Matt think someone is using social media —and you—to distract from the investigation."

"Are they still looking at Elias? Could he have something to do with this?" I ask.

"They're still looking at him. They don't think he has anything to do with this, nothing to tie him to this online shit."

"Wow, she tells you a lot."

"She tells me nothing, except for the online stuff today after I hounded her," he grumbles. "Weston tells me the rest, any information he overhears."

"That could get him in trouble but it's so good he has your back."

"He would do anything for me and vice versa. But it's not all niceness. We clash sometimes." He laughs.

I'm jealous because I don't know what that is. Most people have siblings they complain or gush about. "I would have loved to have a brother or sister to argue with and be complicit with. Someone to stand by me like your brother is doing with you."

The way he takes my hand in his is so natural I don't fight it. It's also perfect, a slight but soft grip. Everything to remind me he's stronger than me, but protective as well.

"You got me."

His voice flash floods my body in waves of warmth. I believe him. He hired me a bodyguard and he would have rented me a place if I let him. He runs to me when I need him and he gets mad on my behalf.

"Thank you. You've done so much. I appreciate it."

"Stop."

"No, it's true. Anyone else would have washed their hands."

He shakes his head. "I'm not anyone else, and I don't want you to be grateful to me. I'm just doing the decent thing."

"You're doing more than that."

"Because I was there too. Because of you. Because it's you." He stands and paces to the other side of the room, looking out into the night. "I can't stop thinking about you."

He says the last part so low, but I hear it, every single word.

And my heart booms like an 808 drum. I'm halfway to him when I stop.

What the fuck are you doing, Mila? Go back to your seat.

Instead, I close the distance. He turns around as I'm at arms' reach.

"This is wrong," I say.

"I know," he replies. In his face, an agony that mirrors my own.

"I can't stop thinking about you either."

He exhales, taking a step forward. "It's not just me."

I shake my head. "There's no way for us. They wouldn't let us be."

He takes another step. "All day you're in my head, at night you're in my dreams. Ever since the moment I saw you, you're everywhere. I think I breathe you, Mila."

My throat tightens and I fight the smile with all that's in me, because this is not a good thing.

This may not even be a real thing. Men love what they can't have. They lie. They confuse love with lust.

And I scream these things at myself but I dream about him. I think about him all the time, too. I lean into him and press my head against his chest. He folds his arms around me.

"I think I breathe you too," I whisper against his shirt.

He hugs me tighter, like he's trying to fuse us together. I splay my hands on his back and blend into him.

Alis doesn't make any other moves but when I tilt my head up to look at him, he's there, staring into my eyes. And all at once, I push on my tiptoes and his head comes down. Our lips touch, feeling our way around each other. Unlike last time, it's slow and we don't do much more.

14

Alis

The One-Night-Stand that Keeps on Giving. How Heir to Ellison Corp is Protecting and Supporting His Corporate Latina Vixen.

I read the headline again, waiting for Mila to text me back. It's weighing on my shoulders how often I start my day like this because I know hers is going ten times worse.

I don't dial her because someone storms into my office. I don't look up. I don't really care. I want to reach her and talk to her.

"Is it true?" my father asks. He doesn't sit. Instead he looms over the front of my desk. "Are you supporting this woman and have set her up somewhere?"

Fuck this day times one thousand.

I keep my eyes on my desk.

"Your mother is beside herself."

"How is that different from Mom any other day?" I ask, finally looking up at him.

His jaw sets and I just know he's measuring his words. "I don't meddle in your life, Alis. What a man does in his own time is his business. I'm trying to make sure you don't ruin things for yourself."

"Ruin things?" I parrot back, which is bound to make him angry, and that's what I want. I want him to be as pissed off as I am right now.

"You don't want to anger the Summervilles. We've known them all their lives and this... situation of yours has been an added annoyance to their pain. They keep having to hear about you and *that girl*. There's still a chance. Lindsay—"

"Stop." I raise a hand and point at him. "I'm going to stop you right there for the last time. I'm not going after Lindsay after I publicly dated her sister."

He stares at my hand in the air. "Time heals wounds and you and she can be a comfort to each other."

I close my eyes and breathe. "Let it go. It's not going to happen."

"I get you're having fun with *that girl,* but either way, this is not an optimal situation. See her if you must, but keep it out of the press. You're obviously not discreet enough if the media is finding out you're supporting her." The reproach is there, as always, creeping into his every word.

"One, I'm not having fun with her, Dad. Two, I'm also not supporting her. Because she is not a girl, she's a woman who works hard and is successful on her own. Yes, I got her a bodyguard. She shouldn't be in fear for her life because these psychos have nothing better to do."

He continues like I didn't speak.

"Who you take to bed shouldn't be public knowledge. You have a reputation to keep. Are you sure she's not selling stories for money?"

I laugh. "That doesn't make any sense. They're constantly harassing her and dragging her through the mud. What is there for her to gain?"

He presses his palms to my glass desk. "I don't know. I don't know her mind. Apparently, I don't know yours either. All your life you've claimed you want to lead this company and now you pull a Weston."

The red takes over and I don't even have to close my eyes. And that's what does it. Pulling a Weston means I'm acting like my brother who fell in love and married a woman of color, defying my parents.

They tried every manipulation in the book, but it didn't work with Weston and Dahlia. It will not work with me and Mila either.

Normally, this is how he pulls the strings to keep me doing what he wants. He dangles the family company before my eyes like a bone to a hungry dog. I'm not in the mood to play fetch for him anymore.

"You know what, Dad? If you don't think I'm the man to lead this company after you, then choose Fred McConnell. I'm sure he'll do a wonderful job growing the company with his great ideas. Excuse me."

I grab my laptop and walk out of my office, telling my secretary I'm leaving for the rest of the day. "I will work from home. Call me if you need me."

I don't call Mila until I get in the car.

She answers right away this time. "This is crazy. How the hell do they know about the security? Only you, me, Grayson, and the detectives know."

"I've been texting Dahlia. She assures me it wasn't Knox or the police. I don't know how these fuckers are getting the information."

"This is a lot, Alis. What else can they use against me?"

I tense because there's the part that she doesn't know. How I'm financing a portion of her place, but that's between Grayson and me and there is no paper trail. I breathe and get to comforting her.

"There's nothing else for them to find."

"Except for the other night."

She means the night I went to her new place.

"Nothing happened. Well...not what they would think."

I kissed her. I held her. I went home after, wishing I had pushed for a little more. For her to let me into her bed, with the new bed sheets she washed while I was there, to get another taste of her.

"I'm serious."

Me too.

"I know," I say instead.

"Someone sent me the article via email. Then I got another text."

My hand stills on the steering wheel. "A threat?"

"Yeah." Her voice is low but enough to wash over me.

"What did it say this time?" I grip the leather wheel tight enough to make my knuckles scream.

"This is only the beginning. It will get much worse if you open your mouth." She puffs out air, creating a wind tunnel on the line. "I don't know what the fuck this person is talking about. How can I keep my mouth shut about what I don't know?"

Confusion, sadness, and the fear she doesn't easily admit, it's all in her voice.

"We need to put an end to that shit. If the police won't do anything, I will. This shit is going to stop."

She sucks in a breath. "Listen, no. Let's leave this to the police. Maybe we should call off Knox."

She's not thinking clearly now.

"What are you saying, Mila? You're in danger and you want to call back the person who watches over you to please some little shits on the internet?"

"I know it doesn't make any sense, but I'm tired of this. I'm tired of getting dragged all over the place. And threatened. I can deal with the dragging, I know, they're just words—"

"How do you know they're just words? How do you know this person is not baiting you to get you to do this exact thing and then strike?"

"Oh God." It's a forced-out whisper that makes me regret my outburst.

"I'm not trying to scare you. I just want you to be safe. I'll be there this evening."

"No." Her answer is so quick. "I appreciate that you want to see me safe, but I think this is part of the issue. We have to stop seeing each other so we don't give these people more fodder to attack. At least until we find out how they're getting their information."

And here we are, back in the same place. She's keeping me at arm's length while she's alone in Baltimore. No, I'm not allowing this again. Leila's words come back to me.

She doesn't need to know all your moves.

"Fine. Call me when you get home."

"I...will." There's surprise in her voice.

We hang up and I immediately dial Jennifer Carey.

"I was just about to call you." Her voice is weary. "My phone won't stop ringing."

"It's about this fucking newspaper article, right?"

"Yeah." She lets out a heaving sigh. "The no comment bit is getting old."

"Then let's comment. I think it's time we gave these people what they want, a statement. Call our lawyer. Let's get it crafted."

15

───────

"Did you read this?" Mary asks, holding up the Baltimore Gazette.

Three months ago, the Baltimore Police Department cleared Mr. Alister Ellison and Ms. Milagros Rosario of any suspicion in the death of Madison Summerville. However, social media has tried and found Ms. Rosario guilty in the court of public opinion. The onslaught of cyber aggression is constant. Her character, professionalism, and all her relationships have been questioned. This has come in the form of a very public smear campaign where racism, sexism, and classism take front and center.

Despite the police clearing her of any wrongdoing, Ms. Rosario continues to be victimized, abused, and harassed. She had to leave her home because her address was revealed and the threats against her life became personal and targeted. She is unable to work in peace due to the constant calls to her employer. She cannot go to eat at her favorite restaurant like any person has the right to.

And now the hatred and vitriol take a more torturing form as gossip bloggers continuously call her mother's job, interrupting life or death work in the name of this defamatory vendetta. The constant digging through her past for more ammunition to continue these senseless attacks is senseless and problematic.

Ms. Rosario is taking the brunt of the virtual ire alone. Although Mr. Ellison was part of the perceived offense, and even though he shoulders more than her share of it, no one comes after him. They are deterred by his race, privilege, and financial status. They continue to toy with Ms. Rosario's livelihood, life, and safety. The constant salacious commentary from the gossip blogosphere, combined with the overtly sexist headlines, have now crossed the line of no return. The offenders claim they're exposing the truth. What they're really doing is bullying in its finest and most insidious form.

Mr. Ellison has had enough of the defamation and threats. He is going to use his assets to track down the originators of these attacks and expose them. He plans on pursuing legal action against the content creators who fabricate and perpetuate lies against Ms. Rosario.

"Girl, you're so lucky. This is so romantic." The sigh is hanging from Mary's lips. My project manager is practically drooling.

And I don't punch my sandwich like I want to. Instead, I push a smile onto my lips.

"Carter, I really love your updates to the audience profiles. I've been preaching that pigeonholing age groups into categories without flexibility is a marketing mistake. I think your research will optimize our ad targeting."

"Thanks, Mila," my data analyst says, adding a check to the list on his notepad. "I hate when people assume Gen X is not on any of the new social media platforms. I'm in all of them."

This is why he's so good at his job. He tackles his research with an open mind.

Mary clears her throat. "Ms. Rosario is taking the brunt of the virtual ire." She looks at both of us with her mouth open but continues before I can say anything. "Although Mr. Ellison was part of the perceived offense... Girl, that is *everything*."

She collapses her elbows on the conference table as if weak.

My eyes meet Greg's across the room. He rolls his eyes and goes back to his coffee.

I grit my teeth and point at the newspaper. "Mary, that's enough. This Brown Bag lunch is not for that."

Nonplussed, she looks at me. "You encouraged us to share and get to know each other. I happen to be happy for you. You've been shouldering a lot of this and it's good to see someone having your back."

I don't bare my teeth like I want to. "Yes, we are to share things like stress busters, work-life balance books, and career-related articles. Even TV and pleasure reading. This is just..."

"Inappropriate." Greg shoots from the coffee area.

"Why?" Mary asks. "Because of Madison? You've been cleared and anyway, everyone knows that girl was getting... hers on the side."

"Yeah, but she's dead. And this is Mila's private life," Greg admonishes.

Carter bobs his head up and down.

Mary waves them away. "It is, but that's all people talk about. I mean, when are we addressing the elephant in the room? Personally, I don't see what the big deal is. If they're feeling each other, why not go for it?"

Heat spreads over my neck and my face. And now she's staring at me with those eager eyes and when I look at Carter, I see the light dancing in his. I walked right into her trap. This is what she wants, to put me on the spot so they can have stuff to gossip about with the others.

Fuck them.

"Mary, thank you so much for sharing your feelings on this. However, we are going to move on from this topic. It's not a conversation that aids any of our personal developments. *Appraisals* at GG are not based on gossip or our opinions on other people's personal lives. Now, do you want to talk about your assignment this week or the book our leader recommended on optimizing your time management for success?"

Mary looks at Carter and then at Greg. Neither turn her way.

This fucking bitch tried to play me. She thought they would back her up.

I stare at her until she looks away.

"We can talk about our assignment if you don't mind," Carter says, bailing her out.

Greg winks at me and walks out of the lunchroom.

I don't tell Mary to fuck all the way off like I want to. "Let's get started."

We go through the documents and what our higher management is looking for. I ask them to refine some data points and clarify in several areas.

"You have fantastic data here that you can use more effectively and meaningfully. Because you're trying to prove a point, I would spotlight your good news—ROIs, ROAS, and ROMIs analysis—closer to the top. You want to get our executives' attention from the beginning."

"That makes sense. Thanks Mila," Carter says.

Mary mumbles. "Yeah, it's good feedback."

"That's what I'm here for. From here on out, I recommend you're more in tune with Grayson's comments in our meetings. He gives the feedback for a reason and expects us to address it. Make sure you're addressing his concerns directly. He does not like to repeat himself."

With every passing second, I get more and more heated. I can't stop thinking how she tried to set me up, and now I have to be a good boss who looks out for her. It's my job, but I don't have to give up my lunch hour to tell them things they should already know, yet here I am.

You're getting petty, Mila. It's time to go.

I text Sandy and ask her to save me and go back into the feedback. "By the way, make sure you run this by one of our editors. There are several typos and instances of Mr. Grayson's word pet peeves, like saying utilize instead of use. We don't need him to call you to the carpet again."

Now that was petty.

Mary's face goes red like that day Grayson tore them a new hole. She opens her mouth, but the intercom beeps.

"Mila, you have a call from the CEO suite."

I excuse myself to take the call in my office. I close the door. Sandy dials my cell phone.

"What the hell's happening?"

"Mary wanted to talk about the press release instead of work. I've spent the entire morning avoiding the topic, fielding calls from reporters, asking me for my reaction. I don't need to deal with this."

"I told you it's probably a bad idea to give people access to you outside work meetings. These hyenas are looking for information. Not to be like them but did you talk to Alis yet?"

My blood is back to boiling at this point. "No. He's not picking up the phone. He's avoiding me. If he had told me he was planning on doing this, I would have said no. This is crazy. Now we have the internet talking about us all over again."

"Hon, they never stopped."

Ugh. She's right. "I don't need the extra attention."

"Don't kill me, okay?" Sandy pauses. "I think it's a beautiful gesture. I like that he's trying to protect you and telling people to back off. It shows how much he cares."

I sigh. "This is only going giving people more ammunition. It's a nice gesture, but it does nothing other than create more fodder. I want to thank him, but I have to make sure he doesn't start going after people. That is not helpful. Of course, he's chicken shit and not answering. He must know how ticked off I am."

I take a sip from the bottle of water on my desk. My throat is parched after my tirade.

"Go see him," Sandy says.

"What?"

"If he's not picking up the phone, go to his office and stir shit up for him like he did for you."

My mouth drops open. "Are you crazy? I can't show up in his office. People—"

"People will what? Talk about you? They're already doing that. Insult you? Check."

I nod. "As much as I hate it, you have a point. It would instigate more."

"It could," she says. "But you need to talk to him and it will do you good to get the hell out of here today."

I turn it over in my head and it sounds reasonable. I pack my laptop and tell my secretary I am leaving early. I'm going to handle Alis, then I am going home to work.

Twenty minutes later, I'm driving south toward Luciana Island with the music blasting.

Mila

I park in the visitor's lot and pull out my phone. Alis hasn't answered my text. It stares at me, time-stamped from the moment I sent it.

ME

You won't answer my calls. I'm coming to your office.

Maybe I should give him a few more minutes.

He's had more enough respond. You made it all the way here already. Might as well get out of the car... or you can turn your ass right back around. Go back to your safe place.

Safe place? Where is that exactly?

I look in the rearview at Knox parked a few feet behind me. Never too far. I owe that to Alis. He's made sure I'm protected, but I can't let him go after people. This is not good. Not for me and not for him.

The press release was entirely too much. My phone notifications are going crazy, which can only mean I'm already getting crushed. I reach for the key, not caring that my bodyguard thinks I'm crazy. I think I'm making a mistake until I remember the tweets.

She must have put that kitty on him real good. He's planning on suing the world to crawl back into it.

He hired her a bodyguard and now a lawyer? Home girl needs to write a book sharing the throat skills. #RealThroatGoat

He's dropping money on her. That's why I say #FuckTheFriendship #GetYours #Snake

I throw my truck door open and push myself off the seat. My heels clickety-click against the concrete parking lot and only Knox's footsteps echo behind them. The glass fronted building is massive, like a giant that can squash me by barely lifting a foot. I'm fully prepared for these people to turn me away and to make a fuss until he comes to meet me.

I cross the threshold and make my way to the desk. A man and woman sit in front of several low monitors. Behind them, in large traditional chunky block letters, Ellison Corporation looms like a threat. The man behind the desk gives me a thorough once over. The woman's eyes eyebrows rise but she puts on a smile. "How may I help you?"

"I'm here to see Alis Ellison."

She nods. "Please go through those doors and the elevator is on your left. You will go up to the 14th floor."

"Thank you," I say, a little taken aback.

Knox clears his throat behind me.

I turn to the reception desk. The man waves a hand to the elevators. "He can go up too."

As we walk away, I'm put off. This seems like a little too easy. To get inside Grayson Global offices, you have to practically scan your retina and provide a blood sample. She didn't even ask for our names...

Oh, we're expected.

And now I'm heated I can hear my own breath. He got my messages. He just didn't bother to answer me.

Why though?

In the elevator, Knox turns to me. "Don't walk so fast ahead of me. You want to look purposeful but not leave yourself open."

I nod. "I'm sorry. I'm on edge today and I need to get this over with."

He says nothing. I don't even want to imagine what this man is thinking. I just got in a car and left work like I'm trying to outrun a forest fire. He's been following me for close to an hour.

The doors open to a long hallway. Ahead are two glass double doors. There's not a sign that says CEO suite, but there doesn't need to be. It's obviously secure as these are sliding doors. Beyond them, there's expensive carpet, furniture, and three women behind the desks.

One looks up and sees me and her lips begin to move. The doors slide open, and I step through them. The reception is beautifully done in light gray walls and navy accents. The brown furniture probably costs more than my car.

She looks at me with a serious expression. "May I help you?"

"I'm here to see Alis Ellison."

The middle woman nods. "Please have a seat."

I choose my chair and seethe in silence, ignoring the fact that she doesn't ask my name either.

The others pretend to work, but I keep catching their glances. Knox takes a seat on one end. I take one closer to the window. Luciana Island provides a gorgeous backdrop. Lush greenery and boats are in front of docks that lead to massive estates. It reminds me of a giant puzzle my mom, uncle, and I put together once. It was so beautiful my uncle taped the back of it. We framed it and had it on our wall for years.

This building, this island, the suite, all of it screams old money and privilege.

And yet, people are passing by and staring. I guess the rich and the poor have one thing in common: both are nosy. There's even a cleaning person who walks by three times. I'm dying to snap at all of them. "Take a picture. It will last longer."

I turn out to the view instead and wonder if you can see Alis' house from here. Which is his? We've never talked about that, only our jobs and our situation.

Why would you talk to him about his home, Mila?

I swipe the thought away and start flipping through my phone, looking at the images we received for the *Lash n' Gloss* X *Autumn Lush* new gift set. It's a new box set of seasonal make up and skin care products. It's going to be a holiday release and I can't wait for the sample box. Normally, the girls in marketing get to try it first so we can describe the products well.

The smooth slide of the door has me snapping my head up. I'm not prepared to see him there, in his navy-blue suit and tie. All shoulders and so impossibly tall from my sitting position. I fight not to let my gaze drift lower, but when our eyes lock, I'm imprisoned by the heat in his.

"Come on in, Mila," he says in a voice that is both stern and polite. And it activates every single nerve ending in my body.

I swear to God if there was a voice dictionary, his intonation right now would appear as a '*yes, daddy*' moment.

I stand and follow him. He turns to the right side of the reception desk. "Please hold my calls."

He opens the door for me and I pass by him, absorbing all the nautical notes of his cologne and the heat of his body even from that one slight second of closeness.

His office is just as I would have expected: wood, glass, and steel. Modern but with all the classic pieces. The solid wood desk is imposing and there are books on the shelves. There's a photo of him, his brother Weston, and a beautiful older lady. It's his aunt, whom he called his soul mom the other night. There's an impressionist style painting of a cottage overseeing the water. But there's also a lot of open space. It's minimalist but not boring.

The scent in the air is woodsy and green, the fig notes building on the visual story of all the pieces. It screams power and money, but it's also seductive. It's him.

"Thank you for coming. Please have a seat."

I stab him with a look because he's acting like this is a social visit. But I sit and wait for him to take his chair. There's glass on the door and I don't have to turn around to know that people are watching us, probably thinking we're about to fuck right here.

His eyes are almost piercing through me, and my mouth goes dry.

"Would you like something to drink?"

It's like he's reading my thoughts, like he's anticipated my needs before.

Stop thinking about that. You need to focus.

"Water please."

He stands and goes to a small cabinet. It's a hidden mini fridge.

He grabs a bottle and hands it to me. I get ready to make a dig but when I take a sip of the Voss water bottle, I fight the urge to close my eyes and sigh.

Instead, I get to business. "You know why I'm here."

"The press release, I assume." He's definitely trying to irk me.

"Yes. While I appreciate the intention, I have to say that was not the smartest move. You didn't even tell me you were doing this. Why didn't you answer my messages or calls?"

"I didn't tell you because you would have argued against it. I did not answer your messages because I'm not interested in arguing with you long distance."

I frown. "What? That doesn't make any sense."

"Doesn't it? You don't want me coming over there, but you want to talk to me."

"So you send out this press release to force me to come to you?"

Ice flashes through his eyes. "No."

"Then explain, because I'm about to get real pissed right now."

"I meant every word in that press release and I had it sent out because it needed to be said. What you're going through is ridiculous." The color is high on his face. This really means a lot to him.

"Thank you. You could've just answered me. It didn't need to come to this."

He sighs. "You fight everything and you want to keep your distance and then you said you were coming down here. If making you angry is what it takes to make you come to me…"

He shrugs.

"You manipulated me." I wish the heat hadn't gone out of my voice by now.

"Did I? Or do you not have impulse control?"

"Apparently none when it comes to you," I say without thinking and wait for the regret, but none comes.

I should be more angry and part of my annoyance is the fact that I'm not.

"I'm sorry if this made things harder for you." He reaches across the table, steadying his hand halfway. I look at it, at the invitation he's extending.

People may watch us. *What would they say if they see us holding hands over the table?*

I can't push myself to care because these fuckers will talk, no matter what I do or don't. If I stay away from him, they'll say I was his jump off and that's it. And I'm already the backstabber.

He begins to withdraw his hand. I reach over and wrap mine around it.

He looks from our hands to my eyes. "Can we go finish this talk somewhere else?"

16

Alis

I don't think I breathe well until Mila's car crosses through the entrance of my garage. I hit the close door button and text Knox to go around and park in the garage behind the house. My housekeeper already has instructions to let him in.

I step out of my Audi and stand next to it, waiting for her. I'm letting her take the first steps. I want her to come at her own clear-of-mind will. I watch the battle of in her eyes just like I watched her from the conference room window, waiting to see if she would dare take the step.

She does, of course. I know that about her. She's not a coward. She may be cautious. Yet when she decides, she commits.

She walks toward me but stops halfway.

"I thought you meant a restaurant or a public place."

I cross my arms and shoot for my business casual smile. I don't want her to see how much I want her in my space. How much I've pictured her in parts of my house.

"Are you thirsty for the stares? I thought we could talk more comfortably in private."

She rolls her eyes, steps right up to me, and smiles. "I may be a fish out of water, but I'm not a dumb one. You got my attention, though. Go ahead and make your moves. Let's see if they pay off."

I didn't set this off. There's no way I could have known she would really come to see me.

"I don't want to make you do anything you don't want to." It's important she knows that.

She takes my face in her hand. It's soft yet firm and she stands on her tiptoes like she's going to crush her mouth to mine. "I'll say this only once. No one forces me to do what I don't want to. Now let's go sit somewhere and talk."

She turns toward the door to the house. Even as my dick throbs in my pants, I follow, praying for the day I can fuck her here, against my car. We enter through the mudroom. I show her the formal living room, but we end up in the family room.

"This is beautiful, you know that?" Then she laughs a little. "Of course you do. This is probably why you got the place."

"It is, and thank you. Glad you like it." That's casual enough, I suppose.

"How long have you lived here? Do you live here alone?"

"Three years now and yes."

Her gaze lands on the food at the table and she turns to me with narrowed eyes. "Not planned at all."

I shrug. "I called my housekeeper on the way here."

"She works fast."

I raise an eyebrow at her. "She does, but the chef made it. *He* has great soup and sandwich skills."

She doesn't answer; instead she walks to the window overseeing the patio and docks. "So pretty and relaxing, right?"

Speak for yourself. I'm anything but relaxed right now.

"That view is my favorite."

Now even more than five minutes ago, because it includes her looking out with her hands on the glass.

"I don't blame you." Her voice is low, almost like a whisper. Then she turns around and, still smiling, says, "Let's eat."

We eat without talking, and I hate the silence. At her place, we found things to talk about. Now it's tense and weird and I don't want this for her when she's finally where I pictured her so many times.

"I didn't fully answer your question. I got this place three years ago. I was living in the cottage house at my parents' place, but I needed privacy. I work with my father as you know. I didn't need to see him on my time off, too."

"Oh. How come?" she asks.

I'm transfixed by the way she dips her bread in the soup and brings it to her mouth. "My parents are intrusive and difficult. Wes and I respect them but keep them out of our lives."

She shakes her head. "I can't picture that."

"You don't know them yet." I half laugh, but *what the fuck*? When is she ever going to meet them? God forbid. "You're close with your mom. I have Leila for that."

"You call her your soul mom. How did that happen?"

I lean back and smile. "She's been there for us since the beginning, but she was closer to Weston. They're a lot alike in what they wanted out of life. They had adventures together. My parents would notice their long absences and questioned it. I would cover for them."

"How come you weren't part of it?"

"I was too busy with the dirt bike my grandad sneak-bought for me. When I got good at riding it, I started following them. I snuck into Leila's photoshoot from a car. I wanted to photo bomb it, so I popped a wheelie. When she screamed my name, I lost control and flipped."

Her hand stills. "That's so dangerous."

I nod. "Dislocated shoulder, scratches everywhere. Almost gave her a heart attack. She cried, which made me feel bad. I was in pain but felt so guilty I'd scared her. I told my parents I fell from a tree. Leila fawned over me for my whole recovery period. She's watched over me since."

"That's sweet. She sounds like a special lady."

"She is," I assure Mila.

She blots her mouth with a napkin and shifts on the seat. "This was fantastic, better than any restaurant."

"Thank you."

She chuckles. "No, thank you."

"Why did you come all the way here, Mila? Just because you can't resist a dare?"

She shakes her head. "I would like to think I'm more grown up than that. Originally, I came to tell you that maybe it's best that we stop communicating, that you stop paying Knox, that you take back that press release."

My heart begins to pound my chest. "And now?"

"I'm not sure... wait, no, I'm not a dishonest person. It's just that I watched the way people reacted at your office. The way people have reacted to us all along and no matter what we do, we're setting them off, anyway. So—"

My phone goes off and I'm forced to glance at it. "I forgot to silence it. Damn, I have to answer. It's my secretary. Can I pick this up and continue after?"

She nods and waves me away.

"Alis, there's an issue with the Franklin paperwork. We received an email from budget management. It requires your immediate attention. Today is apparently the last day to submit the requisition to the state."

"Okay, let me set up in my home office and I'll call you back." I turn to Mila. "I'll be right back. Make yourself comfortable. Kitchen is that way, bathroom is over there, and TV remote is right here." I say and move to the office. I want to forget this requisition and concentrate on her, but we need to get this or let the company follow Fred McConnell's idiotic plan as a backup.

It takes me an hour of constant work with budget management and a big favor from a friend with the state, but we submit the correct paperwork for the requisition and now the wheels are in motion. When I return to the family room, Mila is leaning sideways against the armchair, looking out into the water with half-shuttered eyes. Her eyes open wide the minute I step close.

"Sorry." She smiles. "I relaxed and was falling asleep."

I touch a finger to her cheek. "It's okay. I need a few more minutes. Just rest and I'll come wake you."

She nods and I head back to my office.

I write an email briefing my father and copying everyone on the board. I check on her but don't come too close. She is still sleeping so I keep working.

Forty-five minutes later, I get inevitable call from my father.

"Hey, Dad. I got it handled. I don't know if you saw the email. Everything is now working as it should and we are getting approval from the state as of Monday."

"I read the email. You did a good job, Alis. You have a sound mind for business most times."

And a kink pops up on my neck. "Most times?"

"As proud of you as I am for spearheading and implementing this project, I have to question your judgement for bringing that woman into your office. Why was she there?"

Here we go.

"I invited her."

"Why?" he asks. He hates when he doesn't get his information up front. I love delaying him as much as I can.

"We had business to talk about."

My father scoffs. "What business? She is not an investor. This is a woman you're—"

"Stop," I say, in a forceful voice that I've never heard come out of my mouth. "You will not insult her."

"I'm not insulting anyone. You do not have any professional business with her."

"It doesn't matter," I reiterate.

"Fine, but keep your business with her away from Ellison Corp," he yells, his voice carrying but not echoing.

He's in his car. He wouldn't discuss this at the office.

"Is this all you called to talk about?"

"Why, do you need to get back to your business with Ms. Rosario?"

I set my teeth so hard, it's painful. "I said stop that."

"I'm not going to say anything untoward to her. I need you to think, Alister. You have more to lose than she does. If the Summervilles hear about her presence here, it's going to ruin any chance for you and—"

"Jesus Christ, don't you know when to stop?" My voice rises. "I told you I'm not doing that. Lindsay and I will never happen. Madison was a person. So is Lindsay. She doesn't deserve to be treated like one of mom's broken antiques. One sister does not substitute for the other the same way Weston and I are not interchangeable. Give it up."

"Fine. If you don't want to stop flaunting whatever it is you have with that girl out of respect for the Summervilles, then do it for the company you keep saying you want to run."

He's the king of gaslighting and manipulation, and I finally have Mila where I want her, I don't have time for this. I need to get him off the phone now.

———

Mila

One second, I'm floating in the heavy sleep I haven't gotten in what feels like forever. The yelling yanks me upright. I look around for a second, not recognizing where I am. Then I hear Alis' voice, and I remember. I'm at his house.

"So now you question my dedication to the company because I'm not doing what you want?"

I push to my feet and walk toward the sound of his voice, yelping when I transition from the area rug to the cool tile floor. It jolts me out of my half stupor.

When did I take my shoes off?

"You know what, Dad? If you think someone else can do a better job, then choose someone else. I transformed this company, I work late every day to increase our revenue, and you keep making excuses. I'm done."

I walk down the long hallway, passing a couple of closed doors, until I find the office. It's an enormous room with a massive desk with two leather chairs in front. He's sitting behind the desk with his back to me, staring out of the massive glass window.

"I'm not going to keep doing this with you. Every time I don't do everything you ask, you threaten me with Ellison Corp. With other people you think could do a better job. I'm also tired of you constantly throwing Weston in my face. If you think he would do a better job, go ask my brother to come and deal with all this shit. Good luck convincing him to leave his life's work to come deal with the board of archaic prunes who would love nothing more than the status quo. Think he and Dahlia will move down here so he can work for you?"

"Stop being a child, Alister." His dad's voice booms through the speaker phone.

I hear his father's words clearly, as if he was standing in the room with him.

"You know what, I'm signing out for the day. I did everything that needed to be done and beyond. If McConnell and his team did what they were supposed to, I would not have had to call in favors."

His father says something I can't understand.

"We'll talk later. Have a good weekend, Dad."

He hangs his head, staring at the floor. He doesn't even turn when I come in the room and make it around the desk.

"How much did you hear?" he asks, without looking up.

"Not much. I woke up to it."

His head snaps up, his gaze locking on mine. "I'm sorry. You were resting so comfortably."

I hate the turmoil in his eyes.

"You have a great couch."

He chuckles low. "That's true."

But his head goes back down, as if he needs more time to stare at the tile. I come around the desk and stand in front of him.

"I guess I'm not good company," he says.

"You don't need to be. I can go home if you want?"

His arms shoot out, snatch me by the waist, and fold around me. I suck in a breath, but all he does is press his face against my chest. "I don't want you to go."

The way he says it feels both warm and scary. There's his desperation, the muffled movement of his lips, and my insides crumble.

"I don't want to go." And my words don't surprise me. I already know that I enjoy being around him way too much. This is what got me where I am today. I also know that I'm starting to not care for the shit that stands between us. It will be there regardless.

"Stay with me."

"I... can't." My tone is as flimsy as my resolve.

He rolls his head back to look up at me. "Why not?"

"Because..." I trail off, unable to finish the sentence.

"That's not an answer."

"I want to, but it's only going to cause us more issues." Part of me wants to fight it.

"How? The world is talking about us. They're whispering and dragging you when they don't know anything about us, Mila. They make up shit or dig into your past and I don't think it matters what we do. They won't stop."

His words make sense because even though I locked myself away and didn't give any interviews, they still talk and still dig, and still put me down.

"We're damned anyway, right?"

"I guess so. And I don't care. I don't care what the internet says, or the people around us. I don't even give a fuck about my father using the company to try to control me. All I seem to want is the one I can't have. You."

And I stare at him, thinking of how much more I want him every time the world seems to turn against him. No matter what, I want *him*. And why shouldn't I?

"Who says you can't have me?"

His head rears back and those coastal blue eyes turn dark indigo and then almost black. I can't look away. Even as he stands, our gazes remain padlocked together.

"I don't care about any other who. Are *you* saying I can have you?"

For the first time in two months, I'm completely sure of one thing. "I'm already yours, Alis."

So many emotions scroll over his eyes as he takes my face in his hands. "We were only pretending you were mine last time. This time, I'm going to fuck you so good, neither of us will be able to walk it back."

I'm feeling bold and almost vibrating with desire. "That's what I want. You're what I want."

"Take me then, Mila." He opens his arms. "I'm all yours."

The blood rushes through my veins and I've never felt this hunger for someone. I'm starving for him.

I climb on my toes, and crush our mouths together. I feel that first taste of him everywhere at once, in all my nerve endings. It's a flash-back to that moment in the car when I knew it was all lost.

"All it took was a brush," I whisper against his lips, tracing my words.

He nods like he understands and flickers his tongue against my mouth. Then he captures my lips again. I soften against him, almost into him. His hands are on my lower back, while mine can't stop roaming up his arms. I find the buttons in his shirt and start undoing, one by one, not breaking the fusion of our mouths. And then he's working the buttons of my slacks and he pushes them down my legs. He only lets go so I can shrug his shirt and undershirt over his shoulders.

Before he can touch me again, I unbuckle his belt, undo the buttons, and send his pants and underwear to the floor. He's naked before me, so beautiful he snatches my breath. He reaches for me. I shake my head.

"You offered yourself to me. I'm going to take you at your word, all of you."

He doesn't react. Just stands there, staring so intently at me my scalp tightens. I'm so wet and achy for him. But I want my mouth all over him. I press my lips to his chest, run my hands down the planes of his stomach. I follow the trail down with open-mouth kisses, licking and nipping, until the floor meets my knees. He's in front of me and I sigh. Alis shudders and his scent sneaks into my nostrils, man, skin, cologne.

And that's all I need to take him in my hands, stroke my way down him. He bites his bottom lip. I smile, almost tasting him. I can't wait anymore. I take him, getting the mouthful I've been dreaming about for months.

"Wet and hot," he hisses, low and reverent, like a prayer.

I take him deeper, enjoying his moans, letting them wash over me. His fingers tangle in my bun, untying as I work him with my lips, pressing with my tongue. He pulls away the bobby-pins as I retreat, only to go back in, yanking a moan. His fingers tighten on my hair and he pulls it free.

"Look at me," he commands and I obey, staring up at him.

"I needed to see this again, your hair down your face, my cock in your mouth, the fire in your eyes. I want to fuck your face."

The wave of heat that flushes to my pussy makes me tremble and I shift my hands from his hips and place them on my thighs. It's an invitation I've never made before.

He takes control, thrusting into my mouth gently. I open wider, and he goes deeper, grunting and picking up the tempo.

His rhythmic grunts amp my growing need and I reach between my legs.

"No." The word freezes me. "I want to do that."

He pulls out of my mouth and pulls me up to him. His smile is devastating.

"I'm all over your mouth." He licks the trail of spit and plunges his tongue into my mouth. "I can taste me, but I want to taste you." He takes my hand in his and pushes it between my legs, past my nether lips, and strokes me with it. The sensation shocks my entire body and sends me into a frenzy. I'm so slick. I need him so badly.

I free my hand from his and bring it to his lips. He laps my fingers with his tongue, sucking one into his mouth, his hand rubbing my clit, and I'm losing my mind.

"Fuck me. Now."

He doesn't stop rubbing me or sucking on my finger. The friction and suction build, and I'm practically clawing at his arms.

"Now. Fill me."

And that's what does it. He slides my panties off and settles me half on top of the desk. I spread my legs wide and the moment his cock enters me, it's slow and magnified. His girth stretches my tight muscles. My skin bumps all over. "It feels so good."

I meet his every inch with a gasp or moan. He's deliberate and I'm desperate. I buck my hips, but he stills them with his hand.

He's biting his lip, trying to keep his strokes precise, but I'm beyond waiting. I rear up and kiss him, stroking his tongue with mine like he did my pussy to work me up.

He picks up the rhythm with faster strokes, bringing me to the brink, and then slamming his hips against mine until the stars burst behind my eyelids and I throw my torso at him. My face on his neck, kissing and sucking on his skin, I ask him, "Let it go, baby. Come for me."

He grunts a couple of times and the rough sigh caresses my ear.

He pulsates, the slick warmth spreading between us.

17

———————

Alis

Mila snuggles on the outdoor sectional while I get the fire pit going. There's a nice breeze and the sky's full of stars. I couldn't have scripted this better if I tried.

"I can't believe you don't come out here and use this patio every day." The wonder in her voice makes me pause and look at her.

I look around at the stone patio. "I use it sometimes. The other day, I had lunch with Leila and Weston out here."

"When did you use it before that?"

I search my brain but can't think of it. "Maybe last month?"

"What's the point?" she asks.

"Huh?"

She shakes her head. "It's not a judgement. I just mean you have this gorgeous outdoor space. Why not maximize and sit out here?"

"I'm barely here during the day and at night..." I stop short of saying I'm not going to sit out here by myself. I turn it on her. "What would you do with a place like this?"

"Eat all my meals out here, looking out at the water. Read, talk on the phone, snuggle up to someone." She reaches out to me. I take her hand and sit next to her. She throws half the blanket over my shoulders and scooches closer. "Like this."

I chuckle. "This is a different side of you."

"Not really... we know very little about each other. You've only seen me in defense mode."

"And the sexy woman at the restaurant. She was something, wanting to educate me about Jersey life."

"I had to let you know."

Her phone rings, stopping her mid-sentence. She flips the screen to show me.

It's Knox. She answers and switches to speaker.

He jumps right in. "Something's happened and you should know about it. Is it okay if I join you?"

Weariness creeps up into her eyes like the unease percolating up my spine.

"Okay," she says and hangs up. "What now?"

I scratch my chin and try not to jump to conclusions. "I don't know but whatever it is, we're not letting it ruin our time together."

She wraps the blanket tighter around her chest. Her gaze is over my shoulder, out into the darkness.

Knox clears his throat. I find him still near the door and wave him into the patio.

"I'm not going to beat around the bush but I just got some information through a BPD connection. This morning someone died at the Java Cup. The police suspect it was poison."

The name of the place sounds familiar and I get ready to ask why when Mila beats me to it.

"At what time did it happen?" she asks.

"7:45 in the morning."

She gasps, her gaze ping-ponging from Knox to me. "You and I were there this morning."

My stomach goes rock hard as I finally remember where I heard about the Java Cup. "That's where you get your coffee."

Her hand goes to her mouth and she stands.

"Shit. It can't be a coincidence," I say, standing because I can't sit anymore.

"There are no coincidences," Knox agrees. "The cemetery, the ramen place, now this? Yeah, this is all too connected."

"Someone really wants me dead."

I look around for my phone but I left it inside the house. I point at Mila's. "We need to call Dahlia and the Baltimore PD."

"No need. She already knows. Her department too."

I don't believe it. "She would call to tell us."

He shrugs. "Maybe she can't."

But she can call you and have us find out indirectly.

"What did they order?" she asks.

"Coffee light with sugar."

"That's how I get mine," she says, looking at her hand like she's holding the cup.

"You asked her for nutmeg today," he reminds her.

She nods. "Is that what saved me?"

"I don't know," Knox says. "We'll need to be more careful now. You'll have to make coffee at home. Let me know if you need me."

He leaves us and I cross the distance between us but Mila takes three steps back.

"It got so close to me," she says, her hands bunching into fists in front of her chest.

"It didn't get to you. It won't get to you," I insist, placing a hand on her shoulder.

"Are people dying because of me?"

I shake my head. "This is not because of you. We don't even know this is about you."

"There are no coincidences, remember?"

I wish I had not said those words now. I hate the semi-panicked look in her eyes. "Yes, but you're protected—"

"I was protected this morning. Knox was right there. Someone died and that could have been me."

I pull her to me, my arms securing her tight against my chest. "We'll be more careful now. Whatever it takes to keep you safe."

"Alis, I'm going to lose more freedom. I can't even get coffee like a regular person."

I kiss her temple. "It's temporary. I swear this will pass."

"When?" she pulls back. "I know you can't answer that. We were having a good time and it never fails. Someone always brings us back to fear and uncertainty."

"I hate this for you. I wish whoever this is came after me," I say, closing my eyes.

"I don't want that," she whispers. "I don't want anyone going after you anymore than I want them going after me. I would worry too much."

"It would be easier for me."

She frowns and we stare at each other for a minute. "I don't want to think about the asshole that's after me or the internet or anyone. I want to feel good and feel safe."

I squeeze her tighter. "We can manage that. Let's lose ourselves in each other this weekend. Let it be only about us. We can deal with everything else on Monday. Can you do that?"

She doesn't answer me for a while, then she lifts her head to look into my eyes. "Make me forget."

———

Mila

Me and my thoughts sneak out of bed. I can't breathe with the knot of worry that wound itself into my stomach the minute my eyes flew open. I prayed, meditated, and even tried to tap into Alis' even breathing. I would only end up waking him with my tossing and turning. So I grab my laptop from my bag and head into his office.

There, in the early morning quiet, I let myself channel my energy into my work, first checking the email. Monday, I have a long day at work. I make my list and the first item is to talk to Mary and Carter. Only a small portion of the feedback I provided them earlier in the day is reflected in the briefing, prompting several questions from Grayson. I also need to talk to Greg about his answers to Grayson's suggestions. He's focusing on the last one and missing the overall inquiry. He keeps digging the hole deeper and deeper for himself, creating more inquiries from our boss.

I jump in because I can sense Grayson's annoyance as he continues to refer to his previous questions and pointing out where things don't make sense to him.

It takes a few minutes to dig up the different data figures and answer. Then, I send Greg, Mary, and Carter meeting invitations for mid-morning on Monday. I go back to reviewing the sales numbers from last month and the direct correlation to the three campaigns we are A/B testing for the graphic tablets. The reach numbers are comparable with all three, but people react more to the ad with the artist teaching children to draw. It has a higher engagement, especially click and share values.

"I didn't do my job well," Alis says from the door.

He's standing at the door naked except for a pair of boxer briefs. I take him all in—the wide, muscular shoulders with the gorgeous tribal tattoos, narrow waist, and defined thighs—and press my legs together.

"You did. I just had a nap this afternoon. I didn't want to wake you. Since I was wide awake, I might as well do some work."

"You should have climbed over me. I would've loved that."

"Noted."

"You were smiling, so I assume all is good." He nods at my laptop.

"Yeah, one of my campaign concepts did really well last month."

A small message window follows the ping from my work communicator. It's Grayson.

Thank you for answering all my questions. Exactly the information I was looking for. Now please, log off work. It's two in the morning. Monday is around the corner.

I type, *Yes, sir. Finishing up and will log out. Good night.* I promptly exit the communicator.

Alis is standing next to me. "You got busted."

I nod, and we both laugh.

I log out but pull the files from the campaign. "This is the ad I was talking about."

I show him the video of the teacher, showing a group of children how to paint in a classroom where every desk had the Grayson Global tablets. The ad then transitions to the students transferring their designs to canvases.

"Wow, this is stunning, from the images to the concept and the actors chosen."

"I was also in the talent casting and wrote the script." *Am I bragging?*

"Nice. I am 100% sure Grayson loved this," he says.

"I got the idea from a video I saw of his wife. She was one of the original testers for the tablets. She spoke about the ease of it and how the canvas mode perfectly emulates painting on cloth. She used it in her pieces and it's easier to explain sketching to her students and how to translate it into their work."

"So you created a classroom of the future with all Grayson Global technology. I didn't miss the desk." He taps at his own desk, touches a button under it, and it switches on.

"Oh God. I had my ass on company property."

He laughs and shakes his head. "Hey, do you still have your hiring portfolio and the one that got you this job? I've been curious since you told me about it."

I pull them up and show him.

"This is brilliant. You mixed images and actual video ads. Who did your visuals? They're poignant and very high quality."

"Thank you." And all my pride goes into the two words.

"Are you done with work?"

"I have to be. My boss ordered me to log off because it's 2 a.m." I shut down my computer.

"And yet he's also working."

"That's the real tea, but he signs the check, so I don't question it."

"You're a smart woman, Ms. Rosario." He stands and takes my hand. "And may I say you look great in my t-shirt?"

"I only have my gym clothes in my truck and didn't want to dirty that up, so I have something to return home in."

"That's a long time away," he says. I don't correct him and tell him we only have today and tomorrow. I leave on Sunday evening.

We walk back to the bedroom. He stops us at the door. "No clothes zone."

"I'm a stickler for the rules," I say, shrugging off his T-shirt and leaving it on the hallway floor. I step into the room and peek over my shoulder at him.

He slides his boxer briefs down his body and throws them on the floor next to the shirt. I get another full look at him. I don't think this can ever get old for me. He's so beautiful from head to toe. It's almost not fair. We climb on the bed on each side, sliding over the silk sheets, and meeting in the middle.

"I love how soft your bed is, and it's so good for the hair." I touch the bun on top of my head.

"So that's why you buy silk sheets."

I frown. "Yes. Wait, is that why you got them?"

He doesn't answer me, turning to grab a remote from his nightstand. A small light flashes and the piece of art on the wall switches from the beautiful woman with her back to us to a network TV channel.

Damn, I need to step up my TV game, but first, I need to reassure his manly feelings.

I climb over him like it's becoming my routine and rest my head in the crook of his neck. "There's no need to be embarrassed. I love that you did this. It's thoughtful. I like thoughtful acts."

"Yeah?" he asks.

"Oh yeah." I stroke the side of his face. "Let me give you a bonus fact about me. I'm about the actions. Show me, don't tell me. It's..." I stop short of saying the way to my heart. That would be so inappropriate.

"It's?"

"Nothing." I slide my hand down the side of his torso.

He flips me on my back and I don't even have time to react. I'm now under him and his face is hovering over mine. "Finish your sentence."

"I was going to say that show me is my love language. Along with food." Ugh, this makes me sound like a total girl. "It's a dumb joke, Alis."

"Why does it bother you that I know you love language?"

I can't shrug because his full weight is on top of me. "It doesn't bother me. It's just weird to be using the word. I didn't want you to misinterpret me."

Now I made it worse because he stares at me and there's a hint of a smile on his lips. "How can I misinterpret love language?"

"Not love language. It feels like too much to be talking about this."

"You don't think I feel or know how to show love?"

I can't read his face. Now he's serious, and this is getting too weird and uncomfortable.

"Forget I said anything. I was trying to be funny. Just forget it."

"No. I don't want to." And it's the teasing in his eyes that sets me all the way off.

"Fuck off."

He's taken aback. "Mila—"

I shake my head, not caring he's on top of me or that his cock is nestled in my apex. "Don't gaslight me. This is the second time. I fucking hate that."

I don't back down and don't look away.

"I'm sorry," he says and his eyes are warm, his face a little red.

"It's fine."

"I wasn't trying to be an asshole. I just don't understand why you just didn't want to say something everybody says…"

I sigh. "Because you're not just anybody. We've known each other for a short time, but we've been through so much. And I don't know what this is, but I have no expectations and I don't want to bring those in. I want to enjoy this for however long it lasts."

He says nothing and I'm sorry. I read too much into it and overreacted. My face tingles and my eyes start to well. I take a few breaths, hoping to get a hold of myself. I'm going to get off this bed and take a quick walk to cool my head.

"You know what my love language is, Mila?"

I shake my head, not trusting my voice. I want to tell him it shouldn't fucking matter, but... I introduced this conversation and I want to know how he likes to be loved.

He strokes my cheek with his thumb. "It's touch. Now, I'm going to show it to you."

18

Mila

"*Mami*, I'm really okay. We're just hanging out."

"*Amor*, do you think that's wise? If people find out..." I hate the heaviness of her voice, how she's constantly worried about me.

"People are going to talk regardless, and I'm in a safe place. I'm protected, Mami."

"Yes, thank God for the bodyguard." She's talking about Knox and that jars me because I was thinking about Alis. *I feel safe with him in his place.*

"I'm going to cook him a meal when I come to visit you."

"Who?" I ask.

"Knox, Mila. *Tienes que star enamorada.*"

You must be in love.

Her words freeze me. "Why do you say that?"

She laughs. "Because, *mi hija*, your head is in the clouds today."

She's right. I woke up in the clouds pressed next to Alis' body. His bed is heaven and the way he pounded me into it, my outline is carved on it and not just because the mattress numbers are adjustable.

"I finally got some serene sleep."

Mami snorts. "Yeah, right?"

The heat flares over my face, and I open my mouth, then close it. What can I say that won't make things worse?

Nurse Rosario to reception.

"Gotta go, *Amor. Te amo.*"

I sigh with relief. "Me too, *Mami.*"

"*Cuidate, Dios te bendiga, y que los Santos the acompañen.*" She hangs up right after.

"What does that mean?" Alis asks from the door.

"Take care, God bless you, and may the saints be with you. It's a Dominican thing."

He smiles and I want to eat him alive. He looks so good in his gray sweats and nothing else.

"Breakfast is ready. I was on my way to bring it here, but I got a call. Seems like your boss recorded a segment with a national network. They asked him about you and he took the opportunity to clear the air."

I jump off the bed and we head to the family room. He turns on the TV and we dig into our breakfast while we wait.

"What did your mom say? Is she doing well?"

"Yeah. She was a little worried about the media finding out I'm here. I told her I'm safe."

He nods. "We have a lot of security and Knox is here."

It's funny how he thinks the same as Mami, but once again I was thinking of him for safety. I need to file that away and make sure I don't blurt it out like the love language debacle.

That got you magnificently fucked.

We eat in silence, next to each other and picking off each other's plates. We are barely done when the interview comes on. Grayson answers questions about our last numbers, using the figures I gave him overnight.

"He should talk about your ad, share that news."

I smile at him.

"Mr. Grayson, the tragic death of Madison Summerville affected your company recently."

"Yes, Madison was a valued member and a great asset to Grayson Global and all those who knew her. Her absence has been devastating. We are all hoping for justice and healing. We continue to keep her family very present." He means it. It's in his eyes and he cares about all his employees.

"It had to be exacerbated by the involvement of another one of your employees, Milagros Rosario, in the situation."

My spine stiffens. Alis slides a hand over my thigh.

"There was no involvement of Ms. Rosario. The police cleared Mila early on in the investigation."

The interviewer pushes. "They were professional rivals, though. Ms. Rosario got the position after Madison's death. You can understand why people would think it could be related."

"Madison and Mila were colleagues and friends. They were not professional rivals at the time of Madison's death. I had already selected Mila as the Chief Marketing Officer for GG. She was informed the day before. I informed Madison the same day as Mila, but in the afternoon."

I'm stunned, staring at the screen, and then my gaze snaps to Alis. He looks surprised as well.

"She knew?" the interviewer asks.

"She did. My intention was to make the job announcement that week. I had to notify the runners up before I could do that."

"Was Madison number two behind Mila?"

"I'm not discussing that, Charles. The only reason I revealed Madison's prior knowledge of my selection is because I would like to stop the narrative festering in some dark corners of the web. It's time the world stopped bullying someone who had nothing to do with Madison's death, as the Baltimore Police Department has stated many times."

"You're the second person this week who has championed her."

"That's none of my concern. The only thing I care about is that Mila Rosario is a creative force, an employee above reproach, and I'm excited to see what our marketing department can accomplish under her capable hands. Grayson Global is 100% behind her."

"It would probably be helpful to Ms. Rosario if she gave an interview. While we do our best to clarify misunderstandings, sometimes it's helpful to hear it from her."

"Well, that is her story, and she had the right to tell it how she deems appropriate or not. She's in a no-win situation here, Charles. If she speaks, she's feeding the trolls who refuse to accept evidence and facts. The police department investigating the crime has cleared her. She had an alibi. The motive people thought she had has been debunked, and yet, the harassment continues. The narrative is nonstop, so are the physical threats, and she's been doxed. Do you know how dangerous that is in our current climate?"

"Where information is at our fingertips," Charles says.

Grayson nods. "Exactly. Technology is the highest of commodities these days, but it has come at a steep price. It can be weaponized in the hands of the irresponsible. That's why I'm trying to make sure Ms. Rosario is protected."

They segue into other company topics, but I'm still staring at the TV, floored that my employer would do something like this. It's not just the support, it's him going above and beyond.

"He's really got your back," Alis says.

I turn to look at him. "He does. You do too."

"It's the least I could do. It's rare for Grayson to do something like this. You mean a lot to that company. He's expressed it enough..." *Shit, I fucked up.* It's only exacerbated by the sharp look in her narrowing eyes.

"He's expressed it enough to you?"

I tread carefully, giving just enough of the truth. "Well, he expressed it the two times I've called to ask for your contact information?"

"You did? And he gave it to you?"

I shake my head. "No, the first time was after you left the police station and I needed to talk to you. He refused and cited all the good employer reasons he couldn't."

She crosses her arms. "And the second time?"

"After you were doxed. He said if I wanted it, I had to get it from you. So I did." And because I'm an asshole, I smile at her.

She rolls her eyes. I breathe discreetly.

But that scrutinizing gaze is aimed at me again. "I didn't know you were close with Grayson."

"We don't call each other to shoot the breeze every day, but since I met him, we've shared some experiences and project interests."

"Like what and why you never told me before?"

I shrug. "It was some of the work we are doing for communities."

"Oh, the sustainable and humane projects, right? The water in the villages?" Her gaze brightens.

"You remember that?"

She bobs her head up and down. "Of course, you were so genuine when you talked about it."

"What makes you think I wasn't just trying to impress you?" I ask.

"Were you?" Then she shrugs. "I don't think you were, but either way, you did a good job."

Now is my turn to be shocked and for her to smile.

I lean to kiss her, but my doorbell goes off.

We both pull back. I reach for my phone and look through the app.

The blonde at the door waves my way.

I look up at Mila. "It's Lindsay."

"I'll go to the bedroom," she says.

"No, I'll see her in the formal living room."

———

Alis

The shock doesn't wear off, even after I open the door and let her in. I give a small hug. "How are you doing?"

She shrugs. "Well, I guess."

"How are your parents?"

"A mess. Mom won't stop crying. She sits in Maddie's room every day. Dad is... I don't know. He's trying to keep busy with everything except the one thing he knows how to do, work. He's taken up gardening and does a lot of golfing and hangs out with the horses."

I lead her to the formal living room I barely use. "Can I get you a drink?"

She shakes her head. "No, I have to get home soon. It's not a good day for Mom. I assume you saw Spencer Grayson's interview this morning."

I nod. "Just watched it."

She tips her head toward the family room. "I figured you would have. We got the heads up yesterday. He wanted us to know what he was going to say. He also wanted us to know he was going to reveal what he told us when Maddie died."

Now this is interesting. "You knew about her not getting the job?"

"Of course, I did. Who's the first person you call when you have a big letdown or when something goes wrong? Maddie and I were not twins like you and Weston, but we were best friends. She called me right away."

"Why didn't she say anything to me?" I really meant nothing to her. It's still a shock that she didn't even share the minimal. *How did she ever think we would get married?*

"She was embarrassed, Alis."

"We were dating. You share those things."

A sad light flashes in her eyes and Lindsay looks away.

"Oh," I say. "My bad. I was dating her but..."

She stands and comes to sit next to me. "Please don't think badly of her. You're very successful and everyone on the island talks about all the sound decisions you make. She lost the job to her coworker. Someone she saw as scrappy and equally talented. They got compared all the time."

Mila never said that to me. "Were they really?"

"Maddie heard it all the time, but she and Mila were cool. She wanted to keep the one friend she had in Baltimore." She closes her eyes for a moment. "She was in love and in way over her head."

"With Elias Saunders?"

She doesn't look away. She stares me in the eyes and says, "Yes."

"But she thought she was going to marry me?"

"Alis, how long have you lived here? People on this island don't marry for love. But she was hooked, and she's my sister... I can't bring myself to use the word was."

Her eyes fill with tears and she presses a fist to her mouth. I grab her hand and I'm surprised when she takes it.

"When she disappeared, I thought she was hiding and giving Mila the cold shoulder. I told her she was playing with fire when she asked her to go to dinner with you."

I want to pull away, but I don't let go of her hand. "That's crazy. She should've just cancelled and broken up with me. I would've gotten over it."

"Or under someone else quickly." She chuckles through the tears. "You and I are so much alike. Anyway, normally, I'm the one she would have called to cover for her, but since I was in Cabo, she asked Mila. She thought it would be the same."

"It wasn't."

She grunts. "No, but you knew Maddie, when she got something in her head, no one could dissuade her. And no offense, but I was like, she had her heart broken at work, she might as well have a good evening with the one person who made her feel good."

"I'm okay with it."

"Well yeah. You moved on." Her smile is so sad I almost can't stand it.

"It's not like that."

"I'm not judging you. You would've had to move on, anyway. Maddie was too far gone. She knew all there was to know about that man, a fucking piece of work, by the way. But she loved him and accepted him. And he loved her. I went to see him."

"Are you crazy? He could've hurt you."

She shakes her head. "I don't think so. He's broken up about her. I don't think he did it."

"You don't know this guy. He was the last one to see her alive."

"No, Alis. I don't think he was. She was seeing someone else."

The earth shifts under my seat. "Everyone knows she had something going on with Elias."

Lindsay shrugs. "It didn't stop her from dating you and sleeping with someone else."

"Did he say that? He's trying to throw mud at her, maybe using you to clean himself." This is crazy.

"Alis, they had a different kind of relationship and honestly, I was stupid enough to think she was just getting hers. I should've made her tell me who this other guy was."

"Did you tell the police? Call Dahlia. This is important. They have to know." I'm calling her right after this conversation.

She reaches out but withdraws her hand. "They know. I told them from the beginning."

Something in my chest churns. "Everyone knew but me."

Her gaze drifts away briefly. "You were a player, and it was only a matter of time before you went back to your old ways. I hated to see her sad. Unfortunately, the ship with Weston had sailed. I was hoping she would get you both in bed and out of her system."

"Jesus, Lindsay."

She shrugs. "I can't help it. It's my nature. Maddie went and fell for Elias. And now she's gone. I don't even know who killed her. I'm living my worst nightmare. Life without her."

No matter what I'm feeling, it doesn't compare to her pain. "I don't know what to say to you. I can't even imagine what you're going through."

She sighs. "I wake up every day and hold my family together. It was a shock to everyone that I have smart thoughts and that I can keep a business and my family afloat. You should see their faces at meetings. It's like I'm an alien."

"You were the consummate socialite man-eater."

She laughs. "Those were the days. I never wanted to get serious about anything. You know why?"

I shake my head.

"I knew there would come a day when I had to and I wanted to live my life before I got trapped. The only thing is that I thought I would have my sister to bitch to every day. That she would laugh her ass off as I complained."

Her pain radiates over her face and my chest constricts. I hug her. "I'm so sorry."

She holds on for a bit, then lets go of me. "I'm sorry she didn't tell you the truth. I'm glad you are moving on, though."

She keeps saying that, which leads me to believe it's why she's really here. "Lindsay—"

"Oh, I need to tell you so you hear it from me and not anyone else. I punched Melinda Ford at the country club this morning."

"What?"

"She hinted that now that Maddie was no longer with us, I should try to shoot my shot with you."

I don't know what to say, but there's a little worry worming its way up my spine. Does she think about that? I open my mouth but close it when she continues.

"I'm tired of people thinking I'm a replacement for my sister. It's like one sister died, insert the one next to the island's most eligible bachelor. I told my parents and your mom that you and I will not sail into the Luciana sunset together."

"I told Dad the same thing. I don't think they're listening."

"Even my pastor was talking some bullshit about David and Bathsheba finding comfort in love after the loss. I swear my mom must have put him up to it. I told him we would find comfort in many many many other people. Your person just came before mine."

Her words drop my stomach down like a stone. *She is here to talk about Mila.* And now my back is up because as much as I care about Lindsay and commiserate with her, I'm never going to let her or anyone hurt Mila.

"I'm guessing you also came to talk about her? Mila had nothing to do—"

"I know that. I spoke to the police—by the way, Dahlia is nice. Tough, but so kind. No wonder Weston fell in love with her... Anyway, I want you to know that I intend to talk to Mila. Just not here. I don't think she'll tell me what I need to know with you around."

"How do you know she's here?"

She smiles. "I need some answers." Her phone rings and she looks down. The smile vanishes and is replaced by a flash of agony. "Unfortunately, or maybe fortunately for all of us, I don't have the time today."

I frown at her, and she waves me away.

"I'm serious, Alis. Don't get in the way of this. She wouldn't take it too well if you don't let us talk. I don't think that Jersey girl would forgive you if you make her look like a punk."

19

Mila

I haven't been inside the building for ten minutes yet, and I'm already fighting annoyance. It only took walking through the doors of Grayson Global for me to go from the complete privacy of Alis' house to being on full display like a fish in a restaurant tank. All eyes on me, again.

I no longer stop anywhere before I come to work, so I am forced to go to the break room. The men milling around, talking about the Ravens' game, pause to smile and look me over with bold interest. The women are eagle eyed and their smiles half cold but no questions. That's the text I got from Sandy this morning. No one is to question me about my personal life or allowed to harass me. Grayson has my back yet again. And today we got free breakfast. It's the little things in life.

My boss believes me, I'm wearing my killer blue outfit, and Alis is in love with me. I still don't want to be around these people, but I force the smile. "Good morning."

I don't wait for an answer, just grab coffee and, though they have my favorite breakfast box, I choose another. Today, I feel different, and I want something else.

Greg intercepts me halfway to my office. "Hey, thank you for the email to Grayson. I was planning on responding to him today since he always insists on us not working past our regular work schedule."

"It's no problem, G. I just wanted to make sure he got his answers. The thing with Grayson is that he will continue to come back unless he gets the information he needs."

"I've been working for him for ten years. We went to college together. I watched him go from dirt poor to nipping on the heels of Jeff Bezos. I know how he operates." His tone is biting like February morning air.

Heat flashes over my face. *What was that?* "I know you have. It's just Grayson was starting to get impatient. He also clearly needed the answers for the interview."

"You would know better than me since the interview was about you, right?"

I tighten my hand around the coffee cup. Why is he upset with me? "Greg—"

"Hi Mila. Hi Greg." We turn to Carter as he joins us. "Greg, I need to run something by you when you get a chance."

Greg turns away from me to face Carter. "Yeah, let's go now."

I open my mouth, but he stalks away. Carter looks at me, his confusion mirroring mine.

"We'll talk in the meeting," I say and head to my office.

What the hell was that? Did I overstep in my haste to answer Grayson's questions?

I unpack my laptop and breakfast, still unsettled by the conversation. I take a couple bites of my breakfast sandwich and power up my machine. I'll set up a meeting with Greg and figure out what's going on.

My phone pings and there's the text Alis promised he would send when he got to the office.

ALIS

Bet you're regretting it already.

ME

Nope. Our boss got us breakfast and really good coffee.

He doesn't make me wait.

ALIS

That's nice.

But you're not naked in my bed.

I can't lick the corners of your mouth or…

All the things we did yesterday morning and why our breakfast got cold while he imprinted me into his mattress and the memory into my brain. Just remembering makes me a little wet and wishing I had stayed there today.

ME

You just ruined breakfast for me. All because I like to stay employed.

ALIS

Grayson wouldn't have fired you. Work at home day.

I shake my head like he can see me.

ME

Who can work with you around?

His reply is swift.

ALIS

I would let you work. We need breaks after all.

I laugh.

ALIS

Have a good day and a good meeting.

I'll come up to have dinner this week.

We are getting into too deep but I reply right away.

ME

I'll be ready.

I hit send and put my phone away. I grab my sandwich again and take a small bite when Sandy knocks on the glass door.

I wave her in and hug her.

She's smiling from ear to ear. "You look gorgeous. No wonder these nosy bitches are dying right now."

I laugh. "I'm getting lots of looks."

She drops herself into one of the chairs across from me. "I dare them to say anything after Saturday's interview. Did the two of you watch it together?"

I don't play coy. "We did."

She leans forward in her chair. "And?"

"We both thought it was a good interview. Very nice of Grayson."

"Oh definitely. But what I really want to know is how was the weekend." Her eyes are dancing, catching the window light.

"Weird, interesting, and mostly hot."

She bites her lip. "Yes, girl. You only have to take one look at him." She winces. "No offense."

I chuckle. "None taken."

"Is this officially a thing now?"

"I'm not sure about officially, but it's definitely a thing."

She air-high-fives me. "About time."

I fill her in about my visit to his office when it occurs to me. She almost never comes downstairs at this time unless she is delivering a message.

"Wait, why are you here?"

"Oh. Grayson sent me. He wants you to go to our building in Canton and see Simone De Castro."

Simone is one of the top company attorneys for Mr. Grayson. I met Simone before, at a couple of other events. She gave one of the most impactful sessions at the company's annual conference. Her session was on women, power, diversity, and inclusion. I stayed after to talk to her and pick her brain.

"Do you know why?" I ask Sandy.

She shakes her head. "I just know that I was to come deliver the message. Read between the lines."

He wants no record of this.

"Okay. When does he want me to go see her?"

"Now. Get your things and we'll walk out."

I send out an email to my staff, switch our scheduled meeting, lock my computer, grab my purse, and follow her out. I tell my secretary that I have an important meeting on the executive floor.

When we go in the elevator, Sandy turns to me. "Girl, that booty is popping. No wonder everyone's staring."

"Yeah. I learned long ago I can't hide it no matter how much I want to, so I work with it."

"Not mad at you. If I had an ass like that, David wouldn't let me out the house."

I laugh.

We ride the elevator halfway when she inserts the key, and we are taken to the top floor. We get out and she walks me to the other end of the floor, where there's another elevator. "Never mention that you know about this elevator."

She presses the button, the doors open, and she motions for us to get in.

"This is why we never see Grayson come in or out of the building. I swear he's like James Bond."

"He's just as hot, too. I said the same thing to Winter. She just laughed and told me not to tell him. She doesn't want him getting a big head."

"You speak to her like that about her husband?"

She nods. "Winter is chill. She's crazy in love with him, but she is the first one to tease him. I've known her since she was pregnant with their daughter. I was the one that sent her the preview of the article where they said he works harder than the devil. She got a kick out of it."

"Yeah, she seems nice."

Sandy taps her chin. "You should get to know her. You're both with high profile rich men. I bet she can give you great advice."

I tilt my head and focus on her. "Do you really think she wants to talk to me with my scandal-riddled ass?"

"She's had to deal with a lot of scandals being with him. Their relationship has been tested. When Grayson's brother-in-law went to jail, a reporter thought it would be cute to call her a Yoko. Grayson shut that down real quick. Kinda like your prince did with you."

"Prince?" I almost laugh thinking of Alis' face if he heard that.

"Yes, he put on his cape, grabbed his sword, and set out to slay the dragon for you."

"You've been reading too much historical romance," I say. Those are her favorite novels.

"Don't be disappointing. I know a lot of shit has gone wrong lately, but you have to stop and see the fairytale side of this. I think most men are shit, but this guy has stood by you. He could've washed his hands of you, sat back and enjoyed no one getting on him. Instead, he's hiring you security, making sure you are always safe, and giving press releases."

I don't tell her about the breakfast in bed, walks in the woods, and sex on his patio under the stars. I swish it over in my head and she's right. "He is romantic, isn't he?"

Knox meets us in the garage. Soon we are on the way. I take the conversation with Sandy with me all the way to the Canton building. As quasi-annoyed as I was at the press release, I'm smart enough to realize I cannot throw it all away. He didn't have to do that, but he did.

It makes me smile again. And no matter what the hell else happens, I'm going to latch on to that. I'm going to fight for us because I think I'm in love with him, too.

We arrive in Canton seven minutes later. Even though this is a smaller building than our headquarters, "the tower" is near the seaport. We take the elevator to the top floor and Knox stays in the waiting area while I'm shown right into Simone's office.

She's waiting for me but holds up one finger. "Please set up the meeting with Mr. Saunders for 5:00 p.m." She's silent briefly, nodding a couple of times. "I'll definitely be there. Tell Grayson I wouldn't miss this for the world. As his lawyer, of course. Thank you."

The smile on her face is the true meaning of impish. Then she sets her eyes on me and her gaze softens.

"It's good to see you, Mila. How are you doing?"

I smile back. "I'm okay."

Her eyes narrow. "I say more than okay. You're glowing. It's good to see after these past weeks."

"Thank you," I say.

"Before we get started, one thing: you never called me for mentoring. Not that you need it, you're doing amazingly well on your own. However, let me reiterate: you can reach out to me anytime."

"I'm sorry I never reached out to you like I was supposed to. Things got crazy after. And thank you for being willing to mentor me despite all this... stuff."

"Girl, I work for Grayson. I'm his main lawyer, despite what you hear from little men with no personalities. All I do is deal with fires for him. Plus, and off the record, Madison's office romance was the most public secret ever."

"Why didn't anyone do anything? Is that not an actual rule?"

She smirks this time. "You will learn today that it is very much a rule. Let me explain in a way HR never did during your new employee training. The reason the rule is in place is to protect subordinates and non-management employees and prevent workplace harassment of any kind. It's easy for you to tell your peer I'm not interested or that is not appropriate. There's always a person above you can run to. It's trickier to tell someone in higher management or key positions. The reason is that we are all human and we react different to rejection."

I nod.

She continues. "Grayson and I talked about this in the early inception of Grayson Global. He wants to avoid his company coming into any scrutiny and it is important to him that his employees are protected. What some people don't realize is that when they take mentorship roles, the company watches them closely. If you are going to pull off an office dalliance, you need to be extra careful because once one person realizes what is going on, the rest of your office will and then the floors below and above inevitably follow."

"Wow," I say, thinking back to how Maddie would talk about what they did. Sometimes she would be loud in the break rooms. She also would outright flirt with him when he visited our floor.

"You don't have to protect her anymore, Mila." This is the second time I hear the same phrase.

"Old habits die hard."

Simone taps her finger on her desk. "I guess, but they're the ones that put this out there. The rumor mill was alive and spreading after he came to your floor, and they had *their quasi-session* in the conference room."

I press three fingers to my forehead. I told Maddie so many times. All people talked about was the way she leaned on the table and how close their faces were to each other. They licked their lips and found reasons to touch.

You know they're not talking about work. I remember being trapped in one of the bathroom stalls while people talked all their shit.

Doesn't she have a boyfriend?

Look at Mr. Stiff, trying to put the moves on someone.

When she is named CMO, we all know the conference room was her casting couch.

There was no way I could come out and defend her like I had before. After the "mentoring" she went up to their floor and they went into his office. I just waited for them all to leave.

"She was just in love."

"We can't help who we love, but I wonder if she knew who he really is."

And then a thought hits me. "Is that why I got the promotion? Did Madison disqualify herself?"

"Stop it right there," Simone says. "First, this was never on Madison. She was not the one with the power in that relationship. Her mentor was. Second, Grayson doesn't do defaults. You got that job because you worked your ass off."

I remember what Lindsay told Alis. "I heard Maddie knew exactly all there was to know about Elias. I think Alis and me were the only ones in the dark about it."

Simone's eyes widen but the moment is way too brief.

"It's interesting that she knew. It makes it more confusing, but then again, I wonder if she was just one of those ride-or-die chicks."

"I'm confused."

"I'm sorry, I know. I can't say much more right now. I think after today, you'll begin seeing new things and the pieces will start falling into place. But that aside, the reason you are here is that Grayson wanted me to give you some prep about the weeks to come."

"Okay." I still don't understand.

"Because of Grayson's public defense of you, the media will continue reaching out to you. We're getting a lot of requests for interviews with you. I need to advise you not to talk to them. We can't control what people outside our organization say to the media or press releases, but your words can sink you more. We want to help you craft a strategy. If you allow me to work with you, I can coach you on how best to address this situation."

"Of course. I need all the help I can get."

She nods. "Very well—" Her phone rings. "Sorry, got to pick this one up. It's our boss."

She answers and listens and her mouth drops open, her gaze snapping at me. "You're kidding me. Okay. Okay. I'm headed that way."

She hangs up and gets up. "We have to go back to the office. There was an incident."

"What kind of incident?"

She shakes her head and then stops. "Did you have breakfast at work this morning? The one catered?"

I nod. "I didn't get to finish it."

She pulls me from the chair. "Come on."

I get up and follow her.

On the way out, she spots Knox, who stands right away. She asks him to follow us and go in the elevator.

"There's a car downstairs. I need you to go to St. Raymond's right away."

"The hospital? For what?" I ask.

"You need to be checked for poisoning. One person is in the hospital right now. Grayson thinks some of the breakfast items may have been poisoned."

————

Mila

"Are you okay?"

I close my eyes and pray for strength. It's not my mom's fault that I've answered a variation of that same question what feels like hundreds of times.

"I'm fine, *Mami*. They have me under observation and they tested my blood. Nothing yet."

"Did they do an arsenic test? And what about ethylene glycol? You know what? Let me talk to your doctors."

I hand over the phone to the attending nurse, sighing. "It's my mom."

The woman blinks a couple of times but begins talking into the phone. "Yes, yes. The doctor ordered those, but it doesn't seem like that matches what the other patient has." She is paging fast through her notepad. "Yes, ma'am, I understand. Let me tell you what we ran."

I smile for the first time and tune them out, laying my head back against the pillows. My mom is the most thorough of people about hospital procedures. I close my eyes and concentrate on breathing. I need to call Alis. I want to make sure he hears this from me. Before this shit-show makes its way to the press. Simone has been checking in. We are keeping everything quiet until we find out if there are any more victims, but with the office the rumor mill already going all cylinders, they're bound to find out.

I get comfortable and take slow breaths, inviting calm. I center myself thinking about Sunday, walking through the woods with Alis again, sitting in the front of his house, staring out at the lake. I want to be there now, turn back the time and be where it's safe.

The warm touch on my arm almost makes me come off the bed. My eyes fly open, but it's just the nurse.

"Sorry. You were finally falling asleep."

I shake my head. "I was just summoning calm."

"Your mom will call you right back. She's having the doctors in her area looking at the information in your electronic chart for today. She assured me she has access. I did not give her any information."

I chuckle. "She does. I'm sorry she's questioning you so hard."

"Don't even worry about it. Parents are like that. Your mom has so much more knowledge... she's a good nurse. I can tell. She asks more questions than our head nurse."

"She is good," I say with so much pride. "She's won all the awards several times. The Pathway, the Order of St. Jude, the Nightingale."

"Wow. You're lucky."

"I can't even cough in peace before she is on me with a stethoscope." I close my eyes as she takes my blood pressure again. I don't sigh like I want to.

The nurse laughs this time. "I get it. My mom was a nurse too and..."

I open my eyes up to see what stopped her. My heart squeezes inside my chest. There's a man outside our double doors. His back is turned to us, but it's him. I know him. Then he turns around and I see his face. Almost the same face, same height, but this guy's frame is smaller. And then I remember watching him across the cemetery. It's Weston, Alis' brother.

He smiles and walks through the threshold.

"Dr. Weston." The nurse's voice is excited, inviting, and giddy like a teenage girl with her first crush.

"Nurse Phillips. I got it from here. Kim is requesting you at the desk."

"Oh, thank you." She smiles way too bright and tucks a hair strand behind her ears.

He waits until she exits the room and turns to me. *God, he looks so much like Alis.*

He offers his hand. "It's good to meet you, finally. I hate that it's under these circumstances."

I shake his hand. "Good to meet you, too."

"Your mom is causing waves. She's asking all kinds of questions through your chart. She's also contacted our administrators."

I grimace. "She won't stop."

He shakes his head. "She's a mom away from her child and something big is happening. This is how she feels she is contributing."

"I know. I know. My patience is just dwindling."

He stops paging through my chart and looks at me. "Well, you've been through a lot."

"Are you supposed to be doing this? I mean, I kinda know you…"

"No," he says. "I was about to get off work and I heard what happened at GG. I saw your name and stayed on duty. There's a lot of you guys here. They need all the doctors they can get."

"Ah okay."

He clears his throat. "By the way, my brother is on his way to Baltimore. He says he's been calling you since he found out, but can't get through."

I can't help the thump in my heart. He's coming to me again. "How did he hear about it?"

"I guess someone must have told him."

I open my mouth to say that this has been confidential, but he's not looking at me and I think there's my answer. He told Alis.

"I just wanted to wait and see. I don't think I'm contaminated with anything."

He leans closer. "Honestly, and I never said this. I don't think you are, either."

"How's the person who got poisoned?"

"She's stable. Thankfully, she ate very little, and they got her here on time. The first couple of bites made her sick."

Because of me. The thought hits me so hard. And my heart speeds.

"Someone's trying to kill me. There are just too many coincidences. First my favorite ramen spot, the coffee house, and now at work." I press the heels of my palms to my temples.

The panic bubbles are expanding and becoming larger.

Weston places a hand over mine and pulls my hand from my temple. "I understand, but right now, I need you to relax and let the police do their work."

"You don't get it. People are not safe around me. I'm never going to make it through this mess."

The bubbles begin to burst, and I start to feel it. All morning I was in my haze from this weekend. Now it's getting to where I just don't know what to do.

"Hey," he says, and begins massaging circles near the base of my thumb and index fingers. "How come you didn't follow in your mom's footsteps and became a nurse?"

I freeze, look up, and frown. "What?"

His thumb is moving and pressing. "Mama Rosario is a decorated nurse. It would only be normal her daughter wanted to follow in her footsteps and go on and win some awards of her own."

"I win awards. I just don't have the stomach to patch wounds and watch things ooze from someone's skin."

"Oh, you let that little thing get in the way? What a wuss."

I laugh. "That's what she said too."

"Blood jokes aside, I know she has to be proud of you. You're a big exec in a global corporation."

I nod. "She is..." The pressure in my chest eases. "What did you do to me?"

"Acupressure. Whenever you feel like your anxiety is climbing, take your right thumb, press it here and draw circles." He takes my hand and shows me.

"Ahem."

My gaze snaps to the door and standing there is Detective Dahlia Wicker.

"Detective," Weston says.

I might as well not be here by the way she's watching him. "I got my eyes on you, Ellison."

"I hope so."

She rolls her eyes and turns away, but not before I can see the small smile. She keeps walking but then stops. "I'll be back, Mila."

Detective Hunter meets her halfway and they talk to Nurse Phillips.

"Oh God. I don't want to talk to them."

"They're good cops. They want to keep you safe."

I look up at him. "I'm so tired of talking to the police. I'm tired of being the center of attention."

There's no anxiety in me. I'm just exhausted.

"They're going to find who's doing this. Right, Detectives?"

Dahlia comes to stand by him. Detective Hunter stays at the foot of the bed.

"Dr. Ellison, can you give us a few minutes?" She doesn't look at him, but I don't miss the way he passes way too close to her, the way his hand brushes over her ass, or the way her gaze lasers after him.

He walks out into the hallway and closes the doors behind him.

"It was acupressure," I blurt out.

Her gaze is back on me. "He's a good doctor."

I nod. "I wouldn't…"

She presses her hand on top of my wrist, just like he did. "Relax. We don't want to bother you too much. We just want to talk about what happened today."

"I don't know much about it."

"Tell us what you do know," Detective Hunter finally says.

"I grabbed breakfast and a coffee from the break room, and I went to eat in my office."

"Is that what you normally do?" Dahlia asks.

I shake my head. "I get coffee on my own but when we get catered breakfast, I sometimes stay there and socialize, but that's not a thing right now."

"How come?" he asks.

"I'm don't like to feel a fish in a tank, Detective Hunter."

Detective Hunter jots something down. "Call me Matt. What did you get? Were all the breakfasts the same?"

"No. They always order three or four combinations and the same amount of each. I got the cheese, egg, and sausage sandwich."

"Is that your usual?"

"Normally I get the scrambled cheesy eggs with kielbasa."

The detectives exchange a brief look. I see what I need, though.

"That's what was poisoned?"

Dahlia's face is impassive. "You know we can't answer that. What happened next?"

"I was in my office when Sandy came down. She's Grayson's secretary. She started asking me questions about my weekend—"

The slight lift in Dahlia's eyebrows tells me she knows where I was.

I continue. "Sandy came to tell me that Grayson had scheduled a meeting in Canton for me. I was to go there."

"To meet with Ms. De Castro?"

I nod.

"How much did you eat?" Matt asks.

I shrug. "Not much, only a few bites. I mostly had the coffee."

"How come only a few bites?"

"Sandy and I got distracted talking and then we left the office."

"Did anyone say anything weird to you? Or push you to take any type of food."

I rub a circle into my wrist like Weston taught me. "People mostly stare at me these days."

"You'll need to be very careful about what you eat. I would get into the habit of preparing my own meals for a bit. Until we find out what's really going on."

I don't groan like I want to.

"Mila—"

The door flies open and this time my heart slams against my ribs and my body goes haywire. Alis walks past Matt, and he doesn't stop coming toward me until he has my face in his hands and his lips crush against mine. It's a slow kiss and we are not alone, but I don't care. I don't care who sees and what they have to say. I only care that he's here.

20

Mila

We pause outside the black iron door. This quiet part of Fells Point is charming, but I look back at the car with a longing heart. It's still so close. I would only need to take a few steps and I'll be back in it. I know I could convince Alis to return to my place instead of being here. God knows I could talk him into something dirty without much effort.

He tugs at my hand. "Hey. Listen, if you don't want to do this, we can just go back to your place and find something in your kitchen."

I look down at our interlaced fingers and then at his face, and there's something there. Some kind of anxious energy. *He wants this.*

I push a smile onto my lips. "There's not much in my kitchen. I don't see you eating ramen noodles and eggs. I'm okay. The day has me jittery. Let's do this."

He frowns and stares for a bit. "I don't want to force this."

It is important to him.

"You're not. I'm the one who said yes when she asked. I just need to transition her from a cop suspecting me of murder and into a person."

There's no turning back now. The door flies open and Weston is standing there. "Get in here."

We go inside and Weston gives me a hug. "Thank you for coming."

I smile at him. I see what Alis says about him. He's like a comforter-in-chief.

He and his brother lightly shove each other. It's manly cute.

He shows us to the living room and we meet Dahlia halfway. She's wearing joggers and an off-the shoulder burnt orange top. It's a complement to her beautiful skin. I would put her in an *Autumn Lush* ad for golden eyeshadow and highlighters palettes.

"Hi," she says, hugging Alis first and then turning to me. To my surprise, she hugs me as well.

"Hello," I reply, fighting the urge to call her detective.

"Welcome to our home. Please make yourself comfortable." She points at the sofa.

I nod and sit, my purse next to me.

She extends her hand for my purse. "Let me take that."

She's trapping you here.

I don't hesitate because if I do, I would let all my apprehensions talk for me. I'm being ridiculous, but this woman has been watching me like prey for the past months. Alis takes my hand in his again, his fingers tightening around mine.

She looks down at our hands and then at Weston.

"I'll go find us some wine."

He turns and heads for the kitchen. Her gaze turns to Alis. "You should go help him. Make sure he doesn't pick a bottle that has us hungover tomorrow."

God, she *is* trapping me.

Alis turns to me and the question is all over his face. He wants to know if he should stay.

Dahlia stares at me.

Don't punk out.

I turn slightly to look him in the eyes. "You should go help him. We definitely don't want to be hungover tomorrow."

He leans over and kisses me, then gets up and walks away in the direction Weston disappeared.

When I turn back, Dahlia is smiling. "You're hanging in there?"

I shrug. "I'm swimming, not drowning. Thank you for not asking me how I'm doing. I hate that question these days."

"I get that. Thank you for not chickening out."

My back stiffens. "Meaning?"

She sits next to me and places a hand on my arm. "It's a good thing. I know we didn't meet under the best circumstances, and I always do my job, even when it's uncomfortable."

The question must be written all over my face because she laughs.

"Matt and I could tell you didn't do that to Madison early on. However, we have to treat everyone like a suspect, especially when they lie to us."

I wince. "I didn't exactly lie…"

"You just didn't tell the whole truth and I get it. It was a hard truth to tell, but you put yourself in the middle. Both of you did."

"Yeah, but you didn't suspect Alis."

"We didn't suspect you either. I just needed to know what you knew."

"Which was nothing," I say. "Did you find out who's the other guy Maddie was sleeping with?"

She shakes her head.

"What about Elias? He has to know something."

She places her hand on her knee and leans in a little. "Look, I really can't talk about an ongoing investigation but I will say this, trust us. You don't see any movement but there is. We intend to get whoever did this."

"Okay," I say but it's not. How long will this take? How long will I be in danger?

"Let's put this away for tonight. I want you to feel comfortable here. I'm not Detective Wicker, I'm just Dahlia."

"Why?"

She shoots a look to where the brothers disappeared. "I think you know."

I nod. "It seems important to him."

"It is. I like you're not delaying this. I think you and I can get along."

And it hits me. "Because it was not that way with Maddie?"

Her eyes widen a bit. "You catch on quick." She sighs. "I tried... I just feel like we were not compatible."

Well, no. She was hung up on your husband...

"It was complicated," I say.

"He won't admit it, but it was also hurting Alis. So, I kept trying, but it's not in my nature to kiss ass and she seemed more and more uncomfortable with time."

"She was a good person. It was just weird for her."

We fall into a silence but I don't want to take off running.

"Are you working from home tomorrow?" she asks.

I nod. "We all are. It's crazy how we keep getting sent home. I heard Karin is stable and should go home in the morning. We are all just glad no one was badly hurt."

"Yeah. I wish the people at the coffee house and restaurant had been that lucky."

My gaze drops to the floor. "They're dead because of me."

"They're not dead because of you, Mila. They're dead because some crazy person is trying to get to you. It's not the same thing. I'm mad we could not crack this."

"Do you have any leads?"

She shakes her head. "Let's not talk about this. We all need a reprieve from this case. Matt is getting his in a house full of kids and a pregnant wife. You, me, and the twins are going to have some wine and a nice evening."

"Okay. I think I can do that."

Her eyes narrow. "Let's talk about the elephant in the room."

"What's that?"

"You're Dominican. I'm Dominican. And we both got an Ellison brother."

I laugh. "You really got Weston. Alis and I, it's... new."

"And hot. Enjoy it. He cares about you. Don't question it."

"How do you know that?"

She shoots me a don't be stupid look. "That man practically ran here from Luciana Island today. He throws caution to the wind every time anything happens around you. He's even got into it with me a few times, and I know for a fact I'm his favorite family member after Leila."

"Why?"

"He felt we were not doing enough to protect you."

I can't help it. I smile. She does too.

"He has been consistent."

"You're using your work words?"

I laugh again.

"Here's the wine," Alis says, his gaze lasers to mine. The question is clear. He wants to know if I'm comfortable.

I nod and take one glass from him.

Dahlia takes the other and waves him away. "We're good here. Make sure your brother doesn't burn the food."

"How would I know how to do that?" He looks so perplexed we both laugh.

"You don't know how to cook?" I ask.

He glares at Dahlia and then answers me. "I've never had to."

She stands. "Let me go check on the food."

I hold out a hand to him. He sits next to me, in the spot she left vacant.

"It's okay, you don't know how to cook," I say and lean closer to his ear. "Your other skills more than make up for it."

His hand flies to my thigh. "I feel like I need to put them on display tonight. I'm being attacked and need to prove my worth."

His fingers move to the inside of my leg. "Yeah, you should definitely prove your worth to me. All night."

"You're offering me all night?"

I lean my head on his shoulder. "I don't want to be alone. No, scratch that. I want to be with you tonight."

"You got me." He throws his arm around my shoulders.

"I'm having a good time. She's funny."

"Yeah? We heard you laughing. It's good to hear you do that."

I turn and press my lips to the corner of his mouth. "You heard a lot this weekend."

"I want to hear it more. I want to bring that to you, Mila. I want you smiling more and not waiting for the other shoe to drop. What's the point of having all I have if I can't give you..."

He trails off and I pull his head down to me. I want him to finish that sentence. I want to hear what he will say.

"Someone wants to talk to you." Weston comes back into the room and hands him over his phone. He winks at me.

"Hello, my love." Alis' voice is honeyed and soft. He's smiling hard and I'm transfixed because this smile is so different from his other ones. It's warm and from deep within.

I look down at the phone and there's a beautiful woman on the screen. I've seen her before. She's in photos at his house and his office.

"Should you be calling me your love when you are there with another woman? Have some respect."

His Aunt Leila. And just like that, my chest tightens a little.

Not just his aunt. She's his soul mom, one of the people he loves the most, and she's on the phone.

"Different kind of love..." He trails off again.

She laughs, breaking our eye contact.

"Let me see her face. I need to see it for myself."

He awkwardly hands over the phone and I'm face to face with the most important woman in his life, prettier than any of the photos I've seen.

"Hi," I say. "It's good to meet you."

"Ohhh, you're gorgeous."

"Thank you," I've never been called gorgeous before. "That word is better suited for you. You're so beautiful."

"Thank you. Now you know where he gets his looks." She laughs again. It's clear she is joking, but it's also the absolute truth.

"I think they do."

"So, my boy can't stay away even a day away from you. I knew the day would come when a woman had him chasing her."

"He's been good to me."

She snorts. "As he should. You deserve it. Listen, I'm not going to take a lot of your time, but remember this, fuck those people. Be happy."

Her words rattle me and there's something in her that reminds me of my uncle Felipe. "Yes, ma'am."

"Good girl."

I hand over the phone to Alis and he trades places with Dahlia. When he's gone to the kitchen, she whispers, "Aunt Leila likes you. You're in."

"She's probably being nice. She doesn't know me very well."

She chuckles. "Leila's a straight shooter. She likes the way he talks about you and the way he is with you. It's different..."

"How do you know?" I ask.

"We talked about it. Weston has noticed it, too. He's hands on with you."

"He wasn't like that before?" And that's interesting because he's very invested in all that I say and do.

"By all accounts he was a player, but that changed before I got to know him. Let me tell you something, but I want to preface it by saying I'm not bad mouthing Maddie. Do you understand?" She waits for me to nod. "She called the shots in their relationship. He didn't care."

I open my mouth to say maybe that was their dynamic, but she stops me with a hand over mine. She leans closer.

"That man cares about those he loves. He cares about his company, his employees, the communities they do business in. But he just shrugged, accepted all her cancellations, how cold she could be with him. And I can say that because I saw it. Men sometimes don't notice things, but Leila and I sure did."

"Maybe they were just not right for each other. She was in love." I press my lips together. It still hurts to talk about her this way.

"She was in love with someone else. Meanwhile, I got a phone call from him and a talk from his brother because he called to make sure I'm not trying to ambush you."

"I'm going to kill him," I say and then wince. "I need to stop using that phrase."

"Girl, I say that twice a day. Sometimes about my partner, who's also a cop. Don't be mad at him. He's doing what he's supposed to do. If he doesn't feel protective or a healthy dose of possessive toward you, your time, your life, and interests, is he really in it?"

———

Alis

We leave Dahlia and Weston's house and I can't help how relieved I am. Knox nods at me from across the street and the undercover cop car Dahlia assured me would sit outside is about three hundred feet from mine. Alis opens the door for me and then climbs into the driver side.

He puts the car in drive and we are coasting toward her place in no time. Knox is following close. There's also a car driving ahead of us.

"Those are cops, right?" I ask.

"Yes. That's the advantage of having a detective in the family."

"You are lucky, and me by association." I squeeze his forearm. "I take back all my bad thoughts about her before. Dahlia's cool peoples."

"She is. Gave me a hard ass time about you, but she is good."

"How so?"

"At first, she told me I needed to stay away because people were all over you and you didn't need more attention. She saw you at the cemetery. That's how I spotted you. I was looking at her and then I saw your car. She told me to let you pay your respects in peace."

"I'm glad you didn't. If you had not been there, I would be—"

"Let's not talk about that." He pauses, holding up a hand. "My point is that she didn't want any more mud on you."

"I get that. She was great tonight. I need to send her a gift for how she welcomed me."

"You don't have to do that."

I nod. "Yes, I do. She didn't have to bring me into her home and show me the first relaxing evening out in months."

His gaze snaps to me. "What about last weekend?"

I laugh. "I meant in public company, while I'm dressed."

"The naked time was better."

I swat him. "It was. I just crave socializing sometimes. I wasn't everywhere, but I used to do things out of my place. I used to walk a lot, go to stores, grab takeout. You don't know how much you'll miss the little things until you lose them."

"It won't always be like this."

"But when will it end?"

"Soon. It has to." There's so much conviction in his voice, but I just don't feel it.

"What if it doesn't?"

He stops at the light and looks at me. "Then I'll hire you more security and you'll be like a capo's wife while you go out and shop to your heart's content.

I snort. "Why a capo's wife? You could have said a politician or celebrity."

"Because I feel like the madman who would kill anyone that tries to hurt you."

Warmth floods my body from the tip of my hair all the through my toenails. "I don't want you to kill anyone for me. I don't want anyone dead."

"And I just want you safe. I couldn't take it if anyone hurt you." He takes my hand in his and kisses my open palm.

My skin turns to gooseflesh and I lace my fingers through his. I'm still smiling when the phone rings. It's Knox. I put him on speaker. He doesn't even wait for us to say anything.

"Don't go straight home. There's a car following you. Drive by the office and then East Madison Police Station. The other car is going to pull them over and then we are heading to your place."

My heart slams against my ribs and I turn around to look through the back window. *We're being followed.*

"Okay," Alis says, and he presses the gas.

"Maybe this is a good thing and they can catch whoever the fuck it is."

"Yeah," he nods, his eyes looking straight ahead. "Whoever he is, he's not getting close to you."

I nod. "Don't kill us in the process."

"I'm not. I'm good at drag racing. I used to do it before."

"What?"

He shrugs and speeds through the street. We drive past my job. The neighborhoods shift like a movie around us, going from affluent to commercial, to poor urban. Two blocks after we pass the police station, two cop cars stop behind us and we drive through the light. They're pulling someone over.

Knox calls again. "Let's go home. They'll let us know what they got."

We drive to my place, this time with another police escort in front and one in the back. The cops make it through the gates and they go in first, look at my place, and then Knox does. Finally, we are told it's safe to come in.

Alis is rushing me through the hallways until we are behind closed doors.

The minute we're inside, I take my shoes off and drop my purse on the table by the door. I go sit on the couch. He goes to the fridge.

How much more of this can I take? It's ridiculous. I bury my fingers in my hair and try to massage the tension out of my scalp.

"Let me do that."

I look up and he's standing there with wine glasses. He hands me one.

"We can't even have one nice evening out. It always ends in some bullshit."

He nods but says nothing. Instead, he shrugs off his shoes and climbs on the couch behind me. His fingers dig into my hair and he takes over, massaging.

"I don't want to tell you it will be over soon, but there's a possibility that we finally caught the person tonight. Whoever this asshole is, he'll have to tell the cops why the hell he was following us."

I take a sip of my wine. Unlike him, I can't be optimistic, but voicing my negative thoughts is not doing me any good. I'll just drink to take the edge off.

"Talk to me."

I shake my head. "I'm not putting that out into the universe."

"Okay, let's not talk then."

He tilts my head up to his and devours my mouth. The angle makes it hard to breathe, but I don't need to breathe when he's kissing me and his hand is sliding from my head down my torso. He flickers his tongue against mine and his hand sneaks into my pants. I spread my legs a little and unbutton my jeans to let him in.

He doesn't release my mouth and uses his other hand to touch my breast, his fingers finding a nipple over my sweater and his fingers trace it and draw it out into a hard bud. I moan because he's ambidextrous, talented, limber, working me from different angles, building me.

"I have this fantasy," he says, pulling away as we both pant.

I swallow. "What is it?"

He draws pressured circles against my clit. "I want you to ride my face."

The shudder rocks my body. Because I see it all, I picture it, and I'm flooded with heat because I want it.

I catch his tongue inside my mouth and suck on it. "Okay."

I scramble off his lap and put my wine on the side table.

"One hundred points to you for not dropping that."

"I'm an expert player and I'm feeling like a real winner tonight."

He chuckles and takes my hand, pulling me to the room. He lets go as soon as we're there and sits on the bed. He shrugs his shirt off, dumps it on the floor, and falls back into the mattress.

"I'm ready."

Another shudder rocks me, and I discard my pants and my panties. I freeze, trying to execute.

"Climb over me. That's part of the fantasy, but take off your shirt and keep your bra on."

"You really thought of this."

"All last night and all day today."

"Really," I say, now close to him.

He offers me a hand and I take it. He puts it over his crotch. His cock is like granite against my fingers. "I want it," I gasp out.

"After the first," he says, pulling my face down to kiss me.

"We can sixty-nine, pleasure each other at the same time." I stress my words with a long stroke down his dick.

"Hmmm." But he shakes his head. "Today, I want to worship you."

I'm speechless and so wet I squeeze my inner muscles.

He bites my bottom lip. "Climb on and ride."

My mind goes everywhere at once. We should've showered first. This is not pretty. My ass is going to look huge.

He lays back down and I pause to look at him, his pouty lips, his muscular body. He's mine to do with as I please and as he pleases. And what he wants is me over his face.

My pussy clenches and the urgency flares through me, pushing my doubts far away. He wants me to ride his face and now I want it so badly.

I climb up, and he lifts his head. His lips brush down my body as I crawl toward the center of the bed. My thighs are on either side of his head and his hands shoot to my hips. "This is perfect."

His breath hits my core, the sensation is so powerful I shudder.

"You're so fucking beautiful, Mila."

I concentrate on the moment. Alis presses his lips to my lower folds, tracing the outline with the tip of his tongue. It would tickle if my pussy wasn't already hungry and ready for him. I knead my tits, looking for something to hold on to, trying to maximize on his effort. He kisses my pussy like he would my mouth, open-mouthed, flicking his tongue through the center of my pleasure. My hips flex, creating some friction, sending a burst of pleasure, a promise.

"Mmhmmm." He encourages me, his fingers digging into my ass.

And I start a slow thrust, following the rhythm of his tongue laps, pressing myself against it. He inserts a finger and I writhe against it, longing for the meatier part of him.

"I want your cock," I grind out. I'm climbing up a steep hill, urging him to hurry and make me cum.

He fingers me, licks me, and thrusts harder, chasing the orgasm that keeps taunting me. He presses the pad of his thumb against my ass, making me gasp. But then he sucks my clit into his mouth and I have to brace against the bed, leaning forward, bunching the pillows into my hand as my inner thighs begin to tremble. He keeps sucking even as my body explodes and I bury my face on the pillow and scream. Everything goes silent. My body feels like it's falling and coasting.

He slides out from under me, licking his way out, and I'm too wiped to ask if his tongue ever gets tired. But then again, my pussy is so sensitive, I still shiver where he licks and he commits fully. He licks all the way around, even where I've never been touched before. He's already gone there twice, with his finger and then his tongue.

He kneels on the bed, reaches out, and grasps my hips. He drags me back against him, impaling me on his hard shaft. "I owe you one more."

And he proceeds to thrust and fuck until I'm screaming against my pillow again and he's pressed against my back, panting against my ear.

"No one's ever fucked me so good." And I don't even know where that came from. But I'm bewildered and almost in shock.

"That's what I like to hear." He bites the back of my neck and presses a kiss against it.

21

Alis

No one's ever fucked me like this.

Her words still ring in my ears. I can't help but smile every time I think about it.

Nothing can ruin my day today. My only gripe is that I'm back on Luciana Island instead of Baltimore with her. Maybe I should work there for the rest of the week. I just have to get through this afternoon's meeting.

I text her.

ME

How's everything over there?

I look through two different proposals before I get an answer from her.

MILA

I may need a chiropractor. Other than that,
it's all good.

My secretary comes in with more paperwork. I nod at her and go back to typing my reply.

ME

> Maybe we should get one on retainer. You'll need treatment often.

MILA

> I believe it. How are things there?

I type back right away.

ME

> Boring. Rather be with you.

MILA

> 🤍 Soon?

ME

> How soon?

I want to make sure she is okay with having me there all the time.

She doesn't answer right away. I move back into work mode and then I get the message from her.

MILA

> The cops had to let the guy they arrested go.

I call her.

"Hey, I got to run into a meeting in five minutes." Her voice is rushed like she's moving around from room to room. "But the gist of it is that the person following us was just looking for information to sell to bloggers."

"At least they grabbed them before—"

"Look at your phone." Her voice is so low I don't even want to.

I go to our message thread and there's a link. I click on it, and it goes to a website called Pipin' Hot Tea. On the landing page, it's a photo of us going into Dahlia and Weston's house. Below is another of when we left their house. On top there's a little circle with the closeup of my hand on her lower back.

My blood simmers so quick it should scald my skin from the side. The headline is what sends me over the top. *Guess who's still bangin'?*

"Jesus, Mila."

"Yup. Read the comments." Her voice is clogged and then she sighs. "This is fucking bullshit. No-life-having assholes can't leave us alone. You know what? Fuck them to hell."

And as fucked up as this is, it does my heart good to hear this fire in her voice. "Good. Let it out. They're not going to stop me from being with you or you from being with me."

"No, they can go to hell. And I'm about to do the same in this meeting."

I chuckle. "Give them hell."

"Nobody better try me today. The oven's hot, but it ain't for cookies. Talk to you later."

She hangs up and I just stare at the phone.

I've actually never heard her this mad and I have to do something. I dial Dahlia.

"She called you."

"She's pissed."

"I don't blame her. I would be too. We had to let that fucker go, and he sent out the photos before leaving the station."

"How do you know?" I ask.

"The time stamp. He's also credited."

I want to punch a hole in my desk. "Are you sure he is not the guy?"

"Yeah, he got the tip from someone that you two would be there. He said it was some phone call. We couldn't hold him any longer." Her voice is somber, tinged with edgy.

"No one knew we would be at your house but us."

"Maybe someone overheard. We are looking into the people she works with that were at the hospital."

I freeze. "The people who work with her. It could be one of them."

"I've already said too much. I'm not supposed to divulge this much about an ongoing investigation, but we are watching and looking into everything. Knox is in the apartment with her. She is safe."

"Someone tried to poison her yesterday."

"They'll be working from home for a few days. Meanwhile, the company is taking precautions before bringing anyone back."

"This nightmare has to be over soon." I hope I'm right.

"Hold on a second."

She puts me on hold, and I start formulating my plan. I need to tell my father I'll work outside the office or maybe I should just take a week off.

But I don't know when this will end.

The sigh fills the line before Dahlia speaks. "Um. There's more, but you need to breathe and don't do anything crazy."

"What now?"

"There's a new article. *The Daily Times* just posted an interview with someone who knew Mila in college. They have photos of her at the time and they're trash-talking about her. I have to go. We had a homicide not so far from here. I need to go check it out."

She hangs up and before I can even think of flinging my phone away, it rings and it's my publicist.

"Yeah."

"Alis, I'm sending you the latest two articles. By your tone, I'm assuming you already know. Read it and let me know if you want me to comment at all. I'm already doing some digging about the people behind these blogs. I should have names if you decide to pursue legal action."

"We're going to. I'm tired of playing with these fuckers."

"Okay," Jennifer says and hangs up.

I pull out the article and skim through it.

"It seems like the mud keeps piling on the corporate *mamacita* Milagros Rosario. Just months after her friend was murdered, the spicy Latina is living a full-on tryst with Alister Ellison. Now, one of her former college mates is coming out to expose her as a serial "side-chick." Ms. Blackstone, who went to Ms. Rosario's alma mater, was candid about her experiences with her former friend. "This bitch was screwing my man. She always liked to play the good girl role, pretending she was all into her schoolwork, but we all knew better. We knew she was getting nailed by everyone she was supposedly tutoring." When asked if she thinks Mila targeted Alister Ellison, she was extra candid. "That bitch always wanted what she couldn't have. She hated that she was poor as shit. She saw her friend had so much, she was probably scheming to take her man and we all heard about the job thing. I'm not saying she killed her, but isn't that convenient for her? Her rival drops dead and now she got her job and her rich ass man."

The article continues and this time I flip the phone face down on my desk and walk away from it. Throwing it against the wall will only call attention. The last thing I need is more attention. I take a few breaths to calm myself down.

My computer chimes for me to go to my meeting. I need to set it all aside and take care of this.

I take a bottle of water and head to the conference room, managing a few sips before I walk in. The second I cross the threshold into the conference room, I spot my father smiling and chummy with Fred McConnell. They're laughing and sharing what seems like a private joke. The minute they see me, Fred sits up straighter, but it's the look in his eyes that tells me everything I need to know. This asshole is going to try something today. Good. I'm in the mood for it.

"Son." My father barely looks at me. His gaze goes to the paper Fred gingerly pushes in front of him.

"Good afternoon, all." For a moment, I consider sitting opposite my father, like an opponent. Instead, I take my usual seat because honestly, I want to see his face when they try whatever it is he and Fred have planned.

The meeting gets off as usual and though I'm making mental notes, I keep monitoring my phone. If Mila calls, this meeting will have to wait.

"Before we get into a heavier subject, we want to discuss our annual company donation. We have three organizations we can make our sizable donation to." My father pulls another piece of paper from his folder. "We have two choices already. At the top, we have Windemere Academy. They've asked to get on the list for a new auditorium. There's also the Luciana Police Department. They are looking to update their headquarters and build two new classrooms. We can also donate to the Chesapeake Bay college's new BioPark."

Everyone around the table nods except me.

"What are you thinking, son?" This is one of those times when that word weighs on my neck like a granite block.

"I need clarification."

"How so?" he asks.

I lean against the table in that way my mother abhors. "At the board meeting, we promised to use these gifts in a meaningful manner. Last year, we donated to B'More."

"Well, we can't do that again. Even though that is a wonderful organization that our family patronizes, we cannot be partial. We need to spread the wealth, if you will."

I smile. "So, we're going to throw money at a rich school for rich kids whose parents already pay a hefty attendance price? Windemere doesn't need our money. Chesapeake Bay just got additional funding for their BioPark, despite them tailoring their intake process toward the affluent. And then LPD..." I let my voice trail on purpose, smiling wider. "I think the *generous* donations everyone here makes to their fund should cover the new updates."

People at the table shift on their chairs, the air ripe and thick, but no one says anything.

"So where do you want us to donate? Franklin?" The twist on Fred's lips says it all.

I'm not going to punch him like I want to. I decide to make his day hell on earth.

"Fred, that's a fantastic idea. It shouldn't surprise me. You have always been a generous soul going by how much you give to LPD. Franklin Elementary is in great need of renovation and Franklin High School can use a gym and track field. I can't believe I didn't think this on my own, man. Thank you. I vote for your recommendation."

I clap until the rest of the table joins me.

Fred doesn't protest. He knows he can't.

My father clears his throat, but neither he nor Fred are smiling anymore. "I'm glad you brought up Franklin because we need to discuss this more now that we may have to table establishing our new factory there."

"Oh?" He took long enough to get to it. "Who said that?" I ask, doing my best to school surprise into my face.

"Well, your office did not file the State of Maryland mandated forms on time. So, the window has closed." Fred taps the table in what seems like frustration, or maybe like a gavel sealing a future, as if he's deemed the matter closed.

I turn to my assistant, who is sitting with the other assistants in the chairs away from the table by the wall. "Didn't we file the state paperwork on Friday and it was reviewed by the approving official?"

She nods. "We did. We received confirmation yesterday. I forwarded the email for this meeting's agenda records."

She ruffles through her notes.

"Thank you, Janice." I turn back to Fred. "You see? We are all set."

"You also needed to file working permits, and the state and federal requisitions and we got an email yesterday saying there was no registration in our company's name? It was a shocking error because your office is usually on top of things. The email clearly states that everything else is to be revoked because of that."

"This is not good. Now we are left to scramble and try to find a suitable place overseas. We need a place that does not eat too much cost and is willing to accommodate us." My father's voice reeks of the disappointment that used to propel me to do more and more.

"Isn't that what you guys wanted from the beginning?" I ask.

"We always want to save money where necessary, but we had committed to your idea. It was a great one. Unfortunately, you could not execute it all the way through."

Everyone is looking at us, Fred's eyes alight with happiness he can't contain, no matter how much of a poker face he tries for.

"Well, everyone. I hate to disappoint you."

"It's okay, son. Mistakes happen." *He can act like a caring and under-standing father when he wants to.*

I nod and shoot him my Human Resources-approved smile. "Thanks, Dad. Fortunately, this is not the case for us. Janice?"

She stands and comes to the table, handing my father a piece of paper. "The email from yesterday was sent in error. If you look, it has the wrong request number. The state issued a correction right away. I think you may have missed it, Mr. McConnell."

When they don't move, she places the paper on the table and takes three steps back. I hold up a finger for her to halt.

I'm waiting for their reaction. My father and Fred exchange a look. It's several layers of frustration and that makes me almost giddy. Then my phone rings and it's Mila. I text her instead and tell her I'll call her in five minutes. I stand, done with the whole thing.

"If you all have no more questions, I'm leaving for the day. I'll be working remotely for the rest of the week. Janice is going to route all my calls to my mobile. Please call me if I can clarify any other errors. I am happy that we are on track to accomplish what we set out to do. Good day, everyone."

I exit the conference room without another look at my father and Janice follows close behind. "Things are bound to be a little tight around here. Route any issues to me and let me know if McConnell's or anyone's office gives you any problems. Also, please order me an SUV rental and have it delivered to my house. Use my personal account."

"Will do," she says, and there's a hint of a smile on her face. "I'll pass on anything that pops up."

"Call if you need me. I'm not here for all of them, but I'm here for you and my staff."

She nods. "Got it."

———

Alis

By the time I call Mila back, she's on a call with work, but texts that she will call me back. I head home, pack a bag with a change of clothes and essentials, my work-at-home laptop, and head back to Baltimore after giving my housekeeper instructions.

My mother calls as I reach Luciana Island city limits.

"Where are you? I just got to your house and you're not here."

Thank God. If I would've lingered one more minute, I would've been trapped. "Hey, Mom. I went out of town."

"Your father said you were working from home."

"He must be confused. I told everyone I would be working remotely."

The clipped little breath that comes through the line is only a warning. "Where else you would work from home at if not your house?"

At my girl's? Next to someone who makes me feel good.

"Did you need anything, Mom?"

"I needed to see my son. We live in the same town, but I haven't seen you in weeks."

#Winning

"I'm sorry, I've been caught up."

"Yes, I suppose. Last weekend you had company. You just got back and now you are off again." Her tone is low and soft, not her usual aggressive and demanding.

"I'll try to come to dinner soon," I say because I don't want my mother upset. I just want her to let me live my life.

"I'm not Leila. I know you and your brother don't feel the need to come see me. But I'm still your mom and I love you and miss you."

I rub a hand to the back of my neck to ease the tension.

"Mom, you know I love you. We love you. I just have a lot going on."

She clears her throat. "You keep running after that girl, Alis. You know that's never going to lead anywhere good."

"I will not discuss Mila with you."

She sucks in her breath. "I'm your mother."

"Yes, but I'm a man and I have a private life."

"There's no private life from your mother."

You think.

"Mom, I have to go."

"You're not going to keep me quiet. Please listen, I don't want you to ruin things. Lindsay—"

I slam my fist against the steering wheel. "What is wrong with you and Dad? Lindsay and I don't want to be together. She just punched Melinda Ford for even suggesting it."

"Ugh. That was unfortunate and grief talking. You two—"

"There is no us. I am done saying that."

"Fine." Her voice cracks like a whip over the line. "But where do you think this thing is going with that girl? Every day, some new gossip comes out about her. Did you see today's article? Son, I don't want anyone to use you. People like her are looking for what they call "a come up.""

Her words are straight from the latest article. I keep my voice low. "Mila is not like that. This is a smear campaign. Now, I will see you when I'm back. Love you."

"Me too. I hope you know that." She hangs up.

I focus my gaze out onto the road, concentrating and breathing. I don't know why I let her get to me. There's no love in the way our parents treat us and deal with us. We've always known that. Yeah, they're obsessed with getting Weston back into what they call the fold, but they don't show us love, just try to impose their will on us.

I hit the button on my dash for my favorites and call Aunt Leila.

She answers right away. "I was just picking up the phone to call you."

"You've been thinking about me. I didn't think you missed me anymore."

"Oh no. You talked to your parents."

I frown. "How did you know?"

Her sigh is so strong, I almost feel it against my ear. "You're off your game, my love. And Christine already called today."

"I just got off the phone with her, too. What did she want with you?"

She humphs. "She wanted me to talk to you about Mila. She sent me today's article…"

"Christ. That's what she called about. And to push Lindsay on me."

"Your mother better stop that. I heard Melinda Foster still has a big welt around her eye. That's why she's not leaving her house."

I laugh. "I still can't believe Lindsay did that."

"I can. She's tired of people thinking she's a replacement for her sister and she's grieving. Have you talked to Mila? She has to be angry about the article."

"I'm on my way to her. She's sad. Sounded dejected."

"That's good you're. She needs you. You should go cheer her up." Her voice is warm and I latch onto that.

"Thank you for being you. For being there for me and for not believing the first thing you hear about her."

"You care about her. Dahlia thinks she's great, and so does Weston."

"Now Dahlia thinks she's great?" I tease.

"She actually always has. She just couldn't talk to you or Weston, but she and I talk all the time and she told me all the shit she's been going through. She also said you have a different type of chemistry with Mila."

It rings true. "She's something else. I feel different with her. I feel like I'm a little obsessed."

"Oh honey. I think she is crazy about you, too. I could tell by the way she looked your way while we were on the phone. I can't wait to come back to meet her."

"When is that happening?"

"I don't know, my love. Work is crazy, but if you ever need me, tell me. My sons come before any of this shit."

I want to tease her some more, say anything to make this funny, but I can't. I don't have it in me. "I love you."

"Love you too."

We hang up and I am driving in silence, contemplating what I will say to Mila. What can I ask her about? Though I have no right to her past, it doesn't keep me from wondering about the story behind her and that woman's boyfriend. *Did she love him? Did he fuck her so good he made her scream into her pillow?*

I push away the thought. This is so stupid. That was long ago. Could she still care about him?

My phone rings again and this time is Weston.

"I guess I'm talking to all the Ellisons today."

He chuckles. "Trust me, you're not the only one. Dad called me for some random issue today to talk about how you dropped the ball at work. I didn't tell him you had already filed that paperwork. I figured you would want it to be a pleasant surprise."

I laugh. "You missed it. It was interesting to see Fred sweat and Dad speechless. Seriously, it's his company. He should make Fred's simple ass CEO if he wants to. I would happily start my own company somewhere else."

Weston snorts. "Dad's not stupid. He knows you are the best man to run it. And you know you want that company more than anything. You dreamt about running it since we were kids."

I sigh. "I do. I can do so much more, but I keep wondering if it's worth all the fighting. I mean, I can do adversity at work, but he road-blocks me, Wes. He conspires with others."

"You know what that is?" My brother doesn't wait for me to reply. "He's playing the game he and Mom always play. Leila and I were talking about it earlier. He wants to manipulate you into doing what he wants and they're desperate. Mom is trying to get Dahlia to talk some sense into you."

"Dahlia," I sputter.

"Yeah. She got a call today. Mom is using that whole I'm concerned for my son..."

"Jesus." I can only shake my head.

"How far away are you? Dahlia and I both work tonight, so we won't be able to have you over again, but maybe tomorrow."

I look at my dash briefly. "I'm twenty minutes away and tomorrow you'll both be wiped and not wanting company. We'll be okay."

"We? That sounds like a unit."

"Does it?" But I don't elaborate anymore.

"It does. You're spending a lot of time with her and sometimes going through shit makes the bond stronger."

"Spoken like a tie-down man who wants to drag me into the same jail along with him."

He chortles. "Or a brother who thinks she's good for you."

"How so?" I keep my tone light, but there's a bit of heat stoking in my chest.

"She makes you realize you need more than you were getting and that there is a life outside Ellison Corp. That company has been your only true love for a long time. Mila came to break that up... Wait, that sounded better in my head. I'm sorry."

I wave a hand. "I know what you mean."

"And?"

"I don't know that I'm ready to go there and think about that just yet."

"Okay. The time will come."

We move on from the topic and he tells me about his call with Mom and makes me tell him about today's meeting. I'm in Baltimore fifteen minutes later. I text Mila and Knox to clear me through the security at the front gate. I don't know what I expected to find when she opens the door, but it's definitely not the glowing anger in her eyes or the balling fists at her sides.

"I'm so fucking tired of this shit." She spits out every single word.

I dump my bags by the door and take her in my arms, squeezing her tight, rubbing her back.

"You should be mad. These people keep fucking with you and your life."

She doesn't hug me back, but she drops her head on my chest. "It doesn't change anything."

"I know. I'm sorry. We're going to sort this out, so please don't give up. Scream, cry, punch me if you want to, but just hang on."

She shoves herself off me. "I don't want to punch you."

"I can take it." I stick out my chest for her.

She runs her hand over it. "That won't solve anything. Plus, you've kinda been my rock."

And nothing she could have said makes me feel bigger than that. "Really?"

She nods and then her face goes somber. "Let's talk."

If she doused me with ice water, it would have been less jarring. "About?"

"I'm sure you have questions about everything that came out today. About me and Nathan and Jaslyn."

I follow her to sit on the couch. "You don't have to talk about this. It's your past, right?"

She rolls her eyes. "Of course, it is, but I have nothing to hide. I should be embarrassed about being that dumb, but stupidity is not a crime. And trust me, I'm not mad that this came out. I'm mad that they keep finding shit to use against me."

Since she is offering to tell me I nod. "Okay."

"I met Nathan during freshman year. We became friends. I wasn't trying to get with anyone because I was highly aware of the whole Freshman Twenty in our college. Older students tried to get with freshman girls and basically brag about it in the underground student paper. Double points if she's a virgin. When he didn't insist and we were friends for well into sophomore year, I gave him a chance. He was my first lover."

I fucking hate that guy already.

"You held out that long?"

She stings me with her glare. "That's what you got from all that? Anyway, we had this relationship bordering on *situationship.* I didn't see him every day. He was going to grad school, and I was taking extra classes to graduate sooner. One day, Jaslyn came to my door with two of her friends. They wanted to jump me because I was messing with her man. I was in shock and then so mad, I was about to fight all three of them. I didn't care. Thankfully, four of the other girls on my floor came to my room and she and friends left."

"You were going to fight them? You're feisty."

She shakes her head. "I can't believe the things you're getting caught up on. Do you not care about what is being said?"

I'm honest with her. "It's hard to care about something that happened before you knew me."

"Wait, hold on. Is that your ego talking? Because, my God, that thing is enormous."

"But you knew that."

Her mouth drops open. "I can't believe you. I'm trying to tell you everything, so there are no questions..."

I grab her hand. "I'm just trying to make you laugh. Did you love him?"

She nods. "I did. I was in so deep that I stayed with him for a while longer. He told me he was trying to break up with her but couldn't because she had a mental disorder and he was afraid she would harm herself. He told so many lies and I believed them. Maybe I wanted to? It was easier, and I didn't even want to think about being without him."

Her answer rocks me more than I expected. "What happened next?"

"We went to a party and drank too much. We went back to my room. I conked out. He snuck out and slept with a girl on my floor. I woke up looking for him and someone told me where he was. I went in there and knocked. She opened, I shoved past her. He was still on the bed talking a whole bunch of shit. I grabbed his pants and phone and threw them out the window. Then I went back to my room and went to sleep."

"He deserved that."

"It was childish and didn't make me feel better. Everyone was telling me I was too good for that situation. Even my mom and uncle kept talking to me. But I didn't listen. Seeing it with my own eyes, letting the heartbreak and the pain in pushed me to act."

Now I'm pissed because she loved him and people are using this against her. "Have you seen him since?"

She rolls her eyes. "I saw him at a conference two years ago. He was even flirty. You should've seen his face at the dinner when I went over to say hello to him and his wife."

"He's married? To Jaslyn?"

She shakes her head. "He *was* married to her. Now he's married to her sister."

I'm stunned. "You know you can get on TV and reveal that."

She shrugs. "For what? What would that change? I just don't want you to feel like I set out to do anything with you. I thought you were hot when I met you, but I only went to dinner that night because Maddie said there would be another person."

"I don't think that. My attraction to you was there since the moment I saw you, in your *fuck me* red dress. I had already decided to break up with Maddie. I only went to the restaurant because she insisted on one more try. You know?"

She nods. "I wasn't even trying to flirt with you on purpose."

"It comes natural to us. Everything does. You keep changing things for me, Mila. Even my brother noticed."

"What kind of things?"

I shake my head. I can't tell her. This is not something you say to someone you're not deep in with.

Don't you think you're deep enough? You don't even give a fuck about what your parents say anymore. You don't care about anything that's happened prior to you.

"You made me realize that there are more things than work and the company. You made me realize I want something bigger and deeper for myself."

Her eyes widened. "And what's that?"

"You know the answer."

I can see the truth dawning in her eyes, but she shakes her head.

I'm not leaving anything to interpretation. "I want you. I want us."

Her mouth drifts open but then closes it. Then, she lunges at me, throwing her arms around my neck. "I want us too."

22

———————

Mila

It's bordering on nonsensical now. They keep digging people from my past to say the dumbest things, and the world is lapping it up. We are watching a YouTuber followed by millions interview a classmate. It takes everything in me not to burst into laughter.

"We were supposed to be close, and she went and interviewed for the same internship. They called us for a group interview and it's like she knew all the answers and she kept smiling at them. And there were two men on the electing panel. Of course they gave her the job."

Alis' face is red. He keeps shaking his head. I can't hold back anymore. I burst out laughing but can't stop, no matter how much I try.

"Why the hell are you laughing like that?"

"It's so stupid." I wait until I'm calm to continue. "Our public relations professors told us all about the internship and encouraged us to apply. That chick and I were sitting next to each other. Everyone was putting in for it. The week before, the company sent us fifty questions to prepare. From those, they would choose fifteen for the interviews. I got started on them right away. I knew all of them better than my birth certificate. I even researched the companies and their current initiatives."

"And that's how you knew all the questions ahead of time."

I draw an exclamation point in the air. "Who knew studying was such a foreign concept to her? Anyway, after the guy I beat for the scholarship, her, and Jaslyn, I wonder who they'll be dusting off next? Maybe that lady I didn't give free fries to when I was working at the *Fast and Tasty*?"

Alis makes a time out signal with his hands. "You know how to make those fries?"

I throw a couch pillow at him.

Then I sober up. "Don't get mad anymore. It's not worth the energy. This whole situation is now ridiculous. They're digging people because they have nothing."

My phone pings between us and I grab it from the cushion. It's a text message from Dahlia. I read it and reply, forwarding the message to Knox.

"Our favorite detectives are here."

We tidy up, taking the leftover food to the kitchen. He grabs a sweater and I close my work laptop.

By the time he gets back, the doorbell rings. He goes to open while I stay on the couch. While I'm on better terms with Dahlia, I'm still not one hundred percent comfortable with visits from the police.

Alis shows them in, and she smiles, taking the other side of the couch. Matt sits in one chair and Alis takes the other.

"What now?" I say. It's half joking and I even smile, but there's a tightening in my upper body, the foreboding that's yet to fail me, is back in my chest.

"Well, it seems we have new a lead in the investigation. The person we picked up the other night works for bloggers. He has been getting stories from an anonymous source. He and the blogger have agreed to let us dump their computer information."

"Why would they agree to that?" I ask.

Matt and Dahlia exchange a look. "We're not at liberty to say."

I watch enough crime shows to know this means they have something they could use against them and this was a deal they worked out.

Dahlia continues. "We don't have a name yet but, we were able to nail IP addresses for two of the sources. One is from Ellison Corp and the other from Grayson Global."

My stomach roils. Someone at work is passing on information, but who?

Alis shifts forward, his jaw tight and his eyes back to shooting blue fire. "Give me a name and the person will be fired and we are bringing up charges before the end of the day."

Matt holds up a hand. "Not so fast. We are still confirming, but this may not even be real. There are some markers that may point to IP cloning, but this is getting close."

The detectives give hope and also take it away.

"Don't get discouraged," Dahlia tells me, as if she can hear my thoughts. "That we can identify IPs is a good thing. It's only a matter of time. We just need to confirm. We already requested information from your employer."

"If it's a clone—"

Mat jumps in. "We don't know that it is or isn't. We just have clues. Clues are important."

I nod. "You're right. This is definitely a good step forward."

Her phone chimes.

"Oh. Wait, our cybercrime tech says in the last hour there's an address circulating online. 253 Lyndenhurst Lane. Does that sound familiar?"

The blood runs cold. *It's my mom.* My mom's address is circulating online.

"Mami," I whisper because I'm so scared of saying that shit out loud. I don't know when I stand but, the next second, I'm across the room with my phone in hand.

"Mila?" Alis is right next to me.

"They doxed my mom."

"Assholes." Alis is almost crushing my hand.

I'm dialing and she takes forever to pick up. "Hey, *amor*. I'm about to head home. I'll call you from the car."

"No, *Mami,* wait. You can't go home. They have your address."

My mom laughs. "Who has my address?"

"Twitter."

"What?"

"Someone doxed you." I hate that I'm saying those words. She's innocent but also has to deal with this shit. "I'm so sorry, *Mami*."

With the same aplomb she takes on her unit at work, my mom is calm as she says, "You didn't do this. It's these no-lifers who have nothing better to do than harass you. This is not about me and they don't scare me. I have a loaded weapon at home. Let them try to trespass into my property."

Trespass? As in, get to her? Someone being inside my mom's home is the conclusion my brain didn't want. My knees go weak. "You can't confront anyone. These people could be dangerous."

"They haven't seen me with a gun. I'm tired of what they're doing to you."

"*Mami,* stop—"

Dahlia is now next to me, and she extends her hand. She talks to my mom while Alis takes my hand. I hold on to him.

"I'm going to pick her up. I'm going to call Grayson and tell him that I need to leave right away." I turn toward the bedroom, but he stops me.

"I'll send for her. I can have a private jet pick her up. We can go to my house and get away from here."

I shake my head. "We can't do that. I don't know if she will be comfortable with that and..." I don't know what else to say. "I'm not thinking straight."

"Then let me take care of you and your mom. You don't have another bed here. You can arrange for all of that while we stay at my place. It will do your mom good not to be just confined to this place while she gets used to this. I will drive you both back after the weekend."

"You should take him up on the offer, Mila. Shit is a little crazy and your mom will need a little time to adjust." Matt moved closer to us and I didn't realize until now.

"Okay."

Alis nods and turns away. He's on his phone right away. Twenty minutes later, Dahlia has convinced my mom to take some time off. A police escort will accompany her home as she packs and also take her to the airport. Alis has arranged for her to be picked up in three hours.

And the fear biting at my heels is now slowly evolving to the type of red anger I never let myself indulge in.

"They're trying to trace the original tweet, but the account was created an hour ago and has since been deleted." Dahlia rolls her eyes.

"Of course it has. And let me guess, this person won't be found either."

"Our cyber unit is doing everything they can," Matt says and his voice carries that calm-down-lady quality.

But I don't want to calm down. "I'm sorry. This is not for you. I know you are working hard, but this is the last fucking straw. I'm so fucking tired of this. It's one thing to mess with me, but now this threatens my mom. Fuck all of them to hell. You don't fuck with my mother. You can mess with me all day, but she's off limits."

"Mila—"

I don't let Dahlia finish. "Please don't make promises. Don't tell me it will be okay. Or to let this shit ride. It's obviously not going to. They won't be okay until someone kills me, or maybe what they're trying to do is drive me to kill myself."

"Stop!" Alis screams.

"No. I'm not stopping. It's my mom. The one I love the most. The only person I've had always. I can't have her be in danger. I'll give them the interview they want. I want to make sure they know if something happens to my mom, I will kill everyone who shared her address. I don't give a fuck anymore."

He opens his mouth, but Dahlia shakes her head.

"Mila, I know you're angry and you should be. When the people we love get threatened, we see a side of ourselves we never had to picture before, but you have to move smart because these people are waiting for a piece of you. There's someone out there that obviously wants you hurt, but there's no way you should do their job for them."

I walk a few steps from them. "I will not kill myself. I'm just saying that's what this kind of pressure leads to. That's what they hope I do to myself. I'm so tired. You guys don't know how exhausting this emotional yo-yoing is." I look at Alis and I sigh. "I was happy today. I mean, it's obvious you and I can't work in the same room, but we were happy. You're here and even if I'm trapped inside these four walls, at least I'm with someone I like to be with."

He doesn't interrupt me.

"And in a matter of seconds, that shit is gone. They trample over it like elephants with their online bullshit. And as close as it's been, this hits different in here." I point at my heart. "I want to appeal to them. Ask them to leave me alone. Isn't that worth at least a try?"

They all nod and it's probably because they're afraid to disagree with me. "You guys probably think I'm at my breaking point. I'm not. I need to try something else. Not talking hasn't gotten me anywhere. It's giving ammunition to assholes to use my past against me. I'm tired of that. I want to be proactive."

"Okay," Alis says. "But I want you to talk to a public relations group first. Let's see what they advise. I don't want you to go out there and be vulnerable to some jackass blogger to use your words against you. We need something controlled and curated where you can speak your piece and it's not turned against you."

I smile at him because it makes me sad that he thinks we can actually control the narrative. "It won't matter what I say. They will still react the way they want. They will use it for their agenda. I'm just letting them know that I'm not sitting back while they mess with my mother. She's off limits to everyone."

My phone goes off again. It's from work. We are getting pulled into an emergency meeting.

"I have to take this."

I go into my office and close the door.

———

Alis

She's barely said a word since we left Baltimore, just stares out on the road. Her hand keeps kneading her leg, or she wiggles her fingers every so often, signs that her brain is overworking.

"Your mom is going to be okay. We are making good time and we'll be there before her plane arrives."

She turns to me with heavy eyes. "Thank you." Then she looks out into the road.

And we drive in silence some more.

"I'm not good company."

I squeeze her knee. "It's okay. You don't always have to be. There will be days like this, right?"

She sighs. "It feels like every other day for us. I've been thinking that even when people start out like we do, they don't go through this constant drama. I think... Anyway, we have Hollywood kind of drama."

"Maybe because we're epic?"

Her gaze snaps from the road to me, and she laughs. "I love how you can joke and make me laugh when I'm feeling like I want to tear someone's head off."

"That's what I'm here for. Oh, and please stop talking about killing people in front of the cops. Stop snitching on yourself, Jersey girl."

"It's how I really feel."

I get it. It's how I feel every time someone threatens her. "I don't blame you. Your mom is off limits. Actually, you should be off limits too. Why have you never been that mad at what they do to you?"

"What?" The fact that she sounds shocked at the question tells me everything I need to know.

"You're never that irate when people come after you. You get mad, but there's never that fire or energy for yourself. You never want to bust a cap on someone for what they say about you."

"What are you getting at?" Her voice is off, cautious, but also a warning.

"It just hit me today. You should flip out when people come after you in ways that put you in danger, but I think part of you feels like you deserve this."

"Are you crazy?"

I shake my head. "What we did wasn't so bad you deserve to pay for it all your life. Madison and I weren't really together anymore..."

"Give me a break, Alis. Just because we're in love doesn't mean we get to erase history. You broke it off with her that night. The day before she thought you two would eventually get married..."

I grip the steering wheel tighter.

"That's not what I'm doing. What I meant was that we weren't in a healthy relationship. I saw her once a week and texted here and there. I text with you all day long. We talk a few times a day when we're not together. We even have phone sex. And by the way, cut the crap about how she thought she would marry me. Was she going to marry me and spend our honeymoon with Elias Sanders?"

She doesn't take her hand from mine but squeezes back. "Plenty of people are in dysfunctional relationships. I'm sorry she was cheating on you..."

Her mouth drops open, and she looks out into the road.

Something heavy rolls off my shoulders and a knot comes undone inside my chest. It takes several breaths before I can talk again. "You know, that's the first time someone said it? Called it what it was, cheating."

"It doesn't feel good, but I think it's fair."

"Thank you. I have not thought about it like I should. For the same reason as you. I felt I had no room to talk or complain or even feel some kind of way about it."

"Because of guilt?

"No, because of you. I don't feel guilty about how I got you. All that I care about is that I did. I would've risked it all for you anyway. It would have been hard for your friendship with her, but I would have not stopped until you relented."

"You're saying that now." She tries to pull her fingers away.

I tug at her hand. "You don't believe me?"

"It's not that. That night wasn't a good look for us, overall. If we were watching this happen to others, what would we say about a relationship that started when ours did?"

"It wasn't the best moment, but sometimes things happen when they need to." I can't believe what is coming out of my mouth right now.

Her sigh is long, but still feels loaded. "It's true. I wish we could have waited."

"Sometimes there's perfection in the heart of imperfection. The only thing I would change about that night, Mila, is that it ended with us feeling wrecked about her."

"It just feels so wrong. To love that night when someone died."

"Not because of you. Not because of me. Not because of us. Two things in life can be true at the same time. You can be destroyed by her death and still yearn for someone else." I stop talking because I'm saying too much.

And she's not saying enough. She wants us too. She cares about me, but would she fight for me like she's doing for her mom? It's easy to get carried away, but I can't keep throwing my feelings at her and not know what she really feels. The one that cares the most is always on the losing end.

I make it to their airport and park on the side.

"We are a bit early. According to my alerts, the flight should be here in ten minutes and then we'll have to wait for her to go through the check out—"

"I think I love you."

My heart thuds hard against my chest. My hands grip the steering wheel. I brace but I don't know against what. "Don't."

"Don't what?" She reaches for my face and makes me look into her eyes. "I love you."

"Why?" I ask.

Her gaze slices straight through me. "Do I need a reason?"

"Yes."

"Okay then, because you always stand by me. You drop anything to come to me when I need you. You make me laugh and though you're annoyingly arrogant, you have a really good heart."

She has me trapped in her gaze, lost in her as I always am.

"This whole car ride and through this ordeal, I keep thinking you could have moved on, and kept living your life, but you're choosing to be here, in the trenches with me."

"Where else would I be, Mila? I don't want to be anywhere you're not."

She smiles and kisses me. It's soft, and she lingers. The thrashing in my chest wanes into an awareness of how we are breathing. There's no tension or rush between us, just her touch on my cheeks, the silky softness of her mouth, against my lips and then my cheeks.

We stay there exchanging soft kisses, not talking, until my phone rings. Even then, we don't jolt apart, we gradually back away.

"Your mom's here."

Ten minutes later, I'm face to face with an older version of Mila, but not old enough to seem like her mom. America Rosario's skin is richer and her eyes so dark they're almost black. Her straight bob bounces when her daughter throws herself at her and hugs her tight.

"*Mi amor*. No tears. I'm well and so are you."

Her gaze shifts to me, and it takes a second before she smiles.

"I'm Alis. Nice to meet you, Ms. Rosario."

"Call me Meri. Good to meet you. Thank you for arranging for all of this." Her voice holds that polite company quality.

"I'm so sorry about all this." Mila holds her hand.

Meri's gaze goes warm. "You didn't do anything to cause all this. It's those crazy internet people."

I open the door to the rental and help her into the back seat.

"Thank you," she says again, and I get the feeling that Mila is going to hear a lot about this the minute they're alone.

She's hovering behind until I open her door and she climbs in.

The drive to my house is short.

"This is your hometown." And just like her daughter her first time here, it's not a question but a statement. I just can't figure if she likes it or not.

"Yes, I was born and raised here."

"It's beautiful here." Now that's sharper, and it sounds more like an accusation.

Mila's hand goes to my leg.

I take her hand in mine, but I can't shake the feeling her mom is watching and judging us from the backseat.

23

———

Mila

"This house is gorgeous. I can't believe he lives here by himself," my mom whispers, like we are not alone in the guest bedroom.

"It really is. Wait till we take a walk around the woods. You're going to love it."

"Keep your eyes open, Mila. You can't fall for the man and the place."

I don't sigh like I want to. "*Mami...*"

"Look, I just want you to be my smart girl. Don't just think with your heart here." She gestures around us.

"I've thought about it. A lot. I've done nothing else since this whole thing started. I know what I'm getting into."

She stops taking her clothes out of the suitcase and looks at me. "Do you? It's not just the idiots on the internet. It's also the worlds of difference between the two of you. You've eaten fried spam and *platanos*. You've had bologna and American cheese sandwiches. I bet you everything we own, the people on this island don't even know the meaning of those words. He's a nice guy, but he's a rich white guy from a place that's a 14-carat update to the best suburb we've ever visited. You're a brown girl from Jersey who's had to scrape for every-thing you have."

"We've had to scrape. You've given me everything you could and been my rock to get the other stuff." I grab her hands. "I need you to understand about us. Alis is not like that. He's different. He doesn't care about me being middle class or being brown. He respects that I want to do for myself."

She shoots me her worried look. "He's not what worries me. It's the world around the two of you. I can tell he cares about you, but that sometimes is not enough. Have you met his family? What do his parents say about this?"

I choose my words carefully. "I met his brother and sister-in-law. They're both great. She's Dominican too."

"The detective?"

I nod. "Yeah, they have a mixed relationship and are married."

"Is that what you think he wants with you? Has he brought that up?"

My stomach sinks because no, we have not gotten there. And I'm mad at myself for even reacting to the questions with apprehension. "This is too new. We haven't had the chance to talk about that. We're just in the enjoying phase."

My mom keeps a straight face, but her nose flares a little and I can already see this becoming a thing we're not ready for. I squeeze her hands.

"Please, let's not fight. We'll be here for a couple of days. I've ordered a bed and furniture for your room. Can you please just get to know him before you form an opinion?"

"*Mi amor*, I would do anything for you, but it's hard to sit back and act like I don't see where the two of you stand."

Since we've gotten this far, I might as well rip the Band-Aid. "We're together."

"I know. I noticed it before getting out of the airport, when you were standing next to him and in the car. I notice it even in the way the staff treated you. He's made it clear who you are to him. You just need to know that things change and fast. I don't want to see you hurt again. Not like with asshole Josh."

"Me either," I admit. "I'm not a young girl, though."

"No matter what age, a heart is a heart. It can be broken or damaged."

I hate her sayings right now, but I can't let myself think that way. I know why she's doing it and it's everything I should tell myself. "If it happens, thank God I have the best nurse to help me heal mine."

She hugs me. "Go hang out with your man. I'm going to go take a long shower in his spa bathroom."

My man. God. "Mom, you're not planning on being sarcastic the whole time, are you?"

She cackles. "I'm not being sarcastic. He is your man. You're going to be sleeping in his bed tonight. Right?"

I don't hesitate. "Yes."

"Okay, so he is your man." She heads to the bathroom but stops at the door. "I'm not going to be rude to him, *amor*. I am grateful that he's gotten you a bodyguard and what's necessary to keep you safe. I just need you to guard yourself. Love you."

She disappears through the door, and I breathe out in relief. I leave her room and close the door and head out to find Alis. I find him in his bedroom.

"I don't think your mom likes me," he says the minute I cross the threshold.

I walk straight to him and hook my hands around his neck. "She's tired, rattled, she doesn't know you yet, and she's worried about what us means for me."

He's pensive. "She didn't look rattled to me. She was dissecting me without a scalpel. Anyway, is she settling in okay?"

I frown. "She is taking a shower. And I'm serious. My mom is the sweetest. It's just too much going on. She's worried about everything."

"She loves you. I can tell just by the way she looks at you. You're her most precious treasure."

I kiss the corner of his lips. "You're such a romantic."

"I am not."

"You are, and you're sentimental, too. I love that. Who would've thought?"

He squeezes my ass. "So your mom is showering, and you came to sweet-talk me into a quickie?"

I laugh. "You wish."

"Yes." He presses me against him. "Later?"

I wonder if that is his way of asking if I'm staying in his bed tonight. "We can take our time."

He nips my lower lip. "Do you think she'll be okay with you sleeping here?"

"I told her I am."

"That's bold of you."

I chuckle. "I actually confirmed it. She stated I was. I don't lie to her. She's my mom, but she's also the best friend I've ever had, the one that has never let me down."

"That's how I am with Leila."

"What about your mom? You don't talk about her."

He takes my hand, and we sit by the window. "My mom is a complicated subject. She's a product of this island, like my dad. They like status quo. She is a society lady who does charities and keeps things pretty. She was never really hands on with Weston and me. She tried, but it's not in her. Some people don't have it in them."

I use my fingers to rub over the back of his hand. "That had to be tough."

He shrugs. "At the beginning, Leila was only Weston's. Once she became mine too, I stopped believing I would turn out like my parents."

I frown. "What do you mean?"

"I thought that's what I was going to be. I wasn't saving hurt birds like my brother, and I dreamed of running our company since I got a vague understanding of what it does."

"Oh, *amor*. I'm so sorry." I tighten my grip on his hand. I don't understand what he's going through. My mom gives me so much love I sometimes can't breathe, but I wouldn't trade that for the alternative.

"Don't be. I think I'm okay, but don't get the wrong impression. I love my parents. I just know who they are, know that I can't change them, and don't try to. I just want them to leave me alone."

My heart breaks for him. "I'm glad you have Weston and Leila."

His smile is sad, but he shakes it off. "Don't forget Detective Wicker, her brother Teddy, and her mom."

"I didn't know you were close to her family."

He chuckles. "Best Christmas of my life. It was like working in the same room with you with the loud music."

"I'm going to ignore the dig because what I really hear is that being around me on a regular day is like the best Christmas of your life. Got it."

"I don't think that's fair to say. After we spend this Christmas together, we can make a better assessment."

My heart takes off on a mad gallop because it's not forever, but it's the future.

"I think that's only fair."

Alis

The night is clear and the stars are out in full force celebration. The glass paneling, the lush greenery, and the fire pit roaring in the middle of the room all give the effect of outdoor dining. Greenhouse is the perfect restaurant to enjoy a night like this, to make the best first impression. At least it should be.

Instead, it's exposing me in an unflattering light. My inability to protect Mila even in what should be a controlled environment. I brought her and her mother out to dinner. We went out of town, somewhere safe and discreet, where we could be comfortable, but we can't escape our reality.

Because Fucking Fred McConnell and his family are here. It's Fred's daughter's birthday, but they're watching us more than paying attention to her. Their loud comments and quasi-muffled laughter have been turning heads all evening. The serving staff and even the manager have come to apologize. Mila's mother was gracious with the staff, accepting their apologies with a smile. It didn't betray all the times she clenched her teeth and even the time when she braced her hands on the table.

Mila and her mom are giving these rich dicks a master lesson in class. I wait for them to disappear on the way to the bathroom and push out of my chair and make my way to the McConnell table.

"Good evening, everyone," I say. "I hope you're enjoying your time here. Fred, can I see you for a second?"

He stands and I guide him away from his table. He opens his mouth but I cut to the chase quickly.

"You're not going to say a word. You're just going to listen, nod when you understand, and smile. The next time you or anyone in your useless family even looks Mila or her mother's way, I will make it my life's mission to expose you. That means your son's little DUI where he damaged that house in Virginia is going to be on all the papers. Everyone will know about that little arrangement you and your wife made with your last secretary, so she doesn't tell the world about the affair. And don't get me started on your nephew's embezzlement issue. You idiots fuck with Mila, I fuck your life. Got it?"

He blanches but nods.

I walk back to my table, pay the check, and am ready when Mila and her mom return. On our way out, we pass the McConnell table, and no one says a word. The forty-five-minute car ride is agonizing. I get out of the car and open the door for Mila and then her mom.

"Those people hate us and they don't even know us. We shouldn't have been there," Meri says, staring at me.

"I'm really sorry about that. I did not know they would be there." My face is so hot, I can't even look at them.

"You don't have to apologize for taking us out. This is just to show both of you what you have to look forward to. I didn't want to embarrass you and my daughter begged me not to say anything, but just so you know, I gave that lady a piece of my mind in the bathroom."

"Mom..."

"No one is going to insult you in my face. She got the wrong one."

I agree with her. "You did the right thing, Meri. I'm just sorry you had to do that. It's my fault you experienced this."

"Stop apologizing. What you both need is to think this through." She walks away, leaving Mila torn between her and me.

"I'm going to talk to her. She's just upset."

"I know." I cross the distance between us and kiss her forehead.

Car lights illuminate my driveway and my father's black Rolls Royce pulls in front of the house.

"Fuck. Me."

"Who is that?" Mila asks.

"My parents."

Her eyes widen. "Oh God. Not tonight."

Not ever. I don't want them near her or her mom.

"Go take care of your mom. Let me handle them."

She heads inside the house as my father steps out of the driver's side and then goes to open the door for my mom. I stand at the door like a gate keeper.

"Can we come in? I don't want to have conversations outside like common people."

First jab so quick it must be a record. I wave them in.

I lead to the formal living room and he looks around. "It's a private conversation."

"Do you see anyone else here?"

"Don't be like that, Alister. We are just worried about your wellbeing. We want to have an overdue conversation about your life choices." Mom chooses the seat nearest to the window.

"My choices are mine."

Dad harrumphs. "They're ours too when what you're doing has a direct effect on us."

"I don't know what you mean."

"I got an alarming call from Fred. He said you threatened him."

I chuckle. "Of course, your old buddy called you. I did no such a thing. I just told him if anyone at his table hurled one more insult at Mila, I would make it my life's mission to expose each one of them."

"You can't threaten a board member and employee of Ellison Corp."

"I didn't. There was only a threat if any of them insult her again and because they obviously have so much to lose, no one did it again. What's the problem?"

"We didn't raise a thug. People in our circles don't go around threatening people."

"True. We just throw money at our problems to make them go away. But I don't want to throw money at Fred. We're already throwing him too much while he does the bullshit he calls work."

My father waves a hand in the air. "Stop this nonsense. Stop parading that girl around."

"Her name is Mila and no, I will not stop going out with her. We were hungry, and we went out to eat. Get used to it. Next time may be the Country Club."

Mom gasps, her hand clutching at her chest as if looking for her pearls. "What? Are you insane? The Summervilles go there."

"So? Since when do I owe them an explanation? Anyway, I don't think they care."

My father gets in my face. "Alis, you're just trying to ruin your life and hers to make a point and spite us."

"I'm not. You just don't decide my life."

He shoves a finger in my face. "You're acting like your brother. But there's a big difference. Weston is not the face of Ellison Corp. You are. Behave like it."

"I'm not acting like anyone. I'm just following my heart and my head." It burns my stomach that I have to keep saying this.

My father laughs. "Your heart? Yes. Your head? Not even close. You're voluntarily walking into hell. People here will never forget. How long until—"

"The world is not Luciana Island. There are other places where people are not narrow-minded and where there is more than the rich white point of view."

He bobs his head like a boxer waiting for the opportunity to land a punch. "That's true, but you live here. You work here. Unless you're planning on living somewhere else, which I'm starting to think is a good thing. I often question where your head is and, if we're talking honestly, son, I wonder if it's the right thing passing our family's legacy to someone who is erratic."

"Weston!" My mother covers her mouth.

I freeze. He's always hinted at it to force me to do his will, but he's never actually voiced that he has doubts about me stepping up as CEO. The cold rage flowing through my body is swift. I've been working for Ellison Corp since before I graduated from high school. I have plans of inclusivity, equality, and benign practices for the company, but I won't be manipulated into anything.

"You know what, Dad? If you don't think I'm the man to run your company, go with someone else. Frankly, I am tired of you using it like a carrot to force me to move at your will. Go ahead, name someone else. I still have a good number of stocks and will make money either way. Maybe I'll take my talents elsewhere."

"Stop it," Mom screams. "You will not give your birthright that you worked so hard for because you're infatuated. Your father is right. You're willing to risk everything for a woman who makes you feel good today. How long until the novelty passes for both of you? What happens when she is tired of being a constant punching bag? You know what you'll be left with? Resentment. Because all you bring each other is stress and trouble. You know why, my son? Because together you can never outrun Maddie's shadow."

It would've hurt less if she took a sledgehammer to my sternum. I don't move, but her words have bent me and I can't seem to straighten up again.

My dad tags in. "Think about that, Alister. You're throwing away your dream and hers. If this continues, how long do you think her employer will hold out? All she does is bring bad publicity to them. And no one is really turning on you yet, but she continues to be in the middle of the bullseye. If you don't do it for yourself, then stop being selfish for once. Do it for that girl. Her whole life will be a mess because of your ego."

He walks out then, and my mom lingers, looking at his back and then at me. "Don't force his hand, please. Don't give up what is yours." She follows him out.

When they walk away, they might as well leave my dead body on the floor.

I've always had to live without them. I will not live without her.

But what about the people in the company that depend on me? What about the projects that I sponsored? They will undo what I built.

The walls begin to close and I wish I could have her with me to talk this out, to reassure her I would gladly give up everything to be with her.

I walk out into the night to get some air. When I come back, I'll call my dad and tell him I'm resigning.

24

———

Mila

Alis and his parent's yelling reaches all the way to our bedroom and we both gasp in unison when his father threatens to take away the company from him.

I wish I could just run in there and shield him from them. But they're his family, and I'm the one they perceive as the threat. I'm the one they said is destroying him as he is destroying me.

"I can't believe they're so heartless with him."

My mom shakes her head. "They're being harsh and heartless, but they're not altogether wrong. Sometimes the truth comes wrapped in bitterness and you have to taste it before you get to the part that sets you free."

I freeze and then my chest bursts with anger. "I can't believe you're saying that. He's not at fault for what is happening around us."

"He's not and that family in the restaurant were massive assholes. I can't tell you how much my heart went out to Alis today. He was a lion for you. He loves you and that has a place in my heart... but that's not enough, Mila."

For the first time in my life, I look at my mother like I don't know her. But I don't have time for this. Alis needs me and I have to go to him.

We hear the house door slam for a second time. I run to the window. The car takes off and there's only deafening silence through the house. I wait a few breaths until I see Alis walking out into the woods.

"I'm going to go talk to him." I take three steps, but my mom jumps between me and the door.

"Stop for a second and think."

I shake my head. "Think about what? He needs me. Didn't you hear what they said to him? It's hurtful, and he doesn't need to deal with that alone."

I raise my voice at her, something I've never done, but she doesn't budge.

She presses her lips together. "*Amor*, this is exactly what I've been trying to warn you might happen. The two of you don't just have a steep uphill battle. Did you just hear what his parent had to say?"

"Of course, I did." I couldn't help but hear it. "But Alis doesn't agree."

"The parents are classists and prejudiced and they don't think much of us, of you."

"And that's okay." I'm lying, of course. Their words cut through me like a steak knife. "They don't have to like me."

"Would you be okay with me not liking him?"

I shake my head. "It's important that you love him. I don't want him to hurt alone. Please, just step aside."

"He's always going to hurt, you're always going to hurt, as long as you two are together. It's just too soon for this." She gestures around. "His community hasn't healed from Madison's death. She was a beloved daughter of this community. You're the woman that got in the middle. The internet has gone mad with hate for you. It's poisoned everyone against you."

"Mom..." I'm so hurt by her words I can't even form a full sentence. I just want to get to him.

"I'm the last person in the world that would hurt you on purpose.

You know I would cut off my right hand, but this goes with my first instinct to always protect you. I need you to know the truth. I need you to face it and let it guide you. Tonight, his family threatened to yank the company he loves, the one he spoke to you so proudly about, away from him because you are in his life."

"I know, I hate that."

"And take some time to think about someone else. My girl. The girl that studied so hard, the one that didn't have much of a social life in college." She points at my chest. "You had a goal all your life, and you put your head down and made it happen. You fought and went without the things most young women want to be where you are. You didn't go on one spring break vacation. Instead, you were paying for trainings to boost your skill. Now all people talk about is your one night with this man."

I wince like she stabbed me and back away from her to sit on the bed. "I don't want to hear this."

"Sometimes that's what God put me on earth for. To tell you all the things you don't want to hear but you need to. Mila, you're so accomplished, I sometimes cry while praising God for my *Milagro*, the miracle child he gave me. Even as I chose a path that he didn't intend, instead of punishing me, he blessed me with a woman who is strong, smart, and has a heart others can only envy and wish evil upon."

The tears blur my vision and roll down my face. I swat at them.

"You don't deserve for people to pick at your relationship. You don't deserve to be destroyed because you spent the night with a man and started a relationship with him. Those choices were yours to make... you deserve to rise and triumph."

"I can't stop them. If I say something is bad, if I say nothing, they still drag me."

She comes and sits beside me on the bed. "*Amor*, you can't control what they do. You can only control what you do."

"I love him."

"I know. I've been hearing that in your voice for a while and while love is powerful, sometimes it's not the right choice for us as women. Millions of people in the world love each other but cannot or should not be together. Can you say you won't be resentful if you lose everything you've always worked so hard for? Are you strong enough to watch him lose his dreams knowing it's because he chose you? I can't decide for you. But you can't let this relationship keep destroying both your lives."

I sit there, crying in silence. When she tries to hug me, I stand and move out of her reach. I stare into her shocked face. "I can't do what I need to do if you comfort me. I need to comfort him if I'm to break his heart... and mine."

———

Mila

My feet weigh so much I have to drag them all over the house. By the time I get to the family room, I'm exhausted mentally and emotionally. He's not back yet and part of me is relieved. If he's not here, I don't have to say it. I should just run, get out of here while I have the chance, but that's not fair. He doesn't deserve that.

I walk to the window and look out. I can wait for him here. I don't want to look into my mom's eyes because I don't want to talk about this again. I couldn't take that lecture all over again.

Then I see him, sitting on the steps facing out at the water, and I don't even know when I get to that door but I'm there and I throw it open. He turns his head and the small smile when he sees me is an arrow piercing through my chest. I'm so overloaded by how much I love him. *How can I even consider saying I won't be with him? How could I stand not to see him anymore?*

He holds out a hand, and I rush to take it. I don't care. I need this right now. He pulls me down next to him and I sit with my side pressed against his. His arm goes around me and I lean my head into his shoulder.

"This night blew up in our faces." His voice is low and charged.

"I think our world was just settled at the top and murky on the bottom. All tonight did was shake things around and the mud tainted everything around us."

"You're philosophizing."

I chuckle and it hurts to do that. "How are you feeling?"

"I'm okay. I'm sure you could hear us screaming. It's funny because we never yell. It's unbecoming of our stature, you know? The two times we get into a screaming match, you're here and now your mom."

"The yelling is not the issue. Families fight and yell. I think it's what he said. He was so cruel to you." My body goes hot all over again. I hated the careless way his dad spoke.

"That's how they are. My parents are not warm people, Mila. They don't look at us with love and affection. We are pieces to them and we need to behave like it. I'm done playing his game. He can take the company and shove it."

I dig my face deeper into his shoulder. "Don't say that. You love that company. It's your dream and you work hard to take care of it."

He kisses the top of my head. "Yeah, but I don't need for it to be held over me and used to manipulate me. I'll be damned if I let him do that to me again."

"It shouldn't, but so many people depend on you. I can't be what gets between you and your dream."

His arm tightens around me. "You're not, Mila. If anything, you're the only one that can make everything else in the world fade away."

My eyes well all over again, but I breathed it out. "You're the same for me. You make me not care about all the shit that's happening, but we need to be objective about this. We need to think long term."

"I am. I can always do something else. I have an inheritance from my grandfather, not to mention the money I made on my own. I don't really need my father. I can start a company or go work for someone else."

I pull away and sit up straighter. "Why would you when you're on the brink of getting what you worked for? You said your dad can undo your impact on the company and that you would do what it takes to change the course he wants to take it in."

"That was before. He's not going to tell me I can't be with you."

"I don't want to be the reason you don't get your dream. I don't want you to hate me."

He turns to look at me. "Hate you? I love you so much I don't care about any of it."

"You don't care about not being CEO?"

"No." But he looks away.

"You're lying."

His gaze snaps back to me. "I'm not."

I smile at him and touch his cheek. "But you are. We've both been lying to each other by acting like they're going to let this happen. We probably jumped into this too soon."

His mouth slackens. "What are you saying, Mila?"

"There's never a moment to breathe or enjoy. Every single time we have a happy moment, it's only followed by something even more fucked up than before."

"But we move past that together. We take it all head on."

And my chest constricts because he has a reason for everything and I'm almost convinced. I don't want to do this. "I wish I could stay here, in this moment, with you."

His whole body goes rigid next to mine, but he doesn't let me go. "But you won't."

"I can't. This is destroying us as people."

"I don't feel destroyed and I don't think you do either."

"But it's happening. Our dreams are just hanging in the background screaming while the world is trying to take an ax to them. And we owe it to ourselves, to the people that believe and depend on us, to do what is right. It's too soon for us."

"How can it be too soon for something that neither of us saw coming but has changed everything about our lives? Unless that's not what you feel..."

His words cut deep and I almost scream out loud. Does he not know how much this hurts? But this could be a godsend. It would make it easier to break up if I said I don't feel what he does.

I tilt my face up. "I do. The one thing I won't do is lie. I'm talking about this because it's the right thing. We need a break or what we have will trample over everything we worked so hard for. But I won't ever let you doubt how much I love you."

He closes the distance between our mouths, and my hand bunches around his jacket. I kiss him back with everything I have, even as my throat swells and I can barely breathe. But I don't pull away.

"Don't go. Stay with me tonight. We can talk some more in the morning. Let's just be us. Fuck everything else."

Every memory flashes before my eyes, the harassing calls, all the social media messages, the conversation with my mom, the screaming match between him and his dad. All that we've been through collides with everything I'm losing. And I say fuck it all because I'm giving myself the gift of tonight with him.

I nod.

He stands and pulls me along with him. "If we're going to hurt tomorrow, let's make it count tonight."

Ironically, those are the words that sealed our fate together. And like that night, I push away my thoughts of what tomorrow will bring and how much will I hurt without him. I concentrate on him, how much I want him, how much I love him, the things I really need him to remember.

"Let's go to our room."

He smiles, but it's not his usual. It's the smile behind a heart that's already broken and needs to cling to what he's already lost. I know because it's the smile I'm mirroring.

We walk in hand in hand. I avoid looking at the walls. I don't want to carry anything with me. I don't want to remember any of it. All I want to take with me from here is the way his hand tightens around mine, the heat from his body, the taste of his kisses.

In the room, we shed our clothes in silence. We touch each other like the first time, exploring, tasting, feasting on each other's bodies with our hands and mouths. Tracing, drawing, and painting on each other's skins with invisible ink. That way neither of us never forgets.

He pounds into me while I'm on my back, staring up at his face.

My heart trembles, overflowing with feelings I can't contain. He twists and bends me, but we end up back in this position. And when he cums inside me, he doesn't collapse. He still stares into my eyes, gripping my face in his hands.

"No matter where you go, who you meet, and who fucks you, you'll always be mine."

25

Mila

Morning arrives way too soon, the brightness breaking through the windows, making my eyes hurt. I don't blink. Neither does Alis. He hasn't closed his eyes all night. I know because we've been staring at each other.

I wish he was sleeping so I could sneak out of the bed and leave his house like a thief who stole all these moments between us. I wish I didn't have to look at him in the morning light as the sun sets on what we briefly were. Yeah, if he had slept, this would be a cowardly but easier goodbye. Yet, we don't dwell. I get out of the bed and so does he.

"I'm going to drive you and your mother back." His voice is thick. We broke night and a little bit of ourselves. Then his words hit me full on.

Drive us back? The panic bubbles begin to burst and I shake my head. I couldn't bear the thought of being in a car with him like a couple of days ago and then having to say goodbye all over again. "No. I will drive. Just please loan me your rental."

"I want to see you and your mom safely home, Mila. That's all."

I press my lips together, searching for the right words that don't make this harder on us. "I know. I just don't think I can make it through that. We have Knox and I promise I will let you know when we make it there. I beg you, let me go alone."

His jaw works and the struggle is there, in those tired eyes, but he shrugs. "As you wish."

He throws on a pair of pants and a t-shirt. "I'll have the truck ready for when you are. Remember, no one is asking you to leave, so please take your time."

He walks out of the bedroom door, leaving me as the sadness washes over me until the heat flashes up my body. I don't know if I'm more hurt or angry. Angry because fuck him. *Does he think this doesn't hurt me? He knows it does because we've both felt the same pain.*

I go to his bathroom, wash up, and put on some clean clothes. I can shower when I get home. I just need to get away from here before I'm tempted to have this out with him.

I throw all the stuff in my weekender bag and don't look back when I leave his room.

I go get my mom and she's fully packed and ready. She's sitting casually at the end of the bed, waiting for me. I don't know why that pisses me off even more. I told her I would do this. Still, her acting like it was a foregone conclusion makes me feel like I never had a real fucking choice.

I tilt my head to the door. "Let's go."

I roll out her suitcase while carrying my weekender bag. Alis intercepts us outside on the way to the garage. We both freeze. His gaze drifts to my mom and he nods at her. He holds out a hand and takes our bags. We don't look at each other again. I just follow him into his garage and the door is already open to exit. Knox is out in the driveway, standing next to his car. Alis thought of everything.

I guess he must feel the same urgency for me to leave as I do for going.

When he loads the bags into the back of the truck, I say, "Thank you for *everything*," making sure I enunciate every syllable. All I feel is poison flowing in my veins and I want him to feel it, too.

Why did he argue so much last night and today is so easy for him to let me go?

I swat the thoughts away and climb into the driver's seat. There's no need for this. We are both hurting enough as it is.

My mom is watching all of it in silence, but she doesn't get in. Instead, she looks at him. "Can I talk to you for a minute?"

What now?

He nods and moves aside for her. They go inside and I'm left alone to contemplate how happy I was two days ago and how miserable this is. I pull out my phone and there are several texts from Sandy.

SANDY

Girl, send me a smoke signal.

I know you're with your boo but let me know you're alive.

Not even one fucking photo of the place, either.

Come on, I miss you.

I send her a quick text back.

ME

I'm sorry. It's been a lot... Mami is here. Will call you later on today.

Two minutes later, Mami and Alis come back out.

She's dabbing at her eyes, turns and says something to him.

He nods, but his gaze lasers through the windshield into mine.

Once my mom is in the car, I put it in reverse, but I don't wave at him.

"Drive safely," he calls out.

I nod and back out into the driveway, go around Knox, as he follows me into the road. I concentrate on it, looking straight ahead, not even glancing into the rearview. I don't want to watch his house disappear. I don't want to let the finality in.

My mom clears her throat. "I know you're not happy—"

"No, I'm not. But it's done." I can't help the bereft tone in my voice.

"He's a good man, Mila."

I nod. "Yeah, but it doesn't help me or make me feel better now."

"I'm sorry. I hate more than anything being the one that told you this."

I let out a shaky breath. I'm not going to cry. "This is not your fault. You told me the truth, and I did what needed to be done."

"It's not your fault, either. Or his. Later, you two—"

"Stop," I snap and then take a breath. "This is not helping."

"Do you want to know what we talked about before I got in the car?"

I'm dying to know, but it's not going to help. I just want to be alone with my thoughts. "No."

I can feel her staring at the side of my head. This is not like me. She doesn't recognize me. I don't even recognize myself.

"Your bed and the furniture got delivered. We'll just need to make it all pretty for you."

"Okay, *mi amor*." Her voice cracks.

I want to tell her not to cry, but if I do that, I will cry all the same. "Maybe you can make me some hot chocolate tonight and we can watch movies."

"Yeah, I would like that."

"We can also look for pretty things to put in your room while you're here with me." *Yeah, that's good. Let's look forward to anything.*

"I'm not leaving you until you are safe."

Her life is also in the balance because of this bullshit. I'm so angry I might as well be chewing on glass. I let the road in and stare into the lush trees that lead the way out of Luciana Island.

I want to not think about how the two times I've entered this town I've come for him or with him. This time, as I drive away, I don't have the hope of coming back or him coming to me.

I let myself feel the wave of sadness as we cross the bridge out of the island. I give myself permission to wallow in my pain. Because when we return to Baltimore, I'm back to being Milagros Rosario, the

Chief Marketing Officer at Grayson Global. I have work to do, a team to lead, and I'm going to reclaim my life.

I'm going to start by making the new place nice for my mom. I'm going to spend time with her the way I kept wishing we had before. I've never let a heartbreak or a setback hold me back. This will not be the time I fall and don't get up.

———

Mila

The internet remembers. You'll get what's coming to you. You better sleep with one eye open.

I stare at the sentences in the neatly-folded piece of paper that have forged another wave of fucked up shit into my life. It was mixed with all my mail and the first thing I opened.

Now the police are searching every corner of the unit and I'm face to face with Dahlia Wicker, and just like many other times, this is not a welcome meeting.

"It hasn't even been a fucking hour since I've been home."

"I know," Dahlia says. "I'm so sorry. I will try to get the team out of here soon so we can talk."

"No offense to the two of you... but the last thing I want to do is talk."

Matt nods. "We get it, but we need to take your statement and your mom's."

I turn around, searching for her like she had not been by my side a second ago. When I don't spot her right away, my nerves betray me and I turn around, intent on going to look for her.

A hand to the wrist stops me. "She went to the bathroom. She told you before she headed that way. And we already swept it. It's clear."

Air flows back in my lungs though not as easily as it should. I bury my face in my hands and try to take control of my breathing. "I'm sorry. I'm exhausted."

"I would be too." Matt takes me by the elbow and moves to the couch.

Dahlia returns with a bottle of water. I stare at it and hold it but don't drink it. I no longer know what to trust. Is it poisoned and waiting for me, sitting here?

"It's safe. We brought it in."

My gaze snaps to hers. She shrugs. "Can never be too careful."

I nod and twist the top off. In that moment, I couldn't care less. I need something to drink. Maybe it can keep me from having a breakdown.

"Why are you back so early?"

I look between her and Matt. I don't want to say what I'm sure they knew would happen, but they'll find out, anyway. "We needed to get home. I missed my bed and the sooner I settle my mom, the better."

I chicken out at the last minute. I can't make myself say that it's over and we came home because we had nothing else to do there.

Matt walks away, and the knowledge is in the soft pity in Dahlia's eyes.

"Tell me everything that's happened since you got back."

I'm so grateful to her for not asking about him. I can't even say his name in my thoughts today.

"We got here an hour ago. We waited at Knox's while he guided people to bring in my mom's bed and furniture. When we got back, there was mail left at the office for us. In it was the letter saying the internet remembers and I'll still get what's coming to me."

"Do you recognize the handwriting?"

I shake my head. "It's really pretty though."

"It is. But it's not handwriting. It's printed from somewhere."

That stokes my hope. "Are there any markers? Can you you trace it?"

Matt is back to our side. "We're taking it as evidence and sent it to our lab. This is not a traditional crime scene, but because of everything that is happening with you, we are processing it."

I bite back the *gee thanks* that's hanging on the tip of my tongue and settle for a clipped, "Thanks."

"I know it doesn't look like much, but we are hoping there are fingerprints and we can find whoever sent it."

"Well, with my luck, it would be another nosy person who you can't connect to the shit that's happening to me."

She winces and I almost feel bad, but there's a part of me that doesn't care for anything. All I want is to shower and be unconscious for hours. I want to fix my mom's room and sleep so I don't have to think or feel.

"Did you notice anything out of the ordinary when you came inside the apartment?"

Yes, the big man that made it feel less big is not here.

"No. Everything was as I left it."

"Nothing on camera." One officer hooks a finger to the door. "It didn't detect people, but we are going to tap into the feed and check out the entire footage."

"Thank you, Ramirez."

A warm hand settles on my shoulder, and I don't move. I would know that hand anywhere and I lean my head against it.

"Can I talk to you?" Matt asks my mom from a few feet away.

She nods and they go to the other end of the room. I follow them with my gaze, watching her for any sign of distress. She didn't even flinch earlier.

"He wants to make sure he gets anything she may have seen without your memories mingling with hers."

I nod.

Dahlia's fingers settle on my wrist. "We'll be out soon, so you can shower and get some rest. We are also leaving some uniforms outside."

"Thank you. I want my mom to feel protected."

"I want you to feel protected too, Mila."

"I have Knox. I just need to stay locked up in here, which suits me just fine right now."

She squeezes my wrist. "You can call me anytime and we can take you and your mom out for a ride. But it doesn't have to be in a professional capacity..."

"Thank you. We may do that. I'm tired of being scared and in hiding. And I don't want her to just be in here like a prisoner." *Like me*, I don't say. "You know, Detective. I'm annoyed and sick of being fucking harassed and bullied. I can't even have five minutes to get used to my mom being here. Something has to happen to mess that up."

"It sucks ass. We are doing everything we can."

"I don't want to be negative, but right now, that doesn't feel like enough."

"Well, on top of all of that, you are hurting."

My eyes narrow. "Did he tell you?"

"He called this morning to say you were on your way back. He wanted to make sure we knew that. He didn't say anything else and didn't want to talk to Weston. There are things I just know about those two..."

Alis and his brother are too synched. That's how he describes it. Does he not want his brother to know how he feels?

The tear in my heart widens, and it bleeds, fresh and red, all over again. Will this day ever end? When will I close my eyes and get some rest? "I hate to hear that."

"Me too. I like the two of you together. I want him to be happy." She whispers the words in the softest of tones.

And who knew she would be emotional? "Thanks."

"Do you want to move to another unit or area? Maybe we can find you another place away from here."

I think of her words, savor them, and I shake my head. "As long as they can't touch me or my mom, I will be okay."

I stand and don't even wait for them to leave. I begin preparing my mom's room as the cops do what they need. I make her bed and set the pretty lamps I bought for her on the nightstands. Together, we hang her clothes and organize things in the drawers.

"I've never had pillows like this." She runs her fingers over silk covers.

"You'll love them. They're so good for the hair."

We walk the cops out and I promise to call Dahlia. My mom hugs her and Matt like she's known them all their lives. She even offers to make food for them and their families. I don't tell her this is not a social visit. It won't do me any good. She thinks of them as our protectors.

I think of them as what stands between me and some sleep.

We go to our respective rooms after. I shower and wash my hair. I don't bother drying myself. Instead, I put on my robe and climb into my bed with it on. I lay in silence for a while, too tired to sleep, which doesn't make sense. I flip on my TV, turning it to a mindless crime show I don't recognize and don't try to. To my annoyance, I get caught up in the story of the boy who disappears after meeting someone from the web.

I don't even realize when I fall asleep, but I get woken up by the growling in my stomach and the smell of garlic, onions, cilantro. It's not just food, it's my mother's stewed beans. I open my eyes but don't move. Maybe I can stay here, but the hunger beats me. I pick up the phone from the pillow next to mine. It's eight at night.

As much as I want to wallow, my mom is here, and she cooked for me. I can't be selfish. I'll have enough time to myself when she returns home to a safe new place. The wave of fresh sadness that washes over me pushes me right out of bed.

I don't bother combing my hair, simply picking it up and tying it in a bun. In the living room, Mami is on the couch with the TV on but on the phone. "I have to go, *chica*. My *bella durmiente* just woke up."

I manage a smile for her. She used to call me her sleepy beauty when I was a kid. "Smells good," I say when she is off the phone.

"I wanted to make your favorite, but I didn't have everything I needed. Maybe we can get some groceries delivered." Her voice is careful and hopeful, like she doesn't know where to start.

"Okay, we can order some of your yucky squash."

She laughs. "It makes beans and soup taste better."

"Sure, *Mami*."

We sit and eat while she's talking about work gossip.

"They're saying Dr. Barnestein is retiring soon. I don't know who is going to take over for him. I'm praying the administration is thinking about this one. He has a great reputation. I would hate it if they choose someone who doesn't care as much for others."

"Do you have any say in it?"

She laughs. "*Amor*, I'm just a nurse."

"You're the head nurse, and you know a lot of the people on the board. They adore you."

"I guess, but you know some of this is very political. I'm sure whoever they choose next has already started paving their road to it." She angles her head as if she's looking closer at me. "What about you? Have you thought about your next steps at work?"

I swear this is the wrong day to ask. I can only shake my head. "I haven't even had time to settle in."

"True, but you're always thinking ahead about what's next. It would do you good to have something other than work to concentrate on."

Like a relationship?

"I've been thinking about buying a house. It makes little sense to rent here. It's cheaper to buy."

"That's a good idea." She pauses and smiles. "My baby is buying her own house. Do you know what area?"

I shrug. "I've been looking close to the city but with a suburb feel. You know? Like, remember when we would take our drives with Tio Felipe?"

Her eyes go warmer and nostalgic. "Remember how much he loved Bronxville during Christmas?"

My eyes well a little. "God yes. Our sip and see the decorations drives with him is one of things I miss the most about him."

She nods. "Me too. He would know how to make you feel better right now."

My chest tightens a little, but I work around it. I need to learn to let myself feel this. "You're doing great, *Mami*. The beans are everything."

We switch to conversation about what's going on with our family members. Then, we tidy up and by the time I get to bed, I prepare to be up for hours but surprise myself by drifting off the minute my head hits the pillow.

My last thought is that tomorrow I go back to making my life work for me because it can't get any worse than it is right now.

26

———

Mila

The meeting hasn't started yet, and I've been with these people most of the day. I don't want to give anyone else an opportunity to drag me into conversation. So, I stare at Alis' texts and tune out the chatter around me.

> **ALIS**
>
> I heard what happened. I was just making sure you are okay?
>
> I can get you more security.
>
> I get why you're not answering your phone, but if you need more security, let me know.

I need to put him out of my head too. It's not good for me to concentrate on him. It was already painful when I woke up and saw the missed called this morning. He worries about me even when he no longer has to. All I wanted to do was dial him back. I had to put my phone away before I typed something that I would regret or make this more difficult for both of us.

The tapping of Spencer Grayson's expensive shoes announces his presence just as someone whispers, "He's coming." Seconds later, he storms through the door. He's always like a hurricane that disrupts everything—in the best of ways for our products—but can cause damage to someone who is not prepared.

Thankfully, I have been up since early today. I'm not a morning person, but when I make it out of bed around five, I'm able to channel my creativity a little more. Today, since we were coming back to the office and had this meeting, I went over our campaign performances. I knew Grayson would want to discuss in specific the numbers for *GrayMatter, Lash N' Gloss vs. Autumn Lush, and GrayIsh*. The first two are over-performing but GrayIsh is still falling a little behind Amazon and Walmart and I'm thinking it's time to invest more on ads, test them against each other, and try a focus group.

"Let's get started," he says, and we go through the *GrayMatter* and *LnG X AL* campaigns.

We present the spike in sales and provide Grayson with a reason to smile, which doesn't let us breathe because there's still the odd man out campaign to discuss.

"I think the concepts for these two were perfect from conception to execution. I love the *it's about the people* concept. Very pleased. Congratulations Mila and team."

I nod with a slight smile, as if I wasn't dancing on the inside.

"We worked really hard on bringing this concept to life," Greg mumbles under his breath.

Every head in the room turns to look his way, but I don't. I keep my eyes straight. I haven't had a chance to talk to him one on one, but our last interaction left a lot to be desired.

"I know, Greg, and congratulations again. I did not mean to minimize your team's efforts. But... since you bring this up, the reason I singled Mila out is that she came up with the concept, visualized it, and created rough drafts for you all. Did she not?"

Greg's gaze snaps to me. He opens his mouth, but Grayson beats him to it once more.

"I know who works late and, in case anyone forgets, I have access to the creative folders. Both *GrayMatter* and the collaboration of *LnG*

X AL are very important projects for me. Both are family related. *GrayMatter* is my daughter's company, so I want to have a finger into everything that goes into it, including creation of marketing and ads."

If Mary and Carter could move away from Greg, they would be across the street right now.

"I understand, Grayson. I am not questioning Mila's dedication or her amazing talent. Everyone knows her campaigns turn a profit. She's diligent and tries to have a hand in everything here. She still runs each campaign like a project manager meticulously checking every piece. None of us would think of doing anything without her unique and invaluable input *if* she's around to give it."

I don't squirm like I want to. He makes me sound like a busybody when all I'm trying to do is help when I can and avoid the wrath of higher management.

"Well, that's what I was looking for in my CMO. Hence, she is above your entire department now."

"Understood." Greg doesn't physically flinch but he tips his chin down and a visible red appears on the side of his throat.

Grayson stares at him for a few seconds. "It's time to talk about where we need to apply some more work. Let's dig into *GrayIsh*. As pleased as I am with the other two campaigns, the numbers for *GrayIsh* are lacking in ways that make me uncomfortable. Looking at people's reactions to the ads, there's very little we can use. It seems like people see them but don't react. Greg, do you want to provide some insight into this?"

He takes a sip of his coffee and that's already very telling. You never want Grayson to smell blood in the water.

"We received little direction for this one. We executed our interpretation of it."

I straighten, intending to save him from himself, but Grayson shakes his head at me. I keep my lips tightly closed and wait for the fireworks.

"You and your team are not new here. You should be able to execute original concepts from the script given to you. I read it myself. You could have asked for help from someone, including your new boss. You asked for more responsibility. It was given to you."

This is going to be ugly.

"Grayson, our marketing lead is no longer with us." His eyes drop to the table. "And our new boss has been overloaded. We did not want to approach her, as she seems overwhelmed with everything that is going on in her life."

My whole body goes stiff. First, he blames Madison's death and now I'm unapproachable because I don't want to feed gossip about my life.

"Are you saying you can't do your job properly, the job we hired you to do independently with your team, because your direct boss is unapproachable when minutes ago you insinuated she was micro-managing you?"

Greg blinks a few times. The I-fucked-up broadcasts across his expression. "I'm saying we can't even have the kind of meetings we used to have with her before, because it's all about what is being said online. She's always out of the office, working from home or in some other remote location. She's never in here like before to oversee what we create."

Grayson leans forward and opens his mouth and this is the moment Greg can kiss his career goodbye, but I need to be the one to performance-manage my employee.

"Grayson, if I may?"

He turns to me and nods.

"Greg and team, though I don't think I ever gave you the impression that I don't welcome conversation, it seems like there's a mass misunderstanding and we will go through this offline at a team meeting. For the sake of this meeting, we can concentrate on giving Grayson what he is asking for: answers to the poor performance numbers of the *GrayIsh* campaign."

Greg pales, and in that moment, I realize our problems are even bigger. He doesn't have the information. Thankfully, I can cover for him this time. I turn away from him and back to our boss.

"Grayson, after reviewing the data we gathered and analyzing our

KPIs and the poor ROI, we believe we've taken the wrong approach to this campaign. We need to recalibrate and come up with new concepts for the next quarter. Then we suggest running A/B testing to see if it's an approach issue or a quality issue."

Someone gasps low and the rest stare with widened eyes.

Grayson's smile makes me more than my share of nervous. "I invest in nothing but quality and believe our products are the best in the market. And the service behind *GrayIsh* is also the best, but people are not jumping off Amazon or Walmart. I am curious why. I can understand and support the A/B testing approach. Do you have a new campaign angle?"

His gaze shifts from me to Greg. It's sad to see him squirm when he's back in Grayson's crosshairs. My focus now is to salvage the meeting so I jump back in.

"Actually, yes. As I mentioned, we should try the people first type of marketing. The first two ads would be centered on the employees under *GrayIsh*. Explaining to people what they understand the service is, why they chose to work for the company, and how they see it benefiting their communities. We should have some visuals by the end of the week. We are still working on the second concept centered on the clients. Focus on who are the people we want to serve and why? How does *GrayIsh* compare to the other services and the things we offer they can't get from the other two?"

Grayson leans back. "Do you have anything for me to see?"

"I have a very rough draft of it." I slide my folder to him.

He pages through the images and nods. "It's really rough like you said, but the vision is clear. I'm looking forward to you all refining the concept and polishing it. It has a lot of promise."

"Thank you," I say.

"Before I go, I need to say that while your team has one head of marketing, everyone needs to account for their work individually. I'm not a micromanager, but I know what happens in my company. I know where the concepts come from. This is why Grayson Global is successful. I know who does what. I also know the people I choose for key positions and why I stand by them and their choices. Sometimes executives cover because their entire team failed to do their job. It's what separates them from everyone else. Great job on the first two campaigns. Looking forward to *GrayIsh* being on top next meeting."

He stands and leaves the meeting, followed by his advisors.

Once we're alone, I delegate the new campaign work. "I would like to be updated on the progress. We promised Grayson we will have the comps on Friday, so I expect to have them on Wednesday. We can review them together and hold live edits and feedback sessions. Thank you for all the work you do. Let me give you twenty minutes of your time back. Greg, Mary, and Carter, can you please stay behind?"

The three of them exchange worried looks. The rest of the team exit like their chairs are on fire.

"I asked you to stay because we need to discuss what happened today."

Greg clears his throat. "I'm sorry I talked about your personal situation—"

I hold up a hand, stalling him mid-sentence. "I don't care about that. My 'personal situation,' as you call it, is not up for discussion. But since you bring it up, it's interesting how you chose to throw a dead woman under the bus and tried to clean it up with *my situation.*" I air quote the last words for him. "All of that to cover the fact that the three of you showed up at a meeting with your CEO unprepared. This was not on Madison's instructions for the campaign. Those were clear and there are plenty of people you can ask, including me."

"Well, we tried. Carter and I met with you," Mary says.

"I met with you to work. You met with me to gossip about my personal life, Mary, which is none of your business and never a topic of conversation for you. When we finally spoke about work, your questions had nothing to do with design or approach. I answered what you asked, but I didn't want to micromanage you. You took none of my suggestions, and if you had, you wouldn't be in hot water today."

"We'll fix it."

I nod. "You will, and it will be great because, as I'm sure the three of you realize, you are in the place you never wanted to be, under the attentive eyes of Spencer Grayson. And you dragged all of marketing into it."

Mary pales to a degree that's almost laughable. Carter won't look me in the eyes. Greg squirms, and that annoys me even more. He's acting like a little weasel.

"Thank you for your time, and please let me know if you need any help. Even if I am working from home."

I turn my attention to my cell phone.

"Um. Can we see the new concepts you created to help us guide us?"

I try not to disintegrate them with my eyes. Since I keep copies of everything, I hand the folder to Carter.

Once they walk away, it takes all of me not to laugh. It's petty, but I love the way they're dragging their tails today. Greg turns at the door and shoots me a look like he wants to say something, but turns on his heel and leaves.

My office phone rings. It's Sandy.

"Girlfriend, everyone's abuzz with what happened in your meeting."

"What? How? It just ended."

She hums, "Just a heads up. Grayson is all over Greg Nielsen."

"I figured he would be."

That's what he gets for acting like an asshole.

"Greg's been frustrated for a while but he's harmless. It may just be weird that you went from his friend to his boss."

She's right. I definitely need to schedule that private meeting with him.

———

Alis

KNOX

Checking In. All Is quiet.

The text from Knox yanks me out of my what-the-fuck-am-I-reading haze. These proposals tend to elevate and disappoint at times. But I've already relegated it to the back of my mind in favor of the person I can't seem to put away.

ME

Keep me posted and let me know what you need. We can add more people to help you.

His reply is swift.

KNOX

Let me reach out to people I trust. Budget?

ME

Whatever it takes.

I send my reply and get back to my reading.

When I reach the last page on the current proposal, I dump it into the trash pile. It's almost to the height of my chair. The last five days I've discovered that this company can't distract me like I hoped. I still love it and all my projects are moving ahead as planned, but the only thing that's kept my interest is reading through proposals sent to us for our entrepreneur-sponsoring program.

The best part is deconstructing these plans. That's how you find all the flaws and I'm liking that. Some of these people think this is Shark Tank and keep sending quirky ideas like the fully organic meal subscription service that costs more than an average mortgage payment. I shake my head and keep reading only for enjoyment.

I never bothered reading the letters before explaining why this is important for them. I should have. You can read passion and intent in all of them. You can even tell when it's a money grab vs. when it's the person wanting to get better along with their project. I save the letters to read after the project plans.

I loved exactly four of them. I also have a pile for the human-interest sponsorships. Those are the ones we donate to and support. My favorite is the young woman who came up with an idea to start a foundation which creates a series of facilities to house the homeless so they can have a safe place for the night. She wants to capitalize on rental property and use some of the revenue to create the facility. It would be like a storage unit full of rooms equipped with a toilet and sink. There's a communal shower. I liked that she thought of everything. She looked for funding from the state, found other sponsorships, and even looked into crowdfunding. She just needs a boost to get started. That's where we come in.

I dial my brother. He answers in the second ring and yawns into the line. "I'm going to bed."

"I was just leaving you a message. I found us a project that I think you'll love."

"Yeah?" His voice is low and I know he's ready to keel over.

"Go be bed. I can tell you about it another time."

"Are you okay?"

Just peachy. "Yeah. I'm just moving through these proposals."

"That had been sitting there for months... why don't you take some time away from the company?"

I snort. "For what? There's no point. Plus, when I come back I would have to fix all the crap Dad and friends fuck up."

"Have you talked to her?"

He means Mila.

"No. There's no point in that either. Go to bed, Wes."

"Stop." My finger freezes over the hang-up button and he continues. "Did you know I got a message from Dad? There's a board meeting tomorrow."

"Yeah, I heard. Some bullshit he and Fred McConnell want to push. I couldn't care less. I just want to do the work, make sure we are following on the initiatives..."

I stop myself because if I keep talking I'll say the initiatives I gave up Mila up for.

"It's okay to be upset. I know you miss her."

I groan. "This is what we're doing now? Talking about feelings? When Dahlia dumped you, I was playing wingman for you, trying to get you laid and happy. I hooked you up with a woman—" I stop because I remember who I was trying to hook him up with... Maddie. "God, that's a horrible example."

That's when I tried to hook him up with Maddie while he and Dahlia were broken up. Then, Weston dumped her, and she decided to give me a chance, only to not do that at all.

"It's not. Those were good memories. I rekindled my friendship with her, and you got to experience a relationship with her. It ended in tragedy, which is not our fault, but you gave it a chance."

It ended in the worst of ways. "This is not helping."

"Okay, then let me say something that will and that I wish I had listened to when someone tried to tell me: give her time. This doesn't have to be a permanent goodbye. Maybe this is just not the right moment. It happened like that for Dahlia and me."

I refuse to feed the sliver of hope he's stoking. "It's not the same. I think you guys had a chance. Our parents and probably her mom, who I think hates me and I don't blame her, have cemented in her head that we can never outrun Maddie's ghost. That she will always be between us."

"That's bullshit. Neither of you were at fault for Maddie's death, and lots of people started with a hook-up."

"Yeah, but their ex doesn't end up dead and someone is not actively trying to kill one of them." I run my fingers through my hair. "Christ, I can't even be there to take care of her. I could settle for that, to just be close and make sure no one hurts her. She doesn't even want that from me. She wouldn't even let me drive them home. She couldn't get away fast enough once she made her decision."

"Time is the word, Alis. Give it to her and yourself. And don't worry about her safety. Dahlia has people on her and she still has Knox watching over her. I think BPD has additional cars patrolling her area."

"That's good. Anyway, go to sleep. I'll call you later."

"Okay."

I sit back and think of what he told me. Dahlia is watching out for her. I shoot a text to my sister-in-law.

ME

> Please let me know if I need to add more resources to protect her. I can pay for the extra cops.

DAHLIA

😊 Will do.

ME

Thanks.

The next text comes in five minutes later.

DAHLIA

Give her time. It will be worth it.

Has everyone confabulated to give trite advice today? I hate that both she and Weston are so hopeful when I don't feel it. I know there's no hope here. She doesn't want to see me or talk to me. If she did, she would answer the phone when I call her, not just text back polite little messages like

MILA

I'm okay, I hope you are too

Or the worst of all...

MILA

I'm thinking about you.

What the fuck does that even mean?

Besides, we were never just text people. We were phone and video people too.

I'm beginning to hate everything around me, the house because she's touched everything in it, the company that seems like an anchor around my neck. I especially can't stand the sight of my father. He keeps finding excuses to come to my office. It takes everything for me not to walk out of a room when he walks in. He's not at fault for me losing Mila, but he and Mom put ideas in her head. They poisoned the water, and I'm not my brother. Weston's less resentful, but he also has something I don't, the ability to shut them out completely by not having to live and work near them. All this time, he's been the smart one.

The intercom on my office phone buzzes. "Alis, someone's here to see you." Janice's voice is downright cheerful, which tells me it's not my dad.

The door opens without me saying okay and I'm ready to blast whoever it is for barging in and then I freeze as Leila walks in through the door.

She throws her purse at the chair on the other side of my desk and comes around, throwing her arms around me. "My beautiful son."

I hug her tight, holding on to her warmth. I never know how much I truly miss her until she's back with me. "What are you doing here?"

"Your father asked me to come for a meeting."

I laugh. "Since when do you let him tell you what to do, especially when it has to do with the company?"

"Fine, I'm here for you. I hope my room is ready because you know I'm not staying with your parents. Fuck that."

And that sinks my stomach like a stone. As much as I love her, I want to be alone. I want to work until I pass out tired. "I'm not in the best of moods and I'll be shitty company. It's probably a better time if you stayed with Weston and Dahlia."

She shakes her head. "Nope. They will both be working, and I want to be with my grumpy son, not the exhausted one. He needs to use whatever energy he has left to keep his hot cop happy."

I laugh again. "You're staying with me because I have no one. Ouch."

"Stop that. Have you heard from her?"

I don't try to pretend I don't understand. "Yeah, I found out what happened when she got home. I texted her, asking her if she wanted more security. She declined."

"Well, my son, I once told you she doesn't need to know all your moves. I'm sure you can arrange for more people to take care of her without her knowing."

"Isn't that obsessive?" I ask.

She nods. "Maybe, but she'll be safe. You can live with the moniker."

I kiss her cheek. "I love you, you know that?"

"And you already did it, didn't you?"

I'm a fucking chump. "I asked Knox to get more people."

"Good boy."

I move away from her. "I'm a simp, that's what I am."

"You are not a simp. You love her. We protect the ones we love, especially when they're vulnerable."

"Is that why you're really here?" I'm teasing her, but she doesn't smile.

"Yes. Someone has to take care of you." She goes to the chair on the other side, pulls the laptop out of her bag, and gets to work.

I shrug and grab my phone to shoot Grayson a message.

ME

> I have new people for your rental building and a couple for the office. Send me the bill.

His reply comes in fast.

GRAYSON

> You got it. We also have extras in the office as well. Those fuckers brought the issue inside my building. I'm pissed.

I shoot him one last message.

ME

> I get it. Let me know if she needs anything.

<h1 style="text-align:center">27</h1>

<hr>

Alis

"Thank you so much, Andrew. I appreciate your collaboration on this one and you know I don't forget. Let's grab lunch soon." I hang up the phone and quickly shoot an email to my team, letting them know the state accepted our last amendment.

I lean back in my chair and stare at the plan in front of me. We will be ready to break ground in Franklin by the spring. I need to make sure we have the schedule in place for hiring and training. Dad is being extra gracious the past week, signing off on the expensive training, the costs for food for the trainees. I hate to think of the reason. The only thing that makes me feel better is that we are not just using the town of Franklin, but helping build the community as well.

The knock on the door has me snapping my head up. Weston, Leila, and Dahlia walk in.

"What are you all doing here?"

My aunt smiles. "Your father summoned us to the meeting."

"Today? This is a regular meeting."

Weston shakes his head. "Not from what he told us. He even asked me to bring Dahlia because it's important."

"What the hell is he planning now? Maybe he's adopted Fred's sour ass as his new child."

Weston and Leila laugh. Dahlia looks at the three of us. "Oh wait, that's the guy that Weston told me wanted to give the money donation to the rich kids." Then she laughs too.

"How's the Franklin project going?" Weston asks, but he's eyeing the paperwork on my desk.

"Good. We had one minor amendment but we can break ground in the spring. We are also finalizing the hiring and training schedule."

"What about the small militia Fred requested to keep everyone safe?" Leila's smile betrays her tone.

"Fred is an anal wart."

My intercom buzzes. "Alis, you have another call from Andrew Foster with the state?"

Weston takes his wife's hand and says, "We'll head to the conference room and let him know you're talking to the state if you're late."

They head out along with Leila.

I take ten minutes to finish up with Andrew and answer a few more questions for his report.

"You should get your permits in the next two weeks. So sorry for the extra call."

I reassure him. "It's good. As long as this goes through, we are golden."

"It will. You know the federal government likes to make us jump through hoops."

We hang up and I stand, put on my jacket, and make my way to the conference room. Janice is waiting outside.

"Why are you out here?" I ask.

"Your father said I am not to go in. I didn't want you to wonder why I'm not in there."

I have a feeling my father is going to pull the rug from under me. "It's okay. You can go back to your desk. I'll be there after the meeting."

As I reach for the door handle, an uneasy feeling settles in my stomach.

What's the worst that could happen? He tries to fuck up my plans again? I'll just have to work harder to get them done.

I throw the door open, and everyone is standing around the table. There are people here who don't normally attend, and one of them is my mother. She's sitting next to my chair. She smiles at me and it's so big that it's almost unsettling. Because my father has that same horror movie smile as he stands by her side. I find my anchor points, Leila and Weston, and they're both smiling and nodding.

"Son," Dad says, waving me in. "Come stand by me."

I do as he says without rolling my eyes.

"I want to start by telling all of you I still remember the day my sons were born. When I looked in their faces, I pictured this day though I didn't know which one of them would be the one. I see confusion on Alis' face, so I will get on with it. I want to announce I will be stepping away after forty years of service to this company, and in the tradition of my family, I am naming my son, Alister Weston Ellison, as the new Chief Executive Officer for Ellison Corp."

There's a ringing in my ear, and I'm not processing the words fully, but the sounds segue into applause. My dad claps my back three times, but my mom comes around and hugs me.

"I'm so proud of you," she says, lightly tapping at a tear at the corner of her eye, and stepping back into her place.

"Speech," someone yells.

A wave of cold blows inside me. "I don't know what to say."

Everyone laughs, like they get it, not realizing this is the truth.

This doesn't feel like the way I dreamed about it.

"I'll take this opportunity to hug him, then." Aunt Leila comes around and embraces me. "You don't have to say anything if you don't want to. You're the fucking boss of all these people now."

My gaze locks with my brother, who follows in her footsteps. Dahlia kisses my cheek and whispers in my ear. "You can fire Fred now."

It rips a laugh out of me and makes me snap out of the shock. I turn and whisper, "Don't tempt me."

Everyone's focused, waiting for my reaction. I don't make them wait. "Thank you, Dad, for your vote of confidence and entrusting the company to me. I promise you all to lead Ellison Corp with strength, open-mindedness, and fearlessness. I am looking forward to continuing our growth while becoming an example to all other companies with kind practices and the happiest employees... and, of course, making you all richer."

The last part gets the thunderous applause. Five minutes later, after shaking every hand in the room, we get to step out.

Leila hooks her hand on my arm as we walk out. "I think Fred may be sick."

"Don't be petty."

She shakes her head. "*You* can't be petty as CEO. As your mom, I reserve the right to be petty on your behalf."

I don't laugh. I head to my office with her and my brother. In my suite, everyone claps when I walk in. "Thank you all. I hope you know you are all coming with me to the CEO's suite."

My parents intercept us there.

"We are just proud," Mom gushes. "I cannot wait to tell all my friends. Don't make plans for tonight. We are having a dinner in your honor."

"Please don't—"

"Oh yes, we are. It's not every day my son becomes CEO." She starts talking on her phone.

My dad pulls me aside. "I know you probably would have preferred I talked to you first, but I wanted to surprise you."

"Why now? Just a few days ago, you doubted I had what it takes." I spit the words out through my teeth. I don't want to make a scene.

"You showed me you do when you made the company your priority. Thank you for being the son that listened to me. The one that puts the business above his own personal desires."

His hug is brief and perfunctory like flossing after dinner. "We'll see you tonight to celebrate. I have a present for you. Should be in your driveway when you get home."

I find my brother a few steps away.

"How does it feel?" Dahlia asks.

"Like I'm Judas."

I go inside my office and they follow me. Weston closes the door as if he can sense what's coming.

Leila comes to stand by me. "What was that about with your father?"

I chuckle. "He wanted to reward me for my good behavior."

"Christ," Weston says.

"Yeah, only a few days after he questioned if I'm qualified. But you know, I proved myself."

What will Mila think when she hears this? I wish she had been here, by my side at this moment, but she's what I had to give up to have this.

————

Alis

My parents have been smiling all night. What I thought was a family dinner is really a get together for the prominent people on the island. As my father whispered in my ear, "Everyone came to kiss the ring, son."

I don't swear like I want to. Instead, I go along and chat with everyone.

Leila, Dahlia, and Weston have been playing defense, grabbing me at different times so I can get a break and not tell anybody to fuck off.

When I get trapped with the McConnells, Dahlia cuts in.

"Excuse me," she says and turns to me. "I'm going to steal him from you so I can get a dance with the CEO."

They smile and say all the expected pleasantries. His wife even tells Dahlia how good to see her it is and that marriage agrees with her.

While I'm grateful for their acceptance of her, my tongue sours, remembering what assholes they were to Mila and her mom.

My sister-in-law must see it in my face because she takes my hand and pulls us away. "I'll bring him right back..." When we're far enough away, she whispers, "...when pigs fly. Oooh, look at a cop making pig jokes."

I chuckle. "I don't know how much longer I could maintain diplomacy. I hate that asshole and his family, but you, Detective Wicker, I love you. I'm so grateful that I'm going to buy you a Bentley."

"A Bentley?" She mock clutches her chest. "I live in the city of Baltimore. Where would I park? Just to keep it safe, you need to buy me a house in the suburbs."

We both have a laugh at that.

The laughter dries out from her face and morphs into a frown. "Are you going to be okay? Do Weston and I need to quit our jobs to make sure you don't bust a cap on a bitch?"

I nod vigorously. "I would love to see that! I need that in my life. But to answer your question, I'm a CEO with a brand new Rolls Royce. Red leather interior and everything." That was the gift my father alluded to. It even had a bow on the top, which I assume was my mother's idea. It's disgusting.

"Can't expect less from a true pimp. You can drive that thing to the yearly pimp convention."

I laugh. "Is there such a thing?"

She snorts. "Oh yeah. Fun fact, one of our regular perps dreamed of going. He had tickets, but Matt and I arrested him for possession when we were beat cops. He spent the weekend of the convention in jail. The judge couldn't see him until Monday. He had his hair permed and everything. Oops."

I'm so mesmerized and shocked by the story. She chuckles and soon we are laughing again.

"Have you seen her?"

She nods. "I saw her the day she got back. We've been keeping in touch. I get the impression you're both doing the same thing."

"What's that?"

"Burying yourselves in work."

"I have no choice since I have a company to run and I imagine it is the same for her with her team."

Dahlia's brows lift. "Yeah, you're both really busy. Her mom offered to cook for me. I'm going to take her up on it."

Meri never offered to cook for me. All I got was suspicious looks and veiled disapproval.

And there was the *"I'm sorry"* and the tight hug I can still feel in my bones. It was like Leila's, but it surprised the shit out of me.

"You should go. Never turn down good food."

"Or the opportunity to spy for my handsome brother-in-law?" Her eyes sparkle and I don't know if she means that or not.

"Are you teasing me?"

She shrugs. "Maybe. But I have to say we are grateful for the additional people you hired. Knox picked well-trained guys."

"Glad she is safe." I say it like it doesn't burn a hole in my chest that I can't see it for myself. That I can't hold her hand if she's afraid.

She opens her mouth, but the song ends, and she looks over my shoulder. "Your Dad is standing with Fred and a young woman. I think they're waiting for you."

I turn her around, walking the opposite way. We find the refreshment table and a couple of minutes later, my mom joins us.

"Alis, come with me. Your father and I want to introduce you to someone."

"Who?" I ask.

"I don't think you've met Fred's oldest daughter."

Fuck no.

"Alis was about to walk outside with me." Dahlia presses her hand to her belly. "I'm just not feeling well. Weston is dancing, and I don't want to interrupt him." Then she turns to my mom. "I've been so nauseous lately. I don't know what it may be. Do you mind?"

Mom goes pale and shakes her head slowly.

I take Dahlia's arm and walk outside with her. We barely make it past the door before she presses her fist against her mouth. "I swear it's her biggest nightmare."

"What is?"

"A pregnancy for us."

It hits me then and I laugh. "You're so bad."

Weston and Leila join us a few minutes later.

"Mom said you're not feeling well?" he asks his wife.

"She's worried you're going to be a dad," I say.

My brother's eyes almost bulge out of his head.

"I told her I was nauseous to save Alis from getting engaged."

Leila rolls her eyes. "That's why she's been trying to get me to know that boring girl. She's a Lindsay Summerville wannabe. Except Lindsay is actually fun and didn't care anyone knew about her dating most of the island."

"Own your lifestyle," Dahlia adds.

"Exactly. And I don't know what Wes and Christine are thinking. Alis doesn't need that wet noodle anymore. He already got the company."

He's trying to marry me off to a McConnell? "I'm not entertaining that bullshit. I'm tired of them trying to control me. Is this the reason he stepped back? Does he think I'm just going to do what he wants? I'm going in there right now and disabuse him of his notion."

Leila touches my shoulder to stop me.

"Let's take a walk," Weston says, and doesn't wait for me to respond.

He walks toward the end of the patio. I follow him into the woods. We stop at our favorite tree as kids.

"I miss the days when this place was actually enjoyable for me. Now, when I come here, it's for a bunch of shit. Except for tonight. I don't mind tonight because it's celebrating you and the new era for the company."

I don't know what to say. "I'm disappointing everyone."

"Why? Are you going to give in to bullshit practices and start playing politics now that you're *the man?*"

I chuckle. "God knows I'm only waiting for all the paperwork to go through so I can make changes. I have a surprise for all of Dad's people. They will not be working around me. They've had their time, and I need fresh blood in those positions."

"Then you have your plan. You're implementing your vision. You don't have to do what Dad wants anymore. That's your dream, Alis."

I drop myself on the ground by the trunk of the tree. There's something about being with the one person you can open completely to. Someone who knows your heart and your head. "It was. Now all I dream about is... her."

I can't even say her name. And that's a problem I can't seem to cope with.

"Mila," my brother says, staring at me.

I nod.

"I don't want to lecture you, because it's fucking annoying when people do that. But there's nowhere it says that you can't have her and Ellison Corp. Dad may have threatened you, but he's not in charge. When all the paperwork goes through, you're free. He played dirty with you, showing up in your house, and saying things he knew she would hear. Now you can pay him back dirty."

I look at my brother in a new light. I never heard Weston speak like this. "Who are you?"

He laughs. "Someone that gets you. I wouldn't give up Dahlia for the world. The time we were broken up was some of the most agonizing of my life. I lived my life, went to work, and all the motions, but I went home missing her. I was miserable. You are too. I see it."

I look away. I am. I miss her so much it hurts. "How does someone you know only a few months get such a hold in your life? Six months ago, I didn't have a clue she existed other than in Maddie's stories. And when I hooked up with her, I figured I could put her away, like I've done with so many others."

"But you can't."

I shake my head. "Why? I don't understand that."

Weston shrugs. "Who knows? It's all about a moment, I guess. Dahlia was mean to me, but I couldn't shake the image of her shot and still worried about her brother. I couldn't shake her eyes from my memory. You know?"

I do and I nod. I keep playing moments in my head and sometimes I embarrass even myself.

"When I met her, I felt she was for the one for me." I touch my heart. "After all the shit we've been through and seeing her power through it, now I'm positive she is the one for me. I think I'm obsessed with her."

"You may be. It's all part of it. The shit is not really logical."

It's never felt like it.

"We're talking too much about feelings."

"You're feeling them, and it's not like you're talking to someone else."

It's true. I can admit it to him.

"I'm lost."

"You're not, Al. If you had her but had to work somewhere else, you could do it. You have the company, but you can't put her away. I think you know what you need to do, and you have the backup to pull it off. You already have Leila and me. You just need to decide."

He's right. Life is not fair, and I don't need to be. I'm going to deal with people the way they dealt with me.

I'm going to get my girl, even if I have to fight the whole world, the universe, and her, until I convince her.

28

Mila

My phone vibrates in the pocket of my sweater. I pull it out and it's a message from Sandy.

SANDY

Girl, it's going down.

I look around at our table, ensuring everyone's attention is on their work, but to my surprise, all my team members are on their phones.

ME

What is happening?

SANDY

Legal eagle getting his wings clipped.

I read the message twice. Huh?

ME

ES getting canned.

I swish the initials around in my head and then it hits me. Elias Saunders is getting fired.

MILA

Sandy's next message is swift.

SANDY

> Security is waiting to escort him out. He's clearing his office.

I need to get the team through the last page of comps before they get sidetracked by the tea. I send Sandy a quick text letting her know I'll call her when I'm done here.

"Team, let's—"

"OhmahGod. Elias Saunders is getting the boot," Liza announces.

Several gasps echo in the room.

"They sent security for him," Mary says.

Everyone is shaking their heads.

Liza's frown deepens. "He's been working here for so many years. Wow, I guess when the company is done with you, they're really done."

"Or maybe he shouldn't have been *screwing* his mentee?" Greg says, and everyone turns to him. I look at all of them and all I see are hungry hyenas, ready to tear people apart with gossip.

When did Greg turn into one of them? Since our last meeting with Grayson, I find his comments more and more grating. And though I've tried to set up a meeting to speak to him, we keep having to cancel it for one reason or another. I want to get back to the times where our interactions were easy.

I clear my throat to get their attention. "Everyone, let's finish reviewing the last page of comps and finally be done with this part of the project."

"Shouldn't you be going upstairs as part of management?" Greg's question irks me because that's what they want, me to be gone so they can gossip.

I level him with a look. "I'm exactly where I'm supposed to be, making sure my team rectifies our errors and has something ready for Grayson like we promised him. Now let's get this done."

No one says a thing, but their gazes are burning a hole in my head like lasers. Greg stares at me, his eyes like a wounded animal darting to the side.

"I guess this is where we're all supposed to pretend we're sad? When everyone here, including management, used to gossip about them."

"Greg, this is inappropriate."

His lip curls. "It's been inappropriate. Don't you remember when they were practically fucking on the conference room table? I guess now that Maddie's dead we—"

The gasp echoes around the room.

"Enough. In case you forgot, this is a place of business and we are here to work."

Mary stands and moves away from him.

Phones keep pinging but in the next fifteen minutes we reach the end.

"Mary, please incorporate all edits from today. I want to see it laid out in presentation form before we send it back to Grayson. Have a good evening, everyone," I say.

I adjourn the meeting and everyone exits except Mary.

When the door closes behind Carter, she turns to me. "I'm really uncomfortable with Greg. Sometimes, it's like I don't know him anymore. He says really inappropriate things lately, not just today, and he keeps spreading all sorts of gossip. I want to report it to HR."

I don't side eye her like I want to. She and Greg are thick as thieves. I guess when your career is impacted by the company you keep, the tables turn quickly.

I don't fake sympathy I don't feel and instead get down to business. "Tell me what he's been saying."

"This morning he said I was on the rag because I was nagging him about getting his data for the meeting. He keeps talking about Maddie being a slut and how she was getting around. He thinks you've changed since you became CMO and all the power went to your head and you now you think you're the only one that knows how to do anything. I heard him tell Carter that you're a... I can't repeat the word."

When we're done, I stay behind in the conference room and email the HR representative for my team. She replies on our office messenger.

This is the fifth complaint today. I was about to email you. He will get a visit from HR by the end of the day.

My mouth drops. A visit from HR means he's about to get canned.

She gives me instructions to stay away from him and will follow up with steps for me to follow. The company is getting ready to take action against him and it's a shame because he's a good guy. I'm packing up my laptop to return to my office when the intercom in the middle of the table buzzes.

"Mila, there's someone here to see you."

I walk out of the conference room, taking a couple of cleansing breaths. These meetings are always so loaded now. I hate them. I look back at my staff and they're huddling in clumps. No doubt gossiping and sharing details. In the past, I would have lingered to hear what they had to say, but since my life became fodder for gossip, it doesn't hit the same. I go to our receptionist's desk.

"Who is waiting for me?" In my eagerness to leave the conference room, I didn't even ask.

"Ms. Lindsay Summerville."

My stomach tightens, my hands gripping my notepad. *Why is she here?* What could she want with me? She told Alis she wanted to talk to me but about what? I might as well find out what the fuck she wants. I stroll into my office and find her standing on the other side of my desk, looking at my wall art.

My first impression of Lindsay is much like the one I had of Madison when I met her. Gorgeous, stylish, but she has a downright predatory look in her eye Maddie never had. My spine stiffens, but I'm not going to punk out.

"Hi Lindsay," I say.

"Thank you for seeing me. I don't normally show up unannounced anywhere, but I don't think a scheduled meeting would have worked between us. I didn't want to give the media or anyone else the chance to speculate or try to make something out of it."

"I understand." I take my chair behind the desk and invite her to do the same across from me. "I would rather do anything than receive more media attention."

She nods. "That I get. I think you got the second worst part of this deal, after my sister."

If she had punched me in the stomach, it wouldn't hurt this badly. It's true, I've been feeling sorry for myself and yet Madison is dead. "I can't say enough how sorry I am for your loss."

"Thank you." She lets out a long breath. "I hate that, you know? I fucking hate having to acknowledge anyone's kindness about this. It forces me to acknowledge constantly that she's gone. It's one thing to feel it and another to be reminded."

Her words dig so deep in my chest, like they're ripping flesh. "She didn't deserve this."

She rolls her eyes. "Oh God. Don't tell me you're a goody two shoes."

Her tone makes my back ramrod straight. "What?"

"I hope you're not one of those chicks that pretend to be teddy bears. I'm so sweet and so good and even though I'm going through hell, I think of those who have it worse... but I'll fuck your man if you leave him around me." Her voice is monotone meets valley girl, and she lands the blow flawlessly.

As sad as I am for her loss and pain, I'm done being anyone's chew toy. "Oh. I see what this is. No, I'm not a teddy, or a goody two shoes. And I did fuck him."

She smiles. "You still are."

I'm not anymore, but I don't own this bitch an explanation.

"Yeah." I say it with my whole chest, staring her in the eye. Because I don't regret him and she doesn't know we're not together.

"That's why she liked you. You weren't one of those poor girls who got meek around her."

"Okay." I lean forward this time.

She shrugs. "Those are her words. You know Maddie could be bitchy. Just because she's dead, we're not going to act like she wasn't."

The light that crosses her eyes is downright sad. The pain, loss, grief, all are there.

"You miss her."

"Like someone cut off my hand and I don't know how to get around without it." She stares at her left hand like she needs reassurance that it's there. That's the most heartbreaking thing I've ever heard.

"I miss her too."

Her gaze snaps to my face and I think she's going to say another nasty thing. She dabs at the corner of her eyes. "She liked you and I got a little jealous when she told me that she was going to play our game with you."

"What game?" I ask.

"Normally, I'm the one that would run interference for her, be her distraction. She did the same for me."

They even had a name for it. "I didn't know we were playing a game."

She clears her throat. "I know. She was just crazy about him. And you know Maddie. She had to keep all her things. Elias, her love. Alis, the man she had been low-key obsessed with until she got him. The only thing she needed was Weston." She stops and tilts her head. "You knew she never got over him, right?"

I nod. "It was in the way she talked. But she said she was going to marry Alis."

Her sigh is so deep. "At first, that was her plan, but it wouldn't have been possible. By the end, she was too hung up on Elias. I don't know what kind of crack was on that man's dick. I asked her all the time."

I'm at a loss for words. "I don't know what she saw in him, either."

"He worshiped her. She said even the way he fucked her was rough, but reverent. She couldn't even get with Alis because she was banging Elias so many times. Anyway, I didn't come here to talk about Maddie's sex life. I'm sure you knew about it."

Yeah, Maddie talked about sex with Elias all the time.

"Why did you want to see me?"

"I want you to know that I don't blame you. I saw the danger of playing our game with you. I told her not to get you involved. That it would backfire. Too bad that finding out about the two of you is not the worst thing could've happened that day."

She swallows.

Her pain is so blatant I can barely breathe.

"I never intended for it to happen. We got carried away."

Lindsay laughs. It's soft and sad, but the humor is there. "She put you in a romantic restaurant and alone with him. He's fucking hot, has always been. Everyone always loved Weston because of his looks and his heart. He's like a true hero. But all the girls on the island, we all wanted to get into bed with Alis. I did until Maddie and him became an item. He walks around beating everyone with that sexual energy, as you know. Anyway, she thought he would never fall for you. My Maddie had a little ego in her. She was bitchy but good. She didn't deserve this."

I shake my head. "She didn't."

"When you called me, I thought she was sulking about the job. She always worried you would get the job over her, even after all the coaching and strings Elias was pulling."

I freeze. "Strings?"

"Yeah, he was talking to people in HR about her and trying to get her an edge, but unfortunately, he no longer had any influence with Grayson. Maddie said something happened between them and that it was Elias' fault. It was the reason they couldn't be seen out in public."

"It's against company policy." I don't tell her Grayson just fired him. It's not my place.

She shrugged. "It devastated her when Grayson called her to tell her he didn't select her for the promotion. He didn't tell her it was you, but she suspected it. You were the only one with talent that matched her own. I think deep down, she realized she had fallen off.

All she cared about was him. Even though she knew all there was to know about him and she was sleeping with that other guy."

"What guy?"

Her laugh is soft. "You don't have to keep her secrets anymore. She's gone and they don't matter. You know she was sleeping with someone else."

"I didn't know there was someone else until Alis mentioned it." The memory hits me from the night at the restaurant. "Wait, she texted me to say she had another session that night."

"For Maddie, sessions are with different people. Rounds are with one person. What did she tell you about it?"

I shrug. "She said she had another session and would tell me about it later. I assumed it was the usual Maddie things about Elias. The sex was mind blowing, positions and stuff." I flip my palm up. "What did she tell you?"

"She never told me much about the other guy. She talked about the sex being so unexpectedly good. She said she was using him because he was the key to getting some information so she and Elias could be free. But he flipped the script on her. It flabbergasted her that someone so bland could dominate her like he did and how unexpectedly amazing the sex was. I was so intrigued, but she wouldn't say anything else. I learned about him in her computer diary. It's taken so long for me to crack the password, but I did. I just want to know the why."

"The why and the who," I say. "You should turn the diary over to the cops."

"I will. I wanted to talk to you first. I was hoping you could tell me more, but since you can't, I'll let you be. If you think of anything, please tell me. You don't owe me anything, but we both love her, and I think this may have something to do with the way she died."

"Why do you think that?"

"My sister didn't keep secrets from me. This is the only one. And she didn't even trust her diary with the full truth."

29

Mila

I don't know how I let Dahlia Wicker convince me to do this, but after my afternoon encounter with Lindsay, the firing of Elias, and all the office gossip that followed, I needed to cleanse my palate. I'm not sure I am ready for this. I'm already regretting it. I should just be home in bed or watching a movie with *Mami*. The door opens and my heart drops. There's a man standing behind Dahlia. *Alis*. My heart speeds so fast and my hand goes to my chest. Then, he turns around. It's not him, it's Weston.

"Hi," I say, feeling like a complete idiot.

She hugs me, and then he does, and I start feeling more at ease.

"How are you holding up?" Weston asks.

"Hanging in there." It's awkward as hell though because I keep thinking how alike and different he and his brother are. There's warmth in his gaze but none of the edge Alis has.

"You know you can count on us."

I nod.

Dahlia clears her throat. "You got to go. No boys allowed."

He kisses her in a way that makes my skin tingle with envy.

"I'll see you ladies later," he says and walks out of the door.

"Come on in. The girls are already here."

And my anxiety goes up ten decibels. I haven't been around new people in a while, and these women probably know everything there is to know about me. I no longer care what strangers have to say, but to be trapped in a house with them makes me uneasy, almost sick.

"I don't have many friends, but the ones I have are trustworthy and not assholes," Dahlia whispers as we head into the living room.

I blink at her and nod. No one likes to think their friends are assholes, but I believe her. She's been good to me.

We make it to her family room and two women are already there. Right away, you can see the they're related. They look up at us and smile.

"Mila, these are my friends, Saona and Sierra. Two more Dominicans for you to meet. They're sisters. Sierra is also Matt's wife. She's carrying his seed, in case you are wondering."

Saona laughs and stands to shake my hand. "Nice to meet you. Glad you joined us. The more Dominicans, the better."

Sierra pushes off, but I move closer and offer my hand. "Please don't stand."

"Thank you. I can do it, but I appreciate it. This is my third kid, but the other two were not this big."

"You married Sasquatch. What did you expect?" Dahlia says.

Sierra chuckles. "Matt and her are like brother and sister. They constantly tease each other. Just so you know. Also, I apologize if he treated you like a perp at any point. I wasn't here to keep him in check and from my understanding, she is worse than he is." She hooks a thumb at Dahlia, who snorts.

"He's been really nice. She's definitely the hard ass of the two."

"Aww." Dahlia hands me a drink. "What did I tell you? She's definitely one of us."

I sit on the love seat across from the sisters and sip.

"Okay," Sierra says, looking at me. "We know everything that's going on. I read Neighborhood Chatter, The Shade, and watch that bitch ass Lamonde. I think what's happening to you is pure bullshit, and I'm really sorry about your friend."

I nod. "Thank you."

"You don't deserve the grief and terror you're receiving," Saona chimes in. "And now that we got that out of the way, we can enjoy our evening. We just don't want there to be an elephant in the room."

"Thank you," I say again.

And they tell me about what they do and talk about their kids. Saona has one child and another on the way, even though she is not showing as much as her sister.

"It's nice that you're pregnant together," I say.

They look at each other and the look they exchange is loaded with warmth. "Yeah, we like that. If she had not been there for my first pregnancy, I would have gone nuts."

Sierra snorts. "She was so good at it. I was a mess with my first pregnancy. It was rough from beginning to end, which sums up my Emmi. She's a complicated little thing."

But there's such pride in her voice.

"How did you meet Detective Hunter?"

"Oh God. Don't call him by his title. It goes to his head. Mind you, Dahlia and I had to drag him to take the detective exam." She rolls her eyes. "Anyway, we knew each other as kids, but then he moved away. We connected here a couple of years ago."

"He was like a sociopath before her. That's how we got along. But after reconnecting with her, he just won't shut up. He full on opened up. You don't see it because you haven't hung out with him socially."

"He was very serious at the station," I say.

"That's a facade," Dahlia says.

Saona agrees. "Sierra and Dahlia are grumpy, and their husbands are the sunshine of their relationships."

They laugh.

"What about you and Weston's brother? I hope that's still going on because the two of you are hot and someone needs to fuck him until he's unconscious."

"Sierra." Saona shakes her head. "I would blame it on the pregnancy, but no, this is how she really is."

Shock segues into a laugh. "It's okay. But no, we are not together."

"Why? Is he an asshole?"

"Sierra..." Dahlia starts, but I wave a hand.

I don't know why I tell them, but maybe I'm just tired and I need to talk about it. I can't do that with my mom without her feeling guilty or giving me some Bible passage. I'm so fucking tired of hearing this too shall pass.

"No, he's not an asshole. Not to me. But it wouldn't work. We didn't start right and with everything that happened with Maddie, it's just messy things happening one after the other."

"What happened to her is awful, but neither of you made that happen. And people need to mind their fucking business. No one knows what's in a relationship unless they live in it." Sierra takes a sip of water after saying all that. The other two women nod.

"Yeah, but we are too different, you know?"

"So are we from our men. Jax, my husband, and I had so many mishaps in the beginning. Thank God for the bed-burning sex. You should say screw everything else. You like that man. He obviously likes you. "

God, I miss bed-burning sex. Now I'm miserable all over again.

I offer to help Dahlia bring out the food. I don't want to look like I'm sulking.

"Sierra means well. She just blunt."

"Like *you*, but don't worry. I like both of them. It's been a while since I've been with a bunch of girls like this. Since I moved to Maryland, I've lost touch with friends and Maddie and Sandy were the only ones I friended here."

She pulls out a tray full of empanadas. "I never knew how important it was to have a group like this until I met these girls. Well, Sierra forced herself on me."

I'm jealous of that. "Yeah, it makes things easier when you share. I feel a little better tonight."

"Good. That's what I wanted."

"Thank you for inviting me."

"Of course. Like I said millions of times, you can call me anytime."

"Thank you." I go for it and ask what I really want to know. "How is he?"

"He was named CEO of his company like he's always wanted, but he's miserable."

My heart sinks because this is another nail in the coffin. "Why miserable? It was his dream."

She stops fussing with the food and turns to look at me like I'm stupid. "He's miserable for the same reason you are. Because you have your dream job, he has his, and you don't have each other. That's what usually happens when people love each other and are not where they're supposed to be, by each other's side."

My spine stiffens. Her words feel accusatory. "You don't understand."

She puts a hand on my shoulder. "I'm not blaming you. I'm just stating the facts. I know a little thing or two about this kind of situation. I also know a lot about dealing with Weston's parents. I didn't always make the right decision."

I sigh. "Obviously, you did something right. You're together."

"It took me humbling myself and admitting I made the wrong choices. Thank God the man has the patience of a suffering saint. I don't know how he puts up with my grumpy ass sometimes."

"Because he loves you and you obviously adore him."

She smiles. "Yeah. Anyway, hang in there and keep an open mind with Alis. Thankfully, he and Weston are like Leila and not their parents. Wait until you meet her in person. If you love Saona and Sierra, you will worship her."

She says it like it's bound to happen, but I don't argue with her. I want tonight to continue to be light.

"We need your phone number," Sierra announces when we come back into the room. "I need to bug the shit out of you via text."

I recite it for her.

Dahlia serves everyone empanadas. "You don't know what you just did. She's going on a quest to get you laid. Unless you've already got someone."

I can't even think about that with anyone else right now. But the time will come when I need to get under someone to get over him.

"No, I'm in between."

Sierra smiles. "I already like you. You're not resigned."

I burst out laughing.

After saving their phone numbers, I switch to my text app and shoot two messages to Alis.

ME

Congratulations on your appointment. I know how hard you worked for this.

I'm happy your dream came true.

I drop my phone on the couch, and we eat, and Dahlia and I drink sangria. The rest of the evening is fun. The girls share stories about how they met their husbands. All seem so happy that I get a little heartsick.

Saona offers me a ride home. Her husband is picking her and Sierra up. I can get my truck tomorrow.

When we step out into the cold, her husband is outside. He's huge like a football player, but I can barely concentrate on meeting him because on the other side of the street, outside a black BMW, there's a man leaning against it. Not any man...

"There's your man," Sierra says.

I can't take my eyes off him as he crosses the street and comes to stand before me. His gaze is scorching over me, leaving me bare and unsettled.

"Good evening, everyone."

The women and husband say hello.

I manage a "Hi," like my heart isn't punishing my ribs.

"Can we talk?" he asks

"Sure." I turn around to the girls and Saona's husband. "I—"

Sierra hugs me. "I'll call you tomorrow." Then she whispers in my ear. "Remember what I said, unconscious."

I don't get to say it's nothing like that because Saona hugs me. "I would follow her advice. We'll talk tomorrow."

I wave at her husband and cross the street with Alis. He opens the door for me and then goes around. Knox is a few feet away and gets in his car as well.

"I didn't know you knew Saona and Sierra."

"I just met them tonight."

"Oh. You seemed like old friends."

I frown. "It felt like it, too. Why are you here?"

"I'm here to kidnap you."

I chuckle. "Kidnappers don't tell their victims they're being kidnapped. They also don't leave behind witnesses. Anyway, where are you taking me?"

He smiles. "Where no one can see us."

———

Alis

"Seriously, where are you taking me?"

It's the first thing she's said in the past twenty minutes. I guess I should feel good because she's comfortable enough with me to have ridden this far with no doubts.

"We are going to a friend's property where we can't be seen or photographed and where we can talk in peace."

"Okay." Her voice betrays no emotion, and she's way too quiet tonight. Does she no longer feel the need to talk to me?

"You don't have to be afraid, Mila. Knox is following us, and he's there to protect you."

"I'm not worried, Alis. I know you won't hurt me. Not on purpose..."

"What the hell does that even mean?" I ask.

"Nothing bad. We can hurt each other without meaning to. I know I hurt you when I left your house. I hurt myself too."

I nod. "True."

"Congratulations again. I texted you when I found out."

"I was on the way to Baltimore already. And thank you. It was a surprise."

"It's a great thing. You'll do amazing things for the company. You can put your vision in place."

Her words mean more than anything, but I am so tired of hearing my about vision. Did I go around like an asshole whining about what I wanted to do all my life?

"Did Dahlia set me up? Did she tell you I was there?"

"No. I was on my way to your place. Weston called, and he mentioned you were at his house."

"Oh."

Again, I can discern nothing from her voice. "Does it bother you?"

She shakes her head. "I just wonder if this is making things harder for us."

"Probably."

We get through the gates and check in. I make sure both Knox and the cop car get through, but instruct them to stay in the front lot. I park, exit on my end, and go open the door for her.

She doesn't hesitate and takes my hand so I can help her out. She grips mine tight and lets me go way too soon. We walk down a lamp lit path.

"What is this place?"

"A friend of mine owns this property. They use it for parties and weddings sometimes. It's exclusive. It's not accessible to the public, and it's secure. I didn't tell anyone where we were going."

"It's so pretty," she says.

"It's nicer during the day."

"It has to be something. I don't think I've seen any of these many stars from where I live. It reminds me of the sky over your house."

She ducks her head and keeps walking.

"I'm glad you remember it. I keep hoping you think of our time together like I do."

She doesn't look at me. "I try not to."

It's like a knife twisting in my chest. "Trust me, I understand why you don't think about it."

"I never said I don't think about it. I said I try not to." Her accent flares out, coloring every word.

"Do you ever succeed?"

She lets out an exasperated breath. "No. It's always there, mocking me, reminding me. Kind of like you right now."

"I thought you said it didn't bother you."

"It doesn't. It just complicates things. I was working through it and now you went and reset the clock. It was hard to get used to not seeing you or touching you. I can't imagine starting from zero again. I don't want to wonder how I'll feel tomorrow when we're apart again."

"What if we don't have to do that? What if we don't have to say goodbye again?"

She closes her eyes. "Alis, this is just not conducive to—"

"Can you just let me say what I came to say?"

Her voice is contentious. "Go ahead. I'm not stopping you."

"But you're griping like I forced you to come along."

"No, you didn't force me. No one can force me to do what I don't want to do."

"Then you left me because you wanted to?" And it's fucked up because I'm making her mad on purpose, but I hate her composure.

She goes still, her eyes growing cold. "What did I tell you about gaslighting me? I mean, what the hell is this?"

"A warning. I came here to warn you."

"About what?"

"I'm not giving up on you, on us. I'm going to fight for you even if the person I have to fight the hardest is you."

Her mouth drifts open and she starts walking again.

"Do you have nothing to say?"

"What can I say, Alis? You just said I have no say."

"You have all the fucking say in the world. Tell me you don't want me to fight for you, that I mean nothing to you, and I'll leave you alone."

"You know very well I can't do that."

"Why?" I insist.

"I don't have to tell you what you already know."

"Maybe I want to hear it." I hate the pain in my voice. "I need to hear you say it."

"No. It doesn't help us. This is not our time. There's so much shit between us."

I grab her hand and stare into her eyes. "Say it."

She shakes her head.

"Fine, I'll say it. I love you. I'm not letting you go. I couldn't give a bigger shit about being CEO and everything I've gained in the past few days because I'm hung up on the one thing I don't have. That's you, Mila."

She sucks a gasp of air. But I don't let go and I don't relent.

"Six months ago, I had no idea you existed. You were only mine for a short time and now I don't have you and everything feels hollow. The things I wanted all my life don't compare to the one I've only wanted for three months. I can picture myself working somewhere else that's not Ellison Corp. I can't picture spending even a few minutes with a woman that is not you. I can't picture my life without you."

Her face is wet with tears and I let go of her because I said what I needed to say.

"I'm not asking you to be with me today. We can wait until all this shit settles. I just need you to know that I'll be fighting for us when the time comes. That I'm more than happy to give up my whole world to be in yours."

I take a step back from her, but she closes the distance between us and reaches for my face. I think she's going to kiss me and my skin vibrates in preparation. Instead, she wipes my face, her hands gliding over my cheeks. I didn't know I was crying. Then she throws her arms around me.

"When the time comes, I will not fight you."

Part of me is relieved, the other part is disappointed. She's putting us off.

"I'll fight with you... for us. I just want all of this to be over."

"What if it's never over?"

"It has to end. I can't live in this uncertainty forever."

I hold her for I don't know how long. When we head home, it feels more uncertain than ever, but her hand tightens around mine the closer we get to her place.

I park in the front and walk her through the entrance and into the reception area.

"I've only had to come in through here once," I say.

"I see this part when we get our mail and some deliveries, since not everyone can come all the way through."

The man at the front desk intercepts us. "Ms. Rosario, I just called your suite number. A Spencer Grayson sent an important package for you."

A package from Grayson? This late at night?

Her mom comes in as the guy reaches under the desk and hands Mila the package.

"Mom, what are you doing here?"

Her mom looks from her to me in confusion. "I came to pick up the package from your boss."

My eyes go to the brown box in Mila's hand and the word fragile printed outside of it.

No one's supposed to know Mila's living here. Grayson would never...

My heart takes off in a desperate gallop inside my chest, barreling up, and trampling over thought. I swallow and say, "Mila, give me that package."

My voice is soft, and she frowns.

She looks from me to the box in her hand. "What? Why?"

I keep my voice low but firm. "Please hand it to me."

Her eyes round and she stares at it. Her hand shaking and I don't want her to drop it.

"Give it to me," I insist.

She shakes her head, her eyes glazed like she's looking right through me.

I walk over to her and take it from her hand.

"No," she whispers, gripping it.

"Let it go. It will be okay. Trust me." I take it from her and walk to the door. I can't hear anything but the drumming in my chest. At the door, I fling it away from me, toward the middle of the street. Next thing I know, there's a loud boom, and the earth shakes under my feet. I'm knocked back into the reception desk. I land on my side. I twist my head around, looking for Mila, but she's close, crawling her way to me. She's mouthing something, but I can't hear her over the loud ringing in my ears. I stand and offer my hand to her. Her mom is with the attendant. We look at the street and the spot where the package fell.

It was a bomb. A bomb meant for her.

I stare at her face, touching it, feeling my way through it. I grab her hands and palm them. She held that fucking package. It could've exploded. She could've died. I pull her to me, hugging her tight. I don't know which of us trembling more. And I see her mom clutching her chest. And she could've died too. That package could've made it inside their place.

That fucker won't stop until she's dead.

30

———

Mila

Everything is eerily quiet, despite the amount of people outside the office. All I can hear is the sound of my erratic heart. I don't know who's shaking more, my mom or me? And it's layered too. It's part of the drop in temperature. It's gotten cold in the past hour. The door to reception is wide open, with cops coming in and out.

A bomb could have exploded in our apartment and killed us. I held it in my hands. I can't believe I gave it to Alis. The seconds it took for him to get to the door of the complex and fling it away felt like the longest hours of my life. What if it had all gone wrong? What if it had exploded on him?

My brain is on repeat, watching him throw the box and falling back on the floor. I still remember calling his name and not hearing him answer. I try to push it away.

Every minute drags out as we wait for the police to collect the evidence and come to question us. Dahlia and Matt got here a few minutes ago. They came to check in that we were okay, but told us they'll be back.

Alis keeps pacing the length of the office. Carl's hands are shaking around the mug of tea. He's going to spill it. My mom is glued to my side. She's keeping her composure.

"Are you okay?" I ask her.

Her fingers tighten around my arm. "Someone tried to kill you."

Again. It's becoming a routine.

This is just not about me, though. "You could've died too. And Alis."

I look up at him, and he just keeps pacing. He hasn't looked at me in a while and I'm dying to thank him and tell him how he saved us all, but I can't get the words out. And he needs some space. I will hang back and let him work this out, at least until we can talk alone.

"Okay," Matt says, walking in with Dahlia on his heels.

Her gaze lasers between me and my mom and bounces back to Alis. "Are you guys hanging in there?"

I nod for me and my mom, but Alis says nothing.

A couple of other police officers join us and each takes one of us.

Dahlia works with my mom. Matt pulls me aside. The other two detectives work with Alis and Carl.

Matt and I go stand on the opposite side of the reception area from my mom.

"Tell me what happened," he asks, opening his notepad.

"Um... I was out. Alis drove me home. Because I rarely come through here, he was walking me all the way to my unit."

He jots down a few words. "Where do you usually come in?"

"I go through the security gate and park near my unit in the back."

He nods and writes some more. "Tell me what happened next."

"Carl said he had just called my unit because there was a package for me from my employer. He handed it to me." I shudder again. I can still feel its weight in my hand and it could have killed us all.

"Does your employer send you packages here?"

I shake my head. "No, but I wasn't thinking. God, I'm so stupid."

I run my shaky hands through my hair, but Matt's hand closes on my wrist. "You're not stupid. This is something you were not expecting. Any of you. Now, can you please stop beating yourself up so we can get all the facts? We need to catch this delivery guy."

"As he handed it to me, my mom walked in. She received the call and just came to get it for me. That's when Alis asked me to hand him the package. At first, I didn't know why, but he repeated it."

My breath stalls, and I need a second to compose myself.

"Did you hear any sounds coming from the package?"

I can only shake my head.

"Please tell me the rest."

"I saw his face, the fear, and I didn't want to give it to him, but he asked again. And I handed it over. He walked to the front door and threw it on to the street. Then, there was a loud noise, and he fell to the ground. I thought... I thought maybe he got hit."

My breath is shaky and Matt retrieves my bottle of water from where I was sitting and hands it to me.

"Did you fall?"

"We all did. Carl called 911. Alis called Dahlia to let her know."

"Did you see anyone as you were coming into the building?"

"No, I was out all evening. I was at Dahlia's. After I left, I met up with Alis and we went for a ride."

"Were you expecting to see him tonight?"

I shake my head. "He came to talk. His brother told him where I was."

"How long were you guys gone?"

"Why are you asking me that? You can't think—"

"I don't think he has anything to do with this, but I need to know because the timing is almost perfect. The package had just gotten delivered. You were in the lobby minutes afterward."

"Yeah, right place, right time. Lucky me."

"Mila, did you get any weird emails or texts today?"

I shake my head. "It was pretty quiet. I went to work, came home, and got ready to go hang out."

He nods. "Thank you. We are going to look at the surveillance videos here and out on the street. We should be able to see who delivered the box."

He stands. I open my mouth to ask how long that's going to take when I look over at my mom. She's swiping tears away while still shaking. Dahlia has a hand on her shoulder.

"Can I take her to our unit, please?"

"Soon. We are doing a sweep of the apartment to make sure it's safe. Your neighbors are all being kept in their units. There is no reason to suspect there's any danger on the premises. We just want to make sure."

I nod. "Thank you."

I cross the room and sit by my mom. I drape an arm around her shoulder, but I'm close enough to hear Alis' conversation with one of the other detectives.

"I didn't know something was wrong," he says, his shoulders rigid, his voice charged. "In that moment I asked myself, why would her employer send her a package at home?"

"That's not so weird."

"No one's supposed to know she is here. Her employer knows that. He wouldn't blow her cover that way. He knows she's already in danger."

The detective purses his lips. "You thought about all that in that split second moment."

"Yes," Alis practically spits at him. "She's been in danger for months now. She has a police escort and a bodyguard."

"Where were they?"

"I'm not sure about the police escort. They're supposed to be close by. One of her bodyguards was going to meet us inside. He was parking the car. The others were outside."

"You seem to know a lot about her safety measures."

Alis' back goes rigid. "What the fuck is that supposed to mean?"

"You said you showed up unannounced. You took her somewhere and almost to the minute she comes back, there's a package delivered. She misses the delivery guy, but you knew there's something wrong with the package. You're the one that takes it from her hands and you're the one that throws it where it explodes but doesn't hurt anyone."

My mother gasps, and I stand and cross the distance, but not before Alis reaches back and swings at the cop. Thankfully, Matt is there to intercept it.

"Seriously, Abbott?" Dahlia jumps in the middle and presses a hand on Alis' chest. "Step back."

A few uniforms walk back into the room. One of them raises a thumb. "Clear."

"Ramirez, escort Alis, Mila, and her mom all back to Ms. Rosario's unit. It's been swept and safe to be there. Knox is outside waiting." She said the last staring right at Alis.

He turns around and hooks his arms through my arm and then my mom's. We walk out of the room.

Knox is right by the door. "This is so fucked. We were standing right there." The anger on his face is more than I can take.

I walk faster; so do my mom and Alis. The minute we are inside the unit, he locks the door and my mom collapses on the couch.

"Look, I'm sorry I lost it out there. What he was insinuating crossed the line. I would never—"

Mami halts him with her hand up in the universal stop sign. "You almost died today. Just like we almost did. That cop was stuck asking stupid questions, but that's his job. He wasn't there to see the fear in your face when Mila held the box. I lost a few years of my life…"

She sobs and I go sit by her, holding her.

"I'm okay, *Mami*. We all are."

"Someone really wants you dead and we don't know who that is. That person keeps trying and they're going to keep doing it until they get to you. I can't lose you, Mila. You're the only thing I have." She buries her head in my chest in the way I've buried mine in her chest when I need her comfort.

Unlike her, I don't have the words to comfort her or the words that make this better. I look up at Alis and he's standing there, pale faced and speechless like I am.

———

Alis

It takes the better part of an hour for Mila's mom to calm down. I hand her a glass of water and she looks up like she's seeing me for the first time. She dries her tears with the tissue I brought her and sniffles.

"*Mami*, let's get you to bed," I say.

She shakes her head. "I won't be able to sleep. And besides, I need to take care of you. Let me make you some tea."

"No, I don't want any tea."

But her mom is on the way to the kitchen.

"Let her. I think she needs to be busy."

"I want her to rest. This isn't good for her. She's been worrying too much and I haven't been the best company."

I put my hand on her cheek and she presses her face into it, trapping my hand in place with hers.

"Thank you. We would've been dead if it wasn't for you."

My stomach churns. I still see her standing there with that box in her hand. She nuzzles her face against my hand and it brings me to the present. She's alive, okay, and sitting in front of me.

"It came too close to you."

She lifts her face to look at me. "You had my back."

"It's true," her mother says from the kitchen door. "You saved her."

I fear she'll cry again. Instead she grabs some cups and hands them to us. We sit and sip in silence. This time she's on one side of Mila and I'm on the other. But her mom is not calm for long. Her cup rattles and Mila takes it off her hands.

"Come on. I'm going to give you something so you can rest. I have some of that ZZZ-Time Water. It won't knock you out, but it will help you sleep." She offers her hand and her mother takes it.

I stand as they're heading out.

Her mom walks up to me and hugs me. "Thank you. I owe you everything."

My throat tightens into a knot. I can't say anything, so I just nod.

Mila takes her away and I sit again. There are a few texts from Leila and my brother.

Leila's are more erratic.

LEILA

I called but got no answer. Are you all okay?

I text her back.

ME

Sorry, we are dealing, and the police are here, so we are good. Let me call you tomorrow.

Weston's messages came through just a minute ago.

WESTON

I'll stop by after my shift. Did her mom get some rest? I'll bring her a prescription. She must be wrecked.

ME

She is. I think she's going to sleep, though. Don't think the cops will let you in.

The three dots appear on my screen and I concentrate on that because when I focus on something, I don't hear the bomb explode or see the blast.

WESTON

My cop is there. They have to let me in.

My phone rings and it's Leila.

"I know you don't want to talk right now, but I couldn't wait till the morning until I heard your voice."

I can't seem to loosen the knot in my throat, but she talks and I breathe. I spend the next thirty minutes explaining what happened and calming her down.

I tell her to take something to sleep too. She says she can't but her boyfriend convinces her. I thank him and hang up. Mila comes back into the room, her eyes sunken and her lids heavy.

"You should have laid down with your mom."

"I couldn't sleep if I tried. The only way she went down was because I promised her she could sleep now. I can sleep in the morning while she watches over me."

"I'm sorry. Your mom is traumatized."

She nods. "So are we."

She sits next to me with the side of her body pressed against mine. I throw my arm over her shoulder. She leans against me.

"She's so worried that the cops won't do enough or get to me on time if something else happens."

You're the one that takes it from her hands and you're the one that throws it where it explodes but doesn't hurt anyone.

I don't get angry like I did then. My head's straight now. I'm not letting emotion make decisions for me. And he had a point. I can understand what he was saying and what it looks like.

"Mila, what that cop said—"

"They call him Abbott the Asshole. Guess why."

I nod. "What he was saying made sense."

"Only to someone who doesn't know you. You're not some psycho that would stoop to terrorizing me to look good."

"Whoever is doing this understands it clearly. He's muddying the waters."

"And all because of something I'm supposed to know but don't. I still can't decipher what I should keep my mouth shut about." She leans closer, placing her hand on my thigh.

"I wish he would just meet me somewhere?"

"Who?" I ask.

"Whoever is doing this. I wish he would just face me, and fucking tell me what it is I'm supposed to know."

My spine stiffens, but I don't make any sudden moves or grab her by the shoulders to shake some sense into her.

"That's not wise. If he met you face to face, he would probably try to kill you, and being in proximity increases his chances."

She snorts and laughs a little. "You sound like you're talking to someone on the ledge."

"I'm trying not to let myself lose it for a second time, but I want to. Swear to me, you will never go meet him if he tries to get you to."

She says nothing. I tilt her chin up.

"Swear it, Mila."

Her gaze is wild, like a cornered animal. "I just want it to be over."

"It will, and we both have to be okay when it does."

The knock on the door has us turning to it. She holds on tight. I kiss her head and stand to open the door. Through the glass opening, I can see Matt and Dahlia standing there.

I open the door and they come in. Dahlia goes to sit across from Mila.

"We have some news. There was a small envelope behind the desk. Carl didn't remember it until we showed it to him. It's in evidence, but I took a screenshot." She pulls out her cellphone and shows Mila.

You should've kept your mouth shut, instead you're hanging with cops. Boom boom bye.

"What the fuck? I don't know anything. What is he talking about?"

"He still thinks you know something and you just may, Mila," Matt says, leaning against the wall.

"I'm wracking my brain, but nothing. I wish I knew what this fucker is talking about."

A phone rings and we all start looking around. Mila gets to it first. It's hers.

"I don't know this number," she says and throws the phone on the couch.

It rings again.

"Pick it up," Dahlia tells her.

Mila takes the phone in her hand, hits the green button, and then puts it on speaker.

"Hi, Mila."

Her eyes round and I take out my phone and hit the camera and start the video. Dahlia is doing the same.

"Who is this?" Mila asks.

"I think you know." His voice is soft.

"I'm assuming the one who left me the little present tonight."

"There's my girl. Backstabber? Definitely. Dumb? Never." His voice is so plain, almost robotic.

Dahlia eggs her on to continue.

"Who did I supposedly betray? Are you talking about Maddie? Because I have to say, you took that awfully personal."

"You're cute, but I don't care you fucked her pretty boy boyfriend. She probably wouldn't have cared, either. She was too caught up on Elias."

"But not you. She talked about Alis and Elias, but never you. You must have hated that."

I'm so proud of her. She's been brave.

"See? There it is. She said you were cunning, that you had to learn some underhanded shit to make it to the top. I told her you were a lamb. She hung out with you because you weren't like the other broke hoes."

The color drains from her face.

"I don't know what the fuck you want with me..."

"Are you going to beg me to leave you alone? Maybe you can go on TV and cry your eyes out. Maybe I'll walk away and leave you alone."

"Fuck you, you fucking loser."

The sigh blows through the line like a wind tunnel. "It's funny. She said almost the same thing. Birds of a feather, I guess. But I feel sorry for you. She could've died alone but she dragged you in."

"How did she drag me in?"

"She said you knew where she was. She threw you under the bus. Then again, you're not innocent. You broke the code and betrayed her. Now you're going to end up just like her."

"I don't know what you're talking about. Madison didn't tell me a thing. She talked about work, and sex, and broke bitches, but I don't know anything else." She's screaming and I take one of her hands in mine, willing her to calm down.

"She tried to take it back in the end, but I knew Madison was lying. You bitches have no honor. You flip flop when it's convenient. She said you didn't know after she told me you knew. Then she started bugging out. I didn't know if I could trust her or not. And I had already fucked her a bunch of times."

"She was probably scared."

"She should've been. It's just bad manners to sneak around. She was trying to save a man that didn't deserve saving. Watching how broken he is over her death has been as fun as watching you roll in the mud."

"Are you talking about Elias?"

"Ah, my miraculous one. You'll find out in time. I'll be in touch."

The line goes dead.

We're all frozen, staring at her phone. Then Mila raises her head, her eyes rounded, her mouth hanging open.

"I know him. It's Greg."

"That's the guy I met at your office?"

She stands and paces. "Yeah. But it doesn't make any sense. Maddie would never...not with him." Her face contorts. "He's always been our friend."

"Abbott, this is Wicker. You need to check for a Greg..." She turns to Mila. "What's his last name? Do you know his address?"

"Nielsen and he lives in Laurel." She goes through her phone and finds the address.

Dahlia repeats it back over the phone. "He's confessed to sending the bomb to Mila and he's just become the main suspect in the murder of Madison Summerville. He works at Grayson Global. I'm texting you this address. Have someone pick him up."

"This is good. It's going to be over soon."

"I doubt it," Matt says. "I bet you everything he's not there."

"But we know who he is," I say. "And we're going to catch his ass."

31

———————

Mila

The plan comes together so quickly I don't have time to second guess, entertain doubts, or be nervous. My heart's sunken with my mom's soft sniffling as we waited for her to board the plane. That goodbye took every ounce of my strength. I need to know she is safe and away from all this shit before we put things into motion. She only agreed to go after everyone promised her they would protect me. I'm wracked with guilt at not telling her the details. She would have never gone if she had even an inkling.

I'm on exactly two hours of sleep when I cross the lobby at GG. I'm late because we fed information to the media for the first time since this whole shit started. I did a short interview over the phone talking about what I've been through and the bomb.

The first headline comes from the Baltimore Gazette.

Explosive package nearly kills Grayson Global Exec.

The blogs, of course, choose to give it a salacious spin.

BOMB SHOCKER: *Someone attempts to murder Scandal-ridden Vixen Exec Mila Rosario.*

BREAKING NEWS: *Months after taking her dead friend's man, someone's intent on taking her life.*

I don't bat an eye at the shady language in the articles because, as Alis said, "The asshole bloggers did what we needed them to do."

Everyone should know by now what happened at my place. There's not much chance Greg is dumb enough to come to work, but just in case there are cops on every floor. He manipulated this whole situation, and we didn't get a whiff until now. The plan is to come here, show my face, and drop some information. Someone will feed him everything we want him to know.

I take a long breath as the elevator stops on my floor.

Knox places a hand on my shoulder. "Don't walk too fast ahead of me and remember, look sad, but don't look around. Let me do that for you."

I exit the elevator and head down the hallway. People gather around in clusters. It's not a surprise because I emailed my team and rescheduled our nine in the morning meeting to eleven. Also, because they love gossip here. This is a great company to work for, but there are always the gossipers and tea spillers in every big business. I cringe as I pass them. There's concern in some faces and barely concealed curiosity in others.

Fuck all of you.

Sandy breaks through the crowd and hugs me. She's holding a tote in her hand. "Come on, let's go to your office."

Everyone nods at me as we pass. Knox takes his cover as maintenance person and turns on his vacuum cleaner. There are other people cleaning windows who are normally not here. My other security people.

I'm careful not to stare at them, rushing along with Sandy until my door is closed and I breathe. She takes out a thermos, pours some tea, and offers it to me.

I stare at it, my mind still on the people outside, on their gazes. Someone's already telling him all that is happening.

Sandy points her finger at the tea. "I brought it from home. It's been on my arm the whole time. No one has touched—"

I wrap my hand around her wrist. "I trust you. My nerves are just shattered."

"Who could blame you? And now to deal with all these bastards. Sit down and drink this."

I do as she says, taking my desk chair. I take a sip and the aroma of chamomile scent infuses my senses. First the calming smell, then the sweetness spreading over my tongue. "You used sugar."

"I know how you like it." She smiles and I hate the regret and sadness I see there.

"I'm going to be okay, Sandy."

She dabs at the corners of her eyes. "I hate this for you. Thank you for trusting me with everything, but I hate that you're going through this. You could've died."

I nod and strain to stay at the top of my feelings. I can't let the emotion in. "Let's not talk about that. We have to keep our heads clear. What is everyone saying?"

She swallows. "Everyone was shocked. People were pinging me on messenger all morning to ask about you. A lot of people feel bad and are genuinely concerned. Others are just fucking nosy. Greg didn't come in so they don't know where to get their gossip from. I don't know why they think I'm going to say anything."

His name is a bucket of icy water over me.

"Greg's not here?"

She shakes her head. "Didn't even call in from what I gathered. It's weird because you know he's always here early when there's tea to spill." She winces. "I didn't mean it like that."

I wave her off, but her words keep echoing in my head. "It's true, he always knows what's happening."

"Hon, he always got that kettle ready with three cubes of sugar."

"So true. Give me a sec." I grab my phone and shoot a message to Dahlia.

ME

The rumor mill at work is lacking without him.

The three dots appear on my screen.

DAHLIA

We're getting a warrant for his place. He's
gone dark…

I'm clenching my teeth so tight that pain breaks out in my jaw. I pinch my lips together. It won't do me any good to scream my head off. Greg's on the run, which is scarier since we don't know where he is. I need to keep it together, so I type a last message to Dahlia.

ME

Keep me posted. Pls.

"Everything okay?" Sandy's tone is cautious and soft.

"Yeah. I was just telling Dahlia that he's out today."

"Hon, I'm still a little shocked." She leans forward. "He's worked here forever. He went to college with Grayson. Did you know that?"

"I did. He never lets anyone forget it."

"That's why he got hired. Grayson gave him a chance."

I blink a few times. "But he's in hot water right now and may get fired."

"Because Grayson doesn't play games with his company." She drops her voice again. "I'm a little afraid because Greg knows where I live. Dave is locked and loaded."

I grasp her hand in mine. "It's going to be okay. This will end soon."

"I want to stay here with you."

I shake my head. "We have to keep going as we planned. Come on down when you get the signal from Dahlia. "

She presses a hand to her belly, her fear palpable. "Whatever you need me to do."

32

———————

The numbers are not adding. The analytics seem clear to everyone else on the email thread, but might as well be gibberish to me. I have six items on my to-do list, but my hands won't stop shaking. For the first time in my life, I can't hide behind my work. The worst part of it is that I need to act like I'm not affected. Thank God I'm alone in my office, but I wish I would get a call from Matt and Dahlia, green-lighting me to leave.

Alis is waiting for me downstairs, but they keep delaying my departure. What the hell is going on?

I'm not going to call Alis again. He's on edge and so am I. I just need to ride this out and wait. I put on my Airpods and play the only thing that calms my nerves down when they're wrecked, hardcore rap.

I'm flying through my document humming along to a song where the artist turns her nose at media attention, declaring over and over she doesn't need press. I replace her name with mine and declare I don't need no press.

It's ironic how true those words are. I need no more press or media or people calling to try to get me to talk to them. That's what drives me to move through my fear and go through with this plan. I want to live the way I used to. I want to be free to move as I please.

My cellphone rings and my heart lurches, threatening to leap out of my chest. It's Dahlia. She only says three words. "It's go time. Sandy is on her way down. Everyone is in place."

I shut down my laptop and drop it in its carrier. I grab my purse and take my phone in hand. I leave only one headphone in. Sandy taps on my door exactly two minutes later. I get up and walk out.

"You're heading out, hon?"

I smile at her like my insides are not jiggling like Jell-O. "Yes. I'm working remotely the rest of the day."

"Oh, well, Grayson sent you these. He wants you to stop by his desk before you leave."

I grab the folder from her hand and stuff it in my bag. "Walk with me and you can tell me what it is on the way there."

We head down the hallway. Carter's in the supply closet and grabs a ream of paper. He smiles at us. "You're leaving, Mila?"

I nod. "Yes. I'll still be working, so I'll review your report when I get it."

Sandy and I continue to the elevators. I push the down button and she pushes the one up. Mary is now talking to Karin near the reception. There are a few people on each end, all pretending to talk to someone else.

I shift my gaze to them and back to Sandy.

She nods. "If you're not doing anything, I can come by with some wine this evening. It will do you good to relax. David and I have some good selections from the last wine fest we went through."

I love how well she is playing along. "Thanks, amiga. But I'm getting away for a couple of days."

She leans closer. "With…?"

I press my finger to my lips. Then laugh and loud-whisper. "Water, beautiful trees, and my…" I face her as if I'm whispering something, then say "my man" loud enough for them to hear. "That is all I need."

"Who could blame you?" She throws her arms around me and whispers, "Just be careful, okay?"

When the elevator door opens, we jump in and ride it up to the CEO suite. Normally, there are people milling about, but the hallways are empty. The police didn't want anyone here to witness everything, so they made up a pipe bursting.

"It's weird not to see anyone here," I say as we quickly make our way to the other side of the floor.

"Tell me about it." She hits the elevator button. "When this is over, you need to take me to your prince's castle. I've only seen Luciana Island online and in magazines."

"We'll go and—"

The elevator dings and the doors open. My eyes immediately go to the man across from me. It's not Knox. It's Greg and I don't have a chance to react before he swings and hits Sandy in the head. She falls by my feet.

I don't have a chance to scream. He shoves a gun in my face.

"Let's go, miraculous one."

―――――

Alis

I hate everything about this day. I hate being cooped up in this car. I hate the smell of police-bought stale coffee that permeates the air. Mostly, I hate sitting here with my thumbs up my ass while Mila's inside that building. I know she's safe and on her way to me, but I need the jasmine and spice notes of her perfume deep in my nostrils. I want to run my fingers over the silky skin of her arm. I need her breath synched with mine like when we hugged this morning before she had to make her way to work. It's the only way I'll know she's safe.

> WESTON
>
> How are you holding up?

I stare at my brother's text, not knowing how to reply. I go with the truth.

ME

Not good. I have a nasty feeling in the pit of
my stomach.

WESTON

It's called being in love. Or food poisoning.

No, this is not just love. It's knowing this asshole is out there,
trying to get at her.

ME

Hahaha, Doctor Priest. You're a ball of laughs
today.

He sends one more message.

WESTON

Hang in there. I know this feeling all too well,
but it will be over soon for you.

It takes me a second to realize what he means. His wife risks her
life every day when she's working.

ME

You do get me.

I look at the time. We've been hanging for way too long.

"They should've been here by now," I say, typing another message
to Mila.

ME

Are you almost here?

"Abbott, what the fuck is happening?" Dahlia speaks into the two-
way radio.

"It's quiet on this end but someone just called a shelter in place
on the other side of the building."

"Shelter in place? That was not on the plan." She reaches for the
door handle and opens it. Matts does the same on his side but neither
moves.

A knot twists deep in my belly. Something's not right.

"Keep your pants on, Wicker. We're calling the elevator now." Abbott's voice comes through the radio. "Oh fuck. Knox."

"What?" Dahlia yells into the radio.

"Fuck fuck fuck," Abbot says, adding, "We need a bus. Knox is down."

My heart lurches and I am out of the SUV before the thought can fully form, running toward the parking lot entrance to the building. I need to get to her. Dahlia and Matt are running behind me, and we reach the elevators in seconds.

Knox is on the floor of the elevator. His hands clutch at his side, blood oozing between his fingers. Abbott shrugs out of his jacket and presses it against the wound.

Knox points a bloody finger up. "He got her. He dragged her into the stairwell. He knocked out Sandy too. I couldn't get to her inside the elevator. He has a gun."

I turn toward the stairwell but Matt steps in front of me. "You can't go in there like that. You're going to get your head blown off."

"He's got Mila."

Dahlia places her arm on my shoulder. "And if we want to save her, we need to be smart. Let us do our job." She pulls out her radio. "Derek, we're going to call for reinforcement. Make sure everyone stays in their shelter in place. They're in the stairwell. We need a team from the top and one from the bottom."

Matt looks at me. "We're going to get to her."

"Yes, we fucking are. We have to. I'm not losing her."

33

Mila

The stairwell door thunders shut, rattling my skin, echoing against the concrete walls. My heart thrashes like a painful storm, battering my chest. The lights here are not as bright as the hallways but I'm grateful. I don't think I could make it if it was dark. There's comfort in seeing the iron of the railings and gray walls. If I can see, I can breathe.

Until he points the gun to your face and shoots you. He'll be the last thing you'll see.

"Move," Greg says, shoving my head with the muzzle of his gun. All he has to do is squeeze just a little and he'll put a hole in my head.

"We have to help Sandy. I think you hit her too hard." I can't unsee my friend, laying on the floor unconscious. Or Knox bleeding on the elevator floor.

"She'll be fine. Worry about yourself. I may just shoot you and keep going." His voice is so cold. This is not the Greg I worked with for two years, not even the bitter one I've been trying to schedule a meeting with for weeks because I was worried about his change in behavior.

"Who are you? I don't even recognize you. You're wearing all black like a cliché robber. You hurt Sandy of all people."

"Unfortunately, she was in the wrong place at the wrong time. Fucking walk, Mila, and don't make me tell you again."

He shoves me again and the cold of his gun against my scalp is enough to propel me forward. I hold on to the railing because I don't want to trip. My heels are too high and I have to carefully step on my toes first before firmly balancing on the heel of almost five-inch Louboutins.

"It's funny you wore those shoes today."

"Why?" I ask but keep going down. My heels click-clacking against the concrete steps.

"It's like you're trying to be her all the way. Maybe you're trying to die like her too, trying to play me."

I try to turn my head to look at him. "How would I even play you?"

He shoves again. "You came to work acting like all is good when you already told everyone about me. You thought I would fall for it like I'm an idiot. But there's something you don't know about me. I always have a fail safe."

I shake my head before I think, and the gun rubs back and forth against my head. And my stomach turns, threatening to empty out. I need to keep talking. "I don't think you're an idiot, G. I never did. I thought you were sweet and my friend, but you're right. There's so much I don't know about you."

"I was your friend. You were lucky."

"I felt lucky. Tell me why you turned against me. Why you're doing this?" Maybe if I keep him talking, I can buy time. Alis will realize something's wrong. They'll come for me.

He pushes me and my legs almost buckle. "I'm not here to talk, Mila. I need to finish my work and be done with it."

I'm not going to panic. "Be done with it? You mean kill me?"

He shrugs. "I should kill you but you're more valuable to me alive. I can get millions for you. And I deserve it. I was good to you, even though you thought you were too good for me. I respected your drive at work. You were the only one who gave a damn about all those fucking campaigns. You weren't fucking other executives. But you turned against me and betrayed me. You forced me to deal with you."

He says deal like it's a strong talking to, like he doesn't mean to end my life. He already killed once. I don't believe him when he says he's not going to hurt me.

"How did I betray you? What exactly did I do?"

"Don't play stupid, Mila." He forces me faster into the landing, I stumble but brace against the wall. "The minute you got that job you changed. You stopped texting me like you used to. You came down on me, sided with others. You even tried to get me fired with that cunt bag Mary. And I rooted for you. I hoped you got it over Madison. Come to find out you're a two-faced bitch just like her."

He drags me toward the next flight.

My fingers dig into the railing, needing something to anchor me so I don't give in to the panic. "I wasn't trying to get you fired. You're the one that started gossiping and making people uncomfortable with your comments. And I had to change after I felt I someone was out to kill me. But you want to talk about betrayal? You sicced the internet on me. You were behind every lie. You doxed me and my mom. You sent a bomb. You could've gotten her killed."

He sighs. "Your mom's a nice lady like you used to be until you got tainted. I warned you before. I told you to watch the company you kept."

I scoff. "Come on, Greg. What does that even mean? Everyone says that."

"Madison wasn't your friend. You were the rival she kept her eyes on, the enemy she kept close. She liked you, but she didn't trust you. You were a surprise to her. She didn't expect you to be more talented or to be assertive about it."

Same thing her sister said but I can't let him get to me.

I stop and turn around to face him, the muzzle of the gun right between my eyes. The bile rises up my throat but I press a hand to it. "She's dead. You killed her. Don't bad mouth her."

"Okay. I won't." He smiles and now he's back to break-room-Greg near the Keurig. *How the fuck does he do that?*

"How did you manage to poison the others."

He chuckles. "It's a matter of knowing the right people in the right places and knowing how to grease their palms. No one ever suspects the friendly, caring type. You have the personality to do the same if you weren't too busy being a pencil pusher. Maddie was great at that. Except she used her—"

"Stop," I snap.

"Okay, but keep moving."

I do as he says. I still feel the cold metal in my forehead and it's taking all I have not to break down and cry. But my breath hitches.

"Don't do that. Just breathe and do what you're told. I wish you hadn't turned on me with Grayson. I wish she hadn't lied. That bitch would've said anything so I wouldn't kill her."

Huh. "Maddie?"

"I don't know why she's started acting fucking crazy. I wasn't doing anything she didn't like. And she liked everything. I was so surprised. Prissy rich girls don't get down like that, but she liked it in the ass and her pussy at the same time. She whimpered and touched herself, but that night she was acting like she was afraid, like putting my hands around her throat was something new. Can you believe that?"

The images play vividly in my head. Her eyes wild with fear. His hand squeezing. My heart fissures, sending painful waves through my sternum. *Don't let it in. You can't let him in.* I shake my head. "So it was an accident?"

"Kinda." His tone is non-committal like he swatted a picnic ant, not a person we knew and loved. "That wasn't what I set out to do. I could've let it pass, but then she went snooping."

"What was she looking for?" I ask.

"Her death."

"What does that mean, Greg?"

He chuckles. "Our Maddie was trying to free her lover. She wanted what I have on him. Then she broke her own heart. Because he didn't tell her everything. She knew all the little deeds that would send any woman running. But she still wanted a life with him. She just didn't know the one thing that would prevent them for being free."

"What did Elias do that was so bad? I ask.

"No more talking." His voice is harsh, much like the way he presses the gun to the back of my head.

"Come on. You might as well tell me."

"No, Mila. If I tell you, I'll have to kill you and I'm not going to do that. Not when I can make money off you. Call your boyfriend and give me the phone."

———

Alis

Her name on my phone screen sends a flash of relief through my body. "It's Mila."

I swipe right to answer. "Are you okay?"

"How much is she worth to you?" The male voice, without much emotion, is like a knife to my chest, deflating the surging hope.

"Greg, I suppose."

"You suppose well, Alis. Now answer my question."

"She's invaluable to me," I say in an even tone, trying to betray none of the impotence coursing through me.

"That's what I like to hear. Because I want you to deposit twenty million into an account."

"Okay, Greg. Consider it done but I want to speak to her first."

Dahlia mouths, "Good."

"Hi." The hoarse whisper nearly undoes me.

"Are you okay?" I ask and it's stupid. Of course, she's not. She's with a fucking lunatic.

"Yeah, G's treating me well."

There's nothing in her voice. I don't know what her mental state is.

"We'll be together soon, right, Greg? You'll get your money. I get my girl. Everyone's happy."

I infuse a coolness I don't feel into my voice but she needs it and I need it. I can't let on how desperate I am.

"What about the police? Or do you think I'm stupid? You're down there with them."

"I can make them go away. For Mila, I would do anything."

"Aw, that's sweet. Just get me my money and you have no worries. But if I get where I need to and it's not there, I'm going to put a bullet right through the back of your girl's head. You'll get a text you with the number."

The line goes dead and my heart drops down my chest. I can see her already lifeless, with a hole on her beautiful head.

Rage breaks all over my body but it's the darkness I can taste in my tongue that makes my stomach roil. I'm afraid and I'm not even ashamed of it. This fucker can kill her. He will if I don't do what he says.

Matt takes the phone from my hand and dials a number. "When you get the text for the account, we are going to put a trace to it. You're not going to lose that amount, but we will track it."

"I don't fucking care about the money. I just want her safe."

———

Mila

"He didn't even pause at the twenty million. Wow. Maddie must be rolling in her grave right now. First, he dumped her for you. Now, he's willing to pay all that to get you back."

No, Alis didn't even flinch when Greg asked for that amount and I'm holding on to his words. He would do anything to get me back. I know it in my bones.

"You already killed her. Why don't you let her rest in peace?"

He taps me hard with the gun. Pain breaks at the back of my skull, rattling my head, and I have to hold on tight to the railing not to lurch forward. My leg buckles and I use all my strength to hang on.

"Just because he's going to pay for you doesn't mean you're going to talk to me any kind of way. Next time, I'll hit you harder." He grabs my arm and drags me down the stairs. I am barely holding on. He pulls me so rough that I end up falling on my knees.

"If you move, I'll blow your head off." He walks to the door and looks through the glass window. "Fuck."

I bow my head in silence. I don't want to provoke him. My heart's been beating so fast that it should give up any second. I force myself to breathe slow, channeling Alis' voice. He's here, so close. I want to see him again. I'm going to see him again.

"Where the fuck are you?" Greg's voice makes me jump. "Hurry up."

I peer up and he's typing into his phone.

"Can I please sit?" I ask.

"Shut the fuck up."

"I won't look up, I promise. This is so uncomfortable," I insist.

"So is a bullet through your skull." His voice is devoid of anything. He's talking about killing me as if it were talking about the weather by the water cooler. That's how I know he's capable of it. How scared Maddie had to be in her last moments.

And as much as I love Alis, and I want to be with him more than anything, I can't give this fucker my fear anymore. I push back into my heels and sitting in the last step of the stairs.

"Why did you move?" He shoves the gun in my face.

"I can't be on my knees."

He laughs. "Hard to believe. He's willing to shell twenty million on you. It's got to be for something."

"Money like that is something to you cause you've always been broke and have no way of making it. Isn't that why you work for Grayson, because you can't be his equal?"

The smile drops from his face. "You have a death wish."

I shake my head. "It's why Maddie had men like Alis and even Elias on her side. People with real money or real power. Not a mediocre marketing lead."

His cackle is the most diabolical thing I've ever heard. "Look at you, dusting off the claws. I knew you had it in you. Madison did too. That's why she didn't trust you all the way."

I rub my ankle, the pain starting to break through, and I can't walk on these heels anymore. I remove them and rub my swelling skin.

"You keep talking about her but the more you say the more I'm convinced you're making shit up. She would never have been with you. She thought you were an incel."

He levels the gun at my forehead. "She loved to fuck me. She wanted everything I could give her. She liked when I tied her up."

There's a movement through the corner of my eye and my gaze snaps to it. On the other side of the glass window is Elias.

And now my stomach turns because I know I'm going to die. I'm not going to make it through this. They've been working together. I need to make a move because I can't just let them kill me without trying.

"Finally," Greg says, following my gaze. He turns toward the door. I take both shoes in my hand, push to my feet, and launch myself at him. I hit him with both heels on the back of the head as hard as I can.

He hits the wall and the door swings open. I take off running down the steps. The gunshot thunders against the wall. I don't feel pain anywhere and keep running down. I only stop when something avalanches and drops headfirst on the landing. The thud so loud I almost slip.

Greg's body is contorted on the floor. A ragged moan emanates from his body as his gaze shoots to mine. His eyes are wide and desperate. Blood begins to flow from the hole in his chest. Steps above us and I tear my gaze away from his body. I turn around, fully expecting to look at death in the face, but Elias is still pointing his gun toward Greg's body.

"That's for Madison," he says, glaring and wild. "You took her from me. I was never going to let you live. I only got you in here so I could take you out. Fuck you all the way to hell."

He squeezes the trigger and the boom rocks my entire body, my heart beating erratically. When Elias' eyes land on me, I'm sure this is my end.

"Mila!" someone screams and I would know that voice anywhere. It's Alis.

"I'm okay," I say but don't move.

Elias looks at Greg one more time, smiles, and runs up the steps and disappears through the door.

"I'm here. I'm okay." I shoot one last look at the body on the floor, at the unfocused gaze fixed on me, and take off running down the last few steps.

"We're coming up," Alis says. "Are you hurt?"

"No, Greg's dead."

Dahlia and Matt move up the stairs, guns drawn. Alis is behind them.

"Elias killed him. He ran," I say, passing the two cops and jumping straight into his arms. My foot gives out and I sag against him.

"I got you."

I nod and my body begins to shake, and I break down because I finally feel safe again.

34

———————

Mila

My temporary accommodations are messing up my reality. I look around the suite with the amazing views of Baltimore Harbor. The open floor plan with the dividing wall housing a fireplace and huge screen TV humbles not only the house I grew up in and every apartment I've rented, but also Grayson's place. The fire is roaring, and the sun is coming in from glass paneling on two sides. I'm wearing a long sleeve cozy sweater, but I can't seem to get warm. Because this is not my place and I'm only here because I'm afraid to go back to the unit and I can't go Alis' because...

Because Greg's still fucking up my life.

"Mila."

I turn to look at Alis and he's closer than I expected. "I'm sorry, what?"

He reaches to touch my cheek. "I asked if you wanted something to drink."

I lean against his touch and nod. "Tea would be good."

He heads to the kitchenette and I hate how worried he looks. I pull the soft throw blanket closer to my neck and bite down on my nail but I for myself to stop.

337

It's over. I need to shake this.

If only we could start putting this whole thing behind us. There's still so much. At the East Madison Police Station, all we talked about was Greg and Elias. They wanted to hear everything over and over. It's standard procedure but it sucks to repeat yourself so much. I hate to relive those moments.

Alis comes back with the tea and seats next to me. "Talk to me. I think it may help."

I run my hands over my face. "That awful sound as Sandy hit the ground still echoes in my ears. I can't unsee Knox bleeding on that elevator floor. I know they're okay. I spoke to them but it's there like Greg's eyes, staring at me."

"This is normal. It's too soon."

I reach for my wrist and stop. I have a rash from rubbing circles to try and stall the panic attacks.

He hugs me and we breathe together.

The media's still at it. The requests for comments have only intensified after the police revealed how Greg killed Maddie and set off havoc in my life. How he might be responsible for two other deaths trying to get to me.

And this is all still wrecking my life. We're staying at this hotel suite because I don't feel safe at my place. I'm wearing new clothes because I don't even trust myself to go in there. I expect another one of Greg's surprises to be waiting for me. And what about Elias? He let me live but that doesn't mean he can't change his mind.

There's a knock on the door and we jump. There's a lot of security outside, but we still expect the bullshit. When the door opens, Dahlia walks in followed by Matt. There are dark circles under her eyes and she looks like how I feel. She sits on one of the armchairs, across from us. Matt takes the other.

"There's going to be a press conference later today," she begins. "The cap is going to update everyone on the investigation. He's going to reveal Greg was the killer. We have been instructed to keep their relationship down to very minor details."

"What does that mean?" Alis asks.

"We are not going to reveal anything that's going to taint her memory or cause salacious fodder for social media."

Alis and I look at each other.

"I like that. Everyone doesn't need to know. She's dead. Greg's dead. It doesn't help anyone," I say.

He nods and turns back to the detectives. "Do you have any news on Elias?"

Matt presses his hands together. "No, but we found out how he and Greg got into the building and managed to evade us. They came in the vehicle of one of your employees. Carter Hill's vehicle was found abandoned inside Patapsco State Park near a trail. Carter was in the backseat unconscious and bruised."

My hand flies to my mouth. "Is it okay? Was he part of it?"

Matt taps his fingers on the armchair rest. "He's stable. Greg asked him to come over and to help him with something related to his cat. "He forced at gun point to sneak him into GG. They picked up Elias on the way there. The kid is still scared shitless. He never imagined the type of person Greg really is."

None of us did. He had us fooled.

"We are still looking for Elias but he's part of the reason we came to talk to you ahead of the press conference." Matt looks between Alis and I. "The captain will reveal that even though Greg killed Madison, he dumped her body in Elias Saunders' yard."

"What?"

Dahlia takes over. "After her meeting with Elias, Madison left his house and Elias went out. He came home to find her body. He's the one that placed her in the alleyway."

Alis lifts a hand to stop her. "That doesn't make any sense. They were working together."

"We thought the same thing. Well, actually, we thought he killed her and moved the body but we've since got video evidence from his neighbor. It corroborates Elias' story."

"Dahlia, you can't believe that. They were working together. That's why Elias killed Greg."

I place my hand over Alis'. "When he shot him the second time,

Elias said it was for Maddie. That Greg took her from him, and he was never going to let him live."

"Yes," Dahlia says. "That matches everything. Elias was going to be Greg's getaway. At his place we found his bags packed and the cats in traveling cages. We are pretty sure the kitten's hair will match the ones we found on Madison. We believe Elias went through Greg's things and left the cats and everything else behind."

"This is crazy. What did Elias have to do with Greg?"

Matt and Dahlia exchange a look.

"That's part of another ongoing investigation," she finally says.

"What the fuck does that mean?" Alis pushes to his feet.

Matt holds up a hand. "You'll find out soon enough. Just know that we have warrants out for Elias Saunders. One for the murder of Greg Nielsen and the others related to tampering with a crime scene and moving Madison's body."

"If it wasn't for him, I would be dead," I say.

"If it wasn't for him, you wouldn't be in danger," Dahlia explains, adding, "And Maddie wouldn't be dead but we can't say any more than that. Matt and I didn't want you to be caught off guard."

They leave us soon after with more questions than answers.

Alis takes his place by my side again. "This is insane."

"Poor Maddie got caught between two monsters. I still have a hard time wrapping my mind around her and Greg. Why?"

Alis throws his arms around me. "I don't know. Only one person knows the answers. The police need to find him."

I close my eyes and see the hard light in his gaze as he held the gun. I still feel the gush of wind as he flew at me. A shiver climbs up my spine. "It's not over yet."

"We're going to get justice for Maddie but we need to continue our lives. I'm glad Greg is dead, just pissed I didn't get to kick his balls into his throat for what he did to you."

His arms tighten around me.

"I want to put him behind us."

35

Two weeks later

Alis

I pull up in the circle driveway and park behind my brother's car. All the players are here and I don't shake my head like I want to. I don't want to spook Mila.

"You okay to do this?" she asks.

I'm not, but my father's summons was clear. This shit is going to happen anyway, and we might as well get it over with. She, on the other hand, looks ready. Her eyes are clear and her face determined. She's not spooked at all. She's eyeing the house with raised eyebrows.

"This is a Rockefeller type of mansion. You grew up here, Richie Rich?"

I nod. "I did."

"Wow."

She only finds it amazing because she has not stepped inside or met the people who live here.

"Mila, I want you to know that nothing that happens in there is going to change my mind and I'm not letting you change yours."

She laughs. "I faced a murderer that tried to kill me a few times and the whole internet. I didn't run. This summons won't make me run, either. Let's go meet your parents."

"You don't know what you're in for. It may get nasty."

"It's a rite of passage, Alis. We have to get through meeting them and then we continue our life together."

I take her hand and we walk in together. Loud voices come from our formal living room. We make our way there. My brother throws his hands in the air and turns away from my parents. Our gazes collide. He shakes his head.

"Hello, everyone."

Dad barely spares Mila a look and turns his fulminating glare on me. "What part of a family meeting didn't you get?"

"I got the memo. I'm here."

"With her," he snaps.

I tighten my fingers around Mila. "Yes, with her. Get used to seeing her. She's not going anywhere."

"And this is why we're here. I'm sorry, young lady," he says to her. "I tried to shield you from this. Since Alis has no regards for anyone's feelings but his own, now you have to hear what I have to say."

"Let's get on with it, Wessy." Leila's voice tells me her glass has been ready to spill for a while.

He glares at her. "I'm calling an emergency board meeting in the morning. I'm going to ask for you to step down as CEO and for me to be reinstated effective immediately."

My mother gasps, and in the next breath, she is standing in front of my father. "You cannot do this. It will be a scandal."

"It's better than leaving the company in the hands of someone who is not going to put it first." He tilts his head at me when he says it.

"You're right. I'm not going to put the company first. I'm going to work hard for it as I always have, but it will not be the only thing in my world. I have new priorities." I look at Mila to emphasize my words.

He scoffs and walks past my mother to get closer. "You see, Christine? There you have it. The reason I am making this tough decision."

"Who says Ellison Corp has to be first for Alis to do a good job? He's already made so many changes."

"Shut up, Weston. If you're not going to offer to run the company, you have no say."

My brother laughs. "You do know I'm still a stockholder and part of the board, right? So is Leila. We stand with Alis."

"If he wants me to resign, I can. I won't be manipulated with the company anymore." I take two steps toward my dad. "However, if you force me out, I'm going to sell my stocks and then I'm going to go create my own company."

Dad laughs, shaking his head like he always does when he wants to dismiss us. "Who would you sell it to?"

I shrug. "Spencer Grayson. Isn't your boss interested in acquisitions here on Luciana Island?

My question is for Mila. She blinks a couple of times and then says, "Yes, your figures look right and especially with the new spotlight on the Franklin project. Grayson can do a lot with that."

"You can leave with your stocks and even if Leila and your brother follow you, I'm still the major stockholder. I would still have control, no matter who you sell to."

He calls our bluff and I look at Leila and my brother and we're at a loss. Mila squeezes my hand.

"You're not a major stockholder without me, Wes."

We all turn to look at my mother. She's poured herself a drink and is looking straight at her husband.

"Stay out of this, Christine."

"I... will not." My mother's voice fills the room now. "You will not disinherit my son. The company is his birthright. Weston wants nothing to do with it, but Alis has always worked for it. You will not take that away from him."

Her words take the floor from underneath my feet. She's never gone against him.

"This is my family's company and I've worked forty years to build it."

She sips like she has all the time in the world. "True, but it wouldn't be what it is without my father's money. Remember all those dumb investments that blew up in your face? When all your buddies convinced you to go in on one ridiculous investment after the other, my money bailed Ellison Corp out. I didn't know then why my dad insisted on half your stocks. I know now. It is not a family company if it's run by someone outside of it."

"You're going against me?"

She shakes her head, ever so delicately. "No, I'm doing this for us. I called my lawyer and began transferring all my stocks to Alis. When I die, he will have to divide them evenly with his brother. For now, he just needs to be the majority holder."

"Why are you doing this?"

"Aren't you tired of spending time with people who are not our family? We don't get to see them unless we make a stink about it. I'm tired of making a stink about it. When Weston and Dahlia have kids, I want to see them. I'm going to be their grandmother."

"You've gone senile," he accuses.

"I don't want to be alone. Alis is going to move to Baltimore. We will not see either of them... wait." She turns and points to Mila. "I have conditions. You need to make sure he's spending part of the week here. He's not to sell the house on the island. I want to see my son at least twice a month. I'm not getting in the way of the two of you, but you need to meet me halfway."

Mila nods. "Of course. You're his mother, I promise."

My mother smiles at me. "Great. Did you get all that?"

I'm still floored but I know her well. "Are you going to turn around and try to force my hand later on?"

She takes a sip of her drink, the smile never slipping from her lips. "No, I already laid out my conditions, and to prove my good faith, I won't even put them in writing."

She means it and good faith deserves good faith.

"I promise, Mom."

———

Mila

I sip on my wine and look out into the water. The last time we were here was one of the saddest moments of my life. Today, as I stare at the darkness, the sky reflects in the water like rippling black leather. It's chilly and I'm only wearing a sweater, but Alis' body is warm next to mine.

"You're cold. Let me turn on the fire."

I smile because he listened to me. I told him he needed a fire pit by the stairs facing the water. He outdid my thought and had two installed. One on each side. He doesn't have to work on the fire; instead he flips a switch from his app.

"This is the cushiest kind of rustic I've ever seen."

He laughs. "What do you know about rustic, city girl?"

His arm goes around mine and we sip in silence again. I'm glad the heaviness of this day is gone, but it was a whirlwind of lawyers, papers, and hard feelings on his dad's part. But it got done in one day.

"What are you thinking about?" Alis asks.

I don't take my eyes off the water. "It's amazing how quickly rich people make things happen."

He coughs out a laugh. "What?"

I look at him then and get caught up in his eyes, and the perfection that is his mouth. *He's mine.*

I trace his lips with my thumb. "It was supposed to be more of a fight. We went to your parents with a united front, but a 'let's see what happens' attitude. Everything seemed lost at one point, but your mother throws down the gauntlet, for the most shocking plot twist. She's suddenly on our side. Our side overrules your dad. Hours later, the papers are signed. You're practically controlling shareholder on top of CEO. Now, no matter what he does, your father can't kick you out."

He shrugs. "This is not as shocking as other things. Anyway, it's about time our money did what it's supposed to."

Huh.

"Explain, because I'm confused."

"It's simple, really. This was a power play. I'm really touched by what my mom did and sacrificed for me today. I never expected that. But I'm just relieved. All these months, my money couldn't protect you from the internet. From Greg. It could only keep you safe to a point. We deserved an easy win."

His eyes are cloudy. He hasn't celebrated like he should. He didn't want to go out to dinner with Weston and Leila. He said we have to wait for a day Dahlia could be with us. I saw through it, though. He just wanted to come home to silence.

"You're not happy."

He stares at me. "No, I'm not."

I open my mouth to tell him to give it time. It's been a long day, and he's probably tired. But he beats me to it.

"Happy doesn't cover what's in here." He points to his heart. "I'm so full... you know? It's just confusing. I have what I want the most in the world and now I don't know what to do first."

Relief pours over me, and I chuckle. "I think you know exactly what to do. You run that company the way you always dreamed of."

He shakes his head. "We are talking about two different things. I wasn't referring to Ellison Corp."

Oh. "Explain?"

He smiles. "I'm talking about you, Mila. What I want the most is you. I have you now, and I don't know what to do first."

His confession knocks the air out of me and undoes me. I finally swallow and breathe. "What do you want to do first?"

"Well, I calculated the risk. I already got a taste of how good the reward is going to be. Now, I'm going to throw myself into this investment."

I don't follow until he reaches into his pocket and pulls out his hand. Between his fingers he twists a ring with a diamond teardrop. The firelight strikes the stone, reflecting on it like a prism. My mouth drifts open, but I can't form words. I'm caught in the way the fire reflects in his eyes.

"I want us to make it official. I want to be yours forever. I want you to be mine on paper like you are everywhere else. Marry me."

I can only say one word, the one that's always in my heart for him. "Yes."

EPILOGUE

Alis

The sea splits into different colors like a rainbow made solely out of shades of blue. It's a mirage I can touch and dive into. There's aqua, turquoise, azure, and cerulean, all close to me. There's nothing like the peace in those colors or the relaxing rocking of the yacht over the Caribbean Sea. What better to complete this view than my sexy wife standing at the bow with her open arms?

Mila hasn't moved for a while, her face up to the sun, her hair flowing everywhere. I've been happy to watch her in the deep red one-piece bathing suit that clings to strategic areas of her body like paint strokes to a pre-primed canvas. Even though we're moving, there's a stillness to this moment I wouldn't trade for anything. After months of craziness, we finally got to shut off the noise.

She turns around, her gaze lasers to mine, and extends a hand. "Come."

I stand to join her, and she smiles up at me. Her hand latches around mine tight like the moment we finally met at the altar. Our bodies press together, her sun-heated skin against mine, her head on my shoulder.

"You got lonely after a few minutes without me?"

She shakes her head. "You were watching me. I felt you."

"You just made me sound weird."

She laughs softly and carefree. "Love is supposed to be weird. You came out of nowhere, and it got messy and stressful. I could be without my sanity, but I couldn't be without you. If it's not weird, I don't want it."

"Good point. What were you thinking about all this time? I was about to get jealous of the view."

"We've been so many places."

"Yeah, maybe we overdid it with the traveling honeymoon. Four countries in four weeks is a crazy itinerary."

Her head drifts back, and she looks up at me. "Not like that. I mean, yeah, we've been to opposite sites of the world, from Honduras to Madrid to here, but I was referring to our emotions. We went from attraction to guilt, horror to antagonism, and fear to love. Now here we are."

"Man, you were thinking philosophically this whole time, and I was just thinking of ways to peel this off you." I trace the edges of her bathing suit bottom with my finger.

She elbows me, and I laugh, then kiss her forehead.

"I was actually thinking about all the colors you bring into my life and how you stand out brighter and shinier than all. I love the stillness of this part of the trip. We haven't been still with our jobs, the wedding, Gift of Life, and building a life of inclusion with our super blended family. It's good to just... chill."

She sighs. "It is. Maybe we should get a house here so we can get away from everything."

"Here on Isla Saona or the mainland? Maybe Samaná? That was really pretty."

She looks up at me again, half smiling. "I was joking, kinda. Don't we have enough homes? One in Baltimore, one in Luciana Island, the one we got for Mami in Jersey."

I take her face in my hand. "Those are all houses. I only have one home. You."

ACKNOWLEDGMENTS

Thanks to Enchanting Romance Designs for this beautiful cover. Special thank you to Lindee Robinson Photography for the gorgeous cover photo.

Thank you to my book coach Kim Kessler. To my wonderful editors Jody Wallace and Eli Peters for helping me turn writing coal into a polished diamond. I couldn't have done this without you. Thank you April Bennett for proofreading and accommodating me on a short schedule.

Thank you Laralyn Doran for all your help brainstorming, being a sounding board, and advise. Angil, the best Alpha reader in the world, your support is unmeasurable in every single way.

THANK YOU to my assistant Kimberly Costa.

Thank you to my group of supportive friends John, Vivian, Crystal, and Vera, Kakazi, Citlali, The Lake House Writers, The Domingo crowd, the Damned Mob of Scribbling Women, and my LPHIDs.

Thank you to, my amazing family. *Papi*, *Mami*, *Doration*, my brothers and sister, uncles, aunts, nieces and nephews, and my beautiful Trin. I wouldn't be here without any of them.

Thanks to you, my readers for your support.

ABOUT THE AUTHOR

J. L. Lora is a Dominican-American author. Her stories explore the dark side of good characters, people living in the gray areas of life while playing the cards life has dealt them. She loves strong heroines and their equally powerful Men. She currently lives in Maryland, pursuing her dream of writing compelling, sexy, can't-put-down stories about empowered, badass alpha heroines and take-your-breath-away alpha heroes. You can find her and or chat her up on Social Media.

Sign up for her newsletter and learn more about new releases, events, news, freebies and much more at **www.JLLora.com**.

You can also join *SASS*, JL's private reader group with Laralyn Doran & Cate Tayler on Facebook.

facebook.com/AuthorJLLora

twitter.com/jtothelove

instagram.com/jllora

bookbub.com/profile/j-l-lora

BOOKS BY J. L. LORA

The Trinity

BOSS

MADE

STEEL

A Love for All Seasons Series

THE SUMMER I LOVED YOU

THE WINTER OF MY LOVE

THE LONGEST DAY — *Novella*

THE AUTUMN YOU BECAME MINE

THE SPRING OF MY HEART (TBA)

Sometimes Love Happens Standalone Series

SOME NIGHTS

SOME MORNINGS

SOME DAYS

WHEN YOU BREAK GIRL CODE

Free Short Stories

ALL I EVER WANTED — The Summer I Loved You - *Epilogue*

En Español

Ella es La Jefa

Hecha Y Derecha

www.ingramcontent.com/pod-product-compliance
Lightning Source LLC
Chambersburg PA
CBHW060852210726
48293CB00006B/1766